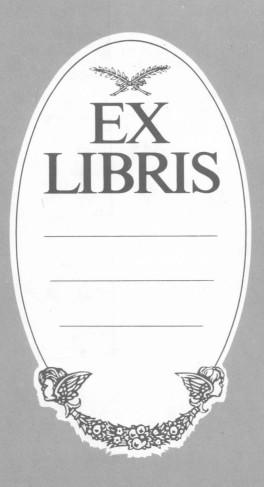

EX
LIBRIS

THE ROMANCE TREASURY
ASSOCIATION

NEW YORK · TORONTO · LONDON

These stories were originally published as follows:

SPIRIT OF THE SUN
Copyright © 1973 by Dorothy Cork
First published by Mills & Boon Limited in 1973

SHADOW OF THE PAST
Copyright © 1973 by Monica Douglas
First published by Mills & Boon Limited in 1973

BEYOND THE SUNSET
Copyright © 1973 by Flora Kidd
First published by Mills & Boon Limited in 1973

ROMANCE TREASURY is published by:
The Romance Treasury Association, Stratford, Ontario, Canada

Editorial Board: A. W. Boon, Judith Burgess, Ruth Palmour and
Janet Humphreys
Dust Jacket Art by David Craig
Story Illustrations by David Craig
Book Design by Charles Kadin
Printed by Kingsport Press Limited, Kingsport, Tennessee

ISBN 0-919860-27-3

Printed in U.S.A.   A028

CONTENTS

SPIRIT OF THE SUN

Spirit of the Sun
Dorothy Cork

Leni first met Kemble Savage in Singapore. She had no idea then that she would be visiting Bali — even less that Kemble lived there.

Leni and her friend, Dee, had dreamed for years of seeing Bali — so when the chance arose to join Dee for a month there, it really was a dream come true.

Beautiful as Bali was, it wasn't quite the paradise they'd expected. For Leni, Kemble Savage's presence spoiled it.

Somehow he seemed to misinterpret everything she did. And while she told herself that his opinion didn't matter, that obviously wasn't true. In fact, Kemble soon became the one person she couldn't ignore!

CHAPTER ONE

Outside the streets of Singapore steamed in the late afternoon heat, but the hotel shopping-arcade's first floor was cool and pleasant. Leni Forrest made her way leisurely to the small store where the saleswoman was to have some dresses ready for her to pick up.

Leni was eager to see the dresses—though they were not for her but for her employer's school-age daughter—but the fact that they were to be ready today depressed her. It was an indication that her sojourn in Singapore had very nearly reached its end. In three days' time she would be back in England and no nearer to realizing the crazy romantic schoolgirl dreams she had shared with Dee Fisher. A life of sunshine and fantasy on some distant tropic isle—the very life that Dee in actual fact was savoring right now. Well, for her it was different, and Leni smiled ruefully at herself as she reached the store and stepped inside.

A tall, broad-shouldered man in a light tropical suit stood at the wide glass counter with its glittering array of Thai silk scarves, batik sarongs, beaded blouses and evening purses. He was running a length of embroidered Indian silk through his hands thoughtfully, almost sensuously, and he looked up vaguely as Leni came in. With a shock, she found dark eyes that held points of fire staring straight into hers. She was aware of quick color suffusing her palely tanned cheeks as the woman behind the counter smiled faintly, her look seeming to say, "Please be patient a moment; this is an important client."

Leni found a brocaded chair and sat down to wait. But soon her glance was drawn back to that handsome arrogant face, with its dark-browed eyes and the very masculine mouth that had an intriguing tilt at one corner. And when the movement of his hands attracted her attention, she saw long, deeply tanned fingers that seemed to caress the brilliant silk while they measured its quality. She started when his voice—deep, vibrant, lazy—asked, "Am I right when I assume that this somewhat erotic violet confection appeals to you?"

To whom? To her? Leni raised dark gray eyes, and he was looking straight at her. She managed to ask coolly, "To me?"

He looked amused as he insisted, "Yes, to you. Apparently you can't keep your eyes off it."

Leni thought, "It's you I can't keep my eyes off," but she studied the silk. It was of a color that sang, a color that resembled a jewel in starlight—an amethyst—extravagant, exotic. It would make her unadorned face look utterly colorless. Its soft sprinkling of pale gold freckles and the straight silvery blonde hair she had cut into a short cap against the Singapore heat were too delicate for such an ornament.

The dark-eyed man waited for her answer. She thought him rather arrogant, so let him wait. The saleswoman stood silent, unobtrusive and serene, as if nothing could surprise her; no kind of odd or unconventional behavior. Leni thought involuntarily, "If Guinevere Raymond could see me now!" and her soft lips curved in amusement.

The man with the broad shoulders exclaimed impatiently, "Here—come over to the mirror for a moment."

Leni told herself she wasn't going to be ordered about like that, yet despite herself, in two seconds she was standing before a great oval glass framed in bamboo. And those long fingers brushed against her bare shoulders tinglingly as they draped the silk about her slender body.

She stood like a statue, staring at herself. Eyes that had never been anything but gray had picked up color from the silk and sparkled like the eyes of a stranger. She pushed back the soft fall of silvery fringe that covered her brow and glanced at the man who stood behind her. His white teeth gleamed in a smile that made him look more incredibly stunning than ever. His eyes looked back into hers.

"Perfect. I'll take it. And thank you"—with a nod to Leni and a quick whisking away of the sari—"for your assistance."

She tried to shrug carelessly, but her heart was hammering madly. Talk about Prince Charming of the fairytales! Yet there was something a little intimidating—even menacing—about this man. The thought of defying him made her nerves tingle. He took her breath away completely. She thought she had never in her life met or seen anyone like him. Was that crazy? Was the spell of Singapore making her lose her usual common-sense attitude to life?

Or *was* there something very special about him?

As she returned to her chair and he leaned nonchalantly against the counter watching the woman wrap the sari she decided that there was. He murmured something in a low voice, and even his voice was hypnotic. Or was it something to do with the soft eastern music that was drifting from a record shop along the arcade? Leni had no idea what he was saying; she only knew that her pulses were stirred. And yet she was a sensible, level-headed girl. Everyone said so—even Guinevere Raymond. Sensible, level-headed and also completely inexperienced in the ways of the world. . . .

The saleswoman said prettily, "Thank you very much, Mr. Savage," and then, with a quick dark smile in Leni's direction, he was gone. The woman murmured, "Please excuse me," and disappeared to fetch the dresses that Leni had ordered on Mrs. Raymond's behalf.

"You had better try them on," she told Leni when she came back. "We must make sure they are quite satisfactory, Miss Forrest."

Leni chose the ivory batik patterned in hibiscus red and delicately veined with a green like leaves in shadow. She was standing before the mirror while the Chinese woman examined the fit critically. The dresses were for fourteen-year-old Emma Raymond and Leni, although she had celebrated her twentieth birthday just before leaving England two weeks ago, had exactly the same slim schoolgirl figure as her employer's daughter. When someone came into the store, she knew, by a tingling in her spine, that it was the Savage man again.

"Pay no attention to me," he said casually. "It's nothing that can't wait. Please go ahead."

Now it was he who took the brocaded chair, he whose eyes were on her, and Leni was uneasily self-conscious. Yet her mirror-image told her that she need not be ashamed. The style of this dress made the most of her slenderness; the long sleeves hid her too-thin arms; the soft simple neckline showed the smooth pale creamy tan of her throat, the graceful draping emphasized her narrow waist and gave a flattering illusion of roundness at the hips and bosom. The dark green sandals she wore matched perfectly, and the saleswoman was murmuring approval.

"I don't think you need try on any of the others, Miss Forrest. They are made to exactly the same measurements. They are for Mrs. Raymond's daughter in

England, aren't they? It's very fortunate you have the same figure."

"Yes, it is," agreed Leni. "I'm sure they will fit perfectly."

She went quickly into the changing room where she divested herself of the lovely dress and unashamedly strained her ears to hear what was going on in the store. Mr. Savage was evidently buying a bracelet now, and she thought as she slipped on her embroidered white cotton dress, one of the few garments she had bought in Singapore, "Of course, he has a wife or girlfriend—or even a mistress! Worldly and sophisticated men often have mistresses!" The silk sari and the bracelet—and the woman who received them would never know that she, Leni Forrest, had been asked her opinion of the silk, had felt its texture against her shoulder; would certainly never know how foolishly her heart had pounded as long masculine fingers brushed against her skin. . . .

Not many minutes later she was in the lift ascending to the sixth floor where Mrs. Raymond had her suite. She tried hard to think of anything but "Mr. Savage," failing lamentably, and she felt impatient with herself. Did Leni Forrest's veneer of common sense hide a hopeless dreamer? Just now it seemed that it did. She wished futilely that she were protected by the existence of someone in England waiting for her to come back. Someone good and reliable like Dee Fisher's Charles. Dee and Charles were to be married in August, though Dee's mother, from whom Leni had received a letter a couple of days ago, seemed a little concerned about that. Dee apparently showed no signs of wanting to leave Bali now that she had achieved her dream and gone there.

As schoolgirls, Dee and Leni had always talked of following in Guerney's footsteps and seeking the sun.

Guerney was Dee's brother, ten years older than she was and an artist, which made him seem a very romantic figure to the girls. He had left home when Dee was twelve to wander about over various islands before he settled for Bali. Dee and Leni promised each other that one day, when they had left school and made enough money, they would join him. Just for a while, perhaps—unless they met someone wildly exciting there and were persuaded to stay forever. . . .

Leni relinquished her dreams almost as soon as she left school. Suddenly orphaned, she was flung into the world on her own and earning a living became a serious business. She worked hard at her shorthand and typing and had to think of tomorrow.

But Dee tumbled in and out of a variety of shortlived jobs and proved herself a trial to doting parents who had always spoiled their youngest child. It had been a great relief to them when Charles Broughton, a young lawyer who worked in his father's firm, came along. He and Dee became engaged and many sighs of thankfulness were heaved.

Then alas! to her parent's despair, Dee broke out again. A windfall from an aunt in Canada, meant quite plainly as a wedding gift, sent Dee to Bali. "A final fling," said Dee gaily. "If I don't give myself this I shall be sorry forever afterward." Surprisingly Charles let her go, but her parents were full of doubts.

Doubts that from all accounts were not unfounded, for Guerney wrote home that he refused to be held responsible for his young sister. He was not specific, but he was quite definite that the sooner Dee went back home to England, the easier he would sleep.

Leni was a little amused, a little envious and a little anxious too. What could Dee be up to?

Then she had a stroke of unexpected luck herself. She was to go to Singapore! And Bali looked such a very short step from Singapore on the map that Dee's mother said comfortably, "You will certainly be able to see Dee while you're there, Leni. You were always the level-headed one. But you're young—she'll listen to you. She'll come along home like a good girl and marry Charles."

But in actual fact, Leni suspected she would never get to Bali. Plane trips and holidays cost money, and she was going to Singapore on a job. She would come back with her employer and that was all there would be to it. She had been Guinevere Raymond's private secretary for close to a year and had loved every minute of it. Mrs. Raymond was a smart and attractive woman of about forty. She had been widowed twice, and she had a daughter, Emma, now at boarding school in England. She earned a very good living writing practical but also rather stunningly offbeat articles on interior decoration. They appeared regularly in one of the glossy magazines, and now, as well, she was writing a book. Leni soon found that she was a woman with a strong and determined character. What she wanted, she got—by using her charm or any other means at her disposal. Many doors were opened to her that were closed to other women engaged in similar work. This book she was compiling had illustrations—photographs she had taken herself—of some of the most beautiful and exclusive homes in England. Once all the ground work had been done, and what remained was a general collation and a sharpening up of the copy, she suddenly announced that she was going to Singapore.

"Bang goes my lovely job," thought Leni in dismay. But her lovely job did not go bang at all. She was to come to Singapore too!

"My dear child, you can't honestly imagine that I

would abandon all the work I've done—break my contract with my publishers! I'm a business woman! No, I said the book would be ready on a certain date, and ready it will be. Besides, there's the financial aspect to consider. However, I must go to Singapore. So—we finish our book in Singapore. Or don't you want to come to Singapore, Leni? Are you hiding some secret and passionate love affair behind that amazingly innocent face?"

Leni had grown used to her teasing, and of course there was no passionate love affair to hide. But she did confess to Mrs. Raymond about the plans she and Dee had once made, and she told her that Dee was in Bali with Guerney now.

"So I do want to go to Singapore, Mrs. Raymond. Though," she had added at the look of quizzical amusement on her employer's face, "of course I don't imagine for a moment that I shall get to Bali."

"But half a loaf is better than no bread? And it will make you almost even with your friend? Well, that's a good sensible attitude to take, and despite such unexpected flights of romanticism you're a sensible girl. I wouldn't have you working for me if you weren't."

And that was that. . . .

Now as Leni left the elevator and walked along the cool carpeted corridor to their suite, she reflected that this little interlude in her life was coming to an end. She had discovered very quickly why they had had to come to Singapore. Guinevere Raymond was, outrageously to Leni who would never have suspected such a thing, on the trail of a man. Her second husband had died over two years earlier, and Leni had imagined that she had built up a full and satisfying life for herself. Her social life as well as her business life was crowded with friends, but her name had never been linked with that of any man. Now suddenly, in Singapore, there was a man—Sam Becker, a Canadian. Leni was not quite sure what he did, but it had something to do with importing, and he was in Singapore on a business trip. It was specifically to "run into" him that they had come. Leni was more than a little shocked by Mrs. Raymond's tactics. She had contacted Sam Becker almost as soon as they arrived with some story of having heard from a friend just that very minute that he was in Singapore! He was invited to the suite, and from then on, Guinevere Raymond divided her time between her book and Sam Becker.

Leni, of course, had to work hard on the book. Far more was left to her own discretion than had been the case in London. Her lunch hour was almost her only opportunity for getting out of doors, and she usually spent it at the hotel swimming pool. The life of the hotel fascinated her, and she loved what she saw of the beautiful clean green Garden City of Singapore. But she was a little timid about going around the city on her own in the evenings, and generally it was a case of too much work and not much company other than her own. Still, she had been cheerful about it. And Guinevere said, "When the book's off our hands maybe we'll have a few days' shopping and sightseeing before we go back to England. That is—unless. . . ."

She had not finished that sentence, but there had been no more talk of sightseeing, and no more talk of "unless." Now the book was practically ready for the publisher; the dresses for Emma had been ordered; tentative bookings made for the flight home. Soon Singapore would be no more than a dream, and Leni, who had up till now been more or less resigned to the fact, felt impatient with herself for the half-formed dreams that drifted wilfully through her mind. Dreams that centered around a man called "Mr. Savage" who was probably married and whom she would certainly never even see again.

How silly could you get! The tropics had certainly gone to her head. . . .

She turned the key in the lock and went into the suite.

Mrs. Raymond was in her bedroom, wearing one of her beautiful hostess outfits and glancing through a magazine as she lay back on the cushioned bamboo lounger.

"The dresses for Emma? Are they exciting enough to please the little monster?"

What a way to refer to your daughter! "They're absolutely gorgeous." She began to unwrap them and wondered if she were imagining it or if Mrs. Raymond was not as interested as she might have been. She held up each outfit separately, and she knew the older woman was thinking about something else.

"Yes—Emma will love them." She dismissed them offhandedly. Leni persisted, holding the ivory and hibiscus red confection against herself.

"She'll go mad about them. This one is utterly fabulous."

Guinevere showed signs of amusement. She said casually, "It suits you. You'd better keep it for yourself, my child. Emma will be happy with the others. She won't have anywhere to wear them—she'll use them to make her friends green with envy, that's about all."

"But . . ." began Leni helplessly.

Guinevere waved a slender hand. "No, I mean it. Besides, you must have something to wear tonight —something better than those pretty little secretary dresses you've acquired lately."

"Tonight? I'm not going anywhere tonight."

"Ah, but you are! Tonight is a special occasion." She

tossed down her magazine and looked at Leni with a mischievous smile. "Sam and I are celebrating our decision to get married. Are you surprised?"

Leni was surprised. She was also a little dismayed. This time her job had *really* ended. She would have to go back to England by herself, watch her money carefully while she hunted for another job. She turned away and began to fold the dresses, and behind her Mrs. Raymond laughed softly, mockingly. Leni, reminded, said quickly, "Yes—I'm surprised. But it's wonderful. I hope that you'll be very happy."

"Of course that quick little mind of yours has picked up the fact that you'll be out of a job."

"Yes," said Leni wryly. She held up the ivory batik and pretended to look at herself in the mirror. She wondered why she felt quite so forlorn and deflated. She would get another job; she would have this time in Singapore to remember. She said slowly, "Thank you for the dress. But let Emma have it. I don't really need it. And—and if you don't mind, I shan't make a third at your celebration dinner."

"Now don't tear at my heart-strings," said the teasing voice. "I know I've kept you cooped up, but tonight you're to step out. And we'll be a party of four—Sam's asked a friend to join us especially for your benefit. So you must look your best and you must pretend to be happy, even if your work for me *is* ended. I'm afraid that just can't be helped. But I've planned a little consolation prize for you. Not the dress—the dress is nothing." Her blue eyes looked bright and she was smiling impishly, and Leni waited, wondering. "What would you say to a month in Bali, all expenses paid, and of course your return fare to London?"

Leni opened her mouth and said, "Oh!" much too

surprised to take it in properly. She sank down in a chair and stared at Mrs. Raymond. She wasn't sure what she felt.

"You can go off and join your school friend—Dee, wasn't it? And that very romantic-sounding artist brother of hers. See what you can do for yourself in Bali! How will you like that?"

"I—I just can't believe it," said Leni, blinking, because tears had sprung to her eyes. She suddenly got up and impulsively kissed Mrs. Raymond on the cheek. "Thank you very much—and I really am very happy that you're to be married—even though I'm sorry to lose my job."

"But going to Bali will help make up for that? And you never know—you may change your mind about going home to England again. In which case you can keep the money for your fare as a wedding present."

Leni looked at her blankly. "A wedding present?"

"Now don't tell me it's not this artist fellow you're dreaming about, for I simply won't believe it. A pretty child like you with no boyfriends—and this impossible dream you've been holding onto."

Leni shook her head. "I haven't seen Guerney for over three years—when he came home for a couple of weeks."

"And you were an impressionable seventeen? Well, we shall see. . . . But you are a little consoled by my gift?"

"More than a little consoled," said Leni. "I simply can't believe it yet. You're too generous."

"I feel generous," smiled Guinevere. "And I know you've been like a bird in a cage here in Singapore. You haven't had a good time at all. I've been too wrapped up in my own personal affairs to take you around. At least I hope you'll enjoy yourself tonight. Sam promises me that Kemp Savage is guaranteed to set any female heart aflutter—even though it is a little engaged elsewhere."

Leni's cheeks flooded with color, then paled again. Kemp *Savage*! Was the name a coincidence, or could the fourth member of the party possibly be the man she had encountered in the arcade shop? Her hands shook slightly as she once again took up the dress she had been given.

"Have a rest, take a shower and look your best, Leni," advised Guinevere. The voice seemed to Leni to come from another world. Her heart was beating fast, and her imagination was racing. Was Kemp Savage her Mr. Savage? And if so, did she still want to go to Bali?

Two hours later, when she went down to the lounge with Sam and Guinevere, she discovered it was true. The lights were soft and music was playing, and she knew she looked her best in the batik dress, her hair gleaming like white gold, her makeup soft and subtle. Yes, she looked her best, but of course she was still far too simple and unsophisticated a girl for the man who could assert his charm on a woman within a few minutes of meeting her. . . .

As she was introduced, she saw his dark brows lift quizzically.

"My little secretary, Leni Forrest," Guinevere said, her arm about Leni's waist. The black magnetic eyes flicked over Leni, over the dress. They seemed to say, "You're certainly onto a good thing, little secretary." Leni, whose heart was lurching madly, expected him to say that they had already met—or at least encountered each other. But he didn't, and she felt vaguely hurt. Even if he didn't remember her, surely he must remember the dress she was wearing!

As she sipped the aperitif that Sam had ordered for her and the others talked of Singapore, of hotels, of the amazing number of times one ran into an acquaintance in the most unexpected of places—she eyed Kemp Savage in a puzzled fashion. He must remember her! He had held a violet silk sari against her body; his fingers had touched the bare flesh of her shoulders. . . . As if aware of her regard, he suddenly turned his eyes her way and smiled at her in an oddly conspiratorial fashion as though the two of them shared some secret. For some reason, Leni did not much like the look in those dark eyes of his. It was so—knowing, so intimate, it upset her equilibrium.

They had dinner in the Dragon Room, sumptuously decorated in black and gold with a motif of marvelous red dragons adorning the walls. Their table was by a wide window that looked down onto the streets of the light-starred city, and as they ate, Sam Becker asked casually, "Are you footloose and fancy free, Kemp? Or is it just a piece of good luck for us that you weren't already booked up for tonight?"

Leni thought of the sari and the jeweled bracelet, and reflected both sadly and wryly that he was hardly free! She put her own interpretation on his careless shrug and grimace, but Sam persisted, "Cristelle Dubois? I'd heard that was serious—and I'll admit I felt happy for you. It would be—"

Kemp Savage made a dismissive gesture with one long-fingered hand and Sam was quickly silenced. He looked at Leni as he said carefully, "Cristelle had another male on her mind. Provocation of that kind is just not to my taste. Besides which, I'm not accustomed to waiting in line for any girl. So—"

"Pity," said Sam with a shrewd look. "There was serious talk that you'd found yourself a wife."

"Serious talk? Or rumors?" Kemp Savage's smile was not altogether pleasant, though his tone was light.

"Hmm. Perhaps we'd better leave that topic of conversation. You're staying on in Singapore?"

"That rather depends. I've been cruising around the hotels for the past month, combining business with pleasure. We've a big board meeting coming up in a few weeks and I have several ideas I want to consolidate before I go back. However, as I said"—and his dark glance again rested speculatively on Leni—"I have no definite plans. For the moment." He turned to Guinevere. "The wedding's to be when?"

"As soon as we can arrange it," she said frankly. "Especially now I know how slippery you males can be," she added with a laugh. "But seriously, Sam and I plan to marry in Canada where we shall be settling. We haven't set a date, but I'd like my little daughter to be there. I suppose it's no use sending you an invitation?"

"No. But thank you for asking. I shall certainly think of you both." He turned toward Leni. "And the little—secretary? Is she off to Canada too?"

Leni shook her head. She wasn't sure what to make of Kemp Savage. It was true that she found him irresistibly attractive, and yet closer acquaintance made her feel unsure of herself, uneasy. The way he looked at her—some sort of undertone that seemed to lie behind everything he said to her. Even the way he had said just now "the little—secretary" with an oddly meaningful hesitation before the final word.

"Leni is off to Bali," said Guinevere.

"And that's Kemp's part of the world," said Sam.

Leni felt her pulses jolt. It was as though she had received a sharp and unexpected blow on the side of the head that made her for a moment incapable of thought. She stared at her wine glass, fingered it unconsciously, so that the waiter hurried forward to refill it. Kemp Savage's part of the world. Bali!

"But of course," Sam Becker continued, "Kemp's on a

kind of business holiday. Kemp," he explained mainly for Guinevere's benefit, but Leni listened hard, "is managing director of the Hotel Selatan Company. You'll have heard of it, I'm sure. And at present he's in search of new ideas. Right, Kemp?"

A careless nod. "Quite right. I've already run a few to earth—maybe the very ones I need."

"But I guess you could still do with a little more relaxation?" suggested Sam slyly.

"You could say that. I haven't taken a vacation for over two years."

"Then what better place to take it than in Singapore?"

"Singapore's fine. But it's not the only place in the world." Again he looked at Leni and there seemed to be hidden laughter in his eyes. "So you're off to Bali, Leni. You certainly strike me as being a lucky young woman. But if you're hoping to find a job there, you may not find it all that easy."

"I'm not looking for a job," said Leni. "Mrs. Raymond is making me a present of a month's holiday." She looked at him steadily, and as he nodded and returned her gaze in a very knowing way, she felt suddenly exasperated with him.

She longed to ask, "What are you thinking? Why do you look at me like that?" She decided her silly infatuation was very ill advised, and that it was a very good thing he was holidaying away from Bali.

"It's not exactly a present, Leni," Guinevere said. "It's more in the nature of compensation." She glanced at Sam with a half-hidden smile. "My change of plans has meant that Leni's suddenly out of a job."

"And that rates a holiday in Bali, does it? You're certainly a very generous employer! But may I know, why Bali? I'll admit I'm intrigued."

"Leni has an old school friend who is holidaying there. Haven't you, my dear?"

Leni said merely, "Yes," thankful that Guinevere hadn't seen fit to make any suggestions about Guerney Fisher.

"Well, I'm quite sure she'll make the most of her month," said Kemp Savage. He pushed back his chair. A few couples had begun to drift around the small dance floor, "Will you excuse us if Leni and I dance before we have our coffee?" He held out his hand to Leni, imperative, lordly. It did not seem to have occurred to him to ask Leni first if she would like to dance with him. And yet she had risen to her feet and was obeying his subtle command almost before she knew what was happening.

Besides, she admitted to herself a moment later as she moved across the floor in his embrace, she would never have forgiven herself if she had passed up this opportunity. Even if she found him enigmatic, aggravating, his attraction was so acute she wanted more than anything to be near him, to look at him, to discover him.

And he, she presently learned, wanted to discover things about her.

His voice close to her ear, he murmured caressingly, "How do you do it, little secretary?"

"How do I do what?" she stammered, taken unawares.

"Come now, you can be frank with me. I've proved myself discreet, haven't I?"

"I don't know what you mean."

"Don't you? Couldn't I have said, the moment we were introduced, that I'd seen you earlier on, taking delivery of those dresses in Guinevere Raymond's name?"

She asked, wide-eyed, mystified, "Why didn't you, then?"

"Because I don't believe in giving away anyone's secrets. *You* gave no sign that we'd met—I took my cue from that." He held her a little way from him and looked down at her in amusement. In the soft lighting, his dark eyes had a strange glitter that was both demonic and benevolent, and Leni felt her bones melting, melting. . . . With an effort, she brought herself back to her senses to protest, "No—but I have no secrets from Mrs. Raymond."

Light only began to dawn when he said flatly, "Those dresses—that dress you're wearing now—were supposed to be for Emma Raymond. I heard it put quite plainly."

So *that* was what he thought—that she made purchases and put them on her employer's account! She flushed hotly.

"The dresses *are* for Emma. But Mrs. Raymond wanted me to have this one. You may ask her if you don't believe me. She's a very generous person."

"She is indeed," he agreed dryly. "But I won't ask her, of course. You know that." They danced in silence for perhaps 30 seconds. Leni felt angry and helpless. She didn't know if he believed her or not.

"A trip to Bali too," he mused. "To join an old school friend. Are you quite sure you're going to join an old school friend, Leni?"

"Of course I'm sure," said Leni, incensed. "Why else would I want to go to Bali?"

He laughed softly and pulled her closer in his arms. "You're an intriguing mixture of innocence and guile. I'll admit I can't make you out yet, Leni Forrest."

Neither of them spoke again. Leni's anger subsided, and despite herself she knew it was exciting to be so near to him. When he took her back to join the others she felt frustrated and was filled with a deep and obscure regret that she hadn't made better use of those few minutes alone with him. Something was over, was ended, and it had never even begun.

"Have a wonderful time in Bali," he said to her casually when the evening had ended.

"Thank you. I'm sure I will." Her eyes were bright and when she turned away she felt the sting of unexpected tears. A chapter was closed. She was misunderstood, and he had not asked to see her again. Obscurely, she had somehow expected that he would. She had best forget him. He would no doubt forget her very quickly as he enjoyed his—relaxation.

CHAPTER TWO

Leni's last two days in Singapore were busy ones as she had some retyping to do where Guinevere had decided alterations were necessary. There was no time for any social life, and of course she saw or heard nothing of Kemp Savage.

Then at last she was off on her own, inwardly a little fearful, flying to Bali to join Dee. She had sent a telegram, but she did not know whether she would be met or not. In any case, she could take a taxi from the airport to the beach where Dee was staying. Guinevere had said, "Don't try to save money, Leni. You'll find I've given you ample for a month, so see that you really enjoy yourself."

It was late evening when the plane landed at the International Airport south of Denpasar, after flying in from the sea over terraced paddy fields, palm trees and thatched roofs. Once through the brief formalities in the airport building, Leni headed for the wide glass doors that led outside into golden evening light and a road where she could see hire cars and small knocked-about vehicles that looked like miniature buses. "Plenty of transportation," thought Leni in relief, but no sign of Dee.

The very next minute her wits were scattered as she was beseiged by half a dozen Balinese, all beseeching, "*Nona*—you take my taxi to Denpasar?" Bewildered, she shook her head and exclaimed, "Kuta Beach!" Then matters became worse than ever. Plenty of transport! Certainly all the drivers were eager to take her to Kuta Beach. They all wanted to charge her a different fare and she simply had no idea what to do. If only Dee were here, she was thinking, when a familiar voice exclaimed with faint amusement, "Your old school friend hasn't met you, then, Miss Forrest?" and she looked up to see Kemp Savage, cool-looking, darker and more handsome than ever in light cotton trousers and short-sleeved shirt of fine cotton.

Leni nearly fell over with a mixture of amazement and relief. She said excitedly, "No! And I'm trying to negotiate for a taxi—but so far it seems quite hopeless."

Kemp Savage made a dismissive gesture to the taxi-drivers, said a few good-humored words, and they all melted away. "Now where is it you want to go, Leni?"

Her spine tingled at the sound of her name on his lips, and at the smile he was giving her. It was enough to make any girl swoon, she thought. She stammered, "To—to Kuta Beach. I'm not sure exactly where—to a *losmen*, whatever *that* is, called Rumah Made."

"A *losmen*?" He looked surprised. "I'd have imagined you'd go to a tourist hotel." Nevertheless he picked up her bag and conducted her to his car, telling her easily, "You'll find the *losmen*—which, by the way, is a kind of small private hotel run by Balinese—rather different from the hotel in Singapore, and also considerably cheaper. You'll be put up for maybe 30 pence a night—and that will include a snack for breakfast! I'd have imagined Guinevere's bounty would run to more than that." He sent her a quizzical look as he ushered her into the front seat of the car. She had still not recovered from the shock of seeing him, and answered nervously, "Yes, of course—I've been given a princely sum." She added, as they drove off, "It was lucky for me you happened to be at the airport. Thank you for rescuing me."

"I wouldn't call it luck," he said, and she saw the corner of his mouth tilt upwards. Casual clothes, she decided, suited him, and she admired the thick dark hair that this evening fell in a slight wave over his forehead so that he appeared less formidable and more approachable. "Perhaps," she found herself thinking, "he's not all that sophisticated after all."

"Not *luck*," he repeated. "I came out to the airport specifically to meet you. I heard from Sam when you were due in, and it occurred to me that you might possibly appreciate a little assistance even if that school friend of yours turned up to meet you. Which she didn't."

Leni said blithely, "No. But it doesn't matter " She felt momentarily on top of the world, and whatever he said, she thought she was incredibly lucky. She had certainly tried hard enough to talk herself out of the idea that she had fallen in love at first sight—and fallen disastrously hard, and disastrously unwisely. But in her heart she was well aware that she had failed. She was hopelessly drawn to Kemp Savage, though she had no idea what sort of a man he really was.

It seemed miraculous that he had actually come to the airport to meet her. After all, he was not even supposed to be in Bali! He was on holiday. Then did that mean—? Leni was sure that it did, and could. How else explain that she was here now, beside him in his car? It was like a dream come true.

"Bali," he said in a musing voice, "is a beautiful island, Leni, and I hope I'll be able to help you enjoy its beauties!"

Now Leni thought she must certainly be dreaming, and she said, her eyes wide, "Thank you. You're very kind."

"Is that what you'd call it?" He sent her a long glance from his dark eyes that to Leni in her present state was almost as good as a knock-out blow. When she had more or less recovered her senses she became aware that they were driving through a narrow village street that was lined with high walls and tall tiered shrines of stone or red brick, most elaborately carved with weird and fantastic figures. Coconut and banana palms and tall bamboos made a jungle of green, and poinsettias and frangipani flowers gleamed like fire and moonstones. Along the side of the street, fat pigs rooted, hens ran, and children squatted in gateways at their play. Leni stared at a little roadside stall with a thatched roof, and at the Balinese girl in traditional sarong and long-sleeved, waisted blouse who tended it.

Kemp Savage said, "That's a *warong*, Leni. In Bali it's the custom for a girl to set up a stall when she's reached marriageable age. That way, she's seen by many people and may attract a suitable husband! I must take you to sample the food some day."

"I'd love that," said Leni. Her month in Bali was already beginning to seem the most wonderful thing that had ever happened in her life.

As they drove on, she heard a deep rhythmic vibrant sound which gradually became louder, and she looked enquiringly at the man beside her.

"The women are pounding rice in the compounds," he explained. "You'll hear that sound often in the evenings."

And now along each side of the road there was a long, long row of yellow hummocks of unthreshed rice, shaped rather like beehives, and in the golden light of evening saronged women walked gracefully, turning them over.

Leni drew a deep breath of happiness and pleasure. "Your island is lovely! I'm going to be happy here."

He looked amused. "You've made up your mind to that very quickly."

"Oh," said Leni, "I've been thinking about this for years—"

"Schoolgirl dreams come true? Well, don't idealize the place—it's not all beauty and light. The people have their sorrows like anyone else."

"Yes, of course." Leni remembered something Guerney had told them. "Didn't one of the volcanoes erupt a few years ago and destroy several villages?"

"That's right. You've been reading it up, have you?" Without waiting for her to confirm his supposition, he continued, "One of these days perhaps I'll take you up the coast and you'll see the black streams of ash that now cover parts of a once-beautiful countryside."

A moment later, he stopped the car at a crossroads and leaning out asked a slim brown boy on a bicycle, "*Dimana* Rumah Made?"

Presently they were driving slowly along a narrow unpaved street where there were many *warongs* displaying not food but batik cloths, blouses and wood carvings. They stopped before a high wall made of coral rock in which a gateway was carved with ferocious figures. At one side of the gate was a small open-fronted restaurant where several Balinese and a couple of young Europeans sat eating.

"Rumah Made," said Kemp, turning to Leni with a smile.

Over the wall she could see thatched roofs and the tapering pagoda shapes of shrines, and suddenly she felt nervous. She climbed from the car, went uncertainly through the gateway and around a projecting wall, which she learned later served the purpose of baffling evil spirits—who had difficulty in negotiating corners! Behind her, Kemp Savage carried her bag, and she wondered what he was thinking. For her part, she thought it strange that Dee should be living in a place like this. She was certain that Guerney had his own bungalow. A brushed dirt path between houses with walls made of woven cane and glassless windows led toward a flower garden. Beyond that Leni could see a cream-washed stone bungalow with green shutters. On the veranda were bamboo chairs and a table with an oil lamp standing on it, not yet lit, for there was still light in the sky. Someone was sitting there reading.

Behind her, Kemp Savage said reassuringly, "This is a family compound. You'll find that various relatives of Made's live in these houses and help with the gardening, the cooking, the laundering, and so on. That's your *losmen* with the verandah, and your fellow-guests will probably be young Europeans looking for a cheap holiday. If you find it too rough—and I rather think you may—then you must move out. I take it your friend stays here?"

"Yes," said Leni. Although he had spoken reassuringly she still felt nervous about going into the *losmen* and wished that Dee would come running out to meet her. But there was only the man on the veranda and a couple of small barefooted brown children running across the path. And a very old man who came through a side gate from the road, carrying a beautiful wicker cage that held a splendid white cock.

Leni drew a deep breath. Well, Kemp would come in with her. Kemp could speak Indonesian. He would find Made and explain who she was and what she wanted. Leni took courage from this knowledge and passed the first of the cane-walled houses. Ahead, a plump smiling woman appeared on the path. She wore a brown and gold sarong with a wide orange waistband and a long-sleeved low-necked blouse.

She smiled at Leni and spoke in a pretty broken English in a soft high-pitched voice. "*Selamat datang*! You are Miss Forrest. I am Made. I have room for you. You come see it?"

"Thank you," said Leni. She glanced at Kemp, whose eyes had narrowed and who looked thoughtful, and once again she wondered what he was thinking. A Balinese woman with a small girl hanging onto her sarong brought a lighted oil lamp from one of the compound houses and hung it in the branches of a tree that bore yellowing fruit like enormous grapefruit. Leni thought it all strange—but it would be fun, with Dee. She followed Made along the neatly swept dirt path. Ahead, the man on the veranda looked up, sprang to his feet and ran down the steps. It was a second before she recognized him in the rapidly fading light. He was a broad-shouldered man of medium height with thick fair hair and—of course! It was Guerney! Leni had hardly made this discovery when he had scooped her into his arms and kissed her soundly and affectionately.

"Leni dear! It's wonderful to see you—I couldn't be happier! You're an angel of light!"

Leni disentangled herself laughingly. Guerney had always been demonstrative. Dee was like that too—extroverted and articulate. "Guerney, how good to see *you*! Where's Dee?" She suddenly became aware that Made was watching smilingly, and that Kemp—Kemp Savage was watching decidedly *un*smilingly! She said quickly, awkwardly, "Kemp, this is Guerney Fisher. Guerney, I met Mr. Savage in Singapore, and he was kind enough to meet me at the airport."

Kemp said curtly, "We've met before, I believe." The two men did not shake hands. Kemp's mouth was hard and his voice chilling as he said briefly, "Well, I've brought you where you wanted to be, Miss Forrest. I can see you're in—good hands, so I'll say goodbye. Enjoy yourself—with your *school* friend." His lip curled, he turned and strode away.

Leni stared after him, her dreams tumbling, her mind churning. Suddenly it seemed to be night, the world was dark, and she wanted to run after Kemp, to tell him, "Wait! You don't understand—" But Guerney had taken her arm and murmured that it was fine that Kemp Savage had been able to drop her off at the *losmen*, but now he would look after her. Despite herself, she was climbing the steps to the verandah while Made went soft-footedly ahead. Leni felt like weeping. She heard the roar of a motor as Kemp's car started up and took off along the road.

She followed Made, who had picked up a lamp from somewhere, into a simple white-walled room with yellow tiles on the floor and a ceiling of woven cane. There was a tall cupboard, a table, a chair and a narrow bed covered only with a sheet. An unglazed window with a wooden shutter looked over a low wall into a courtyard where thatch-roofed shrines made ghostly shadows amongst fruit trees and banana palms.

Guerney said, "Well, Leni, what do you think? Let's have your impressions." He sounded as if he expected her to say she couldn't stay here, but Leni looked at Made's smiling expectant face and said, smiling back, "It's very nice. And so clean!"

"Very clean," Made agreed softly. "I show you wash-room."

The washroom was at the end of the veranda. It contained a built-in trough of sparkling clear water, and there was a scoop, which one used when one wished to take a bath.

"Spring water," said Made. "Very good."

"Yes, it looks lovely," agreed Leni.

"You will eat in *rumah*?"

"Yes, thank you."

Made, satisfied, padded away, and Leni joined Guerney, who looked at her resignedly. "You must learn to say no in Bali."

"I didn't want to say no," said Leni.

Guerney shrugged. "Go and have a wash and I'll take you to the restaurant to eat, and maybe we'll catch Dee as she comes in."

"Where *is* Dee?" asked Leni. If only it had been Dee waiting for her at the *losmen*, she couldn't help thinking, how different everything would have been! As it was, Kemp Savage must believe that she had been deceiving him—and Guinevere Raymond—by pretending it was a girlfriend she wished to see in Bali.

Perhaps it was wishful thinking to imagine Kemp had returned to Bali specifically on her account, but all the same he had come to the airport to meet her, and he had talked as if she could expect to see quite a bit of him while she was in Bali. Then Guerney had materialized and greeted her so affectionately, and Kemp had put his own interpretation on that! And she had heard him say—in Singapore—that he was not accustomed to waiting in line for any girl.

She asked Guerney desperately, the question following quickly on her inquiry about Dee, "Where is the Hotel Selatan, Guerney?"

"A half mile or so along the beach. Do you want to stay there? It's expensive, but really good. Only you'd have to persuade Dee."

"Would she need to be persuaded? I'd have thought Dee would prefer a hotel to the *losmen*—unless she could stay with you."

"She could, but she won't," said Guerney with a decidedly grim look. "But freshen up, Leni, and I'll tell you about it while we eat."

Leni washed and changed for dinner. She tried to think about Dee, who seemed to be causing Guerney some trouble, but instead she thought restlessly of Kemp Savage. She had asked about the Hotel Selatan because she was determined to go there and explain to Kemp Savage that he had made a mistake. After that, it would be up to him. And she simply couldn't believe that he would drop her. Though she couldn't imagine what attractions she could possibly possess for a man so mature and so devastatingly fascinating!

Sitting in the restaurant with Guerney at a small table, she presently asked him once more, "Where *is* Dee?"

"Somewhere around. I just can't keep track of that girl. Look, will you have fried noodles—*bakmi goreng*? It's good." Leni nodded and he ordered it from a slim Balinese waitress. Leni looked around the lamplit *rumah* and saw three Europeans amongst the Balinese. Young, shabby, untidy; vaguely hippy. Not—really—her kind of person. They must be the ones Kemp had spoken of who were after a cheap holiday. . . .

While they ate the simply served—and ridiculously cheap—meal, Guerney talked in a low voice. Leni noticed that the Balinese did not talk, and their curious glances showed that they considered talking while you ate not at all the right thing to do. She felt a little uncomfortable.

"Dee's running around with an Australian fellow she imagines she's fallen in love with—Mike Miller."

Leni stared at him. "But what about Charles?"

Guerney flipped his fingers. "Charles is in England and Dee's moved into the world of her schoolday dreams. Her idea seems to be to have a great and glorious spree before she settles down to sober life. The trouble is, she doesn't seem to realize she could be messing up her whole future.

"Quite frankly, Leni, my little sister is driving me up the wall, and I wish she'd either act responsibly or go back home. She hasn't the experience to handle this sort of thing, and chances are one of these days she'll find she's bitten off far more than she can chew. And then what happens?"

Bewildered and upset at the thought of poor Charles, Leni said, "I'd heard you were finding her a handful, but I never dreamed she would . . . would. . . ." She stopped without finishing and really looked at Guerney for the first time. He was looking more than his thirty or thirty-one years—far more. His thick fair hair was rumpled, and there were lines about his honest blue eyes. There was not a vestige of the romantic artist about Guerney, she thought, and was somehow surprised. For longer than she could remember, Dee's artist brother had epitomized romance.

"You didn't dream she would really get involved in any trouble now that she's engaged?" asked Guerney. "Well, maybe you'll succeed in bringing her to her senses where Janet and I have failed. You were always a level-headed girl, and I've been counting on that."

Level-headed! There it was again. If Guerney could only know how she had let her world be rocked by a man who was practically a stranger, he wouldn't be so sure of himself when he called her level-headed!

She looked across at him questioningly. "Janet?"

"The woman I'm going to marry. She lives in Djakarta—works in the gallery where I sell some of my stuff. I invited her over to stay and see what she could do with Dee, who had managed to involve herself with a man almost as soon as she reached Bali. Dee is engaged and she has no business to be playing around. It's something I don't intend to sanction and I let her know it."

"And—?" prompted Leni, as he paused.

"Janet's remonstrances had no more effect than my own. My little sister packed her bag and flounced off to the *losmen*. Fortunately that boyfriend dropped out of the picture, but in no time she'd found herself another one. Not a particularly attractive one at that. I imagine she's at this moment cavorting with him about this Island of Light. I'm sorry I wasn't at the airport to meet you, by the way. I'd arranged a meeting with a prospective buyer and business has to come first. I thought I'd better see you as soon as possible, however, and put you in the picture. And ask you to do what you can to straighten out my crazy sister."

He signalled to the waitress and asked for coffee, which when it came was thick and black and sweet, with grounds floating on top—a style that Leni learned to like while she was at the *losmen*.

She promised, "I'll do what I can, Guerney, but Dee's hard to influence once she's made up her mind about something. No one could persuade her not to spend Aunt Margaret's money on this trip. And after all," added Leni with a smile, "Dee and I have dreamed about the Bali bit for years and years!"

"You're sympathetic," accused Guerney. "I'm surprised. She's promised to marry Charles. Well, you might yet change your mind. . . . How did you manage the trip to Bali, anyhow?"

Leni told him briefly about Guinevere Raymond and Sam Becker. She described the very generous sum of money she had been given that was meant to last for a month.

"Though if I stay at the *losmen*," she finished, "it will just about last forever."

Guerney turned his attention to lighting a cigarette, then looked at her directly.

"So you have plenty of funds. Well, that makes a difference. I really think the best way to get your money's worth is to stay at one of the big hotels, my dear. They're organized so that the tourists can see everything in the easiest and most pleasant way. There are tours to various parts of the island, visits to markets, and temple ceremonies and dance performances. And there's plenty of entertainment on the hotel precincts.

"You can move around with a group, see everything, buy yourself some souvenirs and generally have a very good time. In my view, that's what you and Dee should be doing." He stopped to consider for a moment, then continued, "I'd recommend the Hotel Selatan—the one Kemp Savage is connected with, incidentally—and if necessary I'll supplement Dee's money to cover it. Have your three or four weeks of sightseeing together—and I stress that, *together*—then take my sister home with you and you'll both have enough memories to last you a lifetime."

Leni, at the mention of Kemp Savage, had bitten her lip, and now she said nothing, but listened as he added persuasively, "Tell Dee you prefer not to stay at the *losmen*. You can find plenty of excuses—cold baths, no air-conditioning or fans, and so on. Moreover, you'll have to make all your own arrangements about sightseeing, and it's not easy on your own. I know an intelligent girl like you will want to see all she can—not just lie about on the beach picking up boyfriends."

Leni colored faintly. But it all sounded very practical and sensible, particularly coming from Guerney, whom she had thought of as such a romantic figure. She was very much tempted by the thought of moving to the Hotel Selatan. That way it would be so easy to see Kemp Savage—to show him that she was completely unattached and that she did have an old school friend.

"I'll see what I can do," she promised.

"Thanks, my dear. You've got lots of sense under that pretty little cap of shining hair. The style suits you, by the way. It gives you a distinctly provocative air. If it weren't for Janet I might find myself looking at you with something rather more than mere brotherly affection."

"I shouldn't like that at all," said Leni in mock horror. "But thank you for the compliment, Guerney. I suppose it was meant to be a compliment?"

"It was. Now if you've finished eating, I'll take you back to your room. You'll want to unpack a few things, and I expect you're tired after your journey too. Possibly I'll see you tomorrow—try to get Dee to bring you over to my bungalow, will you?"

"I'll do that," said Leni. She felt more lighthearted as she went into her room where the oil lamp had been left burning. Guerney's idea was a good one, and it surely should not be hard to persuade Dee to move into the hotel. Once there, everything would fall into place, one way or another. She shivered a little at the thought. Would Kemp think she was chasing him? And come to that, wouldn't it be exactly what she *was* doing? Well, Leni didn't care.

She took one or two dresses from her suitcase and hung them in the narrow cupboard that had a long diamond-shaped mirror on the door. She was momentarily distracted by her own image—slim, pale, faintly ghost-like in the flickering light. She put a hand to her short shining hair. Guerney said it gave her a provocative air. Did Kemp Savage think so too? In her mind, she had already explained everything to Kemp. Her imagination was soaring away to the wonderful time she would have on this—what had Guerney called it? This Island of Light.

"Crazy," she murmured to herself, but her lips curved in a little secret smile. "As crazy as Dee!"

But for her, there was no Charles waiting faithfully in England. Leni could take all the romance that was offered her with open arms. . . .

When she heard footsteps in the garden beyond the veranda, she flew to the door. It would be Dee!

But it was Kemp Savage who stood on the veranda, his dark face lit by the oil lamp that stood on the small table. There was something frightening about the way he stood there, and Leni's heart began to beat quickly. He had her scarf in his hands—the scarf she had worn in the plane—and his fingers caressed it absently as they had caressed that silken sari in Singapore. With a dull shock, Leni remembered that he had bought that sari for someone; he had bought the jewelled bracelet for someone. And she had imagined he had come back to Bali because of her! It probably meant nothing at all to him that she apparently had a boyfriend of her own on the island. All her dreaming fancies of a few minutes ago suddenly seemed silly and childish beyond words.

"Miss Forrest," he said, and her spirits sagged. So formal, so distant, so unfriendly. If only he had said Leni! "You left your scarf in my car. It's a good silk scarf—no doubt another present from your over-generous employer. I thought I'd bring it along to save you chasing after it."

Chasing after him, he meant, of course. Leni accepted the scarf, warm from his hands, mechanically. Her foolish heart cried out, "Please understand!" but her lips said only, stiffly, "It was good of you to take so much trouble, Mr. Savage."

"Not at all."

They stood looking at each other in the light of the lamp. His mouth was hard and his eyes were black mysteries. Yet, helplessly, Leni felt a shuddering warmth steal over her body and into her very bones. She heard herself say, her voice so low it was scarcely audible, "Mr. Savage, you misunderstood the situation this afternoon. Guerney Fisher is . . . is my school friend's brother—"

"Is that so?" He was cool, disinterested. "How very convenient for you, Miss Forrest. . . . But I must congratulate you on your clever deception of Guinevere Raymond. You had me fooled at first too, but now I rather think my second impression of you was the correct one. You're a girl on the make, and a girl who has a very persuasive way with her. When I saw you in that extravagantly beautiful batik that was supposed to be for someone else, I should have summed you up once and for all."

"Mrs. Raymond *gave* me that dress," flashed Leni, although she had paled at his tone. "I told you to ask her if you didn't believe me!"

He tilted his dark head and looked down at her. "It's a bit late now, isn't it? Besides, there's your little fairytale about your old school friend."

"I *do* have a school friend here!" Leni cried. "She just happens to have—to have gone out for the day. And Guerney just happened to be at the *losmen*."

Even to her own ears it sounded weak and unconvincing, particularly since Guerney had greeted her as he had.

She stared at Kemp Savage, feeling helpless and frustrated and very close to tears—hating him, trying hard to hate him. Then on the still night air came the sound of a bamboo flute, sweet, true, oddly eerie. It melted into the air, and the lamp that hung in the branches of the grapefruit tree swung gently, hypnotically. High above, the moon moved into the sky from behind a drift of thin cloud, and the scent of flowers filled the air. Flowers or incense, Leni did not know which. She stared at Kemp Savage, her eyes shining with tears, and he took a step nearer to her.

"He believes me," she thought. It seemed to her that he too was struck by the beauty of the night, he too knew that to distrust, to refuse, to hold back, was wrong. Leni raised her face and half closed her eyes, and her lips curved softly in a trembling smile.

Then from two feet away Kemp Savage said distinctly, "I dislike designing females intensely—women who think they can play one man against another for their own amusement. *You* may have forgotten the fervor with which Guerney Fisher greeted you, Miss Forrest, but I have not. I wish you goodnight and goodbye."

He was gone.

Leni's lids flew up and she watched him through a blur of tears that were half anger and half despair as he melted like a vision into the dark shadows of the strange garden.

She was standing there still, the tears dry upon her cheeks, the silk scarf hanging from her hand when Dee came strolling toward her, one arm entwined with that of a long-haired, shabby-looking young man.

Despite herself, Leni came back to life. Despite herself and the soreness of her heart, she ran down the steps and threw her arms around her friend.

"*Dee!*"

Dee laughed and hugged her.

"Leni darling, how marvelous to see you! I hope Guerney made it out to the airport to meet you. Or was he too *busy*? And I hope you'll forgive me for not being there—I'll explain it all in a minute. Meanwhile, this is Mike. Mike, this is my best friend, Leni. I've told you all about her." Dee, always voluble, ran on gaily.

Mike said, "Hi," without showing a great deal of interest. He flung himself down in a chair, regardless of the fact that there were only two. He was a stringy young man of perhaps twenty-two, with a gaunt face, long dark hair and crumpled shabby clothes—jeans and a tee-shirt. Dee's clothes were similar except that they looked newer and cleaner. Leni thought she had lost some of her plumpness and her pretty pink and white complexion had been spoiled by the sun—her small slightly tip-tilted nose was peeling. The long corn-colored hair that hung about her face was dulled with salt water and must, thought Leni, be uncomfortably hot, from the way Dee was continually flicking it back. She realized that she was staring when Dee asked with a self-conscious laugh, "Well, how do you like my new image?"

Leni made a little face and shrugged.

"You're not impressed," Dee accused. "Guerney's been brainwashing you. But it's the life, Leni—it really is. Lying about in the sun, not bothering how anyone looks, what people think. I feel so absolutely free, so different...."

Mike, who had closed his eyes, opened them to look at her with a half-contemptuous amusement. "It's only skin deep. You're just a little rich girl playing around. But given time I could teach you what life is really about."

"I'm not rich," said Dee. "And I wish you'd get up and let me have that chair. I'm deathly tired."

Mike reached out a foot encased in a dirty canvas shoe,

hooked the other chair with it, and drew it forward. "What's wrong with this one?"

"Leni's going to sit there. Sit down, Len," Dee urged, and Leni sat. She was aware of a faint feeling of distaste for Mike Miller. Why had Dee got herself mixed up with someone so unprepossessing when she was engaged to a nice man like Charles Broughton? And yet Leni could see that Dee was enjoying her new image—possibly because it would annoy Guerney.

It probably amused her to shock and annoy Guerney and now she was enjoying shocking Leni. She had begun to wrestle with Mike, trying to drag him out of the chair he had taken possession of, and eventually he gave in ungraciously and let her have it.

"You want the best of both worlds, don't you?"

"Why not?" said Dee. "I was going to tell you why I didn't meet you, Len. There was a ceremony being held at the Mother Temple in Besakih, and all the kids were going. We set off this morning in the bus. You've just never lived till you've been on one of the local buses, has she, Mike? After about half an hour, we just had to fight our way out and walk."

"You're soft," said Mike, without opening his eyes. "The bus wasn't all that bad."

"I'm not soft," protested Dee. "I walked for miles, didn't I?"

"To save your face. And because there was nothing else to do. But we didn't get to Besakih, did we? Not that I cared," he added indifferently. "Temple ceremonies are just an ordinary part of life here. Each one is the same as the last."

"Not really," said Dee, looking slightly dashed.

"Would you know? You're still dazzled by the gear and the offerings."

"Well, maybe I am," said Dee. She asked Leni again, "Did Guerney meet you, Len?"

Leni shook her head. "But don't worry, I managed all right." She hesitated. Would she mention Kemp Savage or not? She decided against it. Maybe she would never tell Dee about him, and she didn't want to talk of him while Mike was there, leaning against the wall and staring at her. "Anyhow, it's marvelous being here now," said Leni.

"I just couldn't believe you were coming. However did you manage it?" Dee wanted to know. "Tell me the whole story, Len."

Mike heaved himself away from the wall and yawned. "You two can have it on your own. I'm going to bed." He jumped down from the veranda and didn't bother to answer when Dee called out goodnight.

Leni asked a little too brightly, "Does he stay at the *losmen* too, Dee?"

"Yes. There are a few others as well. It's quite fun, really. Makes you sort of realize what a restricted life you've always led. But you were going to tell me—"

Once again Leni told the story of Guinevere and Sam, and Dee sighed and said, "Isn't it extraordinary that both of us have made it? After all, it was never more than a mad dream really, was it? I hope you'll have an absolutely super time, Len. Wouldn't it be fabulous if you met some really romantic type and married him just like we used to imagine when we were school kids?"

Leni smiled back at her, but it was an effort. She had met her "romantic type," but it had come to nothing and it had spoiled her for anything else. Perhaps spoiled her whole holiday.

Dee said, "Sometimes I wish I wasn't engaged to Charles. It's as if I were an old person, and all this had happened to me too late."

Leni said hesitantly, "I noticed you weren't wearing your ring. You *are* still in love with Charles, aren't you, Dee?"

"Well, of course! But I'm not going to sit round like a—like a nun or something now I'm here and miss out on all the fun. And please don't be like Guerney and tell me I shouldn't have come! Once I had the money and the idea I just couldn't *not* have." She changed the subject suddenly. "Do you mind staying here, Leni? I mean, they're very spartan little rooms, aren't they? And that scoop bath! But it's an experience."

Now was Leni's chance to follow Guerney's advice—to winkle Dee out of the *losmen* and persuade her to go to the hotel Selatan. A little earlier she would have done it. But not now—she couldn't do it now, not since Kemp Savage had come and made it plain that he had nothing but contempt for her.

So she said slowly, "I don't mind it, Dee. It's all very clean—and Made is nice."

"But it's not what we used to dream about," warned Dee. "Coral beaches and sapphire seas—well, those are there for anyone. But suntanned heroes with loads of money, exotic feasts and fabulous clothes—they go with the big hotels."

"Isn't there a happy medium?" suggested Leni. "Guerney's bungalow?"

"I tried that," sighed Dee. She flipped her hair back and her pretty mouth grew obstinate. "Guerney's . . . not like he used to be. He doesn't think I should have any fun. He's grown stodgy, Len. I could hardly believe it—I thought he'd be marvelous to live with. Just because I went out a bit, he brought in his girlfriend, who's years older than he is and ferociously ugly. Well, not really, but she's *bossy*. The two of them lectured me day and night—talk about spoilsports! And Peter, the boy I was going out with, was really nice."

Her blue eyes sparkled mischievously, and Leni knew just why she had come to the *losmen* and why she was amusing herself with Mike Miller. Quite likely it would not be long before she tired of her game of tormenting Guerney. . . .

"Heigh-ho," said Dee. "I guess it's time for bed. Sleep well. We'll go down to the beach tomorrow, and we'll see who we can find for you."

Leni shook her head. "Please, Dee—no. I'll take it as it comes."

"Well, as you wish," agreed Dee reluctantly.

CHAPTER THREE

Leni was wakened very early in the morning by the sound of cocks crowing in the yard behind the *losmen*. She lay for a while listening and trying to orientate herself, then climbed out of bed and went barefooted across the yellow unglazed tiles to look at the morning. Poinsettias and hibiscus already showed burningly bright in the early sunlight, and the air that drifted through the window was decidedly hot. Made, in sarong and blouse, crossed the yard carrying a small offering of yellow marigolds made into a decorative arrangement and paused before one of the shrines where similar offerings had already been laid. The banana palms looked cool and green, and in their shade were several of the big cane cages like the one Leni had seen holding the white cock.

The air was still noisy with cockcrow, and after a few minutes she went back to lie on top of the bed and think about yesterday. Futile now to plan going to the Hotel Selatan to explain anything to Kemp Savage! He had made up his mind about her and it was plain that he wanted nothing further to do with her. Right at the start, thought Leni, her holiday had been spoiled. How different it would have been if she had never met Kemp Savage, never fallen in love with him. As it was, she could feel not the faintest stirring of interest in the possibility of meeting suntanned heroes of any kind, rich or poor. . . .

When she heard voices and movements outside, she took her soap and towel and went along to the bathroom. The spring water was cool and refreshing, and when she came back to the verandah in her cotton dress and sandals, it was to find a pot of coffee on the small table.

With it were two cups, two round flat buns, and four yellow bananas.

She poured herself a cup of the thick sweet black coffee and bit into one of the buns, which was fresh and had a little jam in it. Beyond the compound, a Balinese boy on a bicycle had stopped in the gateway and was looking inside. He carried a large cloth bag, and when he saw Leni he came down the path, smiling and showing white even teeth.

"*Selamat pagi, nona.* I have carvings. You buy from me?" He opened his bag and produced an intricately carved bone figure, half bird, half man, about eight inches high, and pointing to himself told Leni proudly, "My work."

Leni took the figure in her hands and examined it closely. She was amazed at the fine detail of the work, but she had no idea what it was worth, and had not yet got used to dealing with rupeah instead of pounds and pence. She thought perhaps it would be wiser to wait until she had seen more samples of craftsmanship before she made any purchases, and finally she handed it back to the boy with a regretful shake of her head.

"Thank you. It's beautiful, but not just now. Perhaps later." She smiled to temper her refusal, and it was certainly hard to refuse, for the boy was so obviously proud of his work. She didn't know if he understood what she said, but she returned to her breakfast, and in a moment he packed up his bag and with a quiet "*Selamat djalan*" went on his way.

Mike Miller appeared on the veranda in time to see him disappearing through the garden.

"No luck? No rich spoils acquired for next to nothing?" he asked, without bothering to wish Leni good morning. "Couldn't you beat him down to your figure?"

Leni didn't care for his tone of voice and she didn't like the way he looked at her as he sat down at the table, reached for a banana, and peeled it efficiently.

She said coolly, "I'm not ready to buy anything yet. I don't know what's available and I don't know anything about prices. I certainly wasn't trying to beat that boy down. Moreover," she added, unable to hold her tongue, "I really don't see why you should make such an unpleasant remark to me."

Mike looked genuinely surprised. His light blue eyes flickered over her pretty dress and sandals appraisingly. "It's my guess you're just another European tourist visiting Bali to buy a few bits of arts and crafts that you can take home and boast to your friends how cheaply you got them."

"Is it?" asked Leni. Her voice was indifferent, but inwardly she was seething. How could Dee put up with such a rude and uncouth sort of person?

"Yeah," said Mike. "There are plenty of your type around here, but mostly they patronize the big plushy hotels. A few—like your mate Dee—doss down at the *losmens* and write home how they're slumming it with the natives. Oh, I like Dee, she's a good kid, and she's learning fast to see things our way."

"Then that's a pity," said Leni coldly. She would have added to that had Dee not appeared at that moment. Mike had just stretched out his hand for the coffee pot, and Dee stepped forward quickly and gave his knuckles a sharp rap.

"That's my coffee! Leni and I are paying extra to have our breakfast here. You push off to the restaurant, Mike."

Mike got up with a lazy grin and gave her a playful pat on the cheek.

"No harm in trying. Your friend and I were having a friendly chat and I forgot what I was doing. See you later on—we'll go down to the beach."

There was a slightly awkward silence when he had gone. Leni wondered how much of the "friendly chat" Dee had heard from her bedroom, and thought it a great pity that Dee was mixed up with Mike. She wore the same clothes as yesterday, and her hair still looked stiff and dull with salt. That was a pity too, for Dee was a pretty girl, and she certainly didn't look pretty today. Yet unconcernedly, she leaned one elbow on the table and drank her coffee, her eyes on the sunlit garden.

"Want to come to the beach with us?"

"I'd like to," said Leni. "Though I don't feel I'll be terribly welcome," she added wryly.

Dee drank down her coffee, poured another cup and dipped her bun in it. She looked at Leni and her pretty blue eyes were laughing. "Never mind. We'll soon find someone for you. What do you fancy? A—a beach-comber type like Mike, or someone more conventional? We could walk over to the Hotel Selatan and—"

"No!" exclaimed Leni quickly.

Dee laughed aloud. "Come on now, Len. You're on holiday—all sorts of things are permissible."

"I don't care," said Leni stubbornly. "I won't go to the hotel, Dee."

Dee shrugged. "Then that leaves the other kids in our crowd. Guerney calls them hippies, but they're not bad. You'll meet some of them this morning."

If the others were going to be like Mike, then Leni didn't feel enthusiastic. Still, she would have to make the best of things. . . .

And when, later, she went to fetch her swimsuit and beach towel, she found herself thinking wishfully that

Kemp Savage might see her on the beach with Dee and realize that she had told him the truth.

He didn't see her, of course. But when she walked along the sand by herself, leaving the others sunbathing, she caught her first glimpse of the Hotel Selatan. It was a big white building, three stories high, with gay awnings over the balconied windows and a garden whose tall palms and tropical trees half hid a number of thatched-roofed bungalows. The sight of a masculine figure emerging from the garden onto the beach was enough to send Leni into a small panic, and she turned back quickly. Of course it was not Kemp Savage, but she knew that she would be unbearably embarrassed if he should catch her wandering about near the hotel.

She scuffed the white sand with her bare feet and looked out over the long unbroken line of breakers to the coral reef and the picturesque *praos* that drifted on the water, their elegant white sails catching the wind from the sea. It was all so idyllic, so beautiful, and yet she could not be happy.

That afternoon, after lunching with Dee and Mike at Made's restaurant, she went with them in to Denpasar, though she knew perfectly well that Mike would have preferred her not to come. They walked up the pretty road from the *losmen*, past the stalls where the batiks and paintings were sold, and at the crossroads where Kemp had asked the way, Mike hailed a *bemo*—a three-wheeled utility truck with a covered back. Two seats faced each other, and the vehicle was able to hold eight people in all. The conductor was a small Balinese boy of perhaps ten, who shouted out to the driver or rapped on the window when he judged it was time to get moving again.

Leni didn't know what the others intended to do in Denpasar, but she planned to look in the shops. Meanwhile she was entertained by the people who clambered in and out of the *bemo*, particularly a slim slight woman with two enormous bags of rice, and three pretty Balinese girls wearing their best sarongs and sweet-scented flowers in their hair. They were quite exquisite with their pale brown skins and limpid dark eyes, and Leni felt herself insipid and colorless beside them.

Denpasar she found to be boisterous, untidy and bewildering, though there was much that was picturesque in its extraordinary mixture of buildings, old and new. The streets were crowded with cyclists and taxis and pedestrians, and the footpaths, where they existed, often required all one's attention as they were apt in places to gape open unexpectedly. Beside them were open drains, deep and wide but, surprisingly, not smelly.

It was not long before she was left to herself. Mike said, "You can poke about on your own if you want to look at the stores. It's irritating to be waiting around while someone's dawdling along, staring at everything."

He indicated a Chinese restaurant. "We'll see you here later on—sevenish. Okay?"

Dee began to protest, but Leni said, "It's all right, Dee. Honestly. It will be best."

All the same, she didn't really like being left on her own—not quite so soon, not when she didn't know anything at all about Denpasar. She walked along slowly, looking in the stores, many of which were open-fronted and kept by Chinese. She was jostled constantly by the crowd and found that to cross the road was something of an ordeal. Horns sounded continuously, and there was an unending stream of bicycles and cars. Pedestrians at the side of the road had to look out for themselves. That was plain, and it was sometimes difficult with the wide drains. She was constantly being offered carvings or scrolls or silver work and she had not yet learned the word for "No." All in all, Leni was not really enjoying herself.

"Taxi? You want taxi?" It was the umpteenth time she had been asked *that* in about 50 yards, and her nerves were jangling. It was hot and she was tired, and suddenly two tears spilled over and ran down her cheeks. She wished that she had never come to Bali where no one—except Guerney—wanted her.

And then, as she turned a corner, almost blindly, she came upon a sight that made her forget her blues. A procession was going by, and the road was lined with people who had stopped to watch. A stream of exquisite girls came down the street, brilliant in their red and gold sarongs and glittering brocaded waistbands. Each one carried on her head a flat silver dish, piled high with an elaborate arrangement of fruit, flowers and colored rice, and above them floated a long silken veil of white. Long-handled, gold-fringed umbrellas rose here and there like exotic flowers, while drums, cymbals, and bamboo flutes made music that was strange and beautiful. Leni stood entranced.

Then, with a leap of her heart, she saw Kemp Savage at the other side of the street, watching too. What had broken her absorption and made her raise her eyes to glance in his direction she did not know, but something had caused her to look. Perhaps the sheer pull of his personality! But he had not seen her—or at any rate he was not looking her way. She watched him for perhaps a minute, and still he did not glance at her. Yet the conviction grew in her that he *had* seen her, that it had been the compulsion of his scrutiny that had made her aware of him. And the fact that he was now ignoring her told her more plainly than any words that he wanted nothing further to do with her. He was finished with her as definitely as he had finished with Cristelle Dubois.

Troubled now, she watched the procession passing, and the sound of the drums and cymbals reverberated excitingly in her ears. When she looked for Kemp Savage again, he was still there, in exactly the same place. But now there was a darkly brooding look on his face, and he was smoking a cigarette. Had his glance just flicked away from her? Leni wondered. Try as she would, she could not get him to look at her. If he had, she was not sure what she would have done—whether she would have smiled, or waited first for some sign of recognition from him. In her heart, she knew she would find it extremely difficult to stop herself signalling a greeting of some sort. Maybe it was as well he should choose to ignore her! That way at least she did not receive an open snub.

When the procession had passed, she went back to the stores, hoping secretly that Kemp would suddenly materialize beside her. "Hello, Leni," she could hear his voice saying. And then, after apologizing for doubting her, "You need someone to look after you, to show you this beautiful island. May I do so?"

But of course he did not come. And after an hour or so of wandering hot and increasingly sore-footed along the pavements, Leni began to think that Bali was not a particularly beautiful island after all. She went into several stores, looking at batiks, looking at art objects. She didn't want to spend any of the money Guinevere Raymond had given her on inferior articles, but she needed a more reliable guide than her own feelings. In the end she bought nothing, merely looked and compared and tried to assess. She was glad when it was time to find the Chinese restaurant where she was to meet Dee and Mike.

It took longer to find than she had anticipated, and it was a quarter of an hour later than the "sevenish" that Mike had stipulated when at last she pushed her way through the crowds to the lighted sign over the dragon.

Mike and Dee were nowhere to be seen. Leni looked inside the restaurant. She even went inside and walked amongst the little tables with their red lamps, all of them occupied and the atmosphere becoming smokier and noisier by the minute. She went into the street and waited again. It was growing dark and lights were springing up everywhere and the crowd was thicker than ever, and Leni knew that it was no use waiting. Mike and Dee were not coming. She was beginning to feel very hungry and very forlorn, and she knew she would never have the courage to eat alone. She would have to go back to the *losmen* and eat there.

The *losmen*. That meant a *bemo*. But where did one find a *bemo*, and how did one know where it was going? Leni looked about her helplessly. It could have been such fun if she were not on her own! But already she was being besieged by taxi drivers, by young men with baskets or bags of paintings, of wood or bone carvings, of silver work. And she was beginning to feel frightened. She had just made up her mind to take the next taxi she saw, no matter how crafty the driver looked, no matter what fare he demanded of her, when a pair of long, expressive black hands, carved out of wood, was suddenly thrust very close to her face.

Somehow it was the last straw. Leni uttered a little shriek of fear and darted down a side street full of flickering lights.

She was in the middle of a market! The air was warm, people milled about her—Balinese people—laughing, shouting, jostling each other, exchanging jokes in their own language. Suddenly Leni relaxed. Here, she felt somehow protected, she didn't know why. Perhaps it was simply the warm friendly atmosphere as the ordinary folk of Bali bought their evening meal. The insistent heckling she had been subjected to before was gone. Now only the piping voices of children called "Hello!" to the foreigner, and Leni eyed the piles of bright strange-looking fruits, the heaps of vegetables, the colored rice, the exotically tinted cakes and biscuits, with interest. She found a little stall surrounded by smoke, from which came the smell of oil, the delicious smell of meat being fried. She began to feel hungrier than ever! She stood looking longingly at the food—at the succulent cubes of skewered pork and chicken being cooked quickly over a small fire. Her mouth watered. How did one negotiate? How did one ask to buy?

"Are you hungry, Miss Forrest?"

Her heart turned over; her bones melted. That voice! Even if it called her "Miss Forrest"! Just now Leni would forgive it anything so long as it spoke to her. She turned and looked up into a dark face that in the flickering light of oil lamps and wreathed about by the smoke that drifted from the *satay* stalls had a faintly satanic look about it. The dark brows were darker than ever and the eyes flashed with fiery points of light. And yet—and yet—it seemed to Leni that there was something kind and even protective in the very slight smile on Kemp Savage's face. Maybe it was no more than a brush-off from the general atmosphere, but Leni moved confidently closer to him as she answered his question, smiling, her eyes alight because of the sudden surge of happiness that had flooded her being.

"Yes, I am—*very* hungry! And I don't know what to do about it—I don't know what's happened to the others."

"You've lost your friends?" His voice was ironical and he put one hand almost roughly on her arm.

"Yes—Dee, my school friend and—" Leni decided not to finish. Mike didn't matter, didn't deserve a mention.

There was a tiny pause. Kemp Savage's eyes narrowed,

then he gave a shrug, and his touch on her arm became a strong grasp. "Well then, what would you like to eat? The *satay*? Or a plate of *nasi goreng*?"

Leni licked her lips. "Both."

Suddenly he laughed. "So be it."

He pushed away through the crowd—he was immensely taller than the Balinese—and led her to a small enclosure where people sat at tiny rickety tables eating the food that had been cooked at the small stalls around. They were barely seated before a young girl came to take Kemp's order. Then with miraculous speed, two dishes of *nasi goreng*, a dish holding *satay*, and a cruet with three tiny pots of sauce appeared on the table, and Leni began eating with relish. All around was the sound of the melodious Balinese language, and everything was colorful and strange and exciting. And beautiful, thought Leni. But the most wonderful thing of all was that she was here with Kemp Savage, and that he was being so nice to her.

"And what have you been doing in Denpasar, Leni"—she was Leni again—"since you lost the—others?"

"Looking in the stores," said Leni. "But I haven't bought a thing," she added wryly.

His satanic eyebrows went up. "No carvings or krisses or scrolls? Not even a silver ring? Why not?"

"Because—because I want to buy something I shan't tire of."

"I see. What delights you today may well bore you tomorrow. Is that how it is?"

There was an undercurrent to his words that made Leni bite her lip on a flash of anger. But if he expected her to ask him what he meant, she was not going to. There were going to be no hasty words tonight if she could help it.

After a second she said carefully, "I want to buy something that's really good, that's—that's true art."

"And you haven't seen anything yet that you'd call true art? Surely you must have seen hundreds of paintings of village life, of rice festivals, of dance dramas. Yet none that struck you as being—true art?"

Leni suspected he was mocking her, but answered thoughtfully, "I've seen many that *looked* very beautiful. Not only paintings, but carvings, and krisses and rings. But how can *I* tell—how can *I* judge?"

He smiled faintly. "You can't, of course. Not unless you know Eastern art very well indeed."

"Perhaps," said Leni questioningly, "they're all good?" Her eyes, serious and trusting, met his in the lamplight, and there was a curious moment of stillness between them. She saw the mocking twist fade from his lips and when he spoke again he too was quite serious.

"The Balinese are an artistic people, Leni. When they're very small, the children learn to dance, and the boys learn to help their fathers to paint and to carve. Art has always been a big part of the way of life here. However, let's face it, in the centers where tourists are beginning to be regarded as a source of income, as in Denpasar, art is becoming an industry rather than simply, like work and religion, one facet of life. So, Leni"—he shifted his position slightly so that she could no longer see his expression clearly—"you had better persuade your . . . friends to take you to visit one or two of the museums. Then, by looking at some of the most beautiful art objects, you may, if you are a discerning sort of person, learn to distinguish the fine from the mediocre.

"Meanwhile, have you had enough to eat, or would you like to sample a cake with your coffee?"

Leni said that she would—mostly because she wanted

to prolong the time she spent with him. She was aware that he had, rather subtly, erected a fine barrier between them. He had shifted his position so that she could no longer read what was in his eyes, and he had not offered to escort her himself to any of the museums. She took what comfort she could from the fact that he had at least talked to her seriously.

She was surprised when later, after he had paid what sounded a great deal in rupeahs but when translated into sterling was a ridiculously small amount, he escorted her as if it were a matter of course around the market. With his guiding hand under her elbow, Leni sauntered in slightly amazed happiness amongst the stalls—past the food section into a maze of little displays of shoes and sandals, batiks and shirts and blouses and scarves. There seemed no end to the stalls with their small lamps and their enticingly spread wares. Everyone was bargaining, laughter came readily and business was brisk.

"Lively, isn't it?" remarked Kemp, as he good-humoredly waved away an offer of a gay shirt obviously too small for his large frame. Leni couldn't quite work out where she stood with him. Maybe he realized she was not a cunning little schemer after all, but had been telling the truth all along. Maybe he was, in his way, apologizing for his harshness. She could somehow not imagine him ever offering her a verbal apology! And maybe he was as fatalistically attracted to her as she was to him!

On the other hand, thought Leni, foolishly happy because his fingers were on her arm, he might simply be sorry for her—all alone and obviously bewildered by Denpasar!

Just for the moment, she didn't really care, so long as she was here at his side, drifting along and smiling at the friendly people who called out again and again,

"Madame—you buy batik, madame? *Bagus*—good—you look!"

The next moment, a length of cloth was whipped from a stall by a graceful Balinese woman and displayed temptingly before her. Leni's attention was drawn by a small brown finger to the figures of Balinese dancing girls in the pattern. Then, with a sudden movement, the cloth was draped around Leni's slender waist as a sarong, and the saleswoman looked smilingly from Leni to Kemp.

"*Indah*!"

Leni remembered that day in Singapore when Kemp had held silk against her body. Were her eyes shining now as they had then? And was Kemp remembering too? She looked up at him shyly, almost fearfully, and felt a sudden shock. All the kindness and good humor had gone from his face—so completely that she wondered if it had ever been there, if it had been no more than an illusion. She recoiled physically from the harshness of his regard, and even the little Balinese woman after a second unwound the sarong and without a word restored it to its long, neat, narrow-folded shape.

Kemp didn't take Leni's arm again. He said roughly, "I'd better get you home. Ask your friends to take you to one of the villages off the tourist route and buy yourself some batik there. And next time you come out for a day in Denpasar," he finished, as he urged her past the crowded stalls, "don't go and lose yourself. You won't always be rescued by me, you know."

Hurt and confused by his sudden brusqueness, Leni stared at him speechlessly, and he continued. "If you have any thoughts of provoking your boyfriend by starting an affair elsewhere, you can count me right out. Moreover, that sort of thing doesn't always have the desired effect, you know."

A pause, while they stared at each other, Leni still shocked into speechlessness. "Another thing—in case you have the mistaken idea in that pretty little head of yours that I came back to Bali on your account, Miss Forrest, understand this—I came because a sudden crisis at the hotel required my urgent presence."

At that, Leni gave a gasp of shock and anger. That hurt! "I assure you it would never have occurred to me that you came to Bali on my account, Mr. Savage," she flashed. "And if *you* have the idea that I'm imagining having an affair with you, then you couldn't be more wrong."

That at least was true—it had never been an affair that she wanted, and right now she wished that she had never set eyes on Kemp Savage. "I already know your high-and-mighty attitude toward women—you want a slave, an adoring slave, who'll never so much as look at another man—maybe you'd be better off with a simple Balinese girl to worship you and run when you call! Goodbye, Mr. Savage!"

She turned on her heel and began walking. She had no idea which way she was going, her whole world seemed to have crumbled, and she was ashamed of her outburst and also of the fact that she had been silly enough to think that Kemp Savage could have the slightest possible personal interest in her. Or that he could have changed his mind about her overnight. She began to think that he had meant—subtly—to punish her for what he thought was her deception by paying her some casual and mocking attention tonight.

Leni walked quickly, pushing her way determinedly through the milling throng of Balinese, consumed by the strength of her futile passions.

"That temper of yours!" said an angry voice close

behind her. And then Kemp Savage's grip was on her wrist and it was as fierce and angry as his voice and it hurt as much as his words had hurt her a few moments ago. "It's going to get you into real trouble one of these days. Is this how you got lost before—walking out on a row of your own making? Where on earth do you think you're going, will you tell me that?"

"I don't know and I don't care," snapped Leni—she, Leni, who was so sensible, so level-headed! "So long as it's away from you."

"Well, it's not away from me, and you'd better start caring, my girl. A few more minutes and you'll be *really* lost. Come on now, about face," he finished grimly as she tried in vain to escape from his grasp, and he turned her about forcibly and started marching her in the opposite direction. "We're going back into the town and I'm going to put you into a cab."

"You needn't bother," flashed Leni, though her voice trembled and she was now close to tears. "I'll manage by myself."

But talk is cheap, and she let him hustle her along. Soon she was sitting in the back of a cab and he was beside her. Neither said a single word as they went through Denpasar and all the way out to Kuta Beach. When they reached the *losmen*, Kemp got out of the cab and escorted her right to her door, and there, Leni could not resist asking him in icy tones, "Just why did you bother about me at all this evening, Mr. Savage? I certainly didn't expect it of you."

It was a good ten seconds before he answered, and his voice was as cold and unfriendly as her own. "I bothered because you're a visitor to the country I've adopted as my own, Miss Forrest. What else can a—host—do about a guest who had found herself in trouble?"

CHAPTER FOUR

Leni tried hard to put Kemp Savage right out of her mind after that. But it was a losing battle. To begin with, she couldn't control her dreams.

She saw Guerney a couple of times and knew he was disappointed that she hadn't yet persuaded Dee to move out of the *losmen*. She tried to pacify him by assuring him that Dee would not get out of her depth with Mike Miller and his crowd. In fact, she thought Dee already showed signs of tiring of the role in which she had cast herself.

Mike had developed a habit of looking Leni over appraisingly every time he saw her and of making disparaging remarks about her clothes.

"All dressed up again?" he asked one evening when they were on their way to the beach to watch the sunset and cool down after the heat of the day. "You must think you're mixing with the rich tourists up at the Hotel Selatan. You're a bit too smart for us simple honest folks at the *losmen*."

Leni, whose clothes were unpretentious, found him irritating. The flowered cotton she was wearing was clean and pretty, but it was not in the least dressy, and though she forced herself to say nothing, she couldn't manage even a good-humored smile. Mike had one arm around Dee while he was speaking, and she freed herself suddenly and bent down to retie the lace of her canvas shoe. Leni wondered if it really needed retying or if Dee, too, was growing as weary of these pointless unpleasant jibes. Mike stared at Leni over Dee's stooping figure and added rudely, "When are you going to start making arrangements of your own and stop bugging us with your company, anyhow?"

Leni bit her lip hard. She had no idea how to answer that. The best thing was simply to walk away and make sure she didn't "bug" them any more, but before she could do that, Dee had straightened up. Her pretty face was flushed scarlet and she said angrily, "Leni happens to be my friend, Mike Miller—and I want her company!"

"Well, calm down," said Mike, scratching his head. "Let's not have a scene. Only does she have to come to the beach in a garden party outfit?"

"Oh, don't be so ridiculous!" snapped Dee. "It's just an ordinary little dress." She turned her back and began walking rapidly along the dusty road.

Leni thought she detected the beginning of the end. Well, it was a rather foolish friendship and unworthy of Dee. Leni was more than ever inclined to think that if Guerney had treated the whole thing more lightly, it would have come to an end long ago. The trouble was, Dee had a very stubborn streak.

The following afternoon, Dee came to the veranda where Leni was writing letters.

"I'm going over to Guerney's. Want to come?"

"I'd like to." Leni closed her writing pad and looked at Dee with a smile. She hadn't yet been to Guerney's bungalow—she had thought it better not to go on her own—and she wondered what the reason for Dee's rather sudden decision to go.

She was soon to know, for Dee said carelessly, "I need to pick up some more clothes. My other pair of jeans has come apart at the seams and I'm too lazy to do any mending. Besides"—with a wry grin—"I'm just a tiny bit sick of this get-up. That's *your* fault, for looking so fabulous all the time."

Guerney's bungalow was something of a surprise. It had once belonged to a very minor French painter, and its ornately decorated rooms were still graced by his exuberant efforts. Guerney said with a laugh as she stared at the painted walls and cupboards where Balinese girls were depicted dancing or balancing loads on their heads, "It's a bit much, isn't it? But part of the furniture."

Dee threw herself down on a divan covered by a hand-woven cloth with a gold leaf design—very sumptuous-looking, and hardly to be treated so casually, Leni thought, and when Dee patted the seat beside her she looked at Guerney doubtfully.

"Go ahead—sit down," he reassured her. "There's nothing special about that stuff—the villagers wear it at their local ceremonies. But maybe you'd rather see through the place first."

Leni, interested, elected to do that.

The rooms in Guerney's bungalow opened one out of the other. Some were painted blue and some red, and they all contained elaborately carved and painted furniture. The unglazed windows were sheltered by the wide eaves of a thatched roof and looked into a green, cool garden with its profusion of palms and big frangipani trees. Leni thought it a great pity that Dee had not been happy here—Guerney and Janet must have been just too critical for her independent nature. When the tour of inspection was complete, they went back to the sitting room and a Balinese woman called Nyomen, who, with her husband Ketut, looked after Guerney, brought a tray with glasses of the thick sweet coffee that by now Leni was quite accustomed to. The three talked lightly and idly, and presently Guerney asked rather pointedly if Dee had shown Leni any of the sights of the island.

Dee replied shortly, "We haven't been farther afield than Denpasar and the beach, if you must know. But why don't *you* take Leni around, if you're so keen? Or are you afraid Janet will hear about it?"

Guerney frowned slightly. "Don't try to make excuses for your own bad behavior, Dee."

Dee jumped to her feet. "I smell a lecture coming up. Excuse me—I'm going to rummage through my bags and find something to wear."

"Then make sure you find something a little more dignified than the gear you're wandering around in today," Guerney said, but Dee had gone.

Leni said a little uneasily, "May I see some of your work, Guerney?"

For a moment she thought he was going to ignore her request and talk about Dee. But he said with a shrug, "Yes, of course, if you'd like to. Actually there's not a great deal to show you—I sell most of what I do, with the exception of a few woodcarvings that Janet likes particularly and I'm hanging onto."

He opened the doors of a tall heavy cupboard and brought out a big folder containing several sketches and paintings, each one protected by clear plastic film. Leni began to look through them with interest. She did not know any artists, and she had seen very little of Guerney's work in all the years of her friendship with Dee. Guerney had been the bohemian artist brother, romantic and slightly out of reach. Now, she found finely detailed pen and ink drawings, acrylics that had the appearance of oils, and other acrylic studies that looked like watercolors. The subjects ranged from the fantastic Balinese shrines and temples, through drawings of village houses and markets, to simple tranquil sketches of boats on the sand, or an old wall with a high gateway and an enshrouding tapestry of bamboo and palm and bougainvillea.

Leni loved them, and yet she was somehow surprised. She had expected, without thinking of it, enormous canvases—works grandiloquent in scale and subject matter, stacked untidily in a huge messy studio that smelled of paint and turpentine.

She was not exactly disappointed, but her idea of Guerney Fisher as an artist underwent a very definite change. There was something very businesslike about these competently executed sketches and paintings—even about the neat way they were packaged and stored.

She looked up into his rather kind blue eyes and smiled.

"I like them very much, Guerney. And they're so exactly Bali! How do you make your sales?"

"Oh, people come along and say they want a painting to take home—they hear somewhere or other that there's an English artist not far from Denpasar. The majority are English or American tourists who want some personal and permanent souvenir of the place. I usually have something that they like—something evocative. I very rarely do a painting to order—I'm not at all keen on that. I have a market in Djakarta as well, and on the whole I get better prices there. Janet works in a gallery and it was her idea—it's brought my income up very nicely."

"*Janet*," said Dee, who had come in while they were talking. She held a large travelling bag and her pretty mouth was twisted disparagingly. "Janet's just too interested in money and business and—and respectability for words. She's a great big bore and she's taken Guerney in hand as if he were a money-making machine instead of an artist."

"That's uncalled-for rudeness, Dee," said Guerney sharply, "and I won't have it. You might tidy up your own life before you start criticizing others. The way you've been playing around since you arrived in Bali is preposterous. If you'd only realize it, you're jeopardizing your chances of happiness with Charles."

"Here we go again!" interrupted Dee, her cheeks flushing. "You can spare me the big brother lecture. Try to remember I'm not a little girl any more. And not ready to hang on your every word. I'd never have come to Bali if I'd known you'd be so . . . so officious. You didn't *used* to be like that. You used to be a nice romantic artist—it's all since you let that Janet get to work on you—"

"Rubbish," interrupted Guerney. "As for being a romantic artist, that's something you dreamed up yourself. Even artists have to live. And as for my officiousness—if you think back you'll realize that you never acted in such an idiotic way in the past. I'll admit you were always unpredictable, but within certain decent limits—"

"Oh, limits! I want to do just as I like on this holiday—after all, it's my holiday. Anyhow, I think it's pretty boring for Leni to have to listen to us sparring. I'm going, at any rate." She looked at Leni. "Coming, Len?"

"In a few minutes," said Leni, slightly distressed. "Stay a little while longer, Dee," she added, hoping that the sister and brother would settle their differences. "I want to see some of Guerney's wood-carvings."

"Then *you* stay," said Dee, relentlessly. "And you might remind Guerney while you're about it what *our* sort of girl is like." She turned quickly and with her head in the air flounced off.

Leni looked at Guerney. "I don't know what Dee meant—"

"Don't you? Well, my dear, it may amuse you to know that Dee has apparently harbored plans for pairing us off in some fantastic future."

They both laughed at the same time, then Leni said, "I hope you didn't think *I* ever thought along those lines."

"I suspected not. And no more did I—you were always like another not-so-well-known little sister. . . . Anyhow, do you want to see my woodcarvings, or do you think you should run along after Dee and soothe her ruffled feelings?"

"Oh, Dee won't hold it against me—especially if she thinks I'm reminding you what our sort of girl is like," laughed Leni, little knowing how much she was to regret her decision later on.

Guerney's woodcarvings were of figures from various Balinese folk stories and dramas. They were simple and beautiful, and Leni particularly admired a monkey with a very knowing look on its face. This was Hanuman, and Guerney admitted it was a favorite of his.

"Just now I don't want to part with him. Maybe I'll give him to you as a wedding present one of these days."

Leni flushed. "I might never get married."

"You're sure to. I'll give you a year at the most. Isn't there someone waiting for you to come back in England?"

"No."

"I find that hard to believe."

"Still, it's true."

"Pity. I won't try to find you anyone here. Holiday romances are extremely risky—even if they happen to be with big-time hotel directors." Guerney looked at Leni with faint severity even though he was smiling, and her face paled. "In any event, as far as Kemp Savage is concerned, I've heard there's already a girl well in the picture—Cristelle Dubois. So don't build up any dreams there, will you, Leni?"

Leni pretended an absorption in Hanuman so that she didn't have to meet Guerney's eyes. She said, with an attempt at lightness, "It's kind of you to warn me, Guerney, but I became acquainted long ago with Kemp Savage's demands—and with his tactics."

She realized that Guerney was looking at her with sharpened curiosity now, and rather unwisely looked up to be confronted by the question in his blue eyes. "Just something I heard in Singapore," she added, trying to sound casual and uninvolved. "Something he said to Sam Becker. Apparently one of his girlfriends actually dared to look at another man, and her stock went way down." She stroked Hanuman's smooth shining head and set him down on the table. "He's really beautiful."

Guerney chose to ignore this red herring. "That would have been the Dubois girl. And so Kemp Savage then came to meet *you* at the airport. Isn't that what you told me? I'm afraid I didn't pay much attention at the time, being rather het up about Dee."

Leni raised her eyebrows. "If I gave you that impression, Guerney, you can forget it. Kemp Savage just happened to be at the airport when I arrived, that's all."

"Then I'm glad. It's been a bit on my mind lately. It's all very fine to have a romantic holiday, but it can be catastrophic if you get your heart broken at the same time. And you're such a serious little person."

"But very level-headed," said Leni lightly.

"You used to be. I'm not so sure now."

"You've seen Dee switch over to a different image, so you think I'll do the same. Well, don't let *me* weigh on your mind, Guerney. I'll have my glamorous month and then I'll go home and live on my memories."

"Taking Dee with you, it's to be hoped."

"Yes," agreed Leni soberly. She liked Charles and didn't want him hurt.

"And I'll be able to get over to Djakarta again, to see Janet and arrange some business. I don't feel like going while Dee's acting the fool, and I can't very well leave you with all the responsibility."

"You *are* a trifle officious, Guerney," said Leni with a sigh. "Don't you realize there's a streak of contra-suggestibility in all of us? So if you don't trust Dee. . . ."

Guerney smiled and touched the tip of her nose teasingly. "It amuses me to hear you talk like that—as if you were quite grown up."

"Well, so I am. And so is Dee," Leni assured him. "And I think it's time for me to go. It will soon be dark, and it would never do for me to be alone with a man in his bungalow after dark, would it?"

Guerney laughed, but he let her go all the same. The sun was already setting as she walked slowly along the beach. A red glow spread all across the sky, making the coral sand appear pink, and fire seemed to dance like tinsel on the indigo surface of the sea, and on the long, long waves that came in smoothly and endlessly to break with whispering sound on the shore.

Leni walked slowly, savoring it all—the peace, the calm, the gentle sounds of nature. Somewhere a long way off she could hear music as some *gamelan* orchestra practised for a village dance performance. For a little while, Leni felt released from all her personal problems. Everything would come out right . . . somehow. She had a sudden and unreasonable belief that anything was possible—that Kemp Savage would fall in love with her and that they would live happily ever after—no matter what Guerney said about holiday romances. . . .

She was smiling to herself when she reached the *losmen* and she smiled still more when she caught sight of Dee sitting on the veranda wearing a hand-embroidered dress of fine cotton, her hair shining and washed and caught coolly back from her neck. Even her sunburned face had been skilfully made up.

But Leni's smile faded as Dee said, looking up through her lashes, "A man came to see you."

Leni's heart seemed to stop for a moment, and then it began to beat painfully. There was only one man who could possibly have come to see her. Yet why should *he* have come? And why couldn't she have been here?

"Who?" she asked huskily.

"He said his name was Savage. It suited him rather," said Dee. "Where on earth did you bump into him, Len? He looked fabulous!"

Leni, who felt her legs were going to give way at any moment, said nothing, and Dee continued, "I told him you were at Guerney's and I asked him if he'd wait, but he said no. He left a little package and wrote you a note instead. I got Made to unlock your door and put them inside for you."

"Thank you," said Leni in a whisper. She still made no effort to tell Dee where she and Kemp had met, but went woodenly into her room. "I told him you were at Guerney's." Oh, why had Dee had to say just that? It could have ruined—if there was anything to ruin!

She had forgotten her lamp and groping about on the table found a box of matches and struck one. She unfolded the note he had written first. It was sealed in an envelope which he must have got from Dee or Made. She had to light three more matches to read it and it would have been a lot more sensible to go onto the veranda and use the lamp there, but she could not.

"Dear Miss Forrest," she read. "I had the idea of apologizing to you for my brusqueness of the other night. However, you were not available. Nevertheless, please believe me when I express regret that I lost my temper with you. I am at your service if you should ever need advice of any kind. Kemp Savage. P.S. The necklace may help you to discern what is good from what is inferior. Perhaps you may even care to wear it. K.S."

Leni felt numb. "You were not available." She opened

the small paper-wrapped package blindly. She didn't light another match. She looked through her window into the courtyard. Two girls with lamps were approaching the ancestral shrine. The banana palms rustled, the long graceful shadows of the girls fell across the neatly brushed yard. In her hand, which was somehow cold, Leni could feel the necklace. She glanced down and from it's pale gleam she knew that it was ivory.

Suppose she had come back with Dee—suppose she had been here when he had come. Instead of "not available"—at Guerney's!

There were tears in her eyes when sudden flickering light came through the door and Dee stood there with a lamp in her hand.

"Leni! You can't possibly see in the dark. Don't you want to know what he's given you?"

"It's a necklace," said Leni, her voice scarcely audible. She handed it to Dee and turned aside to wipe her tears away.

Dee exclaimed, "It's the Barong! Put it on, Len, do."

"Later," said Leni dully. "Not just now."

Dee was examining it in the lamplight.

"But it's beautiful, Len! It's not just bone—it's ivory. It's probably ages old." She clasped it excitedly around her own neck and stood before the diamond-shaped mirror in the old-fashioned Dutch wardrobe. "Aren't you just too lucky! You can see things like this hanging above stalls in the markets by the dozen—but mostly they're bone, and they're coarse. This is so fine it's like lace. And the Barong!" She unclasped the necklace and gave it back to Leni. "Do look—it's terrific! Where *did* you meet this Savage man? And how come he's made you such a fabulous gift?"

Leni said vaguely, "We met in Singapore. He was a

friend of Sam Becker's—you know, the man Guinevere Raymond is to marry. And I—I just don't know why he's given me this. It *is* beautiful, isn't it?"

For the first time she really looked at her Barong necklace. The carving was very fine and detailed, and each small section was joined to the next by a delicate silver chain. Elaborate medallions like four-pointed stars alternated with long oval shapes and at the center was a bar carved into the shapes of flowers and leaves. The central and most ornate piece of all, the piece that Dee had called the Barong, hung from this bar. Leni saw a face staring at her. Not a human face, but the face of some mystical, mythical creature—perhaps a tiger, perhaps a wild boar. It had great round eyes, long fangs and was adorned with elaborate headdress and collar. It was a face that was fearsome and yet oddly benevolent, and for a mad moment Leni wanted to laugh, because she had thought that about Kemp Savage the other night. Fearsome, yet benevolent.

Suddenly, she felt oddly healed, her hurt and disappointment were blurred, receding, and she looked up at Dee with a faint smile in her eyes.

"What's a Barong, Dee?"

"I'm not the best person to ask," said Dee. "But there are these two mythical creatures: one is good; that's the Barong; and the other, Rangda, the widow witch, is evil. That's about all *I* know, but I'm sure your Mr. Savage could tell you a lot more," she finished slyly.

"I suppose so," agreed Leni without enthusiasm. She would never be able to ask Kemp Savage about the Barong. He was "at her service" if she needed advice, that was all. And in any case, she would return the necklace to him. She could never accept such a gift from such a man. She could only wonder why he had made it.

Carefully she rewrapped the necklace and thrust it into a drawer, then turned to Dee brightly. "Shall we go and eat? I'm starving!"

For some reason, the night that followed was the worst that Leni could ever remember. She slept in uneasy snatches, woke frequently to hear motor-bikes, voices, the barking of dogs. Then, even before first light, the cocks began to crow, loudly and long, one echoing another until the noise was almost unbearable. Finally Leni left her bed and went to refresh herself with a scoop bath. When she came back, early though it was, her coffee, breakfast bun and bananas were already on the table—someone in the compound always seemed to know when she was up, and to prepare a tray accordingly.

This morning, a tiny but exquisite arrangement of flowers accompanied her breakfast, and Leni sat staring at it and presently became achingly absorbed by beauty. Pink and cream frangipani, coral-colored bougainvillea, little tight papery buds of palest green and strawberry red, white star flowers with crumpled petals and jewel green centers.

Leni found it strangely soothing to sit and contemplate this miniature work of art, to sip her thick strong coffee and put aside the pain of what might have been, and the stupid hurt in her heart. . . .

Later she thanked Made for the flowers and asked if one of the girls would do some washing for her. It was always done so beautifully, the clothes carefully folded, the scent of incense about them. And the girls appreciated being able to earn a little extra money.

That morning as she tidied her personal belongings Leni thought of her own hot-tempered remarks to Kemp. She longed to apologize to him but suspected that his reaction would be casual, aloof and knew that it was only a dream. It would not put anything right. Nothing was likely to go right between her and Kemp Savage. In effect—nothing was going to happen.

She slipped the Barong necklace into her handbag for safekeeping. She would have to return it some way—preferably without actually handing it to Kemp Savage himself. It would be better that way—better she not see him and make a fool of herself. . . .

That morning, Mike conducted what Dee called a "public opinion poll" amongst the other Europeans who were staying at the *losmen.*

"Did the cocks disturb you last night?" he wanted to know. They were all lying basking on the sand at the beach and they all agreed desultorily and without a great deal of interest that they had. One of the girls, an American called Amy, tall and lanky and lazy, said indifferently, "I hear them every morning. Then I roll over and cover up my ears and go to sleep again."

"Then you're lucky," said Mike. He picked up a handful of sand in which minute fragments of coral showed like tiny pink flowerlets and tossed it at Dee's feet. "I haven't had a decent night's sleep since I came to the *losmen.*"

"The day sure begins early," agreed an American boy, but he didn't even bother to turn his head or open his eyes as he lay flat on his back, soaking up the hot sun.

"What about you two girls?" Mike asked then, casting a sharp look at Leni and Dee.

"Oh, I hear the cocks every morning too," said Dee cheerfully. "But I've become used to it."

"*That's* a flabby sort of attitude," Mike criticized. "I suppose you'd get used to it if someone came and poured a bucket of cold water over you at four every morning. Or is it just because you can afford to get out if it suits you?"

Dee shrugged and refused to begin an argument and Mike turned aggressively to Leni. "Well, what about you? I'll bet *you* don't sleep peacefully through all that racket—you're so damned fussy about everything."

Leni flushed, but said equably, "I suppose I always hear the cocks."

"What is this anyhow?" Dee asked.

"If everyone's in favor I intend to put it to Made that she either gets rid of those damned cocks or she finds her *losmen* deserted. Who's in favor?"

Dee was the only one who answered. She said angrily, her cheeks red, "I think that's despicable! I for one won't have anything to do with it. The cocks belong to the old men—they're their main interest in life. You can't expect to take it all away from them just like that!"

"There are two ways of looking at that," Mike said scathingly. "It's a fact that cockfighting used to be connected with religion and sacrifice and so on, but in case you aren't aware of it, it's little more than a form of gambling now, and quite likely causes more misery than anything else."

"Well, that's not our concern, is it?" said Dee, her eyes still angry. "If you live amongst a people then you accept their customs—the conditions of their lives. I didn't realize before that you saw yourself in the role of a missionary. I thought it was only me you wanted to change."

She stared at Mike and he stared back at her, his light blue eyes completely devoid of any sign of warmth or even liking. Those eyes made Leni shiver inwardly. She couldn't help reflecting that even when Kemp Savage's eyes were at their hardest there was still a glow from the warm fire of humanity somewhere in their depths.

"Waal," said the drawling voice of an American, "I vote we keep from trying to interfere in family life. I reckon you can have it all to yourself, Mike."

Mike looked at Leni, and when she said quietly, "I certainly don't intend to complain," he made an angry face, threw another handful of sand and got to his feet.

"Okay, we continue to be bugged and let Made get away with it. If you were in a European type hotel, you'd pretty soon complain—every one of you."

"Maybe. But at roughly 50 cents a night, I calculate we've still got the best end of the stick," said Amy with wry humor.

Mike turned his back abruptly and strode down to the water, where he plunged into the sea and began to swim.

"He *is* in a rage," said Dee critically. Leni said nothing. Later, she reflected that it was that little idea of Mike's that really ended his relationship with Dee—and that maybe Dee had been glad of an excuse to break with him. That afternoon, she declined to go to Denpasar with him when he asked her briefly, his eyes challenging and unfriendly, "Coming into town?"

"No, thanks." Dee barely looked up. She didn't offer any reason, and after staring at her for a moment longer, he shrugged and went on his way.

Leni and Dee took a siesta. Leni was tired after her wakeful night, but she didn't blame it on the cocks—their crowing was a part of the life here just as it would be on a farm. Later in the afternoon, Dee suggested they walk down to the beach to see the sunset. She had put on a pair of smart white pants and a sleeveless shirt of some silky voilet material that reminded Leni painfully of the amethyst sari. Who had that been for? she wondered and was amazed at herself for not wondering before. Because it had not been for Cristelle Dubois. . . . But she was determined not to start tormenting herself needlessly about Kemp Savage and she called her thoughts to order quickly.

The two girls walked slowly along the white beach together. They didn't talk much as they watched the glorious sunset and enjoyed the touch of a cool breeze that had sprung up to lighten the air after the heat of the day. A little sadly, Leni reflected that all this beauty was the one small part of their schoolgirl dreams that had really come true. How differently everything else was working out!

The sky had faded to dull rose and in a few minutes it would be dark, when they saw Guerney coming toward them.

"Hello, you two! I saw you from the bungalow and couldn't believe my eyes." He meant Dee's changed appearance, of course, and he was looking at her approvingly. "Where's the dreaded Mike?"

Dee made a face, shrugged and said nothing. Plainly, her brother's approval irked her. She hadn't dropped Mike to fall in with *his* wishes, and she didn't want to be praised for being a good girl. Leni hoped Guerney was aware of this as she was and that he would not rub salt in the wound, but he asked cheerfully, "Had enough of Bali yet? Ready to go home to Charles like a sensible girl?"

"No, I'm not," said Dee perversely. "I haven't spent all my money yet—and it's going to last a long, long time at that *losmen*."

Guerney, walking between the two of them, frowned faintly. "Seems to me I should have packed you off to the Hotel Selatan right at the start. That way, you might have got rid of all your money and your nonsense as well in a fortnight. Then what peace would have been mine!"

"Not with that bossy old girlfriend of yours," said Dee, tossing her head.

"Not bossy and not old," said Guerney. His tone was even, but Leni had the feeling he definitely didn't like Dee to talk that way about Janet. "Janet's 33, she has plenty of intelligence and she uses it."

"Not like me?" asked Dee pertly.

"You're right. Not like you. Though at times I see a glimmer of light. At least you're engaged to a good man—"

"You don't know Charles. You only met him once."

"I'm a good judge of character. You're obviously not—except in this one case."

He changed the subject, possibly sensing Leni's unease at having to listen to yet one more family quarrel. "Feel like a cup of coffee and some gateau?"

They had come within sight of the great jungly garden that surrounded the Hotel Selatan, and Leni was suddenly filled with a sort of nervous apprehension. She said, too quickly, "Yes, let's turn back."

"I didn't mean at my bungalow," corrected Guerney. "Nyomen's talents don't run to the making of gateau. And I'm sure even you must sometimes long for a cup of good clear coffee instead of the unstrained stuff we all gulp down each day. No, I'll give you two girls a little celebration treat. We'll go to the Legong Coffee House. After all, it's a long time since Dee has been fit to take into decent society," he added dryly.

Leni felt her heart begin to beat quickly. The Legong Coffee House! That was in the grounds of the Hotel Selatan! She had seen the soft warm lights glowing from it when she had walked on the beach one night, had heard the music of the *gamelan* orchestra that played there sometimes. Part of her wanted to go into the hotel grounds, but she was afraid. She might see Kemp Savage. Yet if she were truthful with herself, she wanted to see Kemp Savage. There was an insatiable hunger in her that made her crave to see him—though it would certainly do her no good at all for him to see her with Guerney Fisher!

Guerney opened the iron gate that led into the hotel grounds. It was guarded on either side by stone dragons, ferocious creatures that were supposed to keep the evil spirits away. Leni hoped that they did! She walked with the others along a raked gravel path between tall palms and rustling banana trees whose huge leaves glowed green and translucent in the light of the ornate lamps that lined the pathway. The air was laden with the fragrance of frangipani flowers and they gleamed like white waxen stars from the branches of the dark trees.

On the porches of the thatched-roof guest bungalows, people sipped cold drinks or talked or played records. Ahead, the high-thatched roof of the coffee house was silhouetted against a sky that glowed softly in the tropical warmth. Soon they could hear the *gamelan* music and in another minute were mounting steps to the red-clothed tables grouped on a tiled floor. Cool breezes blowing in from the sea made the coffee house, with its open sides, a cool and pleasant place.

Leni saw Kemp almost as soon as they entered. He was sitting at a table some distance away, partly screened by one of the tall carved posts that supported the high roof. His companion was a young and very beautiful Balinese girl. She was wearing—and Leni felt a painful shock as she recognized it—the amethyst sari that he had bought in Singapore. At her wrist a bracelet glimmered, and Leni knew that it, too, had been bought in Singapore. She felt a dreadful despair creep over her and remembered her hastily spoken words, "You should find a Balinese girl who would willingly be your slave." It looked as though Kemp might have done just that long before she had spoken. . . .

Deliberately, she chose a position at the table so that her back was to Kemp and the Balinese beauty, and with all her will she tried to forget them. But when she opened her handbag to find her handkerchief, a small tissue-wrapped parcel containing an ivory necklace was there to sear her heart. She could hardly give it back to him tonight! Or could she? That crazy imagination of hers showed her a picture of herself doing so—of the look of amazement and then of displeasure on his face, of the beautiful dark eyes of the Balinese girl raised inquiringly. . . . Leni with an effort brought her attention back to her companions.

After Guerney had ordered coffee, the Balinese waitress, in a gold and orange sarong, wheeled a big carved trolley of cakes to the table. Dee's blue eyes lit up with greedy pleasure at the sight, and she chose three cakes—all cream-filled, all luscious beyond words. Guerney and Leni contented themselves with one each—though Leni was sure she would be unable to eat a single mouthful.

Guerney said warningly, "You'll get fat, Dee!"

"Not fat, plump," said Dee. "Well, I've lost pounds living at the *losmen*. It will do me no harm." And presently, as she attacked her third cake, she remarked thoughtfully, "You know, I'm a little tempted to move into this hotel. How about it, Len? Will your finances bear it?"

Leave the safety of the *losmen*! The thought of coming to the Hotel Selatan terrified Leni even while it fascinated her. What would Kemp think? That she was chasing after him, of course. And now, while she hesitated, Guerney said, "If you're leaving the *losmen*, I think you'd both better come to my bungalow. I don't really think I'd trust you here, Dee."

"But you said," began Dee, then broke off. A young man who had come in from the garden was approaching their table. He was heavily built, with dark reddish hair and a slight swagger to his walk—a rather handsome young man with a wilful mouth and a look that marked him as American. He came smilingly toward Guerney.

"Well, hello! Fancy running into you! I bought one of your paintings a day or so ago, remember! This is really great!"

As he spoke, his eyes went to Leni and then to Dee, and there they stayed. Leni smiled to herself—it was plain why he found this chance encounter really great! Dee was looking charming this evening. The soft lights were kind to her sunburnt nose, and her shoulders looked rounded and seductive in the sleeveless silk top. By comparison, Leni knew she herself must look colorless in her pale silvery blue cotton. Unlike Dee, she didn't think a walk on the beach called for dressing up, but now Dee had recovered from her slumming, she was going to the other extreme and ready to show off all her most stunning clothes.

The American lingered by the table until Guerney rather reluctantly introduced his sister and Leni and admitted, "I'm afraid I don't remember your name."

"Halvorsen—Dwight L. Halvorsen. I'm very pleased to meet you both." He looked specifically at Dee, who was quite aware of what he meant and smiled dazzlingly. "I'm a comparative newcomer here—all on my own. May I join you?"

"Of course," welcomed Dee, her eyes sparkling provocatively as she slipped into a new role. "Do sit down. Are you staying at the hotel—Dwight?"

"I sure am. I hope you are too?"

"Not at the moment. But we've just been talking of making a move, haven't we, Leni?"

Leni agreed that they had, reflecting to herself that nothing would stop Dee now, and immediately Dee proceeded to be amusing about the *losmen* and its short-comings.

Several minutes later, with a start that made her cheeks pale, Leni saw Kemp Savage coming toward their table. He bowed a sardonic recognition to Leni and begged to be excused for interrupting their foursome, then addressed himself to the American.

"The performance of the Pendet dance is due to start in a few minutes, and the girls will make offerings at the shrine of Semara. So if you want to watch, now is the time—"

Dwight looked across at Dee, who shook her head sorrowfully.

"Not me! I couldn't move, Mr. Savage!" She wiggled her eyebrows embarrassingly at Leni. "I've eaten three gorgeous cakes, and quite frankly I shouldn't have put on these sandals to walk along the beach. That coral sand! No, I'm afraid I'd rather sit here. But you go ahead, Dwight."

Of course she knew that he wouldn't go without her—or perhaps she was testing the impression she had made on him. In any case, he said unhesitatingly, "I guess it can wait till some other time. Thanks, Savage, all the same."

Kemp's lip curled a little. He glanced at Leni, at Guerney—impassive, impersonal.

"What about Miss Forrest and—Mr. Fisher? It's the God of Love who's being honored tonight. You might both like to see the regalia—the fruits and the colored rice cakes—the dance ceremony."

The God of Love! Of course he implied that there would be some special significance in that for Leni and Guerney, but his eyes were dark and unfathomable.

Guerney, with a slight movement, settled himself more comfortably in his chair, and Leni thought, "He's not going to leave Dee here alone with this handsome spoiled-looking boy who looks as if he could be a great deal more dangerous than Mike Miller!"

"No one interested?" insisted Kemp.

"No, thanks," said Guerney briefly.

Leni saw the unspoken comment in Kemp Savage's eyes as he cast her a mocking glance. "I've really caught you out this time!"

"I'm interested," said Leni suddenly. She hadn't had the least idea she was going to say that, or that she was going to rise to her feet so quickly. One of her hands was clenched hard on the edge of the bamboo table, and she knew that Guerney was frowning and trying to remind her of his warning about holiday romances. She bit her lip, but still she stood there. She was determined to let Kemp know that Guerney had absolutely no say in what she did or did not do.

"Come now, Leni," said Guerney just a little sharply. "You're going to have plenty of opportunities to see Balinese dancing. Don't be so—eager." He meant, of course, don't be so eager to run off with this handsome sophisticated man.

Leni's gray eyes flicked quickly to Kemp Savage's face. He was looking at her levelly, measuringly, and there was an exasperating quirk at one corner of his mouth. What did he think she was going to do? Sit down? Give in to Guerney? And what did he *want* her to do? Leni had no idea. It could well be that he simply didn't care one way or the other. But Leni knew that she had to go with him. She had to go to make it clear that Guerney was her friend's brother and nothing more. And she had to go because—simply because she couldn't resist the magnetic power that this man seemed to have over her.

She said steadily, looking straight into his dark eyes, "I'd very much like to see the Pendet Dance, Mr. Savage."

The dark brows lifted.

"Then come along, Miss Forrest, or you may miss out," he told her smoothly.

CHAPTER FIVE

He must know now, thought Leni, that Guerney was not interested in her romantically—or he would not so tamely have allowed her to go off without him. She walked rather nervously beside Kemp across the room and down the steps into the garden. A quick glance had shown her that the Balinese girl was no longer sitting at the table she had occupied with Kemp, and Leni wondered where she had gone.

Lamps on carved stone stands lit the garden paths, and coconut palms cast long shadows across the lawns. Leni could hear the waves on the beach, and beyond the garden she could see the lights of the tall hotel building, towering over the thatch-roofed guest bungalows.

"Were I in Guerney Fisher's place, I shouldn't trust you to come out in the night with another man," Kemp Savage said presently into the silence that lay between them. He didn't even look at Leni as he said it, and he kept on walking . . . so quickly that she had to hurry to keep up with him. His remark shocked her a little—he didn't seem to have put the obvious interpretation on the situation at all, and Leni was sufficiently exasperated to exclaim, "Guerney Fisher doesn't care what I do!"

"I find that hard to believe. And if I were you, I wouldn't be too sure about it either. You may well find you've gone too far, one of these fine days." He stopped walking suddenly, and there were dark shadows about them and the sound of leaves rustling in the night wind. The air was heavy with scent and Leni's nerves were tingling. The garden lamps had been left behind and she could not see any signs of activity. She began to suspect he was not taking her to the dance ceremony at all. As she hesitated beside him, he swung round and took her compellingly by her upper arms.

"What sort of a game are you playing, Miss Forrest?"

"I'm not playing a game at all. I don't know what you mean."

"So innocent?" Suddenly he took her chin between finger and thumb and turned her face up to his. "Don't you know what a temptation you are to any man? Your artist friend is a fool to let you out of his sight. It's a foregone conclusion what's going to happen between you and me."

The words were barely spoken when his lips were on hers and she felt herself strained against his body. She was aware of his warmth, of the beating of his heart, of the very coursing of his blood—and of her own. Her eyes had closed and for a dizzying moment she was caught up in the passion of his kiss.

"That's what you get for coming out in the dark with me," he said when at last he freed her. His voice was low and oddly troubled.

Leni was breathing fast. "I didn't exactly come out in the dark with you, Mr. Savage. You were going to take me to see some dancing."

"So I was. But it seemed a far better idea to get this over with. You asked for it, you know—and it had to happen, didn't it? You'd have sought me out or I'd have sought you—until at last it happened. It's best we should get it out of our systems."

"What?" Leni breathed. "I . . . I don't understand you—"

"No? I can't really believe you're as naïve as all that. I think it's pretty obvious that there's something in each of us that draws the other. Isn't it so?"

Leni looked at him wordlessly. She knew that she was hopelessly in love with him and she knew that he was not talking about love. She was engulfed by a hopeless feeling that this game he was drawing her into was far too sophisticated for her tastes. His eyes seemed to be exploring hers through the darkness and she didn't know if there was amusement or some grim intensity lurking in them.

"So," he said, after what seemed an age, "we conduct a very simple experiment. We embrace, we kiss. We discover that this mystical fatal attraction is no more than a matter of chemistry. Are you with me? Are you satisfied on that count, Miss Forrest?"

He was not touching her now. Had his fingers been around her wrist he would have felt the quickness of her pulse, and surely something else . . . some far from merely chemical reaction to his nearness. He must have—Leni was sure of it. And so she should have been glad that he was not touching her.

Yet, perversely, she longed to feel the pressure of those long, strong fingers. She longed for him to stroke back the fine fair hair that had fallen across her brow, or to curve a hand over the curve of her bare shoulder. Chemistry? No, it was not all a matter of chemistry as far as she was concerned; it was something deep and eternal and overpowering and—she was a fool if she did not admit it—completely, utterly hopeless.

She smiled wryly at the thought, and he said, breaking into her reverie, "You're amused, Miss Forrest. We must hope that Guerney Fisher is amused too—that he's considering it all a little matter of chemistry—a test that will be quickly over and forgotten. Perhaps being an artist he entertains such liberal ideas and is ready to accord a corresponding freedom to the woman he loves."

Leni opened her mouth to say, "And that's not me," but he went on tersely, "For my part, I'm not liberal-minded at all. If I love a woman then I want all of her. In my view there are two kinds of love. One has the same quality you'll find in the art objects that are sold in the streets of Denpasar. It's for the undiscriminating. The other is a love that exists because it must. It's comparable to true art—it's fierce and burning and pure and unmistakable to one who has the mystical longing for it in his heart. . . . I could never have done as Guerney Fisher did, Leni. I could never have watched you go out into the tropical night with another man."

Leni leaned back against the rough warm trunk of a palm tree, her legs unaccountably shaky. "Guerney and I are *not* in love—"

"No?" She could see his lip curl. "Didn't you lie to get to him . . . with your pretty little tale about your school friend? Weren't you with him last night at his bungalow?"

"I left at sunset," said Leni tensely. "I . . . I just missed you at the *losmen*—"

"Really? Then perhaps that was a pity. We could have made our little experiment some twenty-four hours sooner. And Guerney Fisher need never have known."

Guerney Fisher! Lini felt exhausted with exasperation. It seemed she was mad to try to persuade this man that Guerney was nothing to her. He was intent on having it his way and she was beating her head against a brick wall. She bent her head and opened her handbag, taking out the ivory necklace that had come adrift from its wrapping.

"I don't want gifts from you, Mr. Savage. Please take this back."

"I don't take gifts back once I've made them. It's yours whether you want it or not. And if you have any sense, you'll wear it. You'll certainly be in need of the Barong if you stay in Bali much longer." He took the necklace from her hands and murmured, almost as though it were a *mantra*, "Symbol of virtue, glory of the high sun—the Barong will protect you from evil always."

Leni seemed half mesmerized as she listened, and then he was fastening the necklace about her throat. His hands lingered at her nape, his fingers stroked for a second her silky hair. . . . Leni shivered suddenly, remembering the girl in the silken sari, despising herself for falling so easy a victim to his charms. She drew away from him.

"Do you always insist that your gifts should be worn by the reciever? Do you always—personally see to it?"

"That means—exactly what?"

"I haven't forgotten the sari you bought in Singapore," she said cynically. "And now I suppose I've missed the dance ceremony."

"Does it matter? Haven't we enacted a little ceremony of our own?"

Tears stung Leni's eyes. She simply couldn't cope with him, couldn't understand him. She thought she hated him, and she began to run back toward the lights and the coffee house and the people she knew.

Of course he let her go. He didn't even follow her.

Dee had quite made up her mind to move. She had dropped Mike completely and lost all interest in the life at the *losmen*. All she could talk about was Dwight Halvorsen.

"Don't you think he's fascinating?" she asked Leni.

Leni said with a smile, "Not really. And I don't think he's nearly so nice as Charles!"

"Leni!" Dee protested. "Charles is in England. I'm here. Can't you get it into your head that the two worlds have nothing to do with each other?"

Leni couldn't. She had some muddled unutterable idea that if you loved, your love went everywhere with you like an aura. At the back of her mind something that Kemp had said was assuming a shining crystalline shape of its own.

"Anyhow," said Dee, smiling up at Leni through her lashes, "that fabulous Savage man of yours is at the Selatan. So of course we must move. No matter what you say, I refuse to believe he's just a friend of this Sam Becker's. If that were all, he'd hardly be giving you expensive presents and cleverly maneuvring you off alone with him on some vague pretext."

"Dee, we were all asked to see the dance. I was the only one who was interested." Leni's cheeks had flushed.

"I don't think you saw much dancing," teased Dee. "You haven't said a word about it. . . . But calm down, Len, I'm not going to grill you—I know how dreary that is. At any rate, we're going to stick together, aren't we? You're not going to stay by yourself at the *losmen*?"

Of course Leni wasn't. If Dee moved to the hotel, then Leni, against all the dictates of common sense, would move too. She would be exposed to the exquisite torture of seeing Kemp Savage—perhaps often. She would be hurt, humiliated, bewildered by him; she would suffer despair and heartache—but move she would.

"We'll take a bungalow," planned Dee, "a romantic thatched bungalow." She hugged Leni. "It's going to be fun!"

Of course Guerney did not approve, but they moved all the same, and the bungalow was excitingly different. No one could have helped being thrilled with it. Dee, embracing her new image wholeheartedly, had a beauty treatment at the hotel salon and, her complexion more or less restored, blossomed forth in all her most attractive clothes. She spent every available minute with Dwight, and Leni found she was largely left to herself.

Dee urged her to "grab" this man or that while he was still available, but Leni couldn't have been less interested. When she encountered Kemp Savage one evening in the hotel garden, he bowed to her formally.

"So you've moved into the Selatan, Miss Forrest."

"But not on your account," she flashed instantly, and then wished she had been more dignified.

He gave a crooked smile. "Naturally not. . . . And the move has Guerney Fisher's approval?"

"No." Once again Leni was too hasty with her reply, but her good sense seemed to desert her completely when Kemp was around. She added, trying to improve matters, "But that's because. . . ." And there she stopped, at a loss. She could hardly go blurting out the secrets of Dee's private life, so she remained lamely silent.

He waited a moment and one brow lifted sardonically. "You must go on some of the tours—see something of the island."

"Yes," agreed Leni. And then to make it quite plain that she wasn't chasing him, "Please excuse me. I have a—an appointment."

"Certainly." Again that bow and Leni hurried on along the path to nowhere.

And later, as she went over and over that encounter in her mind, she thought how crazy it was that such a miserable crumb could give her so much nourishment. She *was* a sad case! At this rate, the sooner she left Bali the better for her. But the next day, she almost changed her mind about that, for by some chance Kemp Savage was at the swimming pool at the same time as herself.

Leni had been swimming up and down the long tiled pool in its setting of coconut palms and telling herself that this was the sort of holiday she had always dreamed about. There were tanned handsome men in plenty, though most of them appeared to be married or at least attached in some way, and a goodly number of them had gray hair! Dee and Dwight were reclining in chairs nearby, and Leni, as she climbed out of the water, decided that Dwight looked more than a little sinister in his dark sunglasses. She had an uneasy feeling that he was the kind of man who would have designs on a girl's virtue, a feeling that Dee, lounging back in her bikini, appeared not to share. Leni glanced not very happily at the Darong necklace that adorned Dee's form. Dee had asked if she might borrow it and Leni had found she could not refuse.

She started when a voice addressed her from the shade of a palm tree.

"You're an excellent swimmer, Leni! You must surely be thirsty after that mighty effort. Will you have an iced drink with me?"

"Leni"—and the offer of a cold drink! Leni blinked unbelievingly. She must be hearing things! Of course she should say "No, thank you"—it would be madness to start on another round of superficial involvement with Kemp Savage—she would only finish up being hurt. But just now, just at this instant—maybe because it was so fair a day and she was suddenly aware of it—just now she felt singularly happy and good-humored and she was not really surprised to hear herself say most agreeably, "Thank you—there's nothing I'd like more."

He sat at a table shaded by a little roof of thatch, and he wore sunglasses too—so that Leni could not see those dark eyes of his. He wore white shorts and a white shirt, unbuttoned to the waist. His chest was darkly tanned. His head was turned to Leni and she knew he was watching her as she came toward him, still shining and wet from her swim. She should have gone to fetch her towel or her robe, but her sense seemed to have deserted her and she walked as one in a dream.

He clapped his hands together lightly and called, "Nani!" and one of the Balinese girls glided up smilingly. Kemp spoke to her in Indonesian and she hurried away, to appear only seconds later with a long cape of white towelling with a crimson fringe. Leni slipped it on over her swimsuit gratefully, with a smile of thanks.

As she sat down two more girls appeared, and all three stood smiling, showing their beautiful even white teeth. They wore the red and gold sarongs that were the uniform of the female staff at the hotel, and they looked so amazingly lovely that Leni would not have been in the least surprised if they had started one of the formal Balinese dances. Kemp soon despatched them to fetch drinks and ice. Then, settling back in his chair, he removed his sunglasses and looked at Leni.

"I hope you're enjoying yourself here, Leni?"

"Yes, I am." Right now, in fact, she was quite besottedly happy, and she knew that her eyes must be shining and giving her away. A tray of drinks had appeared, tiny embroidered table napkins, a silver dish of sweet cakes. The girls smiled, bowed and departed. With the idea that an impersonal conversation would steady her, Leni remarked, "Those beautiful smiles! And they all have such lovely even teeth—the boys and the girls."

"Long canines are reserved for witches and demons," said Kemp, with a lift of his eyebrows and a smile that was, thought Leni helplessly, more fascinating in its very masculine way than any smile she had ever seen in her life. Talk about the moth and the candle! She reached for a cake and tried to hide her eyes. "You've seen those long-fanged ferocious creatures that guard the temple gates and frighten away evil spirits?"

"Yes," said Leni. She thought of those fantastically straight teeth again.

"I'll tell you a secret," said Kemp. "Those lovely even white teeth are the result of a tooth-filing ceremony."

"You mean they have their teeth *filed* to make them even?" Leni's eyes were wide with disbelief.

"Not for that specific purpose—no." Kemp was laughing at her. "Filing the upper teeth is believed to weaken the six evil qualities of human nature."

"Really?" asked Leni, intrigued, and quite at her ease now. She thought of the seven deadly sins. "And what are they?"

"Let's see now." He enumerated them on his fingers. "Laziness, irresolution, indifference. Love of worldly goods, of splendor and luxury, of sensual pleasure. How do you think *you* measure up, Leni? Shall we have to see the priest about a little tooth-filing?"

Leni laughed. She took a sip of the iced drink that had the tang of fruits she did not know and savored it. Even though the conversation had taken a slightly personal turn, she felt no fear of Kemp in this pleasant, half-joking mood. She said lightly, "Well, it's true I'm revelling in the luxury and splendor of your hotel, Mr. Savage—"

"Come now, can't you call me Kemp? I'm pleased you're enjoying the luxury we offer. Tropic island holidays are rather made for luxuries, I think. Provided of course one can by some means or other pay for them."

Leni flushed. "I believe you still think I'm what used to be called a gold-digger, Mr.—Kemp. Batik gowns and expensive holidays . . . and. . . ."

"Ivory necklaces?" he quizzed, his look enigmatic. "Have you worn it yet?"

"No," said Leni. Her color deepened still more. "I've lent it to Dee today." The second before she said it, she had the feeling he knew that already, and now he glanced straight across to where Dee sat with Dwight. Their heads were close together, and Dee was laughing but Dwight was not. The necklace showed creamy against Dee's suntan, above the low-cut bikini.

Kemp remarked dryly, "Perhaps your friend's in need of the symbol of virtue. But I gave the necklace to you—the Barong was to be *your* protector."

"I don't need protection," said Leni casually—and then remembered the other night.

His eyebrows made a sudden straight grim line. "You will wear it," he said.

Leni looked at him quickly, shivering at the deadly seriousness of his tone. She was aware of a strange inward tremor—a communication that seemed to be of another world. Were the gods and spirits that inhabited Bali becoming real to her without her ever actually thinking about it? Did Kemp respect them too? He certainly appeared to. . . . But Leni didn't need protection—it was too late for that, she was so deep in danger already.

"You must see a performance of the Barong dance," he told her after a moment, and now his tone had lightened. "I'll let you know if there's to be one in any of the nearby villages. You'll enjoy it—it will be an experience for you."

To remember when she was back in England, thought Leni. That was what he meant. She thought of the Balinese girl to whom he had given the sari, and she looked at him through her lashes, desperately memorizing his face—the thick blackness of lashes that matched his eyes, the firm decisive line of mouth and chin, the dark hair that fell in a wave across a forehead that was both broad and intelligent. She wished that she had her own sunglasses to hide her eyes so that she could look at him forever. . . .

The next day, he sent a written message to the bungalow inviting her and Dee and Dwight to dine with him that night in his private suite. Leni felt an instant wariness that was completely unfounded. It was as though she must suspect some ulterior motive. . . . It was midday, and Dee, who had been on the beach all morning, was lying on the low divan in the tiled living area. The ceiling fan was whirring and she was glancing through a glossy American magazine she had bought in one of the hotel stores. She looked up as Leni, who had asked the messenger to wait, came into the room.

"You know, I wouldn't at all mind living in America," remarked Dee. "California, for instance. I've developed this insatiable taste for sunshine."

"You'd better see if Charles is prepared to make the move then," Leni said mildly.

"Leni!" Dee's blue eyes were pained. "How can you be so dampeningly matter-of-fact when I'm having such a marvelous time? At any rate, Dwight is getting quite serious about me."

Leni found that hard to believe. Her impression of Dwight Halvorsen was that he was out to get the most in every way from his holiday—just as Dee was from hers. But for now she passed that over and asked, "Are you booked up for tonight, Dee?"

"Not exactly. But Dwight will find something for us to do. Why?"

"Kemp Savage has asked the three of us to join him for dinner."

Dee's magazine slipped to the floor and she sat up and stared. "Honestly? You *are* in luck, Len! I wish a man like that would fall for me! How on earth did you manage it?"

"I didn't," said Leni, embarrassed. "I mean, he

hasn't—fallen for me at all. He probably makes a practice of inviting the hotel guests to dinner."

Dee laughed aloud. "Oh, Leni, you can't possibly believe that!"

Leni certainly didn't want to believe it, but she wondered if she had in fact hit on the truth. . . . But she prompted Dee, "The boy's waiting for our answer."

Dee said, "You go, Leni. Dwight and I can do something else. That's only fair."

"Oh no, I wouldn't dream of going on my own," said Leni, appalled. "He—he wouldn't want that! I'll only go if you and Dwight come too."

"Then in that case, I suppose we must. But I'm sure your Savage man must only have invited us out of a sense of propriety, or something."

That night, Leni wore the batik that Guinevere had given her. It was far and away the best thing she had, and she wanted to do justice to what was surely an occasion. Dee wore a jewel-green brocade—a dress she had bought that afternoon at one of the hotel shops. It looked quite fabulous and made Leni exclaim, "You'll run through your money in no time, if you buy clothes like that, Dee."

"Don't worry. It wasn't my money," said Dee blithely. "It's a little gift from Dwight."

Leni frowned, thinking of Charles, thinking of the look she had sometimes seen on Dwight's face. "You shouldn't take expensive presents from him, Dee."

"Why not? He has plenty of money to throw around—he's loaded. Besides, as soon as I saw this dress I knew I had to have it."

"Love of luxury," said Leni thoughtfully. She smiled a little. "You'll have to have your teeth filed, Dee."

"What?"

"Nothing." Leni's smile faded as Dee picked up the

Barong necklace and clasped it around her throat, her blue eyes looking guilelessly at Leni through the mirror.

"What's the matter? I thought you said *you'd* never wear it. Anyhow, it would look nothing against that patterned batik. With this plain rich stuff, it looks terrific."

Leni had to admit that this was so, but all the same. . . .

"Kemp might think it odd that you're wearing it."

Dee shrugged and admired herself. "It will give him something to think about. You don't want him to get the idea you're too easily impressed, you know. There's nothing like a little provocation to whet the male appetite," she added, the words oddly at variance with the innocence of her round young face.

Leni's heart sank. Provocation of any sort, she knew, was apt to have exactly the opposite effect on Kemp Savage. . . .

"The Balinese like to eat and then to talk," said Kemp, an hour or so later. "It's a custom I've adopted to a certain extent myself over the years, but feel free to talk or not as you please."

Leni chose to concentrate on the dishes that were provided, though occasionally she asked Kemp what a particular one was. Dee being Dee chattered and commented on everything, from the food and the dishes and the beautiful table of teak, deeply carved with birds and flowers and leaves, to the small courtyard beyond the doorway where water glittered from a lily pool.

"May we go and look afterwards?" She looked at her host flirtatiously, not for the first time.

"Of course," he said courteously. Leni knew that he had noted the ivory necklace the moment he had greeted them. His eyes had met hers and there had been something in their expression that had made her feel a deep, troubled feeling of guilt. Stupid! She was too hopelessly stupid and romantic. And gullible. Yes, gullible, to imagine there could be some tenuous secret thing between herself and this worldly man.

She ate her *lontong*—rice steamed in banana leaves—and the delicious chicken simmered in coconut milk, that Kemp called *opor ajam*, slowly and with enjoyment. Yet she could not forget the ivory necklace nor the expression she had seen in Kemp's eyes that was rather more subtle than mere accusation. Dee tasted and tried a bit of everything, and despite Kemp's murmured, "I'd recommend a very little *sambal* for a start," she helped herself liberally to the hot sauce and then had to beg with tears in her eyes for iced water.

Kemp's servants waited on the small party quietly and courteously, standing back in the shadows of the big room with its soft restful lighting, and stepping forward immediately a dish required to be passed. Leni had found her table napkin scented faintly with incense. Small silver fingerbowls held heated water and a slice of lemon. Dwight, dipping his fingers, said with approval, "You sure do yourselves well here in Bali. I'll recommend some of my friends back home pay you a visit next vacation. How's that for advertising?"

Kemp smiled faintly, yet distantly. "I'm sure we shall all appreciate it, Mr. Halvorsen."

Dee sprang up with her coffee cup still in her hands begging to be taken into the moonlight to see Kemp's private garden. She looked back from the doorway to say cheekily, "It'll be your turn next, you two—and I promise to say nothing to Guerney, Len."

Leni felt the color leave her cheeks as she drew in her breath on a little gasp. How could Dee say such a thing! She imagined no doubt that the thought of competition would make Kemp keener! Leni did not dare look at him, but sipped her scalding coffee and felt her eyes fill with tears of vexation.

"Your little friend is very ingenuous," Kemp said dryly. "In fact, she has a quality in her makeup that I'd call—elementary. She wears your necklace knowing very well that *I* gave it to you, and is simple enough to call my attention to the fact that you have another lover. Though of course, I was aware of that already."

Lover! The word made Leni start. "Another lover." Did he think she regarded him as—that? She simply could not meet his eyes.

He added softly, musingly, "I think I like your school friend's frankness, Leni. It's—refreshing."

That, Leni thought, meant that she was not frank. Well, she would certainly not have called Dee's blundering "frankness," but before she could even think how to begin persuading him to forget what Dee had said, he exclaimed sharply, "But I don't like her wearing the necklace I gave to *you*. And I promise you that if it happens again I shall, if necessary, remove it from her plump and pretty neck myself." His eyes went to Leni's throat as he spoke, and involuntarily, her hand flew there in a gesture of self-defence.

In a second he was on his feet and had caught at her raised wrist, drawing her up and almost into his embrace so that she stood close to him, staring compulsively into the dark fire of his gaze. "Why do you do it? Is it to infuriate me?"

She did not answer but stared at him petrified, thankful that with the coffee served the servants had vanished. He bit out, "*One* man is not enough to make your holiday complete. You're intent on stirring up combat . . . complications. Well, don't expect me to participate in the fun."

Leni thought weakly, "There are complications and

combat enough to satisfy anyone when this man is around!" What did he want from her? Sometimes he was so friendly—at other times he was quite cruel and flippant. His fingers with a fiery strength burned into her flesh just as his eyes were searing her soul. "Come," he said tightly. "We'll join the others. Your friend might as well know exactly what it is that she mustn't tell her brother."

Leni felt completely at his mercy as he drew her out past a carved wooden screen and under a thick canopy of purple bougainvillea that glowed like strange fire in the moonlight. The lily pond was a sheet of silver slashed with dark leaves and their shadows, with drifting dreaming pale-petalled flowers. Dee and Dwight stood on the far side of the water. Dee had kicked off her pretty evening sandals and clung to Dwight's hand as she dangled one foot in the coolness of the pool. her coffee cup rested precariously near the edge and, startled at some movement caught out of the corner of her eye as Kemp and Leni came into the garden, she lost her balance and accidentally knocked the cup into the water.

Dee gave a shrill giggle. "Sorry about that, Kemp. We'll fish it out." Regardless of her lovely dress, she threw herself down on the grass and plunged her arm into the water.

"Come and help me," she implored Dwight, and after a second he rolled up his sleeve and did so, though he looked far from pleased.

Kemp said, close to Leni's ear, "Innocence personified. Do you know why that is? She's wearing the Barong. Whereas you—you are unprotected and must therefore take the consequences."

Leni heard the soft rustle of palm leaves behind her, a shadow fell across her eyes and she was caught into his embrace and being kissed. And his kiss was like silk and the scent of incense. . . .

"Do you really think Dee will be able to resist telling Guerney?" Kemp asked mockingly.

Leni didn't know how she made it through the rest of that evening, or how she would ever be able to face Kemp again. When Dee teased her, she had to suffer it until she managed to change the topic of conversation. Yet when she did see Kemp again, he was so casual it was a complete anticlimax. They encountered one another in the surf, and he splashed her and asked flippantly, "Still enjoying your holiday, Leni?"

"Yes—yes, thank you." Leni was disconcerted to find that the mere sight of him was enough to make her forget all her soul-searching, her sleepless nights, her despair over a future in which Kemp Savage would have no part. "Love exists simply because it must," he had said once. She knew the truth of that too well. . . .

After he splashed her, he swam with strong strokes into the sea. Leni watched him for a long time, but he did not turn back and she knew he had forgotten her. She meant nothing at all to him.

CHAPTER SIX

The following day Leni woke feeling strangely listless and fatigued. Dee was spending the day with Dwight, who had hired a car for the week, and Leni decided to spend the day resting. It was particularly hot and she slept on and off all day—restless, uncomfortable, despite the fan which she kept turned on continuously. Just before sundown, one of the maids came to ask if she would like some tea and she said yes. Dee was not yet back, and Leni drank her tea, then decided to stroll around the garden and test her legs and her strength generally. She had not gone far before she realized that her activity was somewhat premature, and it was at the exact moment that she turned back that Kemp came upon her.

"Hello there. I was looking for you, Leni. I hope you intend joining the party at the pool tonight? It's going to be a great feast, I promise you."

The very thought of a feast made Leni feel nauseous. It was all she could do to force her lips into the shape of a smile and to say briefly, "I'm tired tonight. I think I'll go to bed early."

She saw his dark brows lift, felt his quick keen scrutiny and knew that the fading light hid her pallor. She was relieved when after a moment, he said, "Well then—so be it." Then, as she began to hurry away, "I shall probably be driving to Ubud in the morning. If you're interested in the museum, it may be a good opportunity for you to see it."

For the life of her, Leni could not have lingered. If she didn't climb into her bed pretty quickly she would collapse. She mumbled, "Thank you" and hurried on her way. It had been an invitation, she supposed. But right now, she was not interested in Ubud or museums or anything else at all.

Back in the bungalow, she was ill, and then she slept—really slept. She didn't even have time to take one of the tablets she had used in Singapore. When she woke it was ten o'clock. Dee had been in and gone out again—her clothes were dropped untidily about the floor and she had left one of the reading lights burning. Leni stretched. She felt a lot better. She even felt a little hungry. She thought immediately, "I'll be able to go to Ubud in the morning," and this thought did wonders for her. She took a shower and put on a pair of white silk pyjamas that for some reason Dee had discarded and said she might have. Then she went into the living area and telephoned room service, asking for steamed rice and chicken and a pot of weak tea to be brought to the bungalow.

She had just replaced the phone on its cradle when Guerney's voice called from the porch.

"Anyone at home?" The next second he was in the room with her. "Hello, my dear." He dropped a quick kiss on her cheek. "Where's Dee? And how are things?"

"Things are improving," said Leni with a bright smile, and went on to explain, "I've been sick all day, but now I feel better and I'm famished—some food is arriving at any minute. As for Dee, I don't know where she is, probably over at the hotel."

"Still spending all her time with Dwight Halvorsen?"

"More or less. But I shouldn't worry, Guerney. If you fuss, it will only make things worse. Just leave her alone."

"Is that what you're doing? I thought I could depend on you to cooperate and persuade her to behave sensibly. But maybe you're too busy with your own love affairs."

As Leni's meal arrived then, she found it easy to ignore that, and she took her tray out to the veranda where it was cool and pleasant. Her white silk pyjamas were perfectly respectable, and as Guerney had no objection—in fact, she didn't think he was aware of what she had on—she dispensed with a robe. While she ate, Guerney sat with her and talked about some work he had been doing. He had completed a new bird carving, and he had half a dozen sketches and paintings ready to take to the gallery at Djakarta.

"I'd like to take them over personally in the next few days. There are things Janet and I have to discuss that can't efficiently be dealt with by letter. I'll try to persuade Dee to come with me, I think."

"I don't imagine she will," said Leni frankly.

"You may be right. In which case, I'll have to ask you quite seriously to keep a close eye on her. I should hate her to come to grief, and no matter what you think, these things do happen, particularly to the young and inexperienced. I just don't fancy having my young sister ruining her life."

"I'm sure she won't," Leni reassured him. While her opinion of Dwight was not the best, she thought Guerney exaggerated more than a little the dangers of Dee's escapades. As she spoke, her eye was caught by the sight of someone coming along the path toward the bungalow. Her heart leapt. It was Kemp, she was sure. Or did her imagination see Kemp everywhere? One part of her mind noted the comforting fact that Guerney's figure was hidden by the bougainvillea that shrouded the end of the porch, but she still felt agitated. It would be the last straw if Kemp were to witness this intimate-looking little scene, so late at night! He was apt to put an immediate and wrong interpretation on anything that had to do with her.

She prayed inwardly that he would see neither her nor Guerney, that he was intent on making his way elsewhere.

Meanwhile, she tried to concentrate on what Guerney was saying. "I'll be worried sick about this business, Leni. You may not believe me, but I mean it. So come along, there's a good girl, make me a definite promise that you'll stick closely to Dee—"

Kemp was near enough now to hear Guerney's voice, and as Leni watched, a smile quivering nervously on her lips, he turned away abruptly and went back the way he had come. Not for the first time, Leni longed to be able to call him back, to be allowed to explain— But Guerney, quite unaware that anything at all had happened, said insistently, "Will you promise, Leni? Will you set my mind at ease? Or must I give up the idea of going to Djakarta?"

"Yes—yes, of course I'll promise," Leni assured him wearily. She pushed away her chicken and rice scarcely touched. Her appetite had gone. Somehow, nothing ever seemed to go right for her.

When she woke the next morning, feeling perfectly normal again, she remembered instantly and with a feeling of despair that Kemp must believe she had had an assignation with Guerney the night before, and that her excuse of not coming to the poolside feast because she was tired had been just that—an excuse.

She wondered if it would be possible to go to him and say, "I was ill last night. After you left me, I slept, then when I woke I felt better and I was hungry. Guerney just happened to come in, looking for Dee." Even to herself, it sounded unlikely. And then there was the fact that she had been in her pyjamas. She shuddered to think what he would make of that! It would mean a little addendum to her already weak-sounding explanation. "Guerney is like a brother—I just didn't bother changing. . . ."

No, she could not hope to explain away last night. If a man was in love with you—truly in love—then he took you on trust. But Kemp was not in love with her. There was no point in deluding herself on that score. Why then, she could not help wondering, did he seek her out? Yet perhaps he didn't. Perhaps there were half a dozen guests at the hotel who from time to time received his specialized attentions. A thought that was no comfort at all!

She saw him that morning, but he merely greeted her politely and passed on as if he had things to do more important than talking to Leni Forrest. No more was said about the drive to Ubud, and though she knew he did not go, she felt slighted that he had not mentioned altering his plans to her. Obviously, he was not going to bother with her anymore—it was a mystery he had ever done so.

Later, when Guerney came to see Dee, Leni made herself scarce for two reasons. First, she was afraid that Kemp would see her fraternizing and make up another score against her. Second, she didn't want to be called on to take sides if there were any argument about Dee's going to Djakarta. The outcome was as she had known it would be. Dee was to stay in Bali.

That afternoon, she and Dee and Dwight went to a market at one of the beach villages where Dwight apparently tried to find a Barong necklace for Dee. Leni was pretty soon left to herself and finally went back to the hotel on her own. She was sitting on the veranda when the other two returned.

In a foolish sentimental moment, she had put on her Barong necklace, and Dwight, taking one of the chairs, asked her without preamble: "That necklace of yours—where did you get it? I want to get one similar for this girl of mine"—indicating Dee. "We saw some on a stall today, but she wouldn't be satisfied—they just weren't as good as yours, I guess."

"It wasn't that," protested Dee, leaning against the wall. "They were too expensive."

Dwight looked pained. "What you mean is, you think the natives wanted to overcharge me. Well, I don't care a cent about that, and you know it. So—"

"So I just don't want you to spend a whole lot of money on me," said Dee petulantly. "That's all." Leni looked at her curiously. This was a change! She had accepted the brocade dress without a qualm!

"Someone spent a whole lot of money on your little friend," said Dwight slyly. "I'll guarantee she didn't buy that necklace for herself."

Leni said nothing and was thankful that Dee kept quiet too. It was none of Dwight's business where her Barong had come from. She wasn't quite sure why she had put it on this evening. Maybe because Kemp had said so forcefully, "You will wear it." Maybe because—somehow—she felt in need of a protector.

When she and Dee were alone, dressing for dinner —Leni for the modest bistro, Dee for the hotel dining-room—Leni asked curiously, "Dee, why wouldn't you let Dwight buy you a necklace? After all, you accepted the dress."

Dee, intent on applying blue eyeshadow, frowned.

"If you must know, because I think—I think—that Dwight expects eventually to get—something from me in return for his presents."

Leni stared at her. So she was right about Dwight's intentions. She said positively, "You mustn't go out with him any more. You should have gone to Djakarta. If I'd known, I'd never have made any promises to Guerney about keeping an eye on you."

"Oh, pooh!" said Dee. "It's fun to play with fire." Her

blue eyes shone excitedly. "But don't worry, I won't let myself get burnt. That's why no necklace."

Leni said slowly, "I wish you'd accepted a Barong, Dee."

Dee swung round in amazement. "What an extraordinary thing to say! When you've just said exactly the opposite."

"I know. But the Barong would—protect you."

Dee laughed aloud. "Oh, Leni, you must be joking!"

"No, I'm not joking," said Leni, a little annoyed though she felt foolish as well. She was still wearing her own necklace, and Dee said mockingly, "You certainly need protecting, Len—from what I saw the other night! Anyhow, I'm having the time of my life too, with Dwight. It's frightening, but it's fun. Charles is always so predictable, so gentlemanly."

She put her head on one side, winsomely. "You do understand, Leni, don't you? And by the way, Dwight's hired a car and he wants to take me up the mountains tomorrow. Please come—I'll feel so much safer."

Leni frowned. "Dwight won't want me along." But she remembered her promise to Guerney and knew it was not as easy as that.

"Please, Leni," begged Dee. "I really want to do this trip. Maybe we could ask someone else along to make it a foursome," she added brightly. "Kemp Savage, for instance."

Leni, who had blushed scarlet, moved out of her range of vision and hunted in the drawer for her perfume bottle.

"No, Dee, don't you dare! Promise me."

"All right, I promise," said Dee mildly. "I wasn't really serious about that. Anyone can see your bones just turn to jelly when that man is about. You're far too juvenile for Kemp Savage, and if anything, I'd advise you to steer clear of him."

"Excuse me," murmured Leni, dabbing scent on her wrists, "but that does sound rather odd coming from you, Dee."

"You're forgetting something," said Dee sweetly. "I witnessed that very masterly kiss Kemp Savage handed out to you the other night—right in front of me and Dwight! If he acts like that in public, what's he going to do when he gets you alone? And from the stories one hears about him. As a matter of fact, I told Guerney I thought I'd better stay around here to keep an eye on you! So—"

"So that's ridiculous," said Leni hotly. "Anyhow, what stories have you heard about Kemp?"

"Oh, just vague mutterings," said Dee. She grinned across at Leni. "We'll look after each other, Len, won't we? It's rather fun, isn't it, to be pursued by handsome men with evil intentions? But it *is* a comfort to think we're here to look after each other."

With that she was gone and Leni was left to think over soberly what she had said. It certainly sounded as though Dee was getting at least a little close to deep water! And she *had* promised Guerney that she would keep an eye on his sister. . . .

Somewhat reluctantly she prepared to go up the mountains with Dee and Dwight the following day. Her reluctance made her dawdle and she was not ready at the appointed time, so Dee went ahead. It was another five minutes or so before Leni left the bungalow and hurried through the lovely jungle green garden to the thatched shelters where Dwight's hired car was housed. She found herself hoping in her heart that they would have gone without her. She was wearing the Barong necklace and had caught herself wondering seriously is she should lend it to Dee, no matter what dire threats Kemp Savage had made about that. Yet the feel of the ivory at her neck, the glimpse of the strange half-fearsome, half-benevolent Barong, when she bent her head, was both comforting and puzzling to Leni. She could not really understand why it meant so much to her in so strange a way, or why Kemp had made her such a gift in the first place. In fact, she could not work out his feelings for her at all.

She had just caught sight of Dwight's car and given a sigh of resignation when she almost bumped into Kemp himself.

"Hello! I was on my way to look for you."

Leni's heart began to pound at the very sight of him, and she tried instinctively to analyze the tone of his voice. Was he friendly, aloof, polite today? She felt too confused by the unexpectedness of the encounter to decide. She stood gazing up at him and he looked like a god with his thick dark hair stirred by the breeze, and his bronzed face and those dark fathomless eyes, and the high blue sky above him.

"I'm driving to Ubud this morning. My plans went astray the other day, for which I must apologize belatedly. Would you care to come?"

Leni thought instantly, distrustfully, "The polite host who has lapsed and regretted it and is assuming the role again . . . making amends." He probably didn't want her to come, but all the same she would have said yes if she could have. As it was, she had promised Dee.

She looked at him regretfully.

"Thank you, Mr. Savage. But I'm driving up to the mountains with the others today. They're waiting for me."

He looked at her silently for a moment, and his mouth

set in a hard almost cruel line. "Then that's that." His voice was clipped, hard and unforgiving. He bowed sardonically and left her and she hurried to the car thinking despairingly, "I just can't win. He wants it all his own way—he doesn't allow for the little things in life that upset everyone's plans." Though to be sure there seemed to have been an inordinate number of those "little things" continually preventing Leni Forrest and Kemp Savage from making any real and lasting contact with one another. Maybe fate had designed it that way—Kemp was to be a sort of dream, an ideal, drifting through this brief interlude in her life, and that was all. . . .

The next two hours, for Leni, were hideously upsetting and unnerving. Dwight quite plainly didn't want her as a passenger in his car, and though he wasn't actually rude to her, he completely ignored her after his first nod of greeting. She sat unhappily in the back seat while Dwight, as he drove, talked exclusively to Dee—just as though Leni were not there. If Dee turned around to say something to her friend, Dwight apparently suspended consciousness and had nothing to do with either of them. Meanwhile—and this was the really frightful thing—he drove like a maniac, an absolute and utter maniac, thought Leni, incensed and incredulous, as she sat almost rigid with fear in her seat. She knew that the taxi drivers of Bali used their horns continually—the streets of Denpasar were always clamorous with the sound of car horns as pedestrians and cyclists and other cars were warned of the proximity—or the demands!—of one driver or another.

But Dwight, even when they were out of Denpasar and driving through the open countryside or some small village was continually and aggressively making his presence on the road felt. The way he made that car horn blare and scream one had the impression that he was a very bad-tempered man.

Leni was quite unable to enjoy the beauty of the green rice fields, or the out-of-this-world quality of the tiny villages with their many ancient and fascinating temples. Everywhere, graceful women walked along the roadsides carrying on their heads baskets, piled high with fruits or rice or vegetables they were taking to the markets. Mostly they were barefooted, a few were bare-breasted as had once been the custom of the island, but they all walked with the utmost dignity. And Dwight honked his horn at them all. It was no use protesting, though Leni did so. He simply pretended not to hear her and finally she subsided into silence, wondering at Dee who didn't appear to be perturbed at all.

Dwight drove his car madly over narrow bridges that crossed deep ravines where, in the water below, Leni glimpsed women bathing or washing their clothes. His horn startled a group of men and women working on the roads at the very crucial moment when a heavy load of stones was being lifted on to the head of a slender brown-skinned woman. Leni felt she hated Dwight more than she had ever thought she could hate another human being. She wanted to have nothing to do with him, and with all her heart she wished she could get out of this car and walk away. One thing was certain, she would never, never come out with him again.

Finally, the inevitable happened. Dwight drove too close to a cyclist whom he had already unnerved by sounding his horn, and in a moment the boy was sprawling on the roadside. Dwight sped on, and Leni, her heart in her mouth, cried out, "Stop, Dwight—stop!" She swung around in her seat and through the back window saw with relief that the boy was getting to his feet and stooping to collect his bicycle. All the same—"*Stop!*" shouted Leni again.

"Don't get hysterical," said Dwight, who had glanced in the rear vision mirror and seen what Leni had seen. "He's all right."

"Oh, thank goodness!" exclaimed Dee, breathing an audible sigh of relief. "For one awful moment I thought we might have killed him."

"Not us," said Dwight, apparently unperturbed. "I didn't even tip him—I'd have felt the bump if I had. Don't worry, honey—the devil looks after his own. He's probably been drinking *tuak* or whatever it is they get drunk on—a breath of wind would have knocked him over."

Leni hoped that the accident would sober him, but it didn't. He continued exactly as before and Dee, her corn yellow hair blowing back in the wind, began to talk and laugh in a foolishly excited way as though she were actually enjoying herself. Leni's nerves were threadbare when at last he pulled up in a narrow street opposite a row of colorful market stalls.

"Ubud," he said—and Leni's eyes widened. She hadn't known they were coming here. "I hear the shopping's good in this little place, so let's get out."

Of course he was addressing Dee exclusively, but Leni tumbled out of the car as fast as she could. Her head was reeling and for an instant she thought she was going to be sick. Dwight had strolled over to the market, but Dee lingered to ask with concern, "What's up, Len? You look awfully white."

"I feel awfully white," said Leni, unable to manage a smile.

"You're not worrying about that boy, are you? He wasn't hurt—"

"And that wasn't Dwight's fault," said Leni, who simply had to speak her mind. "Just don't ever again ask me to come driving with him, Dee, because I won't. He has no road manners at all—he's one of those people who simply go crazy as soon as they get behind the wheel of a car. I hated every single minute of that ride." By now, her voice was shaking and there were tears in her eyes, and through them she could see that there was a look of impatience on Dee's face.

"You're really making a lot of fuss about nothing, Leni. All because you don't like fast driving. I think it's great fun." Dee tossed back her blonde hair and her cheeks were red. "Don't be like Guerney and develop into a spoilsport, will you?"

Leni blinked her tears away angrily. "I'm afraid I don't call that sort of madness sport. But if you can't see it, Dee, then I give up." At that moment, Dwight began to call impatiently for Dee to join him. "I'm not coming with you," Leni said hurriedly. "I'll go to see the museum. And—and you'd better borrow this." As she spoke she unfastened her necklace and handed it to a rather astounded Dee, then hurried away, turning a deaf ear to whatever Dee was saying to her.

She felt strangely bereft without her Barong and wondered if she were crazy to think it might be any use to Dee. She had acted as if she would not be a passenger in that car again today, which was, to say the least of it, irrational. She would need protection too. She walked along the road quickly, with no idea which way led to the museum, wishing that she could sit down somewhere and have a good cry. Vaguely, she was aware of a tall figure approaching, and with a shock she realized it was Kemp Savage! She felt she could not bear to have him see her trembling on the edge of tears, so she kept her head lowered and made a pretence of not seeing him. Of course it was not as easy as all that, for as he drew level with her his hand shot out to take a grip of her arm and he asked her curtly, "Where are you off to now, Leni Forrest? You're shaking like a leaf, and I don't wonder, after that idiotic ride you've just taken. Where's your boyfriend?"

"I'm going to the museum." Leni refused to raise her eyes to his face. His question about her "boyfriend"—he meant Guerney, of course—she decided to ignore. To answer it—unless she engaged in protestations—would be to admit to what was not so.

After a second's pause he turned her quite gently to face across the street and said amusedly, "Then let me put you on the right road. Puri Lukisan's that way, my girl. So run along." His hand released her and he was gone, and Leni bit her lip hard.

Just now it seemed no one wanted to look after Leni Forrest or to be her friend. She blinked away threatening tears, put her head up and brushed back her silvery fringe with a hand that shook a fraction. Then she actually managed a weak smile when she found she was feeling for her Barong—just as if it were an essential part of her!

Her tears disappeared entirely a few minutes later as she walked through the beautiful garden to the museum. She had reached a mossy stone bridge shaded by trees whose leaves were luminous green in the hot sunlight and paused to look down into the water. As she stood there, revelling in the peace and beauty of her surroundings, footsteps sounded behind her and the next moment Kemp Savage stood beside her. He said nothing and she looked up—rather unwisely—straight into the dark intensity of his gaze. Just for an instant she had the feeling that angry fires were burning there and her happiness, a precarious mood already, was ready to be overturned.

Then he said in a soft, almost companionable way, "You'll like the museum, Leni—and I'd like to help you enjoy it. Your friends aren't coming—I gather their tastes run more to the photographic possibilities of Ubud and to the opportunity of spending a lot of money than to quiet musing over art." Somehow, he had taken her arm and was continuing across the bridge with her. He continued, in a quizzical way that Leni found vaguely unnerving, "On the other hand, if they only realized it, there are quite wonderful possibilities for romance in this beautiful setting, don't you agree?"

Leni glanced up at him through her lashes. Of course he had Dee and Dwight in mind as he said that, but his words brought back vividly the occasions on which he had kissed her, Leni. She said with an attempt at casualness, "This garden is certainly very romantic." She half expected him to take her in his arms there and then, but he answered her with an equally casual air.

"Exactly. But unhappily, in my view, a kiss has certain mystical requirements in addition to the sheerly materialistic and external—however romantic they might be."

They were walking up a long sweeping curve of stone steps, overhung by vines burdened with enormous white and purple flowers. He held her arm lightly and the mad ride in Dwight's car seemed to fade into a mist of unreality. Shadows and sunlight made dancing patterns, there was the sound of water murmuring, and Leni knew a curious admixture of happiness and despair. Happiness just to be here with Kemp, despair that their contacts were always so wrought with misunderstandings.

Restlessly she moved away from the reach of his arm.

"I hadn't noticed you were a stickler for the mystical requirements," she told him, trying to sound sophisticated.

"No? There are certainly occasions when they come as an afterthought."

"And times when they don't come at all," said Leni.

"True. It all depends on the partner one chooses. I had a special kind of recipient in mind when I made my rather rigorous statement."

"The Balinese girl?" wondered Leni. "Cristelle Dubois?" Not Leni Forrest—that was for sure. Kissing Leni Forrest was in the nature of a . . . chemical experiment with easily foretellable results. . . .

She forgot it all as they emerged into full sunlight and saw the lovely simple museum building with its widely overhanging thatched roof. In front spread green lawns and flower beds and a lily pool on whose clear still waters the reflections of tall palms were painted amongst the pink and white lilies.

The museum, Puri Lukisan, seen in Kemp's knowledgeable company, was a sheer delight. Because she was interested, he told her about the modern movement in Balinese art—the movement away from the purely traditional and rather strictly circumscribed forms, that were closely connected with religion—that allowed for a simpler, freer presentation of aspects of life.

"The Balinese," he told her, "have, somewhat miraculously, proved themselves able to assimilate many outside influences in many artistic and cultural fields without losing their identity. Some forty years ago, they were introduced to modern techniques in painting, but their choice of subject and mode of expression have remained their own."

In the wood carvings too, Kemp showed Leni samples of the older, religious work—angular and intricate and detailed, as in her Barong head, she reflected. Contrasting with these were more modern progressive works, simple carvings of animals or birds or human figures, some of which reminded Leni a little of Guerney's monkey, though she kept that little fact to herself! She admired particularly a carving of birds where detail was kept to a minimum and the utmost was made of the flowing line of the wood grain.

Leni forgot all her edginess and uncertainty in pure enjoyment and found it an inexpressible relief to be away from Dwight—and even from Dee, in her present mood. The sad part of it all was that she would have to rejoin them soon and that would be that.

But when she and Kemp had walked back through the delightful garden and across the ancient bridge and into the village street, Dwight's car was nowhere to be seen. Leni's dismay was followed by a strong feeling of relief, but she knew it was merely a matter of putting off the evil hour. They had evidently gone somewhere too far for walking, but they would be back for her. Meanwhile she allowed Kemp to take her to a small restaurant where they ate a Balinese-style lunch and discussed what they had seen at the museum. When she caught him looking at his watch, she felt a stab of uneasy guilt. She had been basking in his company—and possibly forcing her own on him! She pushed back her chair quickly.

"You've been very patient to spend so much of your time on me. I realize of course that it's—it's part of your business."

His frown was ferocious! It almost shrivelled her up, and she knew that what she had said was ungracious in the extreme. He said nothing. He, too, rose from the table, paid for their lunch over a smiling exchange with the restaurant proprietor and accompanied a shaking Leni into the sunshine of the village street. In silence, they walked together along the road, and now Leni looked rather desperately—but in vain—for Dwight's car. It really would be the last straw if they had gone off and left her now! And then, pausing in the shade of a great banyan tree, Kemp said smoothly, sounding completely unruffled—although she had expected a torrent of biting comments from him—"In actual fact, it simply hadn't occurred to me to rate looking after you as—business, Leni. However, if it will make you feel better, there's a small thing you can do for me in return for the time I've spent on you. Though if you remember," he added, an almost imperceptible note of dryness in his tone, "I did invite you to come to Ubud with me, today."

"I do remember," said Leni, feeling small. "But I had arranged to come with the others."

"Yes. I understood you to mean that Guerney Fisher was to be a member of the party. Had I known that it was not so, I wouldn't so easily have taken no for an answer."

Leni blinked. She must be crazy, but it sounded almost as though he were willing to compete with Guerney. Yes, she certainly was crazy, because Kemp Savage would not compete for a woman under any circumstances—and certainly not for Leni Forrest, who had nothing in particular to recommend her anyway! She said uncertainly, "I really couldn't have come—I'd promised. . . ."

"You promised Guerney Fisher," he interjected, sounding displeased. "I inadvertently heard a little of that promise the other night—you'll know the night I mean."

Leni, remembering how late it had been, and her pyjamas, flushed deeply, but she said determinedly, "I promised Guerney that I'd stay with Dee, that was all. With Dee and Dwight."

"There being safety in numbers, I presume."

That was exactly it, so Leni said, "Yes."

"I see. Well, now you can come into this store"—guiding her with a forceful hand—"and help me choose a sarong for Daju."

For Daju! That must be the beautiful Balinese girl.

Kemp was smiling, but Leni felt as though cold water had been dashed in her face. She breathed, "For—for a Balinese girl?"

"That's right. You must surely have seen her at the hotel. It so happens that you and she have very similar figures."

"I wouldn't have thought that figures would matter when it came to the selection of a sarong," said Leni, doing her best to hang back. This idea of Kemp's appealed to her not at all! "I thought it would be more a matter of coloring, and you can hardly expect me to believe that a Balinese girl would be flattered by the colors that would suit me."

"I won't attempt to persuade you," Kemp said blandly and with obvious amusement. Short of making a run for it, which would be extremely undignified, Leni now found she had to go into the store ahead of him. It was a very small shop and materials of every color and design were on show—hanging from the ceiling, stacked on the shelves, draped across the small counter. A plump middle-aged Balinese woman greeted Kemp with an appearance of pleasure. She was the store owner and had an intelligent poised look about her, though Leni was convinced she was a local villager and did not come from Denpasar or one of the big towns.

Kemp spoke to her in Indonesian and she smiled and nodded, then disappeared through a doorway at the back of the shop. While she was gone, Kemp sauntered around fingering some of the clothes on display. Leni, even with her very small experience, could recognize that these were very superior batiks, but she could not give her attention to them, for it was rankling that Kemp should insist she help him buy something for another girl. How could he? she asked herself over and over. It seemed to her a subtle and unnecessary form of torture. She knew she was jealous, and she knew she had no right to be, but she wished that Kemp had not chosen exactly this way to let her know where she stood.

She stood staring at a dark blue and gold cloth, seeing nothing, and almost jumped when he said musingly, "It's remarkable how the same color can flatter both dark and fair good looks, you know. Remember that violet silk I bought in Singapore? That certainly did something for Leni Forrest, but I think you'll agree that Daju looks ravishing in it too."

"Yes," agreed Leni stiffly. "She looks very beautiful." The thought of Daju's beauty was like a knife in a wound. The silk had "done something" for Leni Forrest, but Daju looked ravishing. It was so true that its hurt was incalculable.

"However," said Kemp, "I was thinking today in terms of pattern rather than color. . . ."

Leni didn't look at him, but she was sure he was laughing at her, making fun of her. She said suddenly, "You don't need my help. And I think I'd better go and look for Dee and Dwight. I don't want to miss them." Out of the corner of her eye she saw the owner returning, and with a sudden quick movement, she darted past Kemp and out into the sunlit street.

CHAPTER SEVEN

There Leni had ample time to reflect on her impulsive behavior, as she wandered around looking for Dwight's car and trying to regain her common sense.

At first she hoped wildly that Dee and Dwight would be there—that they would scoop her up in the car and take her away from Ubud, leaving Kemp lamenting. Only of course Kemp would not lament, her common sense eventually reminded her. All that would happen would be that she would have to face that nightmare ride back to the hotel.

In any case, Dwight's car was not there. It was not anywhere to be found, and Leni began to wonder if she had been deserted. Dwight would be quite capable of leaving her stranded—without a qualm—but not Dee. No, she was quite sure Dee would never do that to her.

Leni found a seat in the shade and sat down rather disconsolately to wait. This new worry had temporarily distracted her, but presently she began once more to think about her bad behavior in walking out on Kemp Savage just now—after he had been so kind and attentive to her! The fact was, she reflected honestly, Kemp was far too sophisticated for her to cope with—just as Dee had warned her. She was inclined to take his charming attentions personally, yet those same attentions were probably given to many women. And no doubt many other women, the same as herself, were completely helpless to stop themselves falling in love with him. Cristelle Dubois—Daju the Balinese girl—and Leni Forrest, the least likely of them all to win his devotion. Oh yes, Leni recognized only too well her own shortcomings in being irresistible to such a man as Kemp Savage.

128

She had reached exactly this point in her reflections when he found her and stood looking down at her quizzically. He had a long wrapped parcel under one arm—the sarong, she presumed—and with an effort and a gallant smile, she told him quickly, "I'm sorry I ran off like that just now. It was very rude and unhelpful of me. But I was so scared I'd miss Dee and Dwight—as it is, I can't find the car anywhere." A little breathlessly, she added, "I hope you found what you wanted."

He nodded carelessly. "I managed. I thought, you know, that you'd have enjoyed looking over some good batiks with me. However." He shrugged. "But aren't you being a trifle naïve? Your two friends won't be back for you. Surely you know that. They're only too glad to be rid of you."

Leni flushed, but she shook her head. "Dee wouldn't leave me here, so far from the hotel. How would I get back?"

He said consideringly, though Leni thought there was a smile somewhere in his eyes, "You could come with me. I certainly won't drive away and leave you sitting here on your own."

"Dee wouldn't either," said Leni, her cheeks red. "Thank you for offering, but I don't want to be a nuisance and . . . and land myself on you. Besides, I promised."

"Forget your promises," he suggested coolly. "There are some promises that are made to be broken. Agreed?"

Leni nodded uncertainly, but she could not make up her mind. Of course she wanted to go with Kemp, and it was not only because the very thought of getting into Dwight's car again made her feel sick. But it would look as though she were over-eager—as if she were throwing herself at him.

He said exasperatedly, "Do you want me to sit here

with you and wait for them? I promise you, they won't be back. So come along—if you can't be willing, be sensible." He put out a hand and pulled her to her feet. "Get into my car and forget about your qualms. I'll take good care of you."

"I am out of my mind," thought Leni, as she gave in weakly and went with him. She wondered what the others would think when they came back to Ubud and found her gone. Dwight would be glad, but Dee wouldn't.

As they crossed the street to Kemp's car, her hand went instinctively to her breast seeking the Barong, and she was disconcerted to see a wicked smile flit across Kemp's face.

"I noticed Dee was wearing your necklace," he remarked as he opened the car door. "I had a few words with your friends before we went to the museum."

"Oh," said Leni. She ducked her head and climbed into the car. Then as he settled himself beside her, "I thought you said you'd take it from her forcibly if you saw her wearing it again."

"So I did. And so I would have, under different circumstances." He started up the motor and drove off smoothly. "However, I happened to notice it was gracing *your* little neck early in the day, and I couldn't help admiring your generosity in lending it to your friend. I was a witness to that near-accident this morning, and in my opinion anyone who's mad enough to become a passenger in a car driven by young Halvorsen should certainly take out some kind of insurance—even if it's only in the form of a lucky charm."

"But the Barong isn't just a lucky charm," Leni heard herself objecting. She subsided in confusion at the exceedingly amused look she saw appear on Kemp Savage's face. And she had thought he took the superstitions and beliefs of his adopted country with quite a degree of seriousness!

His next remark, seriously made, reassured her.

"You're quite right, Leni. And it warms my heart to hear you say just that. Don't take any notice if I seem amused. It was a feeling of pleasure rather than amusement that made me smile. Right?"

"Right," said Leni. She smiled back at him and it seemed her heart was warmed too.

She had imagined that he would take her straight back to the hotel, because no matter how tactful he had been, she knew she had more or less landed herself on him. So it was a thrilling surprise to find that he was prepared to give her a delightful afternoon, and one that her mind would dwell on for a long time to come. In Kemp's company, the green countryside with its terraced paddy fields, the saronged Balinese carrying out their daily tasks of marketing and cooking, of working in the fields, of tending their cattle or their ducks, assumed a dreamlike quality of great beauty. Once, he stopped the car in a small village and took her to see a temple where there had been some ceremony the day before. At the temple gates, they both donned a *slendang*—a ceremonial waistband—then went through the *tjandi bentar* that was guarded by grotesque carvings and into a wide courtyard with high walls.

Everywhere, Leni saw stone carvings, mossy with age. Impish stone faces, mythical animals intricately interwoven with plants and flowers, looked down on her from every conceivable part of wall and shrine. All of them were hundreds of years old, Kemp told her, as without realizing it she held tightly to his hand. An old man tending a narrow garden at the foot of stone steps came to greet them gravely.

"I am the temple gardener," he informed Leni in a high musical voice, and when she smiled at him he presented her with a magnificent fire-bright marigold.

"*Terima kasih, pak*," she said shyly, and Kemp took the flower from her and tucked it behind her ear.

"It doesn't become you as well as a white or purple flower would have done," he told her laughingly as he took her hand in his again and they strolled quietly on.

There were three simple thatched pavilions in the courtyard, and these, Kemp explained, were used for meetings, for the temple orchestra and for the preparation of offerings. For the divine spirits must be honored and the evil ones placated.

In the inner courtyard, the ground was littered with discarded offerings, and Leni saw tiny intricate rosettes artistically woven from palm leaf; little bamboo baskets bound with strips of cane and filled with flowers—fading and broken now—red and purple and gold, set in palm leaf cut out like lace. There were flat woven trays of all shapes and sizes that held tiny offerings of fruit and flowers and rice. In fact, the variety was endless. Leni studied them, fascinated, taking care not to tread on any of the scattered ornaments.

"What a shame to see them wasted like this! Some of these things are little works of art, they must have taken hours to create!"

"So they did," Kemp agreed. "But it was a labor of love—and to the Balinese work and play merge curiously into one another. These offerings have served a purpose—they were not made to last, you know, but to beautify the ceremony. This is a form of temporary art, Leni—undertaken in a spirit of reverence for the deities, of service to the religion and the community. The Balinese life is a communal one—everything is shared—joy and sorrow and religion and work and art. Everything. There's scarcely such a thing as solitude." He took her arm and drew her close to his side, in the most natural way. "Look at that little girl with the baby on her hip."

Leni looked. From behind one of the shrines a very small girl in a minute sarong had appeared. Her black hair hung down over her shoulders and her dark eyes were shining as she looked with friendly curiosity at the visitors. On her hip, suspended only a few inches above the ground, was a fat baby, its little head with the silky cap of black hair drooping drowsily.

Leni exclaimed involuntarily, "Oh, the poor child! What a weight for such a mite to have to carry around."

"She's happy in her responsibility," said Kemp. "She's an important little person in the family life. And do you know, Leni, that in Bali a baby is not allowed to touch the impure ground until he's three months old?"

"And then?"

"And then a celebration is held." They stood now in the shade of a banyan tree whose huge twisted roots, carved themselves, were intertwined with stone carvings—carvings that seemed to belong to a world of fantasy; half dream, half nightmare, both beautiful and frightening. "The baby will be given gold ornaments—a necklace, bracelets, even anklets. The local priest will make offerings to the gods, and the infant's feet will be put to the ground for the first time. Children are much loved in Bali, Leni."

The next time Kemp stopped the car it was to show Leni the Elephant Cave, Goa Gadja. Its entrance was a dark gaping mouth with fangs and bulging eyes. Above and all around, the rock was carved with plant and animal shapes and weird human figures. Leni did not much like stepping into the eerie darkness guided by a small boy with a flickering lamp that lit up the various niches and carvings. She was pleased to come out into the hot sunlight again. Kemp paid the guide, then asked her, "Do you feel like an energetic climb, or are those pretty sandals of yours too fragile for enjoyment?"

Leni said firmly, "My sandals are very comfortable, and I think they're quite up to any sort of a climb at all."

"You may yet regret those words," he said, his eyes glinting. Leni thought she had never seen him in so carefree and attractive a mood before, and she was enjoying herself thoroughly. There had been no verbal sparring between them since she had agreed to come in his car, and this itself was very unusual. Leni crossed her fingers mentally as she walked with him down a rough slope that led steeply down to green rice terraces sheltered by a high cliff. She exclaimed in delighted amazement when she found the fragment of a carved head amongst the rocks through which they were picking their way, and she stooped to pick it up. Kemp's head was close to hers as together they examined the ancient pitted surface, the worn features.

"Keep it if you want," he told her carelessly. "I don't want to throw cold water on your pleasure, but there are plenty of finds like this. Your fragment is nothing very special even if it has given you a thrill. The whole of the cliff face was probably carved many hundreds of years ago, but as you see, it's now crumbling to bits. These rocks make so hazardous a pathway that I'm going to insist on taking your hand again." He put her rock fragment in his pocket, and obediently Leni put her hand in his, a faint flush suffusing her cheeks. She wondered if he guessed how she delighted in the touch of his fingers on hers and felt vaguely ashamed of her own reactions.

A minute later she pulled free of him with a casual, "I don't *really* need to be taken care of like a child. I'm very sure of foot." With that, she sprang lightly ahead of him. By now, they had reached the last of the rocks and green grass lay underfoot in long narrow terracelike steps. Hence it was not difficult going, though she acknowledged Kemp's mocking laugh with a wry smile when she slipped and found herself ankle deep in marshy water!

By this time they had a small entourage attached to their expedition—two small girls of six or seven, and a boy even younger. These children chirruped and giggled when Kemp turned to say something to them, and Leni wished she could understand what it was.

"What do they want?" she asked at last, as he repeatedly shook his head and told them, "*Tidak, tidak.*"

"They want to be our guides, and we don't need a guide."

"Where are we going?" Leni, lower down on the terraced hillside, looked up at him, the sun in her eyes so that she saw him half in silhouette above her—dark-haired and broad-shouldered, a menace and a protection.

"There's a small statue of the Buddha I'd like you to see. Nothing special, maybe—but it's in a very lovely spot."

Leni felt vaguely disconcerted, though she did not know why. She turned away, but with a few quick strides he was beside her and had put out a detaining hand.

"Not so fast, my girl. It's I who must lead, not you. And if you won't let me take your hand then you must follow me."

Leni, feeling thoughtful, chose to follow. And still the children circled around them or brushed carelessly by so that once or twice Leni nearly lost her balance—which, although it would have meant no more than another step into ankle-deep water, would still have been a mark against her sense of balance, so highly developed in the Balinese. And for some reason, Leni wanted to show Kemp Savage that she was graceful and sure of foot, even though she had never before felt any particular pride in being the possessor of those two qualities.

Not many minutes later Kemp halted. They had been progressing horizontally for some distance, and to their right the terraces still sloped away down to a gorge where Leni could see the silver thread of a river. But on the left there were now frangipani trees and a tangle of thick bush and bamboos covering a steep rise. The three little Balinese children clamored about Kemp, reaching out their hands. He looked laughingly over their heads at Leni, then produced some coins, which he distributed amongst them with a few words. Instantly they turned and came scrambling back past Leni, their little faces wreathed in smiles.

"*Bagus*," said Kemp with satisfaction. "In other words—fine! Now we're alone and I can show you the little Buddha. Come here." She took a few steps forward and he reached out a hand and pulled her closer. Then with his arm about her, he drew her farther along the path.

She could hear water gushing, and through the thick greenery a narrow stream of crystal-clear water broke from a cleft of hidden rock. Feathery leaves overhung the water, thick and green and tender, and in the shade below, splashed by fine silver spray and touched by flickering gold points of sunlight, a small Buddha sat serenely and enigmatically smiling.

Leni held her breath. He looked so ageless and calm and kind and wise that she felt she could stare at him forever.

When at last she looked up at Kemp, his dark eyes were watching her gravely.

Her spine was tingling, and she had the distinct feeling that she had stepped into a legendary world. She said, her voice little more than a whisper, "He's very old, isn't he? And very wise. He looks as though he's been here for eternity—as though he's seen all there is to see in life, and as if, in spite of everything, he loves humanity—and loves us even for our weakness."

Kemp said nothing; he merely nodded, but his eyes held hers and his hands reached toward her. With an almost trancelike inevitability she felt herself drawn into his arms to receive his kiss. . . .

She was left feeling weak and breathless when he released her, yet strangely serene. Almost—almost as serene as the Buddha. She said nothing and still Kemp did not speak, yet though his lips were still, his eyes were smiling. Leni imagined her eyes were smiling too as she gazed back at him, an eternity in those few seconds. It was all strange and mystical and Leni could not understand her feelings, nor did she have any desire to think or to analyze or to question. Just now, she wanted simply to accept.

It was an experience such as she had never known before, and she felt deeply that she shared it with the man whose gaze was locked with hers. They shared the Buddha and the green, green hillside, the falling water, the sunlight and shadow. The man held her in his arms and kissed her and looked at her now with a true smile deep in his eyes. . . .

It was dark before they finally returned to the hotel. All the way back, Leni sat in a dreamy silence looking out at the paddy fields glittering blue in a flood of soft moonlight, at coconut palms silhouetted against a magic sky, at the pagoda shapes of shrines so delicately beautiful she could hardly believe they were real. Nothing in fact was real; it was all sheer enchantment. Even the eerie road they drove through, whose high and ancient walls were covered with a protective thatch, was a web of the imagination. Leni could make out faintly the grotesque carvings that guarded high gateways so that the people inside were secure in the knowledge that evil spirits could not enter. Weird little winged goblins of stone with huge ferocious mouths and bulging eyes cuddled close to each other as they peered out unexpectedly from the deep shadows of a bamboo thicket, and even while Leni found them ghostly and a little frightening, she still felt curiously at home with them.

Was it because she sat beside Kemp?

Now and again she stole a glance at his profile, and once or twice she caught him looking at her, his mouth tilted enigmatically, his dark eyes unreadable. Not for anything would Leni have said a word that would cause some altercation to arise between them, and when at last they reached the hotel garden and he climbed out of the car to open the door for her, she said a very simple, "Thank you, Kemp—for everything."

"You liked it?"

She nodded, her heart full.

"Then I'm content. Goodnight, Leni."

He was gone suddenly and she stood shivering for a moment, although the night was warm, before she turned and went into the bungalow, welcoming the darkness and the silence that told her Dee was not yet home.

She was casual about how she had spent the afternoon when she and Dee talked late that night. She was already in bed and half asleep when the other girl came home."

"I hope you didn't worry when you found me gone, Dee."

"We didn't find you gone," said Dee cheerfully. "We didn't go back to Ubud. Kemp Savage said he'd take care of you—oh dear, he was decidedly firm about that, and there was nothing much *I* could do about it, and of course Dwight. . . ." She shrugged and gave a half smile, and Leni, blinking in the lamplight, felt a little shock of surprise. So Kemp had practically sent them away—he had said *he* would look after Leni! And she had felt she had been landed on him! He could have reassured her on that point if he had wanted to, but obviously he hadn't wanted to.

There was a short silence while Dee finished undressing, switched off the lamp and got into bed. Leni said, "I'm sorry about that, Dee. I did promise to come with you, though to tell the truth I was dreading another ride in Dwight's car. My nerves were just shot to pieces. He *is* a dangerous driver, and I wish you wouldn't go out with him again."

"His driving's the least of my worries," said Dee. "Besides, I like fast driving—it's exhilarating, so don't start preaching, Len. And you needn't be apologetic. I'd be a poor sort of friend if I insisted you stick to a silly promise when a man like Kemp Savage wanted to take you around. Anyhow, I suppose you thought I was pretty safe with your famous Barong around my neck." She laughed suddenly. "Oh, Leni, if you could have seen the furious look on the Savage man's face when he saw me wearing it! Honestly, I wouldn't have been surprised if he'd grabbed hold of me and choked me with it! He's certainly a forceful character, isn't he?"

"Yes," said Leni faintly, reluctant to discuss Kemp with Dee at all.

"We used to have a sort of wedding bells and happily-ever-after ending to our fantasies long ago, didn't we?" Dee sighed. "But real life is quite different. I don't want to be a wet blanket, but holiday romances aren't serious at all, and you know as well as I do that a man like Kemp Savage isn't likely to really fall in love with either of us, Len." She paused waiting for Leni to agree.

"No, of course not," said Leni, and she said it reluctantly even while she knew that what Dee was saying did make sense.

"And Dwight," said Dee musingly. "Well, he's not romantic like Kemp Savage, but he's the best I could manage. And allowing him to monopolize me is like . . . like playing with something dangerous—a loaded pistol or something. You know you're taking chances, but you go on and on, sort of daring yourself."

Leni began to feel alarmed. Just what did Dee have to contend with in Dwight to make her talk like this? She wished Guerney had not gone away and left her with this feeling of responsibility, and most of all she wished that Dee would behave sensibly. She said cautiously, "Why go on, then, if Dwight's as dangerous as all that? After all, you're engaged to Charles. You don't need to look for . . . for excitement—"

"Oh, lay off," said Dee crossly. "Even though you don't happen to be engaged to Charles or anyone else, aren't you taking a few risks yourself letting a man like Kemp Savage play around with your feelings? Maybe he has more scruples than Dwight—I wouldn't know about that—but he's certainly a lot older and more experienced. You don't know what you might be letting yourself in for, a little softie like you."

Leni, her heart beating hard, said tiredly, "Let's get to sleep, Dee. We're both tired. Goodnight."

"Right," said Dee. "Well, we're both having a taste of the fun we always promised ourselves, aren't we? I will tell Charles, you know—though it will be a slightly edited version! After all, he can't expect me to miss out on all the kicks just because he's not around. He's not the jealous type, at all events, thank goodness. And I'll tell Guerney that you and I agreed to stay out of each other's pockets—that will absolve us both from any promises we made him about keeping an eye on each other!"

In a way, that midnight conversation spoiled Leni's day. She tried to put it out of her mind and not to think about it, which was being escapist and unrealistic. What Dee had said about holiday romances and even about Kemp Savage was probably true, but it was a truth that Leni found hard to face. She would be a fool if she thought Kemp might conceivably be at all serious about her.

The next day, Dee did not even suggest that Leni should come out with her. As she combed her hair preparatory to dashing off, she glanced at Leni, who was frowning worriedly, in the mirror, and her blue eyes were faintly mocking.

"You needn't offer your necklace, Len. I'm not the superstitious type. Except I have the feeling that maybe that thing would choke me if I put it on again. I'd keep remembering the look in the Savage man's eyes when he saw me wearing it!"

Leni decided not to swim in the hotel pool that morning. If Kemp came upon her there with other people all around, she felt that something would be spoiled. Or perhaps she feared to find that the magic of yesterday had simply dissolved away. She went instead to the beach, taking a picnic lunch and a book with her. And it was late in the morning as she was lying on the coral sand and trying to make up her mind to collect the energy to move into the shade of some palms that she heard some women talking about Kemp Savage. They had settled down only a short distance away, and though she was half asleep, Kemp's name caught her attention.

"Isn't he a handsome man?" she heard.

"Fascinating! It would be torture to fall in love with him, though—he looks the type who would expect his woman to be his adoring slave. At all events, I believe men who have lived here any time lose interest in European beauty."

"My dear, you couldn't have said a truer word!" This voice was slightly lower, slightly more discreet, but it had a carrying quality, and Leni, who had altered her position enough to remind the gossips that she was there, could hear with no effort at all. "I have friends who were here earlier on, and they told me a very spicy little story."

"Oh, do tell! I just love a few little gossipy bits when I'm on holiday."

"Then you'll love this. It appears he's attached himself to a little Balinese girl. She's a dancer—a sort of protégée of his—and performs in all the semiprofessional shows put on for tourists hereabouts. Well, as you may know, dancing girls here are just about finished at fifteen or so, and it's speculated that even her day must soon be over. She's apparently reached the ripe old age of seventeen, and it's only her extraordinary talent that's kept her going so long. So the story is—or was—that they were to be married soon."

Leni's head was on her arms; her throat was dry. Was she hearing mere gossip? Or was there more than a grain of truth in it? Despite her distaste at herself for listening, nothing on earth would have made her move now. Having heard so much, she had to hear the rest. . . .

"How madly romantic! She must be that exquisite little creature wrapped in purple silk I saw him whispering secrets to at a rather late hour last night. I'll admit

I did wonder. She certainly didn't look the usual simple village type."

"She wouldn't be, under his tutelage. But wait a bit—I said the story is, or was, because right now it's anybody's guess what's going to happen. He quite recently started an affair with the daughter of one of the hotel board members, and was all but engaged to her."

Cristelle Dubois, Leni noted dully. And he broke with her because she dared to look at another man!

"All but?" It was said with a delighted crow of laughter. "Then what happened? My fertile imagination sees a female scratching party—and I can guess who'd have the longer nails!"

"My dear, unfortunately nothing so spectacular. In fact, it's assumed that the handsome Savage was attempting to rid himself of his addiction to the dancing girl and do the right thing—he does have a certain position to uphold, after all. On the other hand, it could be that his . . . masculinity simply got the better of him for a while."

"Hmm—I see what you mean. The little dancer just could be too delicate a dish to satisfy the appetite of a healthy male. So what's the situation now?"

"I just don't know."

There was a pause while the two women thought over the situation. Leni thought about it too—miserably. Had she ever imagined that she knew the least little thing about Kemp Savage? Hadn't his behavior all along puzzled her? And exactly how did she fit into the mosaic? Assuredly, she was just one little insignificant piece.

A shrewd voice—that of the woman with all the "information"—said emphatically, "Speaking personally, if I were in the English girl's shoes, I'd make it quite plain that unless he was prepared to give up his dancing girl once and for all, he could forget me. I simply wouldn't be involved in a marriage that had to look right if it wasn't. So, if this girl shares my views, he just could be in the process of making up his mind."

"Could be."

Leni felt sick. Was Kemp in the process of choosing between Cristelle Dubois and the Balinese girl? And if so, then why did he take her, Leni, to breathtakingly beautiful places and kiss her so tenderly? Why did he *look* at her as he had done?

Suddenly, she had to get up and move away, and she did so, carefully not looking at the women who were still talking avidly. She reached the shade of a group of palm trees and sat on the sand, hugging her knees and looking at the blue sea and the line of breakers far out on the coral reef. Farther along the shore, some small children scrambled about on a beached *prao*, and the whole scene made such an incredibly beautiful picture it sent Leni's heart aching.

Was Kemp thinking of marrying Daju? Had he upset his own plans when he fell in love with Cristelle Dubois? Leni refused to believe what those women had said about male appetites. Sam Becker had not hinted at any romance with a dancer, she was sure. And yet, thinking back, she wondered if it had been an oblique reference to that affair when he had said, of Cristelle Dubois, "I'd heard it was serious—and I was happy for you." Happy that he was going to do the "right" thing?"

Leni began to feel convinced that Kemp was somehow using her as a kind of light relief while he tried to resolve his own dilemma. She remembered certain things he had said to her about love—things that he had seemed to feel intensely, things that had seemed to Leni to border on the mystical, and that had heightened, if possible, her feelings for the man even though she expected nothing of him in return. Perhaps all those things had been his own soul-searchings. Daju represented the pure and perfect love—Cristelle Dubois was the more worldly. But Cristelle was the daughter of an influential hotel board member!

For the rest of that day Leni felt sick, bewildered, wounded to the core, obsessed by a too active imagination that led her deeper and deeper into hopelessness and despair. She wished with all her aching heart that she had never met Kemp Savage, never fallen in love with him. . . .

That night, as she toyed listlessly with her dinner at the hotel restaurant where she had gone with Dee and Dwight, she heard from some other guests that there was to be a performance of the Barong dance at a village a few miles away. Instantly she thought, "Daju will be dancing," and she knew she must go. Some of the guests were making up a party and arranging transportation, and Dee, Dwight and Leni were all invited along.

Dwight said "No" at once, adding ungraciously, "If we want to go we'll make our own arrangements." But the glance he sent Dee was so patently sensual that Leni's heart sank. They would not go to the Barong dance; Dwight would want to take Dee somewhere on her own. Leni said with determined brightness, "I'd love to go. You would too, wouldn't you, Dee? Even if Dwight doesn't want—"

"Keep out of this, please, Leni," said Dwight curtly, and there was nothing more she could do.

So Leni went to the Barong dance with despair in her heart—despair that concerned both herself and Dee. Several *bemos* had been hired and Leni traveled in one of these to the village where the dance was to be performed.

The theater was a big open-sided pavilion, and there were rows of seats for tourists who would pay for their positions. The sides of the pavilion were already packed with Balinese—men, women, children and even babies. They paid nothing to watch—the dance was part of their village life.

Leni found a seat and was looking with interest at the musical instruments ranged on either side of the platform that formed the stage. There were enormous brass gongs, cymbals, drums and other instruments that were strange to her. Already the members of the *gamelan* orchestra, in gold and orange sarongs, with small turbans tied in a knot over the forehead and topped with a gold leaf spray, were producing softly vibrating music that would later become a fascinating clamor of melodic sound.

Someone nearby leaned across and told Leni, "We're going backstage to see the performers dressing. Are you coming?" Leni, who had already noticed a thin stream of people disappearing into the darkness and wondered where they were going, rose at once and followed. "Backstage" was across a courtyard where the air was heavy with the scent and the smoke from incense. There, in a smaller and very dimly lit pavilion whose carved pillars were draped with flowering vines, the performers were being dressed. Leni joined a small crowd watching two young girls who were to take part in the Legong dance, before the Barong play. They looked exquisite and unreal, tightly wrapped in black and gold brocaded cloth. Eyes and eyebrows were accentuated with makeup, and tiny curved side-curls were painted onto smooth cheeks. On their heads were placed gold headdresses with fine golden tassels that hung scintillating over their ears.

Suddenly Leni recognized a voice nearby as belonging

to one of the women she had heard gossiping on the beach that morning, and with a feeling of distaste she moved away. As she did so, she saw with a slight feeling of shock a third dancer who was being dressed at the far side of the porch. It was Daju, and she was surrounded by a crowd of on-lookers.

Despite herself, Leni's heart was wrung by the girl's beauty. She looked like a fairy creature in her elaborate costume—certainly not of this world, for there was a look in her eyes, and in the whole of her posture—even in the hands, long-nailed and held unconsciously in one of the dance gestures—that set her very decidedly apart from humanity.

Leni was aware of a feeling of awe and completely impersonal admiration as she watched this girl, who seemed completely unconscious of the fact that she was being stared at—even photographed—and turned intuitively rather than mechanically as her dresser fixed the gold leaf headdress, a beautiful work of art in itself, on her shining dark hair.

Leni felt a sudden and awful despair in the face of Daju's beauty. Her own European prettiness, her silvery hair and fair skin were nothing—nothing at all—compared with this porcelain fragility. It was no wonder Kemp Savage found himself in a dilemma! Even if he were in love with Cristelle Dubois, his soul must hanker for this other perfection. The thought came to Leni that she might just as well pack and return to England tomorrow and save herself from further heart-break. She had never seen Cristelle Dubois, but she was certain no human being could compare in beauty with this unworldly looking dancer who stood now within her sight.

At that exact instant, she caught sight of Kemp Savage

himself. His face burned darkly from amongst the other faces in the crowd. Leni thought that in his own way he was quite as remarkable as Daju—one's eyes went to him instinctively. Or Leni's did. She was strongly—too strongly—aware of the magnetism of his being.

She dropped her gaze and turned quickly away to hurry back across the courtyard to the dance pavilion.

CHAPTER EIGHT

She knew without looking whose hand lay detainingly on her arm the moment before she reached the steps, and she felt the familiar thrill go through her, although this time she did her utmost to resist. She took a few quick paces that should have drawn her beyond his grasp—should have, but didn't, for she was free for a mere instant and then his fingers closed tightly on the bare flesh of her upper arm and his voice said, very close to her ear, "Hold on, Leni Forrest. It's only me."

Only Kemp Savage! Leni swallowed hard, halted and managed a smile. Managed even a look of surprise which she hoped would fool him, although he was certainly not an easy man to fool.

"I was hoping you might catch this performance. I tried to get hold of you a couple of times today, but I was particularly busy and you were very elusive!" The dark eyes looked smilingly into hers and the scent of incense drifted about them. "Who did you come along with? Some of the Selatan crowd?"

"Yes," said Leni. Her mouth was dry and her voice husky, and she was very much out of patience with herself. No doubt he would congratulate himself that he was giving the little English tourist the thrill of a lifetime with his attentions, and when she was gone he would continue trying to make up his mind whether he could or could not live without a certain Balinese dancing girl. Whether or not he could live with less than perfection. . . .

"Dee and Dwight?" he questioned.

She shook her head, not wanting him to hear that give-away huskiness again.

"*Bagus.*" They stood close together in the musky semi-darkness. Then in his usual commanding way he had led her into the pavilion, found her a seat—not the one she had occupied before—and was sitting beside her.

"You'll appreciate this better with someone to explain the dances to you."

Weakly, Leni accepted it all; weakly she stayed there beside him. Though she was quite certain that with Kemp there, only half her mind would be on what she saw.

As it happened, she was quite wrong. The dance performances were so utterly enthralling that for long minutes she forgot entirely the man beside her. She felt herself strongly at one with the Balinese, who thronged eager and intent around the sides of the pavilion, dark heads and eyes turned in one direction—toward the stage where the performers moved and where the great gongs of the orchestra were sounded. The people's absorption was like a visible force, and Leni felt amazement that even the tiniest children seemed to be wholly involved in what was taking place on the stage.

The members of the orchestra were the same. The powerfully compelling music with its strange rhythms and vibrations, its resonant repetitions, seemed to penetrate one's being so that Leni felt her physical self was part of the sound. But the musicians themselves watched the dancers—they showed delight, amusement, terror, suspense—they were like children. And Leni was like a child too.

The first dance was the Legone—"the Dance of the Heavenly Nymphs," Kemp told her. "The subtlety of the story is impossible for a European to follow at first viewing. You'll have to see it many more times, Leni, before you'll understand the transfers of scene and character when the actual scene and characters don't change at all. I'll explain as much as I can tonight—there are three female dancers, but the story concerns a king and a captured maiden and a bird of ill omen, and all these you must find for yourself as the girls dance." He smiled at her in a kindly way. "One other thing of interest—inspired Balinese dancers go into a trance before their performance, for the dance is very closely connected with their religion."

Leni made no comment, but she knew now that Daju had been in a trance when she had seen her. She was still possessed, she reflected, as she watched the girl dance. Bound so tightly in the black and gold brocade, it was amazing that she could move with such suppleness. The other two dancers were highly skilled, but Leni could not keep her eyes off Daju—clearly the most talented and dedicated of the three. Her torso arched as she swayed and stooped, elbows and hands held high, fingers with long pointed nails moving expressively into different stylized positions. It was a glittering and detailed performance, eyes and eyebrows playing their part in conjunction with the trembling fingers and the disciplined body, and in the face of such perfection Leni could find nothing to say when the dance ended and the ringing gongs of the orchestra had faded into silence.

The Barong play was completely different, spectacular, sometimes terrifying, the costuming wonderfully elaborate. The Barong itself—the protector of mankind—was danced by two men. One formed the forelegs and manipulated the mask, an enormous and fantastic version of a wild boar, an intricately worked gold head-dress and breastplate mingling with a huge and hairy mane and beard.

"Made of human hair," Kemp said, "and the most sacred part of the mask."

The hindlegs were formed by a second dancer, and everybody laughed, even Leni, even Kemp, as the extraordinary creature swished its tail playfully or snapped mischievously at some member of the orchestra who reacted with an instinctive flinch. Rangda, the evil widow witch, wore an equally ornate and imaginative costume, but she was wholly sinister and terrifying in her necklace of human entrails, and her loud gurgling cries rose above the shattering resonance of the orchestra.

The play represented the battle between good and evil. Kemp warned Leni, "You'll quite likely be frightened in the final scenes where the kris dancers who are attacking Rangda have her spell cast upon them and begin to plunge their krisses into their own breasts."

"Don't worry," said Leni, with a nervous laugh. "I'm not a child. I shall remember it's only a play."

The corners of his mouth lifted in a smile that was half grim. "Don't be too sure about that. This play is very serious to the Balinese and has tremendous significance. Its object is to strengthen the resistance of the village to the forces of evil, and you'll find the Balinese who are watching are far from light-hearted about it. I shouldn't be surprised if you get more than somewhat caught up yourself, you being—you." A remark that took Leni by surprise and made her widen her eyes questioningly.

Kemp didn't enlarge on his comment, however, but continued carefully, "The kris dancers usually go into a trance, for they are people who take their religion very, very seriously. They will actually plunge their krisses into their breasts. It's not mere play-acting, and I think you should be warned."

Leni was both baffled and horrified. "But—" she stammered in distress.

He smiled enigmatically. "But, Leni, the Barong has a

spell stronger than that of Rangda, and so the dancers become invulnerable to their own blades, which refuse to penetrate their breasts."

The play began then and Leni watched with growing absorption. Then toward the end, despite Kemp's warning, she found her heart in her mouth and she cried out aloud when the dancers, who were staggering about as if they no longer knew what they were doing, began attacking themselves with their own krisses. It was as if a game had turned serious, as if something outside had taken over, and the actors were no longer acting. Their trancelike state was terrifying to Leni, who was filled with a real and physical fear and suddenly found she was holding tightly to Kemp's hand. She could not for the life of her let go until the *pemangku* had revived the dancers by sprinkling them with holy water. And then she sat, white-faced, feeling utterly exhausted.

Many people in the audience sat silent after the play was over, though others, more hardy or hardened, began at once to stream out into the night, talking and even laughing.

Leni and Kemp sat for several minutes and then he said, shattering the mood of fantasy that was still upon her. "Well, are you ready to come home, Leni? Or do you want to wait here while I go and find Daju?"

Leni's heart thudded sickeningly. She was brought abruptly back to earth, to the cold realization that she had been lulled into deluding herself, sitting here so close to Kemp in the incense-perfumed darkness. She said jerkily, "I'm sorry for delaying you. You go ahead, and thanks for sitting it out with me. Thanks for the explanations and the . . . the reassurances. And thanks for the loan of your hand. But I shan't wait—"

"Why not?" His voice was sharp.

"I've . . . I've arranged to go back with someone else."

"With whom?"

Leni said, straight out of her head, two names she happened to know. "With Joan and Ian Menzies."

That convinced him. He asked, more mildly now, "Must you?"

"Yes."

"Why?"

She lifted her eyebrows. "Why do you think?" As she said it, slowly, deliberately, she knew exactly what it would seem to imply. It would imply a reference to a promise made to Guerney Fisher, and Kemp caught on immediately.

He said coldly, "You might give me more warning next time that you're about to step back into line. . . . Well, I'm glad I was of some use."

He looked at her hand lying limply across her knee, and she knew he was remembering how tightly she had held on to the strength and comfort of *his* hand. He got up and so did she, and he bowed his head for a second. "Goodnight, Leni."

"Goodnight," she murmured and, turning quickly, made her way as fast as she could from the pavilion. Her cheeks were burning and her heart was hammering and tears were trembling on her lashes. She would not—could not—ride back to the hotel with Kemp Savage and Daju. . . .

Outside, she had still to leave the narrow road where the dance temple stood and find the street where the *bemos* would be waiting. In her half-dazed state, she started off the wrong way, then became suddenly aware that she was battling against the main stream of people and progressing very slowly toward the heart of the village. With an exclamation of impatience she turned about and started in the other direction. She walked quickly, pushing carelessly if she had to push, brushing the silly tears from her cheeks. As if she hadn't known all the time that he would be thinking of Daju! "Cristelle and I just haven't a hope," she thought bitterly. "No one merely human could make him forget someone like Daju!"

She began to look for faces in the crowd she knew—people from the hotel—but she could see no one. When she reached the road a *bemo* was moving off, and another started up. A woman leaned from the back and called out to her so that her heart gave a leap of hope.

"Are you going in to Denpasar?"

Disappointed, Leni, who was hurrying forward, fell back shaking her head. The *bemo* gathered speed and was off, and in its wake came three others, all of them full to overflowing, none of the passengers even aware of her as she stood waiting.

A small tide of panic began to rise in her breast. But it was mere foolishness—she would get hold of a *bemo* easily enough. That panic must be because she was afraid that Kemp—and the Balinese dancer—would come along and catch her and she would have to ride back with them.

It was this fear that eventually caused her to move farther along the road. She was pretty sure it was in the right direction this time, and that she would be able to hail a *bemo* as it came by. Right now, there was not a single *bemo* in sight. The crowd was thinning out considerably and seemed to consist mainly of Balinese. Leni waited for what seemed a long time, and a quietness began to settle. She became convinced that Kemp had already gone—had probably gone before she made it to the road!

To her joy, at that moment a *bemo* came into sight. It

was coming very fast and weaving a somewhat erratic course, but she had to find transportation home, so she stepped forward into the light of the headlamps and held up her hand.

The driver pulled up at one, and she saw he was a young Balinese. He had one arm around the girl who sat beside him. Without doubt he had been driving one-handed!

"You want *bemo*?" His voice was slightly slurred. "Where to?"

"To the Hotel Selatan," said Leni, her heart quailing a little.

"Six hundred rupeah," said the boy, his white teeth showing in a broad smile. The girl beside him giggled and put her hand over her mouth.

Leni knew that 600 rupeah must be far too much, and after a second she said firmly, "Five hundred." The boy nodded and looked well satisfied. He waited while she installed herself in the back, then took off with such suddenness that she nearly lost her balance. There was no conductor here to look after her well-being and she wished that she had not been so hasty in accepting the first taxi that came along. She held tightly to the edge of the seat, watching palm trees and bamboos careering crazily past, and growing more and more frightened.

A glance through the small window into the front cabin convinced her that the driver had forgotten all about her and was completely absorbed in showing off to his girl-friend.

Leni raised one hand and rapped sharply on the glass as she had seen the conductors doing when they wanted to stop their *bemo*, but the driver appeared not to hear. She rapped harder and called out at the top of her voice, "Stop—stop at once!"

A smiling face was turned to her for a second, then the *bemo* sped madly through an intersection, despite the fact that the beam of headlights showed another car was in the offing. And so the crazy drive continued. Dwight, Leni thought, was almost a model driver compared with this young exhibitionist in his flimsy vehicle.

Soon she had a new fear. She was practically certain they were going the wrong way. They should have turned off at the intersection they had sped through. She began to thump with both fists on the glass, and to shout angrily, "Stop—stop, I tell you!"

This time the girl heard her and looked round, the smile fading from her lips as she saw Leni's angry face. She nudged the driver, the *bemo* swerved madly as he braked, then jerked to a stop that all but sent Leni sprawling. Angry and indignant now, even more than she was frightened, she jumped to the ground and marched up to the front window where the driver was looking out, innocent inquiry on his flushed face.

"You want to get out? You not want hotel?"

"I want the Hotel Selatan, but I'll certainly never get there if I leave it to you," said Leni. "You've brought me the wrong way."

He shrugged and looked injured, but held out his hand. "Five hundred rupeah."

Leni gave him the money, although he certainly didn't deserve it. She thought it was worth it to be rid of him, and when he had roared off she began to walk briskly back along the road, fuming to herself over his impudence and the fact that he was in charge of a *bemo* at all. It was several minutes before she noticed how shaky her legs were, and realized that she would quite likely have to walk all the way to the hotel.

It was not a walk she wanted ever to have to take again.

She was far from certain of the way. And the moon, while it certainly lightened the darkness of the road, also cast weird shadows in the jungle. She was frightened—of what, she did not exactly know. Of Bali's evil spirits, perhaps—because she was not wearing her necklace. She had put it away in a drawer after she had heard the women talking on the beach—only this morning—and promised herself she would never wear it again. Because Kemp Savage had given it to her and she was not going to make a fool of herself by wearing it for him to see.

It seemed a miracle when she saw lights at last—and when she realized they were actually the lights of the hotel. Her fingers were clammy, her legs shaking as she opend the gate into the garden, and once she felt the familiar path beneath her feet she began to run and run. It was as though she could not help herself.

She was still running when Kemp Savage stepped out by one of the ornamental lamps, and somehow or other she continued to run until his arms were about her and her head was laid against his breast. Then she was crying and telling him on a sobbing breath, "If I'd had the Barong I'd have been safe—"

"Calm down, calm down, child," he told her. He stood motionless, holding her, while she sobbed against him, and was comforted by the feeling of strength that she seemed to gain from him. It was greater than the merely physical.

When at last she moved to find her handkerchief, wiped her eyes and her drenched cheeks and blew her nose, he said with matter-of-factness that gave her a little jar of shock, "Now suppose you tell me exactly what's happened to put you in such a state." He added with a touch of humor, "I'm reasonably sure it wasn't the widow witch, so what? Come along now." He gave her a little shake. "Tell me."

Leni began to feel like a fool. She was appalled at her own behavior—running into his arms like that, clinging to him as if she had some special claim on him. Becoming hysterical about nothing at all. How he must be laughing at her!

"I'm sorry." Her voice, though low, had a note of dignity in it. "I'm afraid I just temporarily went to pieces. Nothing . . . nothing happened except I picked a bad driver and he—he took me the wrong way. I'm—I'm tired, I've walked quite a way, and these aren't my walking shoes." She managed the ghost of a smile that was half defiant.

He was not amused. He looked at her in silence. "You'd better get back to your bungalow and take something to steady you down. Right now, you're a mass of nerves, that's for sure."

She attempted no protest—she was too busy composing herself—as he escorted her to the bungalow. It was empty, for Dee was not yet home, and he left her there for no more than two minutes, then returned with a stiff dose of whisky, which he insisted she drink down at once and entirely.

She gulped it, suppressed a shudder and said stoically, trying to keep her tear- and dust-stained face turned away from his probing eyes, "Thank you very much. I shall be quite all right now."

"I'm sure you will," he said smoothly. He sat in a heavy bamboo chair facing her and leaned toward her. And although only the low table lamp with its rose-colored shade was alight, she could see the glitter of his black eyes and the determined line of his mouth. "Now," he said pleasantly, "I want to hear why you lied to me."

"Why I—I lied to you?" she stammered in confusion.

"Yes. You told me you were coming back with the Menzies." She opened her mouth, but he said warningly,

"Don't add one lie to another. Don't tell me you missed them. I've made inquiries and I know you made no arrangement with them. I was, as a matter of fact, on my way to fetch the car and look for you. I came to find you when I got in and you weren't back. The Menzies came in half an hour later—they'd had coffee in town and were astonished when I asked where you were. So what idiotic reason made you refuse a ride home with me?"

She looked at him warily and his face was completely grim. His eyes searched hers, and her glance dropped. What could she say? "I wouldn't come because of Daju—because of my jealousy." How would that sound? She hunted feverishly through her mind, but there seemed no excuse she could possibly give and she was relieved when at last he said chillingly, "I was right, then. It was because of your—other boyfriend, wasn't it? Because of the promise you made him. Evidently you regret that you broke it in Ubud."

"Yes," said Leni dully. "Maybe I do. I should have stayed with Dee. It would have been—it would have been better all around."

He stood up abruptly. "I see. Well, now we both know where we stand, don't we? I'll say goodnight and trust that you'll sleep well. The whisky might help even if your conscience doesn't."

When he had gone she still sat where she was, wondering what he had meant—hating him, hating herself still more, very much aware of her conscience and aware too that *she* certainly did not know where they both stood.

He was right on one count, however. The whisky certainly helped her to sleep.

During the next couple of days she saw him only fleetingly, in the distance. He was leaving her alone and she told herself that she was thankful, but of course she was not. She wasn't rational enough over her feelings to be thankful. Her spasm of hatred had disappeared entirely and her infatuation—it must be only that—had come back in full force to make life miserable for her. She tried to hide it from Dee, to pretend that she was having a good time on this island paradise. It was not hard, for Dee was very much caught up in her own tangled love affair—though it was more in the nature of a dangerous game than a love affair, as Leni knew. The one thing she could approve of in Dee's attitude these days was the fact that she refused to accept any more gifts from Dwight. It looked as if the two of them were playing a game and playing it hard, each determined to win. Dee was fairly frank about it.

One morning as she applied a lavish layer of sun tan lotion to her face before going to the beach she confessed to Leni, "Dwight wants me to be his—his mistress—sort of temporarily." Through the mirror she watched Leni warily for her reaction. "I've told him it's no go—that's why I don't want any presents. But he thinks I'm going to give in, that it must happen sooner or later."

"If he wants that sort of thing," said Leni trying not to sound too censorious, for she knew that would get her nowhere with Dee in her present mood, "it's a wonder he bothers about you, Dee. If you give him *no* encouragement," she added skeptically.

"I've told him it's to stop at a few kisses," said Dee, her cheeks red. "Even you can't condemn me for that, can you, Len?" she added sweetly. "And please don't go reminding me I'm engaged. I've told you I'll confess to Charles in good time, and anyhow he's probably kissed more than one girl while I've been away!" She stopped breathlessly and tried to remember what she had started to say. "I can see you don't believe me, but you can just stop suspecting the worst. I can tell you why it is Dwight keeps on dating me—it's because he's put in a lot of groundwork, and even if he could find another unattached girl, which at the moment is not all that easy, he'd have to start digging himself in all over again, and there isn't all that much of his holiday left. And besides," she added, as Leni raised her eyebrows, "we do, in a funny sort of a way, have a soft spot for one another."

"Hmm," said Leni thoughtfully, and honesty made her say aloud what was in her mind. "Perhaps he's trading on that soft spot, Dee—counting on it to get him what he's after."

"Well, it won't," said Dee shortly, and with an attempt at changing the subject, inquired, "How are things going with you, Len?—you and Kemp Savage, I mean."

Leni said casually as if it didn't matter, "They're not going at all. It's better that way. You advised me that yourself." Her lips twisted humorously, but Dee looked uncomfortable.

"I didn't mean you to take me too seriously, Len. It's just that you're . . . well, you're more intense than I am, more serious. You take things to heart more. I didn't want to spoil your fun."

"You haven't," said Leni mildly. "I'm having a very pleasant time."

"All by yourself?"

"Not all by myself. I've made some nice friends among the hotel guests."

Dee was still uneasy. "Come down to the beach with us this morning, why don't you?"

"Thanks, Dee, but . . ." Leni spread her hands, "you're ready, I'm not. Besides, I have some shopping to do. I must start gathering one or two souvenirs to take home—it won't be long now."

"Then come later if you like," insisted Dee, sounding happier.

She was off in another two minutes, and Leni decided she would do as she had said, but rather than shop at the hotel and possibly run into Kemp, she would go to Denpasar. She would have to face the fact that her holiday was very nearly over—that soon Bali and Kemp Savage would be no more than memories.

She did her shopping and managed to find odds and ends that she thought would please her various friends and relatives. It was steamily hot and she arrived back at the hotel just on lunch time. Exactly in time to see a shining black car pull up under the hotel porch along the tree-shaded path. A middle-aged man climbed out, and a woman—a tall, thin, long-legged woman who had the figure of a fashion model, sleek black hair, large dark eyes and skin the color of magnolia petals. This elegant creature glanced up the steps, and calling "Darling!" began to move forward, her arms stretched out in a somewhat theatrical gesture, just as someone tugged at Leni's arm.

"Hi, Len. You *are* loaded up. I gather the shopping went well." It was Dee, her hair wet from the sea, her beach coat over her shoulders. Leni said, "Yes, it was fine," and turned back to the little scene outside the hotel. She very much wanted to know who "darling" was, and as she had suspected, it was Kemp Savage. He was now shaking the hand of the middle-aged man, and Leni didn't know—and now never would—how he had replied to the invitation of those outstretched hands.

She made her way along the path toward the bunga-low with Dee. She didn't want Kemp Savage to think she was overly interested in him, and she told herself forcibly, "There are probably dozens of girls in love with him—he must be used to coping with lovesick holidaymakers like me—they must even come back again and again because he's given them a good time—a thrill." She also told herself that she, Leni Forrest, had come to the end of allowing herself to be victimized by his charm. She was too unsophisticated to escape without having her heart broken.

The next day, she took Dee at her word, and half an hour or so after Dee had gone to the beach, Leni gathered up her swimming gear and went too. After all, she argued with herself, the beach was big and just because she no longer cared to go to the hotel pool it didn't mean she must go without her swimming and sunbathing. No one would believe she had spent a fabulous month in Bali if she didn't take home a fittingly fabulous suntan!

Dee seemed quite genuinely pleased to see her, and even Dwight was civil and made no objection to her stretching out on the sand in his vicinity. But when he and Dee decided to go into the water, Leni let them have it on their own, preferring to stay and sunbathe by herself. She was roused from a half sleep by two little Balinese girls of ten or eleven, in blouses and sarongs, each with a flat woven basket balanced on a coiled towel on her head. One was selling bottles of lemonade, the other fruit, and each had a little stack of woven palm leaf hats.

Leni smiled at them as they stood looking down at her and sat up.

"Hello. Do you speak English?"

"Yes. We learn at school."

"You speak very nicely."

They giggled and sat down on the sand, putting their baskets beside them. One of them touched Leni's leg with a brown finger.

"We're not like this. You have white color."

Leni said ruefully, "I wish it weren't so white. Will you sell me some lemonade? I'm very thirsty."

The transaction was made and then they showed her their fruit, enticingly—short fat yellow bananas and some small fruit with an almost black skin like the skin of a cobra.

"What is this called?" asked Leni.

"*Selak*. You buy some?"

"If you'll show me how to eat it."

The skin was thin and brittle and broke away easily, and inside were two large segments of fruit—white and smooth and rather hard when Leni bit into it. The taste was delicious—a little like a sweet apple, a little like a strawberry.

"I think I like *selak*," said Leni approvingly.

"You buy some more?"

"Well, all right. *Tiga*," she added, using the Indonesian word for three which made them giggle again.

"And a hat?" they asked persuasively when she had handed over the money. "Because you are too white for the sun."

"But I don't want to stay so white," protested Leni, laughing. A shadow fell across her eyes and she looked up to find Kemp Savage towering over her.

"Are these girls pestering you?" He looked at the fruit lying on her towel, at the small brown hands holding out the hats.

Leni shook her head. Her heart was thumping, and she knew her cheeks had lost their color. She wished she could see his eyes better and yet she was glad she couldn't.

The two little girls scrambled to their feet. "We want to sell her hat," said one of them, while the other raised her basket of bottled drinks and with practised ease balanced it on her small head. "She must not get too much sun at first."

Kemp's face suddenly broke into a smile. He fished in his pocket and handed over some money, took one of the hats and tossed it down beside Leni. "Better see if it fits you."

The girls were delighted with whatever money he had given them and began to hurry off with quick goodbyes. Leni felt embarrassed about the hat, but felt impelled to put it on, and at least it did fit her. To hide her embarrassment, she said, "How gracefully they walk with those unwieldy trays on their heads."

He didn't bother to turn his head to look, but watched her steadily and unsmilingly.

She felt baffled and a little unhappy. Then with her head lowered so that she could see only his tan and white shoes and the cuffs of his beige cotton trousers, she asked unsteadily, "Why have you come here?"

There was a short silence.

"I saw you walking to the beach—a good hour ago." He lowered himself onto the sand and lounged back beside her, looking at her so hard that despite herself she had to raise her face and meet his gaze. He said with a wry grimace that was half a smile, "We can't seem to leave each other alone, can we?"

"I've—I've left you alone."

He nodded. "But how long can it last? Are you so frightened that you've retreated back to the safety of your friend's company? And exactly what is it you're frightened of? Is it yourself, or the promise you made?" He glanced quickly down to the sea where Dee and Dwight were wading hand in hand, then his gaze returned to her face. "Why for heaven's sake don't you tell Guerney Fisher you want to be released from any promise you've made him? If I were in his place, I shouldn't insist on holding you to it."

No, of course he wouldn't. A woman who was not entirely his, body and soul—a woman who looked at another man, thought of another man—would never do for Kemp Savage! She would be fine to fool around with but not to marry. Leni recalled her own mad actions of the other night, when she had flown to him, babbled out her nonsense about the Barong. He must know well enough that she was suffering from a bad attack of love for him. Was he ready, like Dwight, to take advantage of that, when it suited him?

She told him, her voice low, "I must work things out my own way."

"You leave me completely in the dark," he said, his voice harsh. "Just what is your way? And just what is this game you're playing? Is it with me or with Guerney Fisher? Or is the whole business no more than a bit of fun to you? I didn't think you were cut from the same cloth as your flirtatious little friend, but if you're not careful, Miss Forrest, you're going to find yourself completely on your own for the remainder of your holiday."

It was exactly then that Dee and Dwight came strolling up, and with a muttered "Damn!" Kemp sprang to his feet and without another word walked away.

As Leni looked after him, she saw a girl appear from the direction of the hotel garden. It was the tall elegant girl she had seen the day before getting out of the expensive black car—the girl who had called out "Darling!" to Kemp.

She was calling to him again now and Leni heard his answer with a shock that went straight to her heart.

"Couldn't it wait, Cristelle? I told you I'd see you for lunch." Irritably spoken, and yet wasn't there something intimate in the very irritability? Leni turned on her stomach and put her face in her arms. She felt sick through her whole being. So Cristelle Dubois was back and he was going to see her for lunch. That was all it needed.

A spatter of cold water flew onto her back and

Dwight's voice drawled mockingly, "Competition! And from a really gorgeous bird."

"Why don't *you* make a bid for her, then?" said Dee, a nervous note in her voice. "She might be just what you're looking for."

They began to scuffle and Leni closed her ears to them. But she could hear the pulsing of her own blood at her temples, and her forehead felt clammy.

CHAPTER NINE

Leni did some very hard thinking that afternoon. She stayed in the bungalow on her own, for Dee had gone out with Dwight again. Her head was aching and the light hurt her eyes, and she was sure that, as well as everything else, she had had an overdose of sunshine. For a whole hour she lay on the bed with the bamboo blinds drawn across the windows and the ceiling fan on and her eyes closed.

She thought back to the very first time she had ever seen Kemp Savage, in Singapore. He had been buying expensive gifts for someone then. She hadn't known at that stage that they were destined for a Balinese dancing girl, but of course she had known they were for someone.

Yet she had persisted in falling recklessly and abandonedly in love with him. On reflection, she thought it had been unnecessary. Her reasoning should have acted as a brake on two counts—one, he was plainly in love with someone else; two, she was never likely to see him again. Of course, she had seen him again, but even then she knew perfectly well she would have only a month in Bali. Therefore she should have had the strength of character to keep him well and truly at arm's length, thereby denying her love the fuel that is so necessary to keep a fire burning.

Leni moved restlessly and asked herself a tormenting question. *Had she been alone in making the running?* Hadn't Kemp Savage sought her out? He had even brought her a gift to the *losmen*—the ivory necklace. Not a cheap trinket, but a very valuable piece of Balinese craftsmanship. Why, when the perfect answer to his ideal of love was there to be had in Daju? Was it because, against his deepest desires, perhaps for reasons connected with the position he held with the hotel company, he had decided he must do the conventional thing and marry a European?

Leni was brought up abruptly by the turn her thoughts had taken. Her eyes flew open and she stared at the high-beamed ceiling with its overlay of meticulously woven cane. She must be going out of her mind. Kemp Savage would never consider marrying her. Particularly when he believed her to be entangled romantically with another man. He had dropped Cristelle Dubois, or so Leni understood, because she—how was it he had put it that night in Singapore?—because she had another male on her mind. A man of his intelligence would hardly make the same mistake twice.

Leni closed her eyes again. Or was the true story of Cristelle Dubois altogether different? Had it been as one of those women suggested? Was it *Cristelle* who had called a halt, insisting that he drop the Balinese girl completely? And if he had refused—and still refused? Leni felt a tremor shake her. Would she, suppose she ever had the opportunity, accept Kemp Savage on his own terms? Would she agree to become his wife because it was "circumspect" and turn a blind eye to his love for the dancer? No, Leni knew she could never do that. She had her ideals too, and while she didn't expect the man she would eventually marry never to have had a love affair at all, she did expect him to be faithful once they were married.

But now that Cristelle Dubois was back again, how did that alter the picture?

Leni gave a sigh that was half a groan. She could not possibly work out what it implied. She only knew that

Cristelle had called him darling and that today he had taken her to lunch. If she had witnessed their meeting the day before, if she knew whether Kemp had embraced that other girl or not, it would all be a little easier to assess.

Suddenly she sat up and swung her feet to the floor. She would never learn the truth of the matter if she stayed hidden in her room like this!

She changed into her bikini, slipped a pink towelling robe over her shoulders, her feet into the green sandals and headed for the garden. At the door she paused and came back. How about her hair? How about a little makeup? Soft, rose pale lips to match her robe, dusty blue eye-shadow to put lights in her grey eyes, a touch of golden powder. Now her hair. She combed the tapered fringe to one side and wished vainly that she had long silky black hair instead of this pale silvery cap. Oh well, quite likely she would not even see him. But yes, she was determined that she *would* see him—and that he would see her.

Oh, Leni, you are sick!

Rather astonishingly, the first person she saw when she reached the palm grove by the swimming pool was Dee Fisher, lounging back in a cane chair sipping an icy green drink and looking moody. Where was Dwight? Leni paused and scanned the area quickly, and pretty soon she caught sight of Dwight cruising around with his camera.

Leni made her way toward Dee and as she did so, three people came on to the flagged area beyond the pool. Kemp Savage, in cream shirt, tan slacks and sunglasses; Cristelle Dubois, stunning in a sleeveless pantsuit of flimsy white material; and the man who had been with her when she arrived in the black car. The three of them were immersed in conversation. Kemp walked with his head slightly bowed, and he did not even glance in Leni's direction. They chose one of the outdoor tables, and at once a Balinese girl came to serve them drinks. Kemp had sat down with his back to Leni, the other man had his profile turned, and Leni could see Cristelle full face.

So much for her scheme of having Kemp see and admire her in her more than usual makeup!

Dee glanced up and her blue eyes brightened.

"Oh, Len, are you feeling better? Sit down—Dwight's wandered off with a fit of the sulks." She smiled brightly, but behind her eyes there was a baffled, hurt expression, and Leni felt a pang of pity for her—Dee, who should have been content with the man she was engaged to and have had the good sense not to come seeking a romantic interlude in the south.

Leni sat down where she could keep her eye on that other group. Despite Cristelle's big sunglasses, she was sure that right now the other woman was giving her a very hard scrutiny. And that, she decided, was something. She told Dee with a smile, "I feel fine now. Am I imagining it, or are you feeling blue?"

Dee didn't answer straight away. She took up her glass and sipped at the green drink before she said brightly, "You should try some of this, Leni. . . . No, I'm not blue—not really. I don't know—I guess I'm just a bit fed up with myself. This thing with Dwight has gone beyond a joke. I just don't know how to handle it any more. We've had a pretty big row and. . . ." Suddenly her blue eyes filled with tears and to hide them she stopped talking and gulped down some more of her drink.

Leni said gently, "Don't be upset about that, Dee. Keep it in proportion. Dwight doesn't really matter in your life."

Dee blinked away her tears. "That's all very well. But I feel so . . . so uncomfortable in my skin. He must think

I'm a terrible sort of girl. You've no idea, Leni—he said such insulting things to me. But since that dress, at the very beginning, I haven't taken a single thing from him. Not one single thing."

Leni sought for something soothing to say. It was far too late to scold Dee. She said at last, "I suppose the fact is that you and I just aren't sophisticated, Dee. We're soft, both of us." Dee gave the ghost of a smile that had a trace of cynicism in it. "If I were you, I'd tell him I just didn't want to see him any more."

Dee grimaced. "That would be pretty hopeless, wouldn't it? Seeing that we're staying at the same hotel. I'd have to stay in the bungalow all day and have my meals sent in on a tray!"

"You're too literal, Dee. You know what I mean."

"I know what *I* mean too," said Dee edgily. "I just can't face seeing him any more, Len. He looks at me as if ... as if ... oh, I don't know, but I feel so second rate." She gave Leni a quick glance. "I've been thinking, Len. Your love affair's turned sour on you too, hasn't it? The Savage man has cooled off, hasn't he? I know you didn't say so, but let's be honest, I suppose it's much the same as me and Dwight. We're too simple, Leni, too trusting—we're still in a state of innocence. And now there's that international jetset girl who was chasing him up on the beach this morning. Why don't we both call it a day before anything else goes wrong? Pack our bags and go back home. We can forget all the unpleasant bits and remember the fun—the good things."

Leni shook her head very decidedly without in the least intending to do so.

"I want to stay my month out. Besides, neither of us should go before Guerney comes back."

"Why not?" Dee leaned toward her persuasively. "It

would really serve that brother of mine right if he came back and found we'd gone."

"Dee, that's a mean thing to say! What's Guerney done to make you so contrary about him?"

"He's spoiled everything, that's what," said Dee unjustly. "If he'd been more understanding—if he hadn't persuaded Janet to side against me—I could have stayed at his bungalow and had a marvelous time and been perfectly safe. I'd never have got myself into this mess."

Leni couldn't quite follow the logic of this, but she suggested reasonably, "It would still be unfair to go now, especially while there's this ill feeling between you. You wouldn't be happy if you went back to England without seeing him again. He's always been so fond of you; it was only because of that he was a bit too paternal and strict. And after all, there *is* Charles."

Dee had the grace to look a little guilty. "But I'm not going to stay here. I'll tell you what—we'll both move over to Guerney's. Ketut will look after us and we can swim and sunbathe and go shopping in Denpasar—"

For a moment Leni thought about that. Then her eye was caught by Cristelle Dubois, laughing and leaning forward to put her hand over Kemp's, while the older man sat back with a smile, a paternal smile, on his face. Of course, he must be Cristelle's father, the board member! It was a sort of family scene, and Leni felt a wrench at her heart. She very nearly said yes to Dee's scheme. Almost she decided to cut herself off from the hope of ever seeing Kemp Savage again. And then she knew she couldn't do it. No matter what the circumstances she simply had to be able to see him sometimes, until finally she would leave Bali and the knife would go through her heart. By that time perhaps the whole affair would be resolved. By that time, perhaps his engagement to Cristelle would have been announced. Or perhaps Cristelle would have disappeared from the scene for good.

Kemp was right about one thing: Leni could not leave him alone. But hadn't he said, "We can't leave *each other* alone?" Well, that remained to be seen, now that Cristelle was here. Maybe just in these last few minutes he had agreed to put Daju out of his life. Maybe that was why Cristelle's father was looking so smiling and benign. Kemp was doing the sensible thing.

And denying, came Leni's instinctive thought, his deepest beliefs and desires. No, the idea of Kemp doing the "sensible" thing had a false ring about it. He was too strong, too honest, for that.

So she told Dee reluctantly, "No, Dee, I won't go to Guerney's."

Dee looked at her curiously. "Why ever not?"

Leni shook her head. She couldn't possibly explain to Dee. She was, in her way, being even more foolish than her friend. It was ironic, really, that she had been so busy offering good advice and warnings when she was not prepared to take good advice herself, or even to turn back from the precipice she knew very well was ahead of her. "I'm sorry, Dee, but I like it here. I want to stay till it's time to go home."

"That won't be so long," said Dee cruelly. Her glance flicked across the glittering blue green waters of the swimming pool to that little group sitting so intimately together at their secluded table. "You haven't a hope with Kemp Savage, Len. Those few kind words you had this morning on the beach were Goodbye in capital letters, I'd stake my life on it."

Leni refrained from reminding her that she had not heard what Kemp had said to her that morning. "All the same, I'm staying here."

"And I'm not," retorted Dee, cross now. "What sort of a friend are you—" She broke off and sighed. "No, that's not really fair. You don't have to hold my hand when I need comforting. You stay here, Leni, and I'll go to Guerney's. It will be pretty lonely, but I guess I'll make out. And if Dwight comes chasing me up—"

"Ketut will look after you," said Leni hardily. She had seen the slanting look Dee sent her when she made her sad little statement about being lonely, and she was not going to be soft-hearted. It was not as if Dee would be on her own and defenceless at Guerney's. Ketut would look after her with devoted conscientiousness.

She saw Dee settled at Guerney's the very next morning and stayed there to share the delightful luncheon served by Ketut, who seemed truly happy to have Dee there. He assured Leni before she left, "We look after Nona. Then Mr. Fisher return very happy."

Leni felt strangely alone back at the hotel. Determinedly she went to dine in the hotel restaurant where almost instantly she saw Kemp sitting with Cristelle and her father. Leni might easily have fled had not the Menzies asked her to join them at their table. Their company proved some protection from a scowling Dwight, who came in late and glared belligerently around the dining room. Leni wondered if he had only now discovered Dee's escape and decided that she certainly would not tell him where her friend had gone. After dinner she walked on the beach with the Menzies, but she could not keep her mind from returning to Kemp and Cristelle, and she wondered what *they* were doing tonight.

When she woke the next morning, she had a very firm conversation with herself. "If you have even a grain of sense left in that far from level head of yours, Leni Forrest, you'll pack your clothes, pay your bill, and trot along like a good girl to spend a few pleasant days with Dee before Guerney comes back and you say farewell to Bali forever."

She jumped out of bed and showered and pretended not to notice her own woebegone face when she happened to glance in the mirror.

When her breakfast—a large slice of pink juicy papaya, fresh rolls and coffee—arrived, she had already started to pack. She ate on the tiled veranda and looked rather sadly out across the green of the garden. She could see the sparkle of the ocean beyond, and she could smell the frangipani blossoms. A tear ran down her cheek and splashed onto her breakfast tray, and it was only then that Leni saw the small envelope with her name written on it: Miss Leni Forrest. She recognized Kemp's handwriting instantly. She took out the single folded sheet quickly, her fingers shaking, her mind deliberately blank.

"Dear Leni," she read. "Today there is to be a temple festival—an Odelan ceremony—at a village not too far away. You shouldn't miss it. Please be in the hotel foyer at four-thirty. Yours, K.S. (P.S. Be sure to dress up a little; it's good manners.)"

Leni read it over twice, blinking with surprise. Kemp Savage was inviting her to a temple ceremony! She could hardly believe it. And what of Cristelle?

On feet that were suddenly winged, she raced into the bungalow and began crazily throwing her neatly folded clothes out of her suitcase. She felt like singing at the top of her voice. The world was a wonderful, marvelous, fabulous place—Kemp Savage had invited her out, and she was to meet him at four-thirty.

Suddenly Leni stood stock still.

Was she to meet him? *Had* he invited her out? Wouldn't he have wanted a personal reply if that was so?

She went anxiously to look at his letter which she had propped up in pride of place on the dressing table.

"You shouldn't miss it. Please be in the foyer—"

No, of course it was not a personal invitation. Leni's spirits took a dive. Her vivid imagination pictured the afternoon scene—herself arriving keyed up, dressed up, eyes shining. The foyer thronged with hotel guests, all of *them* dressed up, equipped with cameras, expectant. But not in the way she, Leni, would be expectant. A bus waiting outside. . . .

"I won't go," Leni decided. "I won't alter my plans just because he sends me a note."

But of course she didn't repack. Fate, she thought, had intervened, and now she was staying. And she might as well go to the temple festival.

She did one crazy unpredictable thing after lunch. She had eaten at the Legong Coffee House and that way had saved herself the pain of seeing Kemp with Cristelle again. As she wandered back through the garden, she picked a few flowers—white frangipani, some flat purple blooms, two or three marigolds. She bound them together almost absently with a thin strip of palm leaf so that they made a tiny bouquet, and then her feet of their own accord took her to a shrine not far from the gate leading to the beach. She had seen the girls who worked at the hotel going there in the mornings and evenings with their offerings, but she had never been there herself, feeling it was merely curious to pry. Now reaching the shrine, she saw a squat human figure with an elephant's head carved into the stone. A red hibiscus flower had been placed behind one of his ears, and the ancient elephant god looked benignly and a little comically down on Leni as she stood hesitantly before him. After a moment she placed her flowers at his feet, amongst the other offerings.

She thought apologetically, "I'm sorry I'm not so clever or artistic as the girls who made you these other gifts."

She wondered, "Have I honored the good spirits with my offering, or have I propitiated the evil ones?" She had an idea it was the good spirits she was dealing with, that gifts for the evil deities were laid rather contemptuously on the ground. In this strange country, it seemed as if these spirits had a very real existence, and though Leni smiled at herself, she felt much happier as she returned to the bungalow. She told herself, though in her heart she knew it was a long way from the whole truth, "If I can merely see Kemp Savage this afternoon, I shall be satisfied."

Later, she dressed herself with care in the batik gown that had been made for Emma Raymond, and she clasped her ivory necklace around her throat. She didn't look particularly splendid, she decided a little ruefully, but she was "dressed up" as Kemp had adjoured her to be. After all, she was going to a sort of birthday party—that was what an Odelan was, the birthday or anniversary of a temple. It was special in that it happened only once in every 210 days, she had read in a book she had bought at one of the shops. So of course, it would be a wonderful memory to take home.

Though just now Leni refused to think about home....

She reached the hotel some minutes before the appointed time, opened the big glass doors and stepped into the foyer. It was curiously empty, and Leni glanced at her watch. The bus had obviously not arrived yet, and through the glass wall opposite, she could see that there was the usual crowd at the pool. It *was* today that Kemp Savage had said the ceremony was to take place? In another few seconds, Leni would probably have run back to the bungalow in a panic, but at that moment Kemp himself appeared on the curved staircase that led, she knew, to the hotel office suites.

"Oh, there you are, Leni! I hope I haven't kept you waiting." He too glanced at his watch, and Leni blushed and stammered, "No—I've—I've just arrived."

His eyes went over her quickly, approvingly, yet there was a faint crease between his brows. Leni thought dryly, "He's seen me in this get-up a number of times."

He murmured, "Excuse me one moment," and disappeared into a room at the side of the foyer. When he returned he had a red hibiscus flower, cunningly set in green leaves, and before Leni had time to protest or even to think at all, he proceeded to fasten the flower expertly in the soft fall of hair at one side of her cheek.

"How's that?" He stood back, his head slightly tilted, to look at her. Leni wished fervently that she was a beautiful Balinese, or at the very least a chic and self-assured member of the international set—instead of just plain Leni Forrest.

His eyes bothered her, and she said awkwardly, "Thank you. Where are the others?"

His look sharpened. "The others? My invitation was for you—so if you've passed it on to your friends. . . ." There was a whiteness about his nostrils and Leni blanched.

"No. I mean all the others—from the hotel."

He smiled fleetingly. "There are no others." A small group had just come through the doors from the bathing terrace, and more than one glanced curiously at the man and the girl who stood, perhaps two feet apart, looking at each other warily. When they had disappeared in the direction of the lounge, Kemp said softly, "This is not a tourist affair. I just happen to have been invited along. I didn't really know whether to expect you or not." Leni looked at him doubtfully and suddenly he really smiled at her and reached to take her by the arm. "Still, I rather thought you would come," he admitted as he propelled her towards the door.

Leni's cheeks burned. He knew too much about her by far! Of course she had come! He had only to crook his little finger.

"It's not much use fighting against it, is it?" he asked a moment later when they were in his car and he was driving to the road. "We really can't—leave each other alone, you and I, Leni Forrest. Can I take it that you did as I suggested the other day?"

"What?" Leni's voice was low.

"Did you put it to Guerney Fisher that you must be free? I believe your friend's gone off to stay with her brother. As *you* didn't go, I naturally concluded. . . ." He left the sentence in midair, and turned his black eyes, intense and compelling, to meet hers for a fleeting instant.

Leni knew a deep and precarious joy. At least he was no longer under the illusion that she was irrevocably tied to Guerney Fisher. But how much that mattered to him still remained to be seen, and she must not lose sight of that fact. It was no use deluding herself that she had the field to herself by any means. After a slight hesitation, she decided there was no point in telling him that although Guerney had gone to Djakarta, it didn't make the slightest bit of difference to her.

So she looked back at him and smiled, and after that she sensed almost physically a lifting of the vague tension that had been there between them.

Leni settled her head back against the seat and prepared to enjoy herself. Even if it all ended once the Odelan was over, for the time being at least it seemed that the good spirits were looking after her.

He talked to her easily and comfortably as they drove along the coast through numerous small villages.

"The Odelan's a 24-hour festival, Leni. I'd have picked you up earlier if I could have—the celebrations start very early in the day. But as no doubt you know, I've an important board meeting coming up over the next couple of days, and I've had to put in several hours of work on the submissions I want to make."

Leni had not had the vaguest idea he had had a board meeting coming up, though now she thought of it, she recalled he had mentioned it in Singapore.

"Remember that hotel where you stayed in Singapore? They had a very impressive conference room there, plus a banqueting hall, and as a commercial proposition I think such an addition to my hotel would be a tremendous advantage. It would bring in people from all over the world to sales conferences and business meetings and so on. However, I suppose you're not very interested in all this."

"But I am," exclaimed Leni. "As a matter of fact, Mrs. Raymond and I had a look at those rooms you mentioned in Singapore. There was a conference on when we arrived and it was all very social. I think the men had brought along their wives and daughters, and they were having a wonderful time with dinners and dances every night."

He sent her a quick smile. "Exactly. I was thinking along the same lines. Right now, we're pretty well geared toward holidays and tourism, but with this new set-up, we could expand in several directions. I rather think we'd be able to take a more sophisticated line all around—in our entertainments, and in the type of clothing and souvenir we stock in our shops. Well, that's enough about business, but it accounts for the fact that we're arriving at the Odelan too late to see the cock-fighting."

Leni gave a little gasp, and he laughed.

"You needn't tell me—you're only too thankful you don't have to watch anything so barbaric! However, there'll be plenty of other things to see, and we'll be there in no more than another five minutes."

The village, Leni discovered when they reached it, was an unusual one, entirely enclosed within walls. She followed Kemp up a flight of mossy steps and through grotesquely carved gateposts. Inside was a series of grassed terraces, with dwelling places and meeting pavilions on either side. A long procession of girls in crimson and green and blue sarongs all embroidered with gold, was wending its way toward the temple that graced the highest terrace. Each girl carried an offering on her head, in a silver dish—pyramids of fruit, highly colored rice cakes and elaborately beautiful arrangements of flowers. Some must be at least three feet high, Leni decided, as she stared in fascination, while Kemp held her arm tightly.

It was a magic moment, just at sundown, and the music of bells and gongs floated through the golden air.

When the procession had finally disappeared through the great temple gateway, Kemp produced from the pocket of his lightweight jacket two fringed and brocaded *slendangs*. The white and silver he fastened about Leni's waist, the red and gold about his own, and they too approached the temple. Leni looked up at the high gateway. Carved in its ancient stone was a frightful face with gaping mouth, and from its sides splayed hands reached out so that Leni drew back instinctively, afraid. Kemp laughed softly.

"Don't be frightened, little one. That's Kala Makara, and it's not innocent beings like you he wants to catch. It's the evil spirits who endeavor to get into the inner sanctuary."

As he spoke he put his arm lightly about her shoulders and together they stepped through the gateway.

The temple courtyard was thronged with villagers, all dressed in their colorful and splendid best for the festival, and everywhere was the gleam of gold brocaded cloths, brightened by the flickering oil lamps that were being lit as the light faded. The whole scene, wreathed about with the smoke from incense burners, had a curious air of unreality and, above it all, mystically, rose the shadowy tapered tiers of the holy shrines. Leni gazed up as Kemp showed her the shrines of the three main gods—Brahma, Siwa, and Vishnu—and, dominating them all, the tall nine-tiered *meru meru*. Through drifts of smoke Leni could see the piles of fruit and flowers that had been offered to the deities, and shimmering amongst them, many long and beautiful painted scrolls, some of which looked to be ages old.

Ceremonial masks looked down on the crowd from high shrines—huge eyes fixed and brilliant and staring. She recognized with a tremor the Barong and the evil Rangda, and instinctively she felt for Kemp's hand. Those faces looked down on her so fearsomely, the white teeth gleamed, and Rangda with her blood-red lips and long tongue, was truly terrible. Kemp told her softly, "The masks are *sakti*, endowed with magic powers, and that's why they must be kept in safety here when they're not in use."

Leni, shivering, could well believe it. Rangda's red tongue, great fangs, and wild mane of hair looked so violently menacing in the incongruously beautiful setting of flowers and fruits. But the Barong—despite his wild aspect, Leni somehow had a weakness for the Barong!

Still, she was glad when they moved on and presently stood back from the crowd, in the shelter of the temple wall, where they could watch the ceremonies unobtrusively. She listened to the chanting of the *pemangku* who sat before a brazier of burning incense, while the metallic sounds of bells and gongs mingled mystically with shafts of gold struck from shrine and ceremonial dress—light and sound curiously combined so as to seem one and indivisible, gold and metallic. An assistant dressed in shining white brought holy water in a silver container to sprinkle on the heads of those who were bringing offerings, and as the trancelike ceremony continued, Leni felt more and more as if at any moment she must awake from a fantastic dream.

She felt a little exhausted by the time Kemp shook her arm lightly and told her, "Come, we'll go and find something to eat now. Later we'll come back to see the Pendet dance."

In the courtyard outside, the world was once more the everyday world of the island, for *warongs* had been set up, and foods, sweets, toys, magic medicines, and even batik clothes were on display. The atmosphere here was that of a very gay, very informal market, everything seemed noisy and happy and normal, and Leni felt more than a little relieved to escape for a while the strangeness of the scene she had just witnessed.

Kemp joked with a woman at a food stall, who laughed back good humoredly, and soon they were eating bowls of *soto,* and a tasty assortment of meats and vegetables and rice was set out on banana leaves for them. They ate without speaking and yet it was a strangely companionable meal in the midst of the busy market. Leni caught

Kemp's eye often, and sometimes she thought she saw laughter there, and sometimes there was an expression she could not fathom, but that made her drop her own eyes.

When they had finished eating, they went as if by some prearrangement to one of the houses at the top of the terraces. There they were greeted gravely by a black-haired, lambent-eyed young man, who with great courtesy invited them inside. Before Leni could even wonder why they were here, he had produced from the drawer of a heavy ornately carved teak chest a length of cloth, which he displayed before them wordlessly. It was a beautiful glowing strip of a kind of muted vermilion color, patterned in gold and dark purplish-brown. Leni, intrigued, made out the highly stylized shapes of temples and of dancing girls.

She had never anywhere seen anything in the least like this, and now Kemp and the young Balinese were both watching her, waiting for her reaction. She said slowly, inadequately, "It's very beautiful—*indah*!"

The young man bowed, smiled gravely and folded the heavy cloth back into its long narrow folds. He held it toward her, but she hardly dared touch it. She told Kemp hesitantly, softly, "I should like to have it, but—please—what's the price?"

"You like it?" His eyes were quizzical and amused in the light of the oil lamp that stood on the carved chest.

Leni nodded. She thought that if she could take this cloth home with her it would be to her a symbol of all that was most beautiful and mystical on this island. She said aloud, "I like it, and I want it—oh, more than anything I've seen here."

He said with a faint smile, "It's imperfect, Leni," and she wondered if he were making fun of her taste. "But," he added, "you can't buy it. It's a gift."

"To me? From whom?" she asked quickly. But of course she knew the answer. It was a gift from Kemp Savage. But why? And could she—should she—accept it? Her mind went fleetingly to Dwight and Dee, but Kemp could not be compared even remotely with Dwight. Anyway, it was impossible just now to argue or to question, so Leni accepted the cloth with a simple, "*Terima kasih, tuan*," as though she assumed it was the Balinese who was giving it to her.

But the minute they were outside again she told Kemp, "Please, I must pay for this. I can't possibly accept such a gift from—"

"From me?" His dark eyebrows peaked upward in a way that made him look faintly demonic. "Why not?" He touched her Barong necklace with one long finger. "You took this."

Leni colored deeply.

"You gave me no option. But this cloth . . . it's too fine, too expensive—"

"I've told you, it's imperfect," he said lightly. "But let me tell you something, Leni," he continued, deftly putting a stop to any argument. He took her arm and they moved slowly in the direction of the temple as he spoke. Above, in the dark cloudless sky, a small silvery moon swam, and the long-stepped terraces of the village street looked icy blue though the air was soft and warm and scented. "This is one of the very few villages where the *kamben grinsing*—the flaming cloth—is woven. The pattern is kept secret, and a single length may take six years to complete. It's used for ceremonial occasions only and each piece is reverently preserved. Your cloth, as I told you, Leni, is imperfect. It's therefore not fit to be worn as ceremonial dress. Such lengths are greatly sought after, as you may imagine, so you're lucky, little one."

Little one. It was the second time he had called her

that, and Leni could not help being charmed—wooed—by it. But she was exasperated too. She thought, "How can he talk to me like that, and make me such a rare and valuable gift when I don't know in the least what he means by it?" A kind of despair rose within her. Of course she wanted the cloth—and equally of course she wanted to hear those endearing words on his lips—but she could not accept either unless. . . .

She walked beside him in a rather subdued and frustrated silence, his arm companionably linked with hers. "I'll keep it just for now," she thought. "Just for a little while. I'll give it back before I leave Bali . . . and him forever."

Perhaps it was not a particularly sensible or realistic way to think, but just now Leni didn't seem capable of sensible or realistic thoughts. Besides, at the back of her mind a crazy flame was burning—a flame of hope. That Kemp should have brought her here, made her this gift—been so patently satisfied when he believed she had relieved herself of her promises and ties to Guerney Fisher. Surely it all added up to something.

Leni longed only to know what that something was.

CHAPTER TEN

When they went through the great gateway once again, the Pendet dance was about to begin. Leni heard the disturbing, exotic music that was to accompany it as Kemp drew her swiftly and silently around the back of the crowd to a position of vantage, then pulled her to rest against the strength of his shoulder.

All this without a word in the sweet, incense-perfumed semi-darkness.

The eye was drawn away from the lure of the scattered oil lamps now—to the file of girls, sliding like a golden river into the courtyard. They were bare-shouldered, and their long black hair, decked with flowers, flowed down their backs. Silver and gold bracelets caught points of light, slender bodies wrapped in gold cloth swayed gracefully as the girls drifted across the great courtyard, weaving their dance about each of the shrines in turn. They carried small offerings of rice or incense or flowers in their right hands, and Leni leaned back against Kemp's body entranced as she watched.

As the last shrine was encircled—the shrine nearest to where Kemp and Leni stood—some of the girls cast their flowers high over their heads and for a moment the air was full of many-colored blossoms.

Suddenly, as she stared spellbound, Leni caught a glimpse of a beautiful face turned in their direction, and her breath quickened. as she recognized the lovely Daju. Flowers of gold leaf gleamed against the dark of her hair, and a gold spot glittered at her temple. The bright marigolds she carried were tossed upward in a shining arc, and they fell neatly against Kemp's shoulder. He

189

stooped to pick them up, murmuring, "That's a blessing and a welcome." Leni's heart had grown cold, had seemed almost to stop beating, and when she met his eyes, she thought they wore a guarded look.

Did he think she didn't know whose flowers they were, now resting so casually in his hand? Did he think she, Leni, was unaware that the lovely Balinese dancer had deliberately flung her offering to him? And had he, all this time, before Leni had any suspicion that Daju was one of the Pendet dancers, been watching her and her alone?

After that, she scarcely saw the dancers melt away into the darkness, scarcely knew that Kemp was taking her away from the temple, telling her, "I think you've had enough, Leni Forrest. Or do you fancy staying till dawn?"

He had come, she reflected dazedly, to see Daju dance, and now that was over he was satisfied. She shook her head, wondered what her voice would sound like when it came, was relieved to find it almost normal.

"I'm quite ready to go home, thank you." She waited, sure he would say, "Then hang on a minute while I fetch Daju," but he did not. He merely nodded gravely.

"The Pendet dance made a fitting conclusion to the evening, I think. It's a very satisfying combination of beauty and art and devotion, the girls in their trancelike state, each so completely unconscious of self."

Leni said "yes," but her mouth was dry. Did *he* really believe that? Or think that she would believe it? Daju had not been in a trance—her flowers had been for Kemp. Didn't that betray that she was being won over to the West—away from the religion, the culture to which she had been born? She wondered again whether Kemp would after all marry this beautiful Balinese girl who looked so young and untouched and who would be faithful to him within the strict insistence of his idealism.

She moved at his side, down the long terraces of the strange village. Behind them there were music and lights and festivity, but they two were alone. In the moonlight, she could see Kemp's face quite clearly, but his eyes were too dark and shadowed to hold any message for her at all. She was taken completely by surprise when, after they had descended the steps at the entrance to the village, he drew her into the lacy shadows of some palm trees and put his arms about her and kissed her full and sweetly on the lips.

His voice was husky as he murmured against her hair, "Have you been happy tonight, little one? Has it been worth while?"

Worth all the heartache that must follow inevitably in its wake? Leni wondered before she answered him.

"Yes, it's been a wonderful experience, Kemp. I think I shall remember it forever."

"And I too." Still he held her, looking down at her, his lips curving and tender in the moving shadows of the palm leaves. "And now, one more thing before I take you home—I shall be busy with this board meeting tomorrow, as you know, but I want you to keep tomorrow night for me. Will you do that? It will be a very special evening, I promise you that—so long as you're prepared to promise *me*, here and now, that you're quite, quite free."

Helplessly, Leni said, "Yes, I'm quite free, Kemp, I promise you that."

"Then you must wear the *kamben gringsing*. I shall send one of the girls to show you how to drape and fasten it, and I shall see you in the foyer at eight-thirty. Is that understood?"

Again Leni nodded. And yet all the time a warning voice was telling her, "It will be nothing more than another memory, this very special evening of Kemp

Savage's. Because of it, your heart will ache for longer."
And she thought of Hans Andersen's little mermaid who
was given feet at the cost of taking every step in agony.

Leni knew a wild and restless urge to have the next
meeting come—to have it all over one way or the other,
for she was quite certain it must come to that.

He did not kiss her again that night or take her in his
arms. He merely saw her safely to her door, murmured,
"Sleep well, little one—and thank you for tonight." And
was gone.

She knew she wouldn't see him during the next day,
because of the business of the board meeting. She slept a
little late, and after she had breakfasted made her way to
the hotel pool. It was more crowded than usual and she
realized that some of the women there must be the wives
of the board members. They were a sophisticated-looking
lot, and Leni eyed them wistfully, aware of her own lack
of poise. These were the people Kemp must have
continually to mix with. In his position, the social side of
his life must be important, and it made her think once
more of Daju. How would the Balinese girl fit into the
pattern of such a highly sophisticated life? How would she
be received by these much-travelled, clothes-conscious
women with their selective and expensive tastes?

Well, reflected Leni wryly, Kemp was certainly encour-
aging expensive tastes in Daju with his gifts of clothing
and jewelery! The teeth-filing ceremony that had given
her such a beautiful smile could not have dealt very effectively with all her weaknesses. She must have developed
quite a love of luxury and worldly possessions. And the
headdress she had worn last night had been, not of
flowers, but of gold leaf!

Leni's thoughts had wandered, and she realized they
were not very worthy ones. Restlessly, she rose from the

lounger where she had been sitting, threw off her beach robe and in a minute had dived into the blue green depths of the pool and was swimming vigorously.

When at last she left the water and returned to where she had left her things, Cristelle Dubois was sitting there, smoking a scented cigarette in a long jade holder and wearing a simple white dress that looked enormously expensive with its deep band of white embroidery at neck and hem. She watched Leni amusedly from behind her sunglasses, and the younger girl's heart began a mad, half-frightened pounding.

"Hello." Cristelle's voice was cool and assured. "You're Leni, aren't you? I'm Cristelle Dubois. Do you mind if I join you here? I imagine we're both a little bored now that Kemp is so fully taken up with this convention bit."

Leni's smile was nervous. Feeling at a distinct disadvantage in every way—she was dripping wet, and she just did not know how to cope with this half-mocking, half-patronizing attitude—she reached quickly for her robe and said jerkily, "Please sit here if you like." That was as much as she could manage.

She had no real idea why Cristelle should want to talk to her, but she imagined it must be about Kemp, and she was afraid she was going to hear things that she would not particularly like.

Which proved to be the case.

Cristelle smoked in silence while Leni sat down, not looking at her, but at some young people frolicking in the water.

"Did you enjoy your little outing with Kemp last night?"

Leni's heart gave a jump of fright and she felt her cheeks flush. Deliberately she reached for a towel and rubbed at her wet hair before she answered levelly, "Very much, thank you."

"Well, that's fine. He told me he was taking you to some temple festival—he's very generous with tourists in that way, and then—maybe you're aware of this, maybe not—at this particular point in time he's just a tiny bit preoccupied with punishing me for a little lapse in devotion."

She smiled at Leni, openly and frankly. And Leni found herself thinking, "*Your* teeth are far from even—your eye teeth are as sharp as can be. I wonder just which of the six deficiencies is strongest in you?" At a guess, she would have said sensual pleasure. Cristelle, close up, despite her elegant slenderness and the virginal white she so habitually wore, had a distinctly sensual curve to her lips and nostrils.

Leni said nothing at all. She looked at Cristelle as blankly as she could manage and left her to make conversation while deciding with a satisfaction that she found faintly shocking that she definitely didn't like Miss Cristelle Dubois at all.

When Cristelle spoke again her voice had lost its mellow indolence and was definitely sharp. "You certainly look as though you'd made a night of it. You have some hardly flattering shadows around your eyes this morning. You should do something about that."

She was catty. Leni looked away from her and was tempted to gather up her things and go. But running away from facts, however nasty or distorted they might be, would get her nowhere. And Leni knew there were things she could learn from Cristelle Dubois if she steeled herself to stay and listen. The very fact that Kemp had told this other woman that he was taking Leni to the temple ceremony was significant. If he confided his activities to her like that, then it said something about the relationship between them. Leni flinched at the thought of being used to punish someone.

Cristelle flicked her cigarette, crossed her long legs at the ankles and asked coolly, "Did he kiss you in that all-out passionate way he's perfected over the years?" Color surged into Leni's pale cheeks, then receded, and Cristelle watched it clinically. She commented cruelly, "You must have some wonderful memories to take home! Well, I don't begrudge you them. Yet Kemp's horribly jealous if *I* so much as look at another male. Strange, isn't it? But I guess I'll learn to live with it. There's no one quite so—exciting as Kemp, is there?"

Leni said, her lips stiff, "Are you—are you telling me that you're going to—to marry Kemp?"

"How astute of you! That's just exactly what I am telling you. Does it surprise you so much? Did you possibly imagine that you might by some chance lay claim to him?" She laughed aloud, and that set Leni's teeth on edge. She said, trying to keep her voice steady and hoping that she would hurt Miss Cristelle Dubois, "It surprises me very much indeed, Miss Dubois. Because I thought that Daju, the Balinese dancer, was the one Kemp would marry."

"Daju?" The older girl seemed genuinely amazed. "Good heavens, no, Daju's—" She stopped suddenly, removed her cigarette from the jade holder and took out a gold cigarette case.

While she selected another cigarette she looked across at Leni through those baffling sunglasses and said frankly, "I suppose it's understandable you should have thought that. But Kemp's . . . infatuation with the little dancing girl doesn't bother me in the least. One learns to turn a blind eye to that kind of affair out here, my dear innocent girl. But perhaps you're just too English to understand that. Fortunately, my background's partly French, and as well I've lived in the tropics most of my life. So if Daju, and after her some other pretty girl, is necessary to Kemp in some way, then . . ." she shrugged and smiled, "so long as he's reasonably discreet, I shouldn't dream of making a fuss. He can have his dancing girls, if have them he must."

Leni closed her eyes and turned away. Was Kemp like that? Was that what Daju meant to him? Did she satisfy the carnal side of his nature rather than the idealistic? Leni couldn't believe it, not when the girl's very appearance of innocence and purity denied it so strongly. And yet she had thrown her flowers to him. *I couldn't bear it*, decided Leni. She could never turn a blind eye. But Cristelle, she did not doubt it, could and would. Was that what Kemp wanted? Cristelle would be quite content to have only part of him. What had he said once? "The girl I love must be all mine." Was that girl Daju? Was he going to marry Cristelle for purely practical reason, not really loving her; gaining his true happiness from an illicit love affair? It was all so sordid, Leni felt sick.

She scrambled up hastily and with no explanation whatever, beyond a muttered, "Excuse me" she began to walk quickly away from Cristelle Dubois. She hurried along beneath the palms actually shivering, despite the heat of the day. She wondered if Cristelle knew she was going out with Kemp again tonight. Come to that, *was* she going out with him? Was she going to shower and put on her makeup, allow some girl to help her dress in the flaming cloth and then, in that rich cloth, go off to be used as further punishment for Cristelle Dubois? Leni didn't like the thought of it, not one little bit.

She had reached the bungalow now, and mechanically she got out of her bathing gear, showered and dressed. It was lunchtime but she was not in the least hungry. She sat out on the veranda, staring into space, her mind buzzing and confused. "Try to be level-headed," she told herself. "Try to do some straight thinking." Her overpowering instinct was to run away to Guerney's, to lick her wounds with Dee and presently go home. But if she did that, mightn't she always be sorry? She remembered the previous night, the gentle way he had kissed her—it had not been an "all-out passionate" kiss. Then there was his insistence that she give him her promise that she was free. She knew very well he had meant free from Guerney and she had willingly given her promise. In return, he had promised that this evening was to be very special. Another memory? Or was she to be the one he would marry?

It was the first time she had dared to put this thought into words, and now there was an addendum. Was she to be his wife, and Daju his lover? His *current* lover, as Cristelle had insinuated. That thought brought her up short. She didn't know what to do. But she suspected she would go ahead and meet him tonight, just as she had gone ahead yesterday. It seemed to her that it was not Cristelle Dubois who was being punished, it was Leni Forrest. And she was foolish enough to keep asking for more.

A little later, she walked along the beach toward Guerney's and found Dee lying on the sand under a big umbrella, reading a letter. She looked up when Leni dropped down beside her with a cheerful, "Hello, Dee, how are things?" Leni saw that her eyes were angry and her cheeks red.

"Hello." Dee pushed back her corn yellow hair and threw her letter down on the sand. "Of all the cheek! I'm just absolutely wild, Len."

"Why, what's the trouble?"

"This letter from Charles. Saying, would you believe it, that he wishes I'd stop my nonsense and come home." She looked furiously angry rather than unhappy, and before Leni could do more than murmur, she went on, "Charles just *trusts* me, Len—he always has. So I know exactly what's happened. Guerney's written and told him tales that aren't true. It would just about serve that interfering brother of mine right if he came back tonight and found I'd made his tales true, it really would."

"Guerney's coming back tonight?"

"Yes. I got that bit of information in today's mail, too. And as soon as he turns up, I'm going to tell him just how rotten I think his tactics are—if I happen to be around."

"Why wouldn't you be around, Dee?" Leni asked, her heart sinking. Dee had an unpredictable temper and her once happy relationship with Guerney seemed to have disappeared altogether. It was odd, how she put Guerney in the wrong. It never seemed to occur to her that for an engaged girl, she had been behaving pretty badly. Leni was not surprised that even Charles's tolerance had finally come to an end. Dee had probably dropped enough hints in her letters to let him guess pretty plainly what she was up to. Quite possibly Guerney had had no hand in passing on information at all, but it was no use arguing with Dee. It never had been.

"If this load of mail had come a bit earlier on," said Dee, "I promise you I wouldn't have been around. It so happens that Dwight Halvorsen came to the bungalow to see me this morning and I told Ketut to let him in. I'm bored all by myself, Len—no one to talk to, nothing to do. Dwight wanted me to have dinner with him tonight at that restaurant on the beach where we went to the market one day, remember? There are bungalows to let near-by—not particularly class ones—and I know what must have been in his mind. So I said no. I wish I'd said yes now and made all Guerney's mean stories come true. Maybe it's not too late yet, and wouldn't he be just furious if he came home and found me gone? Then he'd really have something to make a fuss about."

"It would hardly be fair to Charles, Dee," Leni said dryly.

"Oh, blow Charles—if he chooses to believe Guerney rather than trust me." She turned her head away and Leni heard a sound that was suspiciously like a sniff. It was on the tip of her tongue to say, "We'll spend the evening together," but she stopped herself. She was going out with Kemp Savage. It was to be a very special evening.

She stayed with Dee a while longer, but at last she rose reluctantly. "I'll have to go, Dee. But I wish you'd promise me you won't do anything silly."

"Oh, don't worry, Len, I'm not entirely irresponsible. Who've you got a date with? Not Kemp Savage, now that other woman is around."

Somehow, Leni managed to avoid a direct answer, and with a half humorous, "Don't do anything I wouldn't do," was on her way.

Back at the bungalow, she lay down on the bed and rested. She wanted to look her best for Kemp and she wondered at her own silliness. In her way she was quite as foolish as Dee, for she was certainly rushing headlong into disaster. Dee had found Dwight exciting, and Leni found Kemp Savage far more than that. Her thoughts returned to what Cristelle had told her about Daju, and she found it almost impossible to believe. But then, as Cristelle had said, she was English and conventional and not at all used to these odd arrangements which were apparently accepted quite casually by people like Cristelle.

She was hungry when she finally rose, but she felt too excited to eat. She would be eating with Kemp, at any rate. She took a long refreshing shower and began to dress, to brush out her hair and fix her makeup in a careful leisurely way. She wondered how Kemp had progressed at the board meeting and whether his suggestions had been well received. She hoped he would tell her about it all.

Finally, she unfolded her *kamben gringsing* and looked at it thoughtfully. It was beautiful, the design delicate, intricate, and probably full of meaning of which she was ignorant. A little shiver ran through her at the thought that it had taken years to make—that it was intended to be worn on ceremonial occasions for possibly a hundred years to come. But because there was some imperfection in it, *she* was the one to wear it. Leni studied it carefully, but for the life of her she could find no fault or flaw. She went to the mirror holding it against herself and admitted that the subtle red became her, especially since she had applied some eye-shadow and darkened her long lashes. There was a discreet knock at the door and a young Balinese girl entered.

"*Selamat malan, Nona.* I am sent to help you dress." It was the girl Nani whom Leni had encountered at the pool once or twice before, and she carried with her two tissue-wrapped packages which she placed on the carved teak table at one side of the bedroom. Then, smiling at Leni, she took the flaming cloth and began quickly and expertly to drape it about the girl's slim body. There was ample length to take it over one shoulder where she fastened it with a small gold brooch. Then, after adjusting the folds to her liking, she took from one of her packages a wide sash made of some fine soft fabric like limpid gold. This she wound about Leni's narrow waist.

The effect was stunning—the bare shoulder, the form-fitting drapery, the wide gold sash. And yet—Leni looked at herself with a feeling of disappointment. There was something missing. She looked too simple, too unadorned.

Then from behind her came a faint rustle and the Balinese girl came toward her carrying an exquisite headdress, fragile and light and delicately wrought, yet in its way simple—composed of gold leaf flowers, its curved flexible headband studded with dark red stones. Leni held her breath as the girl lifted it with care and fastened it on her silver-pale hair. Her fringe showed a little below the headband, and limpid gold tassels hung over her ears.

Leni scarcely recognized herself. Suddenly she looked almost—exotic. She smiled wide-eyed into the mirror, and the black-haired, brown-eyed girl who stood at her shoulder smiled back at her. And yet she knew that her fairness could not compete with the exquisite beauty of the Balinese.

She thanked the girl, and her glance strayed back, fascinated, to her own reflection. Kemp would see her like this. In a few minutes more she would be with him, would see what was in his dark eyes that had been unreadable in the shadowy tropical night.

Her heart was beating fast in anticipation when a voice called from the veranda, "Are you there, Leni?"

She thought in surprise that it must be Kemp come to the bungalow for her and she called back, "Yes, I'm ready." But when she went on her sandalled feet through to the living room, followed by the little maid, it was Guerney Fisher and not Kemp Savage who stood there. His good-humored face was tense, and his blue eyes dark as he asked her sharply, "Is Dee here?"

"Dee? No." Leni stared at him in alarm. Many things

passed through her mind—the letter from Charles, Dwight's invitation, Dee's threat—and in the midst of it all she was asking stupidly, "Why? Isn't she at your bungalow?"

"I wouldn't be here if she were," said Guerney shortly. He was staring in some amazement at Leni's headdress, her sari, but for the moment he made no comment. He drew a folded sheet of paper from the pocket of his cotton jacket and handed it to Leni. "I came home to find this."

She scanned it quickly, while the Balinese girl waited at a discreet distance.

"Dear brother Guerney," she read. "Since you think the worst of me and have been mean enough to wreck my engagement, then I just don't care about anything any more. I'm going to meet Dwight and I probably shan't be home tonight. Dee."

Leni's face was ashen. She stared wordlessly at Guerney, who said grimly, "This has to be stopped before it's too late. Where's she gone? Come on, Leni, you should know—you promised me you'd not let her out of your sight."

"I didn't promise quite that," said Leni quietly. "All I can suggest is that—that she's gone to one of the beach restaurants with Dwight. And I'm sure she won't do anything really reckless."

"Well, no matter how sure you are, we can't afford to take any chances. So come along now, which beach has she gone to?"

"We went to a market there—oh, a long time ago. There are some beach bungalows," she faltered, trying hard to remember.

"So there are at most of the beaches. You'll have to do better than that."

Leni stared at him helplessly. "I can't remember the name. I can tell you how to get there—I think."

"Thinking's not good enough," said Guerney. "You can show me, Leni. Come on—right away. This is an emergency." He took her by the arm and began to propel her toward the door. "From the way Dee's behaved since she hit Bali, I'm not prepared to take any chances."

Leni felt herself torn in two. Of course she would have to go with Guerney, but she could not simply forget her appointment with Kemp. She remembered the day they had gone to market. They had gone in a *bemo*, she and Dwight and Dee, and when they had got there she had found herself deserted while the other two wandered off along the beach. She had seen some women with baskets full of fish that looked as though they were made of silver—and she had seen those bungalows—rather shabby bungalows, half hidden among the palm grooves . . . It shouldn't take all that long to get there and back. She told Guerney, "We'll have to be quick. I'm going out tonight."

"I gathered that." His voice was dry.

Leni ignored his tone. "And I'll have to write a note to Kemp to explain what's happened."

"*Kemp Savage?* My God! You girls are so irresponsible it's incredible!" Out of the corner of her eye she saw his hand go to his head. "I warned you not to play around there. Did he give you that gear you're wearing? And are you gullible enough to imagine he'll want nothing in return?"

Leni's color rose. "Yes, I am gullible enough. And I wish you'd mind your own business, Guerney. I'm not your sister."

She heard him muttering angrily as she sat down at the small writing table, thought hard, then wrote quickly. "Dear Kemp, Dee is in trouble and I have to help get her out of it. I'm afraid I shall be late for our appointment, but I hope you will understand and forgive me, and wait a little. Yours, Leni." She folded it twice, wrote Kemp's name on it and handed it to Nani, telling her, "Please give this to Mr. Savage."

Then she snatched up a light stole to cover her dress and hurried with Guerney through the garden to his waiting car. On a side path she saw Cristelle Dubois walking—tall, slender, dressed in a long white and silver gown.

They had barely driven through the hotel gates when Guerney said abruptly, "You and Dee both had better get on the plane for home tomorrow. I've never met two such hopelessly star-struck individuals in my life. I find it hard to believe that you, who were such a level-headed girl, should be dressed up as you are tonight for God knows what kind of a caper with a man who's long passed the stage of youthful romanticism. I warned you, Leni—"

Leni said wearily, "Please don't go on, Guerney. I don't want to hear. And if you can't leave me alone," she added with sudden spirit, "then please pull up and let me out of this car, or else I shall jump out."

"All right. It will keep," said Guerney coldly.

Leni watched out for the road she was sure led to the village by the beach. She knew very well how she must appear to Guerney, dressed up in these extravagantly exotic clothes that she could not possibly afford. She knew she couldn't explain to him about Kemp. How could she expect him to understand what she did not understand herself? Besides, Guerney was so utterly matter-of-fact and realistic, not at all the carefree, casual artistic type she and Dee had always imagined him. For perhaps the first time, she had an inkling of what had made Dee escape from him and Janet and get away on her own.

You can't dream about a tropical island holiday for

years and then relinquish it all at the drop of a hat. It was a once-in-a-lifetime thing. She and Dee were young, they wanted more than sightseeing and souvenirs. She, Leni, wanted considerably more. Of course, for Dee, it was an added complication that she was already engaged, and in her heart, Leni believed that Dee should never have come to Bali at all.

They found the beach and the restaurant, with the minimum of trouble. Leni stayed in the car, for it would have been embarrassing to appear in her gold headdress and she dared not remove it, for she was quite sure she would never be able to get it back in place herself. She watched Guerney stride off with a grim and purposeful tread to the glow of oil lamps, the sounds of music and laughter, then she sat waiting and shivering, her thoughts divided between herself and Dee.

It was after a quarter to nine now. Would Kemp be waiting for her? Would he understand, or would he be angry about her lateness? She wondered what he had planned for this special evening, and she even thought longingly of dinner, for she was very hungry. Silhouetted against the shining moonlit sea, she could see the shapes of the beach bungalows. Lights glowed from some of them, and on a porch a boy was strumming a guitar. It all looked very idyllic and romantic—just as she and Dee had always imagined it. But the thought of Dee in one of those bungalows alone with Dwight was far from romantic, and Leni felt tense and edgy as she waited for Guerney to reappear.

When he came, he was alone. He climbed into the car and started it up. "She wasn't in the restaurant. I insisted on looking in the bungalows—the fellow didn't like it at all, but I paid him well. She's not there—and neither is Halvorsen. So what do we do now?"

"I don't know," said Leni helplessly, as he drove slowly back along the road they had come by. She couldn't help remarking, "She was terribly upset that you'd told tales about her to Charles, you know."

Guerney looked at her in amazement. "So that's what I'm supposed to have done! Well, I didn't tell tales at all. Charles is no fool. He's probably figured it out from her own letters to him. I don't know exactly what he's done about it now, but had I been in his place I'd have issued her with an ultimatum long ago. In my opinion, it's a pity he hadn't done just that. I've been at my wits' end trying to prevent her from wrecking her own engagement."

"I'm sure she won't," said Leni, a little desperately, for she was not sure at all. Dee was capable of doing quite extraordinarily silly things on the spur of the moment.

"It's a pity," Guerney commented presently, "that you didn't carry out your pact with me. I can see I expected far too much of you." And he cast a disapproving look at the trembling flowers of her gold headdress. "Well, we'll try the *losmen* next."

If only she was there, thought Leni. She was going to be later than ever, but she had to help Guerney find Dee. Anyhow, she would explain it all to Kemp when she saw him, and if in her heart she feared it was not going to be all that easy. . . . "Well," thought Leni, "it never has been easy—not one minute of my friendship with Kemp Savage."

They drew a blank at the *losmen* too, and Leni said, "I'll have to call in at the hotel, Guerney. It's getting so late—"

"Don't worry. That's where we're going next. We may catch up with Halvorsen's movements somewhere there. I should have tried that in the first place instead of listening to your scatterbrained ideas."

That hurt more than a little, for she had genuinely tried to help. And now—she could imagine what Kemp would think if he saw her arriving in Guerney's car. She would have a great deal more explaining to do!

"Please drop me off at the gate," she began, and Guerney broke in irritably, "Don't worry. I haven't the time to interfere in your love life at the moment, Leni. I'm more concerned about tracking down my sister and her would-be lover. I'll carry on without your help."

He let her out at the gate and she saw him drive on ahead of her. She hurried towards the hotel, up the steps, through the glass door and into the foyer. Kemp was not there, but after the first spasm of shock she was not badly worried. He would hardly sit there waiting for her! He'd have left a message at the reception desk.

Leni was feeling self-conscious and a little dishevelled, but she dared not take time to find a mirror and attend to her appearance. She wished she had not left her stole in Guerney's car. . . . She hurried across the cool tiles to the desk and asked the clerk if there was a message for her, waited in agony as he searched in a file, and could not believe it when he shook his head.

"No, Miss Forrest. Was there something in particular you were expecting?"

She hesitated. "I thought—I thought Mr. Savage might have left a letter for me," she faltered.

"I am sorry—no. Mr. Savage is at dinner with the visitors to the conference. Is there something I can do for you, Miss Forrest?"

Leni shook her head. She felt dizzy and suddenly very very sick. Was it to the *conference dinner* that Kemp had invited her? She turned away and found a chair half hidden by a tall palm in a metal pot where she would not feel so conspicuous, dressed as she was. Of course, she should have realized that his "special" invitation was to something like that! She should have known that dinner parties and dancing were inseparable from conferences, even in the limited apartments at present attached to the hotel. And Kemp had invited her, Leni, to that! It would be a far from intimate meeting, and yet all the other women present would be the wives and daughters of board members! It was certainly to have been a special evening, and she knew it was a great honor to have been invited. By now, the dinner must be nearly over. She could not possibly go in. If Kemp had wanted her to, he would surely have left a message to that effect.

But he had left no message at all! It was incomprehensible to Leni. Hadn't he understood? And if the dinner couldn't wait, couldn't he at least have suggested she should join in the dancing afterwards?

Or was he just so hard-hearted he thought she should desert her friend who was in trouble?

Leni wondered anew what had happened to Dee. But she simply had not the strength now to go and look for Guerney. She was feeling faint and ill. She leaned against the tall back of the chair, and beads of perspiration formed on her brow. Suddenly the featherlight headdress seemed too heavy, the gold sash around her waist too tight. "I must be hungry," she thought. She had eaten nothing since her light breakfast. She closed her eyes—and for a moment lost consciousness. . . .

A murmuring of voices brought her back to herself, and she saw through the palm leaves that shielded her a group of people cross the foyer and begin to mount the long curved stairway that led to the private lounge on the first floor. They were distinguished-looking people, some of the men silver-haired, all of the women fashionably and beautifully dressed. For a second, Leni pictured herself amongst them, standing out in her lovely Balinese style dress, her shining leaf crown.

And then she saw Kemp, more handsome and dark than ever in evening dress, and at his side, Cristelle Dubois in white and silver, looking up into his face, laughing. With lightning clarity, Leni understood it all. She understood perfectly why Kemp had gone ahead, had left her no message, and she wondered at herself for being deluded so long. Cristelle had told her, and she had preferred in her silly star-struck state not to believe. Cristelle had said, "Kemp is using you to punish me." Now she knew it was true, and now she knew Kemp had decided that Cristelle had been punished enough. Leni, mattered no more.

She had half risen to her feet, but her shaking legs refused to support her and she sank back in the chair again, thankful that he had not seen her.

There would never, ever again, be a message for Leni Forrest from Kemp Savage.

The voices and laughter died away, the foyer was empty except for Dwight Halvorsen and a red-haired girl who came in from the garden. Leni thought dimly, thankfully, "So Dee isn't with him." And then she thought, "I shall have to get something to eat." There seemed nothing else she could think of without bursting into bitter, anguished tears.

She didn't know how much longer she stayed in that chair, but finally she rose to her feet and reached the bungalow. From there she telephoned and asked for a tray to be sent to her room. She looked at herself in the mirror, and the gold headdress, the beautifully draped sari seemed a mockery. Leni thought that this evening held the bitterest, most shattering moments of her whole life. Guerney was right; she had been a stupid, gullible girl, far more foolish than Dee had ever been. Her holiday on the Island of Light would be an unbearable memory for a long, long time.

She turned away from her white face and stricken dark eyes at the sound of a discreet knock on the door. In the living-room, her supper tray had arrived, and close on the heels of the Balinese waitress came Guerney Fisher, and a bright-eyed, unrepentant-looking Dee.

Guerney said, "Dee was in the Coffee House. I saw your light and thought you'd like to know. What's happened to your date?"

"It's off," said Leni. She tried to smile, but she couldn't. She was aware that Dee was looking at her get-up in amazement, and she wished that they would both go away and leave her to weep or to sleep. Instead they sat down, and Guerney said, "Go ahead with your supper—you're hungry," and Leni forced herself to eat some of the rice savory and to drink the black coffee. She was aware that Dee was looking uncomfortable and a little guilty now, and she wondered if she had played a trick on them all—pretending she was going off to meet Dwight when she had no intention of doing any such thing. It would be like Dee to have done that to Guerney, upset as she was over Charles's letter.

"Dee's going home tomorrow afternoon," Guerney said. "How about you, Leni? Have you had enough fun?"

Yes, Leni had had well and truly enough fun, and all the heartache that went with it. She didn't want ever again to see this island, or Kemp Savage, or Cristelle Dubois. She had been made sport of, and she would be forgotten as soon as she had gone. But for Leni, the forgetting was going to take years.

She told Guerney, "Yes, I'll go with Dee." Her eyes were bright, her tears unshed. "I'll pack and come along with you now."

"The morning will do," said Guerney practically, after casting a quick glance around the room at her various belongings. "You have to pay your bill, and I imagine you'll want to return all that finery to whoever—lent it to you." There was just a shade of pity in his blue eyes as he finished abruptly, "We'll be on our way and leave you to it."

"Guerney wants to lecture me," said Dee with a brightness that was forced. "He hasn't caught on yet that lecturing is the worst possible way of dealing with girls like me. Charles is going to be sorry he tried it, too. I'm really looking forward to my next meeting with Charles." She made a face and grinned at Leni, but it was an uneasy grin. Leni and Guerney were so obviously outside her cheeky, defiant mood.

Guerney said roughly, "Come along, Dee—can't you see Leni is dead tired and wants to have some peace?"

They went, but Dee came back to hug Leni and whisper, "I didn't mean to ruin it for you, Len—I was just playing a trick on Guerney, to give him a fright. And you look so beautiful—and you missed your date because of me! I am sorry, Len. Truly."

Leni said nothing. She knew that if she spoke she'd break down altogether, but she managed a forgiving smile, hugged Dee back and let her go.

Once the door was shut and she was alone, she shed her tears. She knew they were futile, but it was a long time before she regained control of herself and began to move about the bedroom, packing her things ready for her departure in the morning. It was no use going to bed yet.

She would only lie awake and probably begin crying with self-pity again.

She had gone into the living room for her stole that Guerney had brought back when the door was suddenly flung open and she was confronted by the dark towering form of Kemp Savage.

CHAPTER ELEVEN

Leni's heart leapt. Had he come for her, after all? How lucky that she had not changed out of her sari! A minute or two at the mirror, and she would be ready to go with him. Makeup would hide the traces of her tears. . . .

A smile was trembling on her lips when she realized there was no answering smile from him. His dark eyes raked her over coldly, cynically, and then he said in a voice that cut like a dagger of ice, "You're back early from your little jaunt, Miss Forrest. I saw your lights from the balcony upstairs, and it seemed to me there were a few words to be said that might as well be said now."

He had stepped inside and closed the door behind him, and Leni watched him in a kind of fear as he came closer to her. Three slow, purposeful steps. Then he reached out and put two fingers under her chin and raised her face, not in the least gently, so that for a moment her eyes met his fully, and then her lashes came down. She felt strangely faint. Of course she meant nothing to him. Of course it was as she had realized, and her moment of hope had been like the last tongue of flame licking up from a dying fire. Cristelle had been punished enough and Kemp Savage had no further use for Leni Forrest. For that reason, he might have left her decently alone.

"You've shed a few tears, haven't you?" he said, and she could feel the warmth of his breath on her forehead, he was so close. "I'm glad you've been chastened, Leni Forrest. Girls like you only learn the hard lessons of love through anguish·"

Leni's eyes closed tightly, she willed herself not to tremble. Could he have said anything so heartless, so cruel? How crazy she had been ever to think he had any feeling for her at all! She knew that the tears she had shed for him showed plainly in her face, but what had she ever done to be spoken to like this? "Girls like you"—girls with innocent hearts who fell hopelessly and devotedly in love. Did girls like that need to be chastened, anguished? And what of men like Kemp Savage, whose ruthless charm made a mockery of such love?

She said on a tense uneven breath, "You didn't care that I couldn't come tonight, did you? I should never have asked you—expected you—to wait."

"You surely shouldn't have. It's not the simplest thing, to delay a formal dinner for twenty guests, not by any means." She dared a swift glance at him through her lashes. His hand had dropped from her face and now he was lighting a cigarette. And because her legs were shaking, she groped for a chair and sat down, but he moved too, and stood like a dark shadow over her.

She said with an attempt at dignity, "I'm sorry about what happened. I wrote you I was sorry. And," she added with a flash of spirit, "You didn't let me know it was a . . . a dinner for twenty I was invited to."

He drew on his cigarette and two minute red lights showed in the blackness of his eyes. "You thought you were to be dressed up"—and he nodded casually at her attire—"just for me? That I'd sent Nani with Daju's golden flowers to adorn you for a little private tête-à-tête?"

Daju's golden flowers! What kind of a fool had he meant to make of her? Leni bit hard on her lip. Cristelle would have recognized those flowers, and how she would have laughed to herself. She'd have snapped her fingers at the whole ridiculous escapade. Cristelle was so broad-minded she could tolerate the man she loved having a dancing girl as mistress. She could look on cynically while he amused himself—to punish her—with a foolish young girl on holiday.

Suddenly the golden headdress seemed to prick Leni's scalp, and she raised her hands to it and with fingers that shook searched for the fine clips that held it in place. She wanted to tell him to take his flowers, to give them back to his dancing girl, but her lips would not move and her voice would not come. She felt his fingers curve over hers as he stooped and found the clips with a quickness and surety that betrayed that he had handled this headdress many times before. Then he lifted the beautiful flowers from her head and laid them casually on a table nearby.

"I hope," he said chillingly, "that Guerney Fisher was impressed by your appearance. It's good to know that someone had the benefit."

She stared up at him wide-eyed. "Guerney Fisher?"

His lip curled. "Wasn't it with Guerney Fisher that you left the grounds tonight—no more than a few minutes before you were to have met me? No lies, please."

Leni felt her face go deathly pale. "Yes, it was, but . . . but I explained to you. Dee was in trouble. I had to go with Guerney to help find her. If I'd known you saw us, I'd have—"

"You'd have what?" he drawled. He was looking at her without pity, without belief. "You'd have thought of some other more convincing lie? Actually, I didn't see you, Leni, but I drew my own conclusions when I was told you'd left with a "handsome fair-haired fellow." I'd read your little note, and I'd already remarked to myself that you were being more than a little unimaginative in falling back on your too-accommodating friend once more for your excuses."

Her voice was low. "I wasn't making excuses. Guerney

was worried sick about Dee. We didn't know where she was."

"No?" His dark brows tilted disbelievingly, and now there was nothing benevolent about him; he was all demon. "You'd not have had far to look, seeing she'd been at the poolside and then in the Coffee House here from about six o'clock on. Even if you hadn't been aware of it, then I think her brother would have been. In any case, why the alarm so early in the evening? Your friend—like you—is obviously no innocent."

Leni said tiredly, "I don't think it's any use trying to explain to you. Guerney has been worried about Dee for a long time now, and when he got back from Djakarta tonight she'd gone, and left him a note that was meant to worry him . . . and did."

She looked up at him hopefully. His eyes had narrowed, he looked at his cigarette, stooped and crushed it out in an ashtray. Leni thought that his hand was shaking, but that must be her imagination. When he straightened up he did not look at her, but through the window into the lamplit garden.

"I see. Or at least I am beginning to see, all too plainly. So Guerney Fisher has been away in Djakarta! Hence your . . . freedom! You know, Miss Forrest, for a girl of such tender years you've certainly done a very sophisticated job of deception. You've really had me fooled, for quite some little time. And that's an accomplishment. I'm not easily deceived. I never go into anything with my eyes half-closed, never. I can see now that I should have been even more on my guard after that first performance you put on in Singapore, of the nice young English girl following a dream—and a schoolgirl friend."

Leni put her head up. She had reached the end of her endurance. "You'll be glad to hear then that there won't be any further performances, for your benefit or for anyone else's. And—and I'm sure you'll have no trouble finding another unwitting accomplice to dance to your tune while you're carrying out one of your—your *punishing* plans. We shall be leaving on the plane for Singapore tomorrow and . . . and you can go ahead and arrange your future without any further help or hindrance from me. And now—I'm tired, Mr. Savage. I wish you'd go away and leave me alone."

He stared at her for five seconds without speaking. Then, slowly, "After tears comes forgiveness. . . . So you're leaving."

"Yes," said Leni.

He took up the gold leaf flowers, and they scintillated and shone mockingly. "Then this is goodbye, Leni Forrest."

Leni said through lips that were hard to control, "Yes, it's goodbye, Mr. Savage. I shall leave the sari for you at the desk in the morning. And the ivory necklace," she added.

"As you wish," he said unsmilingly. And in a moment she heard the door shut behind him.

In the morning after a ghastly night (had she ever thought she had spent a bad night before?) Leni rose early, finished her packing, and with scarcely more than a glance in the mirror at her ravaged face, took the package containing the *kamben grinsing* and the Barong necklace to the hotel to leave with the clerk. She knew she was safe from the chance of an encounter with Kemp, for the conference would be under way once more. She took her time about moving over to Guerney's bungalow, reluctant to face Dee's regrets or the questions that she and Guerney would be sure to ask.

In fact, it was not nearly so bad as she had feared. Tact

or sympathy or both kept brother and sister from mentioning last night, and as well Dee was quite cheerful and excited about returning to England and having her little battle with Charles.

They were taking the luggage out to the car after lunch, and Guerney was complaining good-humoredly enough about the amount of extras Dee had collected, when Kemp Savage flung the gate open and strode into the garden. Leni uttered a silent moan of anguish, and felt the color drain from her face. He was carrying the packet she had left for him at the desk, and shrinkingly she recalled his arrogant, "I don't take gifts back, Miss Forrest. It's yours whether you want it or not." She thought she would die rather than take those "souvenirs" back from him.

He sent her one dark unsmiling glance, then addressed himself abruptly to Guerney. "I hope you're planning to give this girl a good life in England, Fisher." Guerney stared at him uncomprehendingly, and he continued, "Is it altogether too objectionable to you if I insist she keep a couple of small gifts I made her?"

The two men stood face to face, and their mutual dislike was patent. After a hostile second, Guerney shrugged. "Leni can please herself what souvenirs she takes away with her. Once I've packed her off home they can't do much harm."

Kemp frowned and his eyes narrowed. "Do I understand that you're not leaving today?"

"No, I'm not leaving today." Guerney turned his back and lifted two suitcases into the car. He could not have said more plainly or more rudely, "You're not welcome here." Dee's face was alive with curiosity, and Leni stared down at her neat court shoes, trying to pretend that none of this was of any interest to her.

"Then you're not planning to marry Leni right away?"

Guerney swung around in astonishment. "Good God, no! Not right away or ever. What gave you that idea? I'm engaged to a girl in Djakarta, though none of that is any of your business. . . . Just one thing I'd like you to make a note of, however—Leni is definitely taking off on the plane today. And for your own future reference, I'd advise you to take care who you choose next time you want to hand out a helping of sophisticated holiday fun."

Kemp said pleasantly, "If I didn't have other things on my mind I could knock you down for that remark, Fisher. However, you go ahead and take your sister to the airport or marry your girl in Djakarta or whatever. But Leni," Leni knew he was looking at her now, but she dared not to raise her eyes, "Leni is staying here. I have things to say to her that are hardly in the nature of—holiday fun. Well, Leni?" His voice had sharpened. "Is that clear enough?"

Leni had no idea what to make of it all, and in her heart she begged for mercy. She had taken enough in the way of shock treatment in the past twenty-four hours. It was almost a relief when Guerney said briefly, "We've made our plans and we're sticking to them. You stay out of this, Savage."

"Leni?" Kemp insisted softly.

Close to her, Dee whispered, "Stay, Leni. I think you should—you don't have to come with me."

Kemp said once more, "Leni?" and he came to put his hand gently on her shoulder. "Look at me, Leni . . . tell me."

She raised her head slowly, and there was that faint smile, deep, deep in his eyes, that she had seen once before—the day he had taken her to see the little Buddha and kissed her in the sunlight on the green hillside. She said helplessly, "Yes, I'll stay."

"You damn well won't!" snapped Guerney, and moved forward as though he was going to tear her forcibly from the man who still touched her shoulder and looked down into her eyes.

Dee cried out indignantly, "Let her do what she wants, Guerney. You have absolutely no right to tell Leni what to do."

"No right at all," agreed Kemp smoothly. "Leni is going to marry me."

Leni gasped. He simply could not have said that! She stared at him stupidly. "Cristelle Dubois—Daju," she thought wildly. "I could never turn a blind eye." But she looked back at Kemp, and in a whisper she said—and was appalled at herself, "Yes."

The next few minutes seemed not to exist. Dee hugged her and said, "Oh, I'm glad, Len! It's just like we always dreamed." And Guerney said with cold disapproval, "If you need me, Leni, I shall be back soon." And then the car had carried them both away, and she stood in the garden alone with Kemp.

Very, very much alone with Kemp.

She said weakly, "I thought you were at a conference."

"I walked out on it."

"You'll have to go back."

"Presently. But right now, you look as if you might run away from me. I don't want to have to lock you up—and I shouldn't feel sure of you unless I did." His lips smiled but his eyes were deeply serious and questioning. "So Guerney Fisher is engaged to a girl in Djakarta."

"Yes. He has been for a long time. But," she added warily, "I don't need to be consoled, thank you."

His dark eyebrows went up. "It's not consolation I'm offering you." He glanced at the bungalow with its shadowed eaves and wide windows. "This is no place for us to talk. Come. We'll find somewhere more to our taste."

He took her through the garden and along a pathway by the beach, to a grove overhung by bougainvillea. And there, without a further word, he took her in his arms and kissed her until she was breathless.

"So you're going to marry me, Leni Forrest."

"Yes," she said on a sigh. It was useless to resist. "But. . . ."

"But what?"

"Cristelle . . . I thought—"

"Then you must stop thinking. Cristelle and I had a brief affair, but it was over before I met you."

"But you—"

"I stay on good terms with her. It's politics. Her father's an important board member," he said dryly.

"You took her to the dinner last night when I wasn't there."

"Never. There was an empty place beside me—yours. And an emptier place in my heart."

They looked at each other for a long moment, but there was something else Leni had to know. "Daju," she said painfully. "Daju is—important to you?"

"Yes," he said simply, and she felt a stab of fear. "Daju I've known since she was an infant, Leni. I was present at the ceremony when her little feet were first put to the unclean earth. So," his smile was tender and thoughtful, "Daju is very special to me. I've seen her grow up, I've seen her wonderful talent develop. Rather sadly, I've seen her change from the sweet simple village girl she once was, develop more sophisticated tastes and wants. Now she's to realize a great ambition. She's been asked to join an international dancing troupe, and she leaves this island in a few weeks' time, possibly forever.

Hence the rather lavish gifts I've made her, and of which I sense you disapprove."

Leni shook her head. She didn't in the least begrudge Daju her gifts now that she understood.

"And—me?" she breathed.

"I love you, Leni Forrest. I want all of you. Is there a shred that belongs to Guerney Fisher?"

She pushed him from her a little and said mischievously, "Guerney Fisher I've known since I was a little girl. I thought he was a romantic artist—which he's not. He thought I was a level-headed girl—which I'm not. He's my big brother as well as Dee's," she finished, "and he's never thought of me as more than a sister."

He looked down at her quizzically. "I find it hard to believe that any man can think of you as no more than a sister. You're so exquisitely beautiful and alluring, my little silver and gold girl. How many times have I tried to deny that allure, because I thought I must share it with another man! Do you remember that night in the market at Denpasar when you looked at me with your eyes shining and that cheap batik cloth draped across your body? My God, what I suffered on your account! I've always been too proud to compete for any girl, and yet you I couldn't leave alone. Such pride is a serious fault. Do you think, if I promise to try to temper it, you can put up with me for a lifetime, Leni?"

His arm was about her and her head rested on his shoulder, and she looked dreamily from the green shade to the strip of white coral sand and the glitter of blue sea beyond, and said on a sigh of complete happiness, "Yes, Kemp. Forever."

SHADOW OF THE PAST

Shadow of the Past
Monica Douglas

Sara knew something had to be done — and she was the one to do it.

Too busy enjoying her work in the United States to give the family business any attention, she had believed her half-brother David's assurances. Now David was dead, and she arrived home to find Blake's Store faced with bankruptcy.

If only her mission didn't include facing Brent Maxwell! That arrogant, intolerant man wouldn't be likely to grant any favors.

Still, she had to try. Sara was determined to save Blake's; and seeing Brent Maxwell was the first step!

CHAPTER ONE

It had been raining when Sara Blake stepped off the plane from the United States, and it was still raining steadily when the taxi drew up at the apartment block that was her final destination.

She stood for a moment, looking at the dreary prospect, and her already low spirits sank even further. It was exactly, she thought, as if the skies had decided to form a fitting background to her sad and sudden homecoming.

She turned as the attendant came through the ornate doors and greeted her questioningly.

"I want Mrs. Blake's apartment, please," she said.

"That's the penthouse floor. This way, madam."

He picked up her case and she followed him through the luxurious entrance hall into the elevator, which swept them quickly upward, then along a thickly carpeted corridor to a door halfway along it.

He rang the bell and, as they waited for it to be answered, said conversationally, "Mrs. Blake's in, I know. She doesn't go out much, not since Mr. Blake's death. That was a very terrible thing, wasn't it, madam?"

"Yes," Sara answered briefly. She was relieved when at that moment the door opened; she knew she could not bear to talk about her half-brother's recent tragic death with a stranger.

"Sara! At last! I was beginning to think you'd never come."

Valerie Blake flung her arms around her sister-in-law, taking no notice of the attendant who still stood, holding Sara's case, watching them with interest.

Sara kissed her and loosened the clinging arms.

"I came as soon as I could, Val." She turned to the attendant. "If you'll bring the case in, please. . . ."

She waited until he had put it down in the square hall, then tipped him and said firmly, "Thank you. That will be all."

"Thank you, madam," he answered, then made a dignified exit.

"I wish I was as good as you are at getting rid of all the nosy people," Valerie sighed.

Sara took off her coat and flung it over the nearest chair, shaking back her thick honey gold hair.

"Has it been very bad, Val?"

"Yes, simply terrible. I don't know how I've managed. Why didn't you come before, Sara? You must have known how much I needed you."

"I'm sorry, dear. Johnnie and I were traveling around the country and your telegrams were delivered to my apartment. I didn't get them until I arrived home. Johnnie got me on the first available plane. What happened, Val?"

Valerie opened a door at the end of the hall.

"Come in here and I'll tell you all about it. I've made some sandwiches. Do you want coffee or tea?"

"Tea, please. Gallons of it. I'm so thirsty."

Sara followed her into the ultramodern kitchen, one part of her mind noting the expensive equipment while the other was concentrated on what her sister-in-law was telling her between nervous puffs of the cigarette she had lit.

"Was he killed . . . instantly, Val?"

"Yes. I couldn't believe it at first. David was always going to Paris. He was used to the traffic there. It didn't seem possible that he could have been killed."

"No."

"It was awful, Sara. I thought I'd go crazy in those first few days. I don't know what I'd have done without Terry. He saw to everything."

"The funeral?"

"Yes. He went over to Paris and arranged it all. David was buried over there. I thought it best," she added defensively.

"You were probably right, dear," Sara said, but in her heart she wished passionately that circumstances had allowed her to be there to follow her beloved half-brother on his last journey. "I'm glad Terry was still at Blake's to help you."

Valerie looked at her in surprise. "Why shouldn't he be?"

"Oh, no reason."

Sara's reply was casual because she did not want to put into words her own conviction that Terry White was ambitious and thrusting. She wouldn't have been surprised to hear that he had gone to work for another company where his opportunity for promotion was better than at Blake's Store.

But apparently she had been mistaken, and she was thankful now that he, with his valuable knowledge of the family firm, would still be there to help them.

"He's taken charge of the store, you know."

"Has he? How's the business going, Val?"

"I've no idea." Val's voice was offhand and uninterested. "You know I don't know anything about it. David never discussed it with me. Even after he sold the house and used the money on the store . . . my money, Sara, because my father bought the house for me . . . he didn't tell me what he was doing."

"He didn't tell me much either," Sara said, remembering guiltily that she had been too engrossed in her own job to have any time to spare for Blake's. "I only heard from him when he wanted me to back him as the only other shareholder."

"Terry says I'll get David's shares now because I'm his wife. He says I'll be in control, so he's been telling me all about everything, but I don't understand half of what he says. It all sounds so depressing, too."

"Terry told you that? But. . . ."

She stopped, and after a moment Val asked inquiringly, "But what?"

"Oh, nothing really. What's so depressing about everything?"

"Oh, I don't know. He was saying something about the business being deep in debt to a man called Maxwell. At least I think that's the name."

"In debt? That's not possible. And who's Maxwell?"

Valerie shrugged. "I've no idea. Anyway, I may have the name wrong. You know I'm no good at business things, Sara."

"Never mind, love. I'm here now and I'll see to everything for you."

"You're going to stay, then?" Val asked eagerly.

"For a week or two, anyway."

"Is that all? Oh, Sara, you can't go away so soon and leave me here all alone. I'll never be able to stand it. . . ."

"But we're so busy, Johnnie and I. Things are pretty hectic in our particular world of finance. . . ."

"Oh, he can spare you, I'm sure. You can't be all that necessary."

Sara smiled. "Johnnie thinks I am."

"Does he?" Val looked at her eagerly, her volatile mind immediately diverted by the implication she thought she could read in Sara's answer. "Is he in love with you, Sara? Are you going to be married?"

"Here, don't go so fast!" Then as she saw the disappointment in Val's expressive face, she added, "He says he is, and I've never met anyone I like better than him."

"I'm so glad, Sara. I hope things turn out better for you than they have for me." Val's china blue eyes filled with tears. "You don't know what it's like to be left alone so suddenly."

Sara took her hand in both of hers.

"Don't cry, Val. And remember, you're not really alone. You've still got Jamie."

"But he's away at school all the time."

"Hasn't he been home at all?"

"No. The principal said it'd be better if he didn't come."

"He was probably right."

"He was not! My son should have been here with me. Oh, Sara, what's going to become of us both if there's really no money?"

"Who said there's no money?"

"Terry."

"You must have misunderstood him, Val. Blake's has always been a profitable business, and the last accounts I saw looked very healthy."

"Did they really, Sara?"

"Yes. Now stop worrying. I'll go and see Terry tomorrow and get everything cleared up."

Val smiled at her gratefully. "I'm so glad you've come home, Sara. Now everything will be all right, I know it will."

It was late when they went to bed that night, and Sara did not wake as early as she had planned to the next morning. It was afternoon when she left the apartment to go to the store, but she was not worried. In spite of what

232

Valerie had told her, she was sure there was very little to worry about.

She had taken a good look at the apartment that morning and had been astonished by its luxuriousness. The rich carpeting, curtains and furniture must, she was sure, have cost a great deal of money, and if David had been able to live there, there could be very little wrong with the family business.

She felt a nostalgic stirring of memory as she walked along the street where Blake's Store had been since it was first opened by her father.

It had been a small fabric shop then, but as time went on he had bought the stores on each side. It had remained a conservative and rather old-fashioned fabric store, and while Sara had sympathized with her half-brother's desire to modernize it, she had felt sad that in the process it was bound to change.

But she was not prepared for the drastic changes that had taken place, and had walked past the store before she realized she had done so.

She went slowly back again, seeing the magnificent new windows, the costly window design and the imposing entrance, and knew the first stirrings of doubt.

Nothing David had told her in his infrequent letters had prepared her for the extensive alterations that had been made. She could hardly recognize it as the same place.

People passed her, but she didn't see them, though the business side of her brain, so well trained by Johnnie, noted that the site was still a busy one, as her father had always said it was.

She shook her head and went into the store, the glass doors opening automatically and closing behind her as she stepped on and off the mat. The store was brilliantly lighted and very busy, but it was all completely strange to her. It took her a while before she got her bearings.

Three years earlier, when she had left home to go to the United States, a dark staircase had led to the upper floor where the workshops and her father's office had been.

Now, at the rear of the store, an escalator moved upward. She stepped on to it and was whisked into an opulent, perfumed foyer with a white and gold table set on a rich deep blue carpet. The color was picked up in the velvet upholstery of a number of fragile chairs, and the whole room was reflected again and again in the mirrors lining the walls.

There was no one seated at the table and she hesitated, wondering where she could find Terry. As she did so she saw with relief a woman walking toward her along a side passageway.

"Excuse me, could you tell me. . . ." Sara began, then started forward, her dark eyes lighting up in a smile. "Mollie! Is it really you? Am I pleased to see you!"

The woman stared at her in astonishment.

"Why, Sara! I didn't know you'd come home."

"I only arrived yesterday. How are things going here?"

Mollie hesitated.

"All right, I suppose," she said at last. "Not that I know very much about it. We certainly seem busy enough, but there have been a lot of changes, as you can see."

"Yes, indeed. It looks like something at Palm Beach. It must have cost a mint, Mollie."

"I suppose so. It seems to be paying off all right."

Sara looked at her, puzzled by her tone.

"Don't you know? I'd have thought in your job. . . ."

"I'm not head of sales any more, Sara, so I'm out of touch. Céleste is in charge now. Mr. White brought her over from France a couple of years ago. I'm in the sewing room, a kind of glorified storekeeper, really."

Mollie's voice was harsh with the bitterness of failure, and Sara put her hand gently on her arm in an attempt to comfort her.

"That's a very important, job, Mollie. You know what Dad always said . . . the store couldn't function without an efficient sewing room and storekeeper. That's true, isn't it?"

"I suppose so. I'm lucky to be here at all. Most of the old hands have gone now and those of us who are left . . . we don't know from day to day what's going to happen."

She broke off, and Sara realized for the first time that this woman, who had been with her father for so many years, was no longer young and that she was afraid, deeply afraid, that she might lose her job. Perhaps she would find it difficult or even impossible to get another one.

"Don't worry, Mollie. I'm back now and I'll see you're all right," Sara said impulsively.

Mollie smiled.

"Thank you, though I don't suppose you'll want to stay here. You'll have grown away from us all, and I wouldn't blame you for that. Ah, but things have changed since your father died."

"He would have been the first to say we ought to move with the times," Sara reminded her.

"Yes, but not run past them. They do say that things are pretty bad. That Brent Maxwell is the real owner. . . ."

"Brent Maxwell." Sara echoed the name, remembering Val's mention of it the previous day. "Who is he, Mollie? And how can he be the owner? We're the owners, Mrs. David and me."

Mollie flushed uncomfortably.

"I'm only repeating rumors and gossip, Sara, something I've never done before. But there's a lot of unrest and conjecture in the store. What am I thinking about?" she added, obviously changing the subject. "Going on like this and never saying a word about your loss!"

"It's all right, Mollie. It's . . . it's difficult to believe, but. . . ."

"Those Paris drivers! Everyone says they're a menace! Though Mr. David had been over there so often you'd have thought he'd be well used to them, wouldn't you? And his lovely car he was so proud of, all smashed up, too. I suppose it was a case of familiarity breeding contempt," she finished with a sigh.

"I expect so. I'd better go and find Terry. Is he still in the same office?"

"No. He moved into Mr. David's after . . . the one your father used to have. That way, Sara."

"I see," Sara said slowly. "Thanks, Mollie. I'm glad you were the first person I met. It's made me feel less . . . strange."

CHAPTER TWO

Sara watched her until she was out of sight, then went slowly along the passage toward the office that had been her father's, then David's, and which had now been appropriated by Terry. Her feet made no sound on the thick carpet.

She had accepted what Mollie had said without showing any reaction, as if she had thought it a perfectly natural thing for Terry to have done. But beneath her calm exterior she was aware of a resentment out of proportion to the offense.

She stopped outside the white door, remembering how often she had turned the handle and run into her father's office when she was a child. The paintwork had been dark and chipped then, giving no indication of the fairyland of color waiting for her inside.

It had been like walking into a magic cave in those days, because the room was always filled with patterns and bolts of material in all the colors of the rainbow, piled on every available surface and filling the office with gaiety and brilliance.

Perhaps this memory was responsible for the nervous hesitation that made her reluctant to open the door and go inside. Then she squared her shoulders resolutely. Why should she be afraid? This was not a "Pandora's box" she was about to open. She was merely going to see and talk to a man whom she had known for years, who, when she was a schoolgirl, had been a kind of hero to her in those impressionable years before she had gone to the United States.

She pressed down the ornate gilt handle quickly and

went in without giving herself any more time to think. The two people standing behind the huge desk in the meticulously tidy room turned quickly, their expressions startled.

Terry was the first to recover.

"Sara!" He came to meet her, both hands held out welcomingly. "So you got here at last? When did you arrive?"

"Yesterday. I came as soon as I knew," Sara said defensively, sensing an implied rebuke behind his words and not liking it very much.

"I cabled you right away, and sent a follow-up one when you didn't get in touch."

"I know, but you sent them to my apartment and unfortunately I was away, traveling around the country with Johnnie. I didn't get the telegrams until I returned. If they'd been sent to the office, someone would have let me know at once."

"I'm sorry, my dear. It never occurred to me. Anyway, you're here now, and it's good to see you."

"I'd like to have a talk with you, Terry."

Sara looked pointedly at the tall woman who had not spoken since she had come in, and Terry said quickly, "This is Céleste, Sara. She's in charge of the fashion departments now."

Sara smiled.

"Hello, Céleste."

"How do you do, Miss Blake," Céleste said coldly, then moved toward the door. "I'll see you later, Terry, when you're free again."

"Right, Céleste. I'll let you know."

He waited until the door closed behind her, then put a casual arm around Sara's shoulders.

"It's certainly grand to see you again after all this time.

Living in the States had done you good, Sara, or maybe it's only me who's forgotten how very pretty you are." He indicated the chair behind the big desk. "Come and sit here."

She shook her head, feeling embarrassed by his compliment.

"No, thanks, Terry. This one will do."

She sat down in one of the armchairs, trying to fight the wave of aversion that swept over her when she contrasted these expensive and opulent surroundings with what the office had been like when her father was alive.

"As you wish," Terry said casually, and took the chair which she had refused, settling himself into it with an arrogance that was new in Sara's knowledge of him. "Well now, what do you think of the store? It's quite something, isn't it?"

"It must have cost a fortune, Terry. Where did the money come from? I know David sold the house, but even so . . . it couldn't possibly have paid for all this."

"It didn't . . . that's the trouble."

"You mean, it's not paid for?"

"Exactly."

She was silent for a moment, then said with a resolute lift of her chin, "How much is still owing?"

He moved restlessly, flashing her an oblique glance, which made her feel even more uneasy.

"We, or more correctly, you and Val, owe Brent Maxwell nearly thirty thousand pounds."

Sara stared at him in disbelief.

"Thirty thousand pounds? I can't believe it. For what?"

"For everything. You see, as well as owning a wholesale cloth warehouse, he manufactures all kinds of textiles. He also has a carpet factory. Then he's a consultant architect, too, so as well as supplying all the

furnishings, he was also employed by David to advise on
the alterations."

"And he hasn't been paid?"

"Apparently not. Since David died he's been putting
pressure on us to settle, and we can't do it."

"Won't the bank help?"

He laughed. "Be your age, Sara. We've already got a
massive loan, with the building as collateral."

She stared at him, moistening suddenly dry lips,
appalled by the knowledge of how much worse the
situation was than anything she had visualized.

"But David told me he'd raised enough money to pay
for everything. What's happened to it?"

Terry shrugged.

"How should I know? You'd better ask Brent Maxwell
that."

"You mean he's had it and. . . ."

"Oh, come now, Sara! I didn't say that at all. Don't
put words into my mouth."

No, she thought silently, *but that's what you meant to
imply. Why?* But she could think of no reasonable answer
to that question.

"Have you asked him for time to pay?" she said at last.

He laughed shortly.

"Of course. He just says he's waited long enough."

"But doesn't he understand what it means to us?"

"None better, and he doesn't care. He'll tell you he's in
business to make profits, that there's no time for senti-
ment. Believe me, Sara, there's only one thing to be done.
You'll have to sell out. Val agrees with me."

"Does she? She didn't say anything about it to me. In
fact, she doesn't seem to have understood anything you
said to her. Are you sure, Terry?"

He flushed. "Of course I am. I told her we'd had a very

good offer—all debts paid and most of the staff kept on—and she agreed that the best thing to do was to close with it."

"I see. And what will be left for us? Anything?"

"Naturally, I hope there'll be something," he began smoothly.

"Rubbish," she cut in. "You're not talking to Val now, you're talking to me. Don't forget I've been Johnnie Acton's assistant for nearly three years. I may be only 21, Terry, but there's nothing much you can tell me about the finances of running a business."

"All right," he said sulkily. "So you know it all. Maybe there won't be very much for you and Val, but I think the offer I've had is too good to turn down. At least it will keep Blake's open."

She looked down at her hands, clasped tightly together in her lap, and was surprised at the pain that darted through her at his words. The business that her father had built up so lovingly and patiently through sheer hard work was being disposed of as casually as if it was nothing of any importance.

"If these people are willing to buy, they must have faith in the business," she said at last. "Shouldn't we have faith, too?"

He moved impatiently. "They've got the money to pour into it. We haven't. Faith by itself will never solve anything."

"Neither will selling. If we accept this offer, Val will be penniless, won't she?"

His glance shifted away from hers. "There's no alternative, Sara."

"I don't accept that. Suppose I go and talk with this Brent Maxwell?"

"Appeal to his better nature, do you mean? You'd be wasting your time, because he hasn't got one. He's as hard as nails. Anyway, what good could come of it? Let me close with this offer, Sara," he added coaxingly. "Believe me, it's the only way, if we're to save anything at all from the wreck."

She shook her head.

"No. Not until I've seen Brent Maxwell," she said stubbornly.

He got up, the angry color flooding into his face.

"You must be crazy! What do you hope to gain from it?"

"Time," she answered quietly. "Time to think, to make a plan. What's his telephone number?"

For a moment she thought he was going to refuse to tell her, and she braced herself mentally for an unpleasant battle with him. Then, as suddenly as it had come, the anger that had sharpened his features was gone, and he was his usual charming self again.

"All right, Sara, you must do as you wish." He pulled a pad toward him and wrote briefly on it. "There's the number, but I still think you're wasting your time."

"Perhaps I am, but at least I'm doing something constructive." She moved toward the door, but turned before she reached it. "Who's using your old office?"

"Nobody."

"Then I'll take it over. Please have all the books put in there for me to go through."

"Now look here, Sara," he blustered. "The auditors. . . ."

"I have no doubt they've done their job," she interrupted. "Mine is a bit different. If I'm going to make the decision you're pressing for, I've got to know what I'm doing. So see the books are ready for me tomorrow, please."

He shrugged.

"All right, if that's what you want."

"Thank you," she said, and opened the door, closing it firmly behind her.

But she did not walk away at once. Terry's news had come as a shock to her and she had not yet had time to adjust to it, particularly to the knowledge that there would be no money left for Val and Jamie.

She pressed her hands together, facing up to the fact that she alone was to blame. She had accepted what David had told her and had been too immersed in the fascinating life she had been leading in the United States to give the family business the attention she should have. She, of all people, should have been aware of what was happening. Johnnie always said she had a nose for trouble, but it seemed to have deserted her in this particular instance.

That being so, it was up to her to do all she could to put things right, so that Val and Jamie did not suffer through her neglect. So although everything she had heard so far about Brent Maxwell made her feel loath to ask him for any favors, there was nothing else she could do.

Unless Johnnie . . . but she pushed that thought away from her at once. He was already deep in a deal that involved millions of dollars, and everything he had at that time was tied up in it.

Of course he would help if she asked him, she knew that without question. But she also knew that the smallest thing could upset the balance of this deal they had been working on, the biggest thing they had ever handled.

No. This time she was on her own. This was her big chance to show what she could do. But first of all she had to see Brent Maxwell. Until she had done that she couldn't make any plans at all.

She looked around, getting her bearings, then went along the passage, turning at the end into another, vastly different one. With its worn linoleum and dark paint it might have been in another world.

Near the end of it she stopped and opened a chipped door leading into the small, unpretentious office that had once been Terry's. She sat down at the desk and lifted the telephone receiver, giving Brent Maxwell's number. Her heart thudded nervously against her ribs as she waited for the reply.

"May I speak to Mr. Brent Maxwell?" she asked, when at last it came.

"I'll see. Who is calling, please?"

"Sara Blake, of Blake's Store," she said, and her hand tightened around the receiver when a deep voice said curtly,

"Maxwell here."

"I'm Sara Blake."

She paused, annoyed with herself because her voice sounded breathless and very young, more suited to a schoolgirl than a woman who was facing a situation which she had known more than once in the States. Only then it had affected strangers, not herself and her family.

"What do you want?"

"I understand from my manager, Mr. White, that Blake's owes you a considerable amount of money."

"Yes, that's so."

"I'd like to talk to you about it."

"Why? I don't see the necessity. I've made the position quite clear, I think."

"Perhaps you have." Her voice was edgy with annoyance at the brusque replies she was receiving. "But my sister-in-law and I are the owners, not Terry White. You should have seen us."

She heard him let out his breath in a long-suffering way.

"I did try to see your brother's wife, Miss Blake, but I was told she didn't want to meet me. And you were in the States and hadn't bothered to reply to the telegrams that had been sent to you."

Sara felt the hot color flood into her face, and had to exercise a great self-control to stop her voice from trembling with annoyance as she answered him sharply, "Well, I'm home now, and I want to discuss the whole situation with you."

There was silence for a moment, then he said, a note of annoyed resignation very clear in his voice, "Very well, although you're wasting your own time and mine. Yours may not be valuable, but mine most certainly is."

She closed her lips tightly on the blistering retort she would have liked to make to this arrogant man, knowing that she could not afford to alienate him. She had to ask him for a favor that was valuable to her and she was now sure it was not going to be easy to obtain, so she only said quietly, "When can you see me?"

"Tomorrow at 11 o'clock. At the store."

Suddenly she knew that she did not want to meet him for the first time in the place that Terry, in some obscure way, seemed to have made his own.

"No, not at the store," she answered quickly. "I'd like Val, my sister-in-law, to be there. Will you come to the apartment?"

"Oh, very well, if you insist. Where is it?"

She gave him the address, trying not to allow the exasperation and irritation at his curtness sound in her voice, a curtness that, in her present ultrasensitive mood, she interpreted as undisguised boredom that he was going to have to deal with somebody he classed as an unmitigated nuisance.

"I'll be there at 11. I hope you won't delay me too long, Miss Blake. I'm a very busy man."

"I won't," she said, and carefully replaced the receiver, though she would rather have banged it down in anger.

She rubbed her hands over her face, feeling frustrated and worried. Terry had warned her that she would be wasting her time in appealing to Brent Maxwell, and she knew now that he had been right. After talking with him she would have preferred to have nothing at all to do with him, but she knew that would have been impossible.

She had to see him, for Val's sake and for Jamie's. It was their future which was at stake and which must be safeguarded, even though it meant that she must swallow her own pride and beg for favors from this arrogant, impatient man.

CHAPTER THREE

Sara did not tell Val about the appointment she had made with Brent Maxwell until breakfast time next morning, thinking that her sister-in-law would probably lie awake all night worrying about it. Even so, she was not prepared for her reaction to the news.

"I won't see him, Sara," Val cried. "You've no right to interfere. Terry says you've ruined everything."

Sara looked at her blankly.

"What are you talking about? Don't you understand, Val? If we sell the business now, there'll probably be no money for you and Jamie."

"You don't know that. Terry says there will be when everything's fixed up, but if we don't accept this offer, then we'll all be ruined. He's trying to do the best he can for me. You shouldn't meddle in things that don't concern you."

"Don't concern me? You're talking nonsense, Val." She stopped, restraining herself with an effort, realizing that her sister-in-law did not really understand what she was saying. "When did Terry tell you this?"

"Last night," Val said sulkily. "He phoned me after I'd gone to bed. The extension's in my room. I won't see that man, Sara. I won't! Terry says he's awful."

Sara's lips tightened. So Terry had already tried to sabotage what she was hoping to accomplish. Why should he do that? Why tell her one story and Val another? What did he expect to gain personally from the sale of the store? Money, or perhaps position and power? He had surely achieved the last two aims . . . unless she decided to stay in England and take charge.

Suddenly Sara knew this must be the right answer. She had always thought he was ambitious and self-seeking, but had not blamed him for that. Anyone who wanted to get on needed those traits. But while she had no objection to him trying to make sure of his own future, she was not going to allow him to do so at the expense of David's son.

"It's too late to put Brent Maxwell off now, Val, but you don't have to see him if you don't want to."

Val moved impatiently.

"I don't know why you're so against selling, Sara. It was different for David . . . it was his career. It isn't yours. You'll want to go back to the States and get married. It all seems quite pointless to me."

Sara's lips tightened as she realized how well Terry had primed her sister-in-law, but she only said quietly, "I suppose it does, but it's something that goes deep with me. Ever since I've known anything, I've known about Dad's shop. It's part of my life . . . just as it was part of David's."

"Part of David's? That's putting it mildly. It was all his life. He didn't care what he did to me, as long as the store was all right. He uprooted me from my lovely house . . . the house I chose and that my father paid for when we were married. That had to be sacrificed like everything else because he wanted money for his wretched business."

Sara looked at her in surprise, knowing that for the first time she was hearing the truth from her sister-in-law, and wondering why she had never realized before the depth of her antagonism against David's obsession with the store.

"David told me in one of his letters that you'd suggested you should sell the house and rent an apartment," she said.

"Me? I did nothing of the kind. He made up his mind

to do it and nothing I could say made any difference. Just as he refused to send Jamie to a decent school instead of to one nobody's ever heard of because he went there himself."

"You can hardly blame him for that, Val."

"Oh, it's no use talking to you! You think he could do no wrong. You'd have changed your mind if you'd had to sit here day after day alone in this apartment while he went off to France to enjoy himself. He never once took me with him."

Sara smiled, knowing that she had now reached the truth of the matter.

"He probably thought you wouldn't be interested in the buying and bargaining he had to do."

"I wouldn't have bothered about that. I could have enjoyed myself in other ways, but he would never take me. He always said he couldn't afford it," Val added scornfully.

"It could have been true," Sara pointed out, thinking that Paris was the last place she would turn her chic and extravagant sister-in-law loose in.

"Nonsense! But even if it was true, then there's all the more reason to take this offer Terry's had. Then I'd have enough money to do what I want, instead of worrying where the next penny's coming from."

Sara frowned, hearing a note almost of panic in her voice.

"Are you in any difficulty, Val?" she asked quickly. "Do you have money troubles?"

Val shook her blonde head.

"No, of course not, except as far as we all have money worries . . . never having enough of it," she finished, and laughed.

But to Sara her laugh sounded forced and artificial,

and she looked at her, wondering if she should press her further to find out the truth. Even as she thought it she realized it would be a waste of time. She knew Val too well. Her father had always shaken his head and said he never knew when she was telling the truth, that she had all the obstinacy of a weak character. Long before she had gone to America, Sara had discovered that to be true.

"Then you won't see Brent Maxwell with me?"

"No, I won't. And I might as well tell you now, Sara, that as soon as all David's shares are transferred to me, I'm going to outvote you and sell. Terry says he had the majority holding by far."

"Then you don't know about the trust?"

"What trust?"

"Dad's. He had most of the shares and they were left in trust, first for David and then for David's eldest son. David and I were joint trustees. Now there's only me."

"What does that mean?" Val asked suspiciously.

"That I'm the one who administers the trust on behalf of Jamie."

Val stared at her in disbelief.

"You mean I get nothing?"

"You'll get David's own shareholding, I think."

"How many did he have?"

"David and I both held a fifth of the shares each. Dad made no difference between us over that, even though I was 18 years younger than David."

"And that's all I get? Is it true? Is it, Sara, or are you just trying to outmaneuver me?"

"You know I wouldn't do that, Val. Won't you change your mind now and see Brent Maxwell with me?"

"No, I will not. I won't talk to him or to anyone. This is just one more thing David's done to me. Why didn't he make things right in his will so that I was the trustee instead of you? Any other man would have seen that his wife was properly looked after, but not him. Oh, no! Not David Blake!"

"Val, don't say such things! It wasn't David's fault. There was nothing he could do about it. Don't you understand?"

"No, I don't, and I never will. I'm going to my room now. When Maxwell comes see him yourself, and much good may it do you!"

Val rushed out of the room, banging the door behind her, and Sara sighed, feeling depressed and weary. If only she could dismiss her responsibilities as easily as Val seemed to! But she couldn't. Her training with Johnnie and her own nature made it impossible for her to consider it for a moment. She would have given anything not to have to see this arrogant man and plead with him for the time she needed to save the business for Jamie and Val. She knew now she would get no thanks for doing so.

She walked restlessly across the thick off-white carpeting, automatically straightening a brilliantly colored satin cushion on the luxurious sofa, and wondered for the first time who had paid for all the expensive furniture in this big penthouse and whether the cost of it was included in the debt that Brent Maxwell said was due him.

When at last the doorbell rang, just as 11 o'clock was striking musically from the French clock in the living room, she gave no sign of her inner feelings as she answered it.

"Miss Blake? Good morning. I'm Brent Maxwell."

He was nothing like she had pictured him. He wasn't an ogre, nor a hard business tycoon as she had imagined. Instead she saw deep-set blue eyes in a face with sensitive lines engraved in it, eyes which, though unsmiling at that moment, were set in laughter lines.

"Yes, I'm Sara Blake," she said. "Please come in."

She led the way into the sitting room and saw his eyes look quickly around, as though assessing the cost of what he saw. She thought with relief that he had probably no hand in furnishing it.

"Would you like something to drink?"

"No, thank you. I've very little time to spare, so let's just hear what you've got to say and cut the formalities, shall we?"

Her lips tightened at his curt words and she looked at him with annoyance and dislike.

"That suits me. I don't wish to keep you a moment longer than you want to stay. Terry White told me yesterday that you intend to ruin us all in order to get the money you say is owing to you. Is that true?"

He frowned, his eyes wary. "Basically, though it's not the way I'd have put it."

Sara made an impatient gesture. "That's beside the point. I want to know the truth. Does our business owe you thirty thousand pounds, Mr. Maxwell, and do you refuse to wait any longer for repayment?"

"Yes," he said shortly. "I've waited more than a year now, and while David was alive I agreed not to press for payment. But that's all changed, since his death. You may not understand why. . . ."

"Give me the benefit of some sense," she interrupted angrily. "I'm not completely inexperienced, you know. I've been working in the States for a finance house for nearly three years. There's very little you can tell me that I wouldn't understand."

He raised his eyebrows.

"In that case why bother to see me? You ought to know that I'm doing the only possible thing under the circumstances."

"I'd have thought it was obvious."

"Not to me, and I'm not considered to be particularly obtuse. If you're so well versed in financial matters you ought to know that when I lent money to Blake's I was backing a man I trusted. A man who I expected would forge ahead. Now he's gone, there's nothing left for me to do but make sure I'm paid in full as quickly as possible."

She colored at the weary note in his voice and would have given anything at that moment to walk away without asking him for the help that only he could give. But she knew she dared not do it, that she was indulging in dangerous wishful thinking.

That realization only served to deepen the dislike she had felt for him from the moment she had spoken with him on the telephone.

"Well, Miss Blake?" he asked impatiently. "What is it you want to say to me?"

"I want you to give me time," she said, without wrapping the request in flowery language, "so that I can find out what's been happening at Blake's."

"What good will that do? Whatever has happened can't affect the result now. It must be obvious to you, if you are as knowledgeable as you claim to be, that it would be better to go into liquidation voluntarily or to sell as a going concern."

"Perhaps, but I don't want to do either of those things."

"Why not?"

She hesitated, wondering if she could tell him the truth, if he would understand the deep feelings that were driving her. The reluctance to see all her father had striven for and built up gone as if it had never been, and Jamie and Val reduced, perhaps, to penury.

He frowned, looking at her with suspicion. "Don't try to hide anything from me," he said sharply. "I've got to know the whole truth if I'm to make a decision which involves my company."

"I don't want to hide anything from you. I'll be quite frank with you. David sold his home, raised every bit of money he could, to pay for all the alterations and furnishings, yet you say you haven't been paid anything. So what's happened to the money, Mr. Maxwell?"

He looked at her in disbelief, the lines beside his mouth deepening in anger. "How dare you? Are you accusing me of taking your brother's money when he was alive, and asking for it again now he's dead?"

For a moment she quailed before his anger, then thrust that sudden stab of fear aside, knowing that she was right to ask that question.

"It's no use getting annoyed, Mr. Maxwell. I think it's a reasonable thing to ask."

"Do you? Well, I don't. Do you realize what you're saying? Do you?"

She felt the color recede from her face at his angry words, but stood her ground, determined not to be intimidated by him.

"You're deliberately misunderstanding me."

His lips set sternly. "Then you're not accusing me of embezzlement?"

"Of course not. I'm only trying to find out where this money's gone to, if it hasn't been paid to you."

"Then you'd better examine the firm's books."

"I intend to, as soon as I can. Will you do as I ask, Mr. Maxwell? Give me time to investigate?"

His lips curved in a reluctant smile which altered the whole character of his face.

"Well, if you don't take the prize for being completely illogical! Handing insults to me one minute, then expecting favors from me the next. Why should I consider you?"

She found herself answering his smile reluctantly, feeling her resolution not to give way to this man weakening in the face of his sudden, unexpected charm.

"You've just told me I'm illogical. Do you expect me to have a reason?" she asked lightly.

He did not answer immediately, looking keenly at her as if trying to read her mind.

"Take my advice," he said at last. "Cut your losses."

"No, I won't do that, not until I've had time to look into things. That's all I'm asking for . . . time, to do the best I can for Val and Jamie."

"You won't succeed."

"Maybe not, but I still want to try. Will you let me?"

"Is your sister-in-law in agreement with you?"

She colored under his steady gaze. "She doesn't properly understand. . . ."

"She wants to sell, doesn't she?" he asked drily.

"I've told you, she doesn't understand that if we do sell there may be little or nothing left for her."

"What if she outvotes you in a showdown, Sara Blake? Have you thought of that?"

"Yes, but she can't do it. My father held three-fifths of the shares and they passed in trust to David and then to Jamie. David and I were the trustees. Now there's only me. So you see, I'm in control, not Val."

"I see. Does she know?"

"I told her this morning."

He was silent for a time, frowning down at his clasped

hands, and she watched him, silently willing him to give her the answer she wanted.

"Well," she said at last when the silence became unbearable. "What's your answer?"

"I'll do as you ask, Sara Blake." He looked at her steadily out of keen blue eyes. "I'll give you three months to get to know the business and put things right if you can."

"Three months?" she echoed in dismay. "It isn't long enough. I'll never do it."

He got up abruptly. "That's my offer, take it or leave it. If you're only half as good as you say you are, it ought to be plenty of time. And I'll give you all the help I can."

She felt a wave of anger shiver through her and wished passionately that she could give way to it, could throw back this man's ridiculous offer in his face. But she did not dare. She had to accept it because it was her only hope, even while she despaired of carrying out all her plans in such a short time.

"All right, I'll accept. Thank you," she said, with an effort.

"Good. *Au revoir*, then, Sara Blake."

"Goodbye," she answered with emphasis, telling herself that she would have to be in great difficulties indeed before she took up his offer of help. But she was uneasily aware of the amused look he gave her as he opened the front door.

She stood where she was when the door closed with a decisive click behind him, feeling panic rising within her. She had accepted his terms, and somehow she had to succeed without the help she was too proud to accept.

And in addition to undertaking an almost impossible task, she would not be able to go back to the States to Johnnie. He was relying on her to come back and help him to put through the complicated deal they had been working on when she had heard of David's death, and she was going to let him down. Not only that, but she was going to miss him badly.

Dear Johnnie, so loved and so needed. She could see him in her mind's eye, his thick fair hair falling over his forehead, his eyes bright with enthusiasm and eagerness, and knew an intense longing to be with him, to draw strength from him.

Instead she had only Brent Maxwell, a difficult, strange man, as unlike Johnnie as anyone could be. If only she need never see him again! But remembering the amused look in his eyes and his voice saying *"Au revoir,"* she knew there was little hope of that.

She had invited him into her life, and now had the uneasy feeling that however much she might dislike it, he had every intention of staying there.

CHAPTER FOUR

Sara went into the store next morning by the staff entrance, joining the others who were hurrying or dawdling according to their natures. Some of them looked at her curiously, while others pushed past unseeingly, snatching their cards from the rack and punching in with a sublime disregard for anyone or anything.

They all seemed to know each other and called out cheerful greetings. Sara felt lonely as she went quickly upstairs to the office she had requisitioned, wondering if Terry would have put the firm's books in it or whether she was going to have to battle with him to get them. But when she pushed open the door of the dark little office and went in, switching on the light, she saw that she need not have worried. On the scarred desk was a pile of ledgers.

So she had misjudged him, she thought, as she hung up her coat in the cupboard. He was going to cooperate with her after all. Yet under the feeling of thankfulness that she was not to be faced with a struggle to get the information she wanted, there was one of faint surprise at his easy capitulation.

She sat down at the desk and opened the first ledger. Before she could do more than glance at it, Terry came in.

"Hi, Sara. You're early. Got everything you need?"

"I haven't really looked yet, but thank you for letting me have the books so promptly."

"Think nothing of it. I had them put in as soon as Val phoned to tell me Maxwell had been to see you and you'd managed to win him over. I expected you to come in yesterday."

Sara pushed back her thick honey gold hair from her forehead.

"I meant to, but Val wasn't well in the afternoon, so I stayed with her. When did she phone you?"

"Before lunch."

"I see," Sara said slowly, remembering her sister-in-law's attack of hysterics and her insistence afterward that Sara not leave her. Yet before that she had been capable of phoning Terry and letting him know what had happened. For the first time she wondered just how real Val's attack of nerves had been. "Did she tell you about the shares?"

"Yes, though I already knew that. Don't forget I worked with your father and David for a long time."

Sara frowned, wondering if he was telling the truth or if he was trying to hide what he had been planning.

"If you knew that, why did you try to persuade Val to sell, telling her she would be able to outvote me?" she asked.

"Nonsense, Sara, I did nothing of the kind. I merely told her the real situation. You're not suggesting I should have hidden the truth from her, are you, unpalatable though it is."

She colored at the implied rebuke in his words.

"No, of course not. I only wondered why you said she would have all the shares and be in control."

"I didn't. Val must have misunderstood me. You said yourself that she didn't seem to know what I'd been talking about." He looked at her speculatively. "Have you thought what you'll do if Jamie doesn't want to come into the business when he's old enough, Sara? If, say, he decides he'd rather be a doctor or a lawyer or something?"

"I'll face that problem when it comes."

"You may be sorry when you've spent years toiling to pull the business up, and it all comes to nothing."

"That's a risk I've got to take. Up to now he's always seemed keen enough."

"Boys have been known to change their minds."

She sighed.

"I know that. What I must make sure of is that there's still a business to inherit, if he does want it."

"And if he doesn't? What then?"

"We'll have to sell, I suppose, but maybe we'll be able to drive a better bargain."

He flicked her cheek with a casual finger.

"Always the incurable optimist, Sara, but I love you for it. Anyway, I didn't come through to talk about that. I want you to come around the store with me to see what we've been doing and to meet some of the staff."

It took a long time to make the tour of the store. Terry showed her everything, and she talked for awhile to a number of the staff. They seemed friendly enough, yet somehow Sara could sense a constraint, almost an antagonism among them, particularly among the department heads. Yet how could that be? They didn't know enough about her to be antagonistic toward her, because without exception they had joined the firm after she had left England.

She said as much to Terry as they walked toward the model gown department, and he shrugged lightly.

"I suppose they feel unsettled, Sara, and tend to blame you, as part of the Blake family. That often happens when staff feel there may be a change in the air."

"I suppose you're right. Terry, everybody I've met today has been new. I hoped I might see some of the old friends I used to know. What's happened to them all?"

"I expect they've left from time to time. The usual

wastage, you know. None of us are getting any younger."

She frowned, looking back over the past three years, remembering the staff she had known then.

"Perhaps, yet I don't think they were so old, Terry. I doubt if any of them were much more than 50. Yet they've all gone. It seems strange to me."

"I don't see why it should," he said indifferently. "People get set in their own ways and resist changes. And there've been a lot of changes here in one way and another, as you can see."

"Yes. Is there only Mollie left?"

"How did you know she was still here?"

"I met her that first day when I came to see you."

She stopped, thinking suddenly how short a time had elapsed since she had come back from the States. Yet it seemed to her that she had been home for weeks. Almost as if she had never been away.

It wasn't her life now that was strange, but rather the life she had spent in the States during the past three years that had become vague and dreamlike, as if it had never happened.

At that moment it was an effort for her to conjure up the image of Johnnie, who had been close to her every day during that time.

"Well now, this is the real *pièce de résistance*."

Terry's voice broke in on her thoughts and she pushed them resolutely to the back of her mind, concentrating once again on the task of trying to assess the cost of the changes that had taken place and what effect they had had on store sales.

She looked around her, seeing the thick pile carpet, the catwalk surrounded by gilt and velvet chairs, the huge windows shrouded in white nylon curtains, the brilliance of the chandeliers reflected in the mirrors lining the walls, and gave her brother full marks for his foresight and originality.

Whatever it had cost, and there could be no doubt that the cost had been great, it was in itself an achievement and gave a final touch to the new look for Blake's Store.

"Good morning, Miss Blake."

She turned quickly at Céleste's cool greeting and smiled into the tall woman's expressionless face.

"Good morning. This is really a very beautiful room. How often do you have dress shows?"

"Two or three times a week by invitation. You know we make gowns for the trade as well as for individual customers?"

"Are the workrooms still in the same place?"

"Yes, although much bigger now."

"I'd like to see them."

"You won't find them very interesting, Sara. David didn't get around to fixing them up."

"Still, I may as well visit them. Then I'll have had a look at all departments, won't I?"

"Just as you please. Come along, then."

He began to walk along the corridor, but stopped when Céleste called imperiously, "Just a moment, Mr. White. Could I have a word with you?"

"Of course, Céleste. I won't be a moment," he added to Sara, and walked quickly back to where Céleste waited for him.

Sara watched them talking to each other in low tones, too quietly for her to hear what they were saying. Only part of her mind concentrated on them.

"All right, do that," Terry said in a much louder voice, and came briskly back to Sara. "Sorry about that, my dear, but these little problems do arise. This way."

They walked to the end of the passage and climbed a

flight of uncarpeted stairs leading to the attic rooms. As Terry had said, nothing had been spent on them and they looked dingy and rather grim.

But when he pushed open a door in the narrow passageway, the whole picture changed. Here was all the color and brightness which she had known in her father's time.

She stood in the doorway, her dark eyes shining with memories, though in those days there had been nowhere near the number of machinists who were employed now. They sat in long rows, the hum of their powered machines filling the air. Sara had never seen so many collected in one room in all her life. What a change from the modest half dozen which was the most her father had ever employed, even in his most flourishing period.

She turned impulsively to Terry. "It's terrific! How on earth do you keep them all busy?"

"Very easily. We do a lot more work now, making for the trade. Come to the next room where the hand sewers are and where all the model gowns are made."

He led the way down the machine room. None of the sewers stopped work as they passed, to Sara's surprise.

"Well, time's money to them," Terry said, when she commented on this. "They're on bonus, you see, and earn colossal amounts every week. Which means we have to pay the hand sewers comparable salaries, otherwise we couldn't get them."

Sara walked slowly past the sewing women, seeing the tables covered with beautiful materials, stopping now and again to admire the work being done. Here the women had time to speak to her, to explain what they were doing.

"Who thinks up the designs?" she asked.

"David used to. He was in close touch with the Paris houses, of course, but he always gave the designs the Blake touch."

"What will you do now?"

"We're all right for this season, but after that I'm not sure. We'll probably have to employ a designer, but it isn't going to be easy to find one. Céleste and I have already started to make some inquiries, and I'll probably go over to Paris soon to see if there's anybody there we can use."

"That's going to be quite expensive, isn't it?" Sara said, then her eyes lighted up as Mollie came through a door at the end of the room. "Oh, here's Mollie. How are you? I'm glad I haven't missed you."

"Good morning, Miss Blake, Mr. White."

Mollie's voice was as expressionless as her face and Sara looked at her in surprise, hardly recognizing the warm, friendly person she had met earlier.

"What's wrong?" she asked, with concern. "Are you feeling all right?"

"Of course. I'm very busy just at present, so if you'll excuse me. . . ."

Sara stared after her in astonishment as she went quickly through the room and into the one Sara and Terry had just left. Then she turned to Terry, a question on her lips that was destined never to be asked, because as she looked at him it occurred to her with startling suddenness that Mollie had snubbed her only because she was with Terry. And that thought perplexed her.

If it was true, it must mean that Mollie was afraid of him, yet why should she be? Terry seemed affable enough with her and with all the members of the staff. Then she remembered. Only Mollie seemed to be left of those who had worked at Blake's when her father was alive, who knew the old régime. Was she really so afraid now that David was dead that Terry might find some excuse to get rid of her, too?

Well, if that was so, then somehow, she told herself, she would make sure that Mollie's job at Blake's was safe.

Everything that was happening was tying her more securely to England, was making it that much more difficult for her to go back to the States and Johnnie.

"Well, now you've seen everything, Sara," Terry said briskly as they walked back to the office. "What about coming out to lunch with me?"

She looked at him, her eyes still mirroring her troubled thoughts.

"No, thank you, Terry. I meant to get through such a lot of work this morning and I've done nothing."

"I wouldn't say that, my dear. You've seen the store and know now where all the money's gone. And you'll have to have lunch somewhere."

"It's too early yet."

"Not at all. It's past 12, you know. You haven't realized how quickly the time's been passing. Please come," he added coaxingly, "Just to show you forgive me for trying to persuade you to sell the business."

She laughed. "All right, Terry. Give me a few minutes to tidy myself up a bit."

"As long as you like. I'll meet you at the main entrance. See you, my dear."

He left her at the office and she went in, doing automatically all the necessary things while her mind still concentrated on what she had seen that day and she tried to sort out all the impressions she had received while going around the store.

But it was no use. Everything was too close for her to assess it in a sensible way and in the end she had to acknowledge that she was probably doing the right thing in going out to lunch with Terry. Perhaps after she had been away from the store for a while she might be able to get what she had seen and learned into perspective so that it would be of help when she began to make her analysis of the firm's books.

She looked at her watch, realizing that she had taken longer than she had intended, and picked up her purse from the desk before running out of the office and down the stairs to the main entrance.

Terry was waiting for her with a taxi.

"I was just coming to find you," he said, opening the door for her, then getting in and sitting down beside her. "I was beginning to think you'd stood me up."

"As if I would! I'm sorry I was so long, Terry. I've no excuse, really."

"That's all right." He smiled down at her. "Now you're here, will you promise me one thing?"

"If I can," she said cautiously.

"You can. I want us to have our lunch without once mentioning Blake's, to forget all that's happened and just enjoy ourselves. That's easy enough, isn't it?"

She put out her hand impulsively to him. "Of course it is, Terry. Thank you. You've been very kind to me today and I appreciate it."

He put his own lightly over hers. "It's fatally easy for me to be kind to you, my dear. It always was. Don't you remember how one look from those big dark eyes of yours made me like putty in your hands? They still have that power," he finished ruefully.

She made some reply, flustered by his extravagant words, and was glad when the taxi drew up in front of the restaurant he had chosen and she could withdraw her hand from his. She was beginning to wish that she had not come out with him.

She didn't welcome this sudden and unexpected change in him, and yet she was loath to upset him, when he was trying to be kind to her, by letting him see that she had no wish to be reminded of those years when she had hero-worshipped her father's good-looking young assistant.

She need not have worried. Terry said nothing further

to embarrass her but was a charming companion, interested in hearing about her life in the United States and making no reference to Blake's, so that she too was able to keep her part of the bargain they had made.

It was when they were drinking coffee that she first looked at her watch and said with a startled exclamation, "Heavens, it's almost three o'clock, Terry. Do you realize how long we've taken over lunch?"

"Yes, but I hoped you hadn't."

"We should have been back at the store ages ago. You'll have been wanted there."

He laughed. "Oh, I don't often get the chance to play hookey, my dear, and it's worth taking a bit longer over lunch to see you lose that worried look. Mind you don't let it come back," he added. "You look a lot prettier without it."

She colored. "Maybe, but we really ought to go back now."

"Just as you like. I'll meet you downstairs. Ask the doorman to call a taxi, will you?"

The taxi was waiting when he rejoined Sara, and they were almost silent until they reached the store. She waited while Terry paid the driver, then they walked in together through the imposing main entrance.

Sara stopped just inside the automatic doors and said gratefully, "Thank you, Terry, for a very enjoyable time. You were quite right . . . I needed an hour or two away from it all. I'd been getting things out of proportion, letting them get on top of me."

He put his hands on her shoulders, his fingers tightening comfortingly.

"I'm glad to help, Sara love. We must do this again. What about having dinner and seeing a show with me one evening?"

She hesitated, not knowing what answer to give to this unexpected invitation, but before she could say anything a voice behind her said furiously, "Next time you make an appointment wih me, Miss Blake, please see you're there to keep it!"

She whirled around, looking into Brent Maxwell's angry eyes in astonishment.

"What are you talking about? What do you mean?" she demanded.

"Don't play the innocent with me," he said contemptuously. "Perhaps it's your way of trying to look important, bringing me here and keeping me waiting to suit your convenience. Well, it doesn't work that way with me. Remember that in the future."

She stared after him as he went quickly past the counter to the main door, hardly able to understand what she had heard. Then as she saw the interested glances of the assistants who had heard everything he had said in his deep, carrying voice, the brilliant color flooded into her cheeks and her puzzlement changed to anger.

"How dare he speak to me like that! I don't know what he's talking about. I didn't make any appointment with him."

"Are you sure, Sara?"

"Of course I'm sure. I wouldn't be likely to forget that. I'm not so stupid, as I'd have told him if he'd given me the chance. He's . . . oh, he's self-opinionated and arrogant, and I wish I didn't have to have anything to do with him!"

"Well, there's no need for you to. I hate to say I told you so, but you've got to admit that I did warn you about him. Why won't you be sensible, Sara, and do what I advise, then you need never see him again."

She shook her head, "I can't do that, Terry, no matter how much I want to." She looked around suddenly, seeing again the covert interest the nearby staff were taking in their conversation and said quietly, "We can't talk here. Let's go up to the office."

She walked over to the escalator and he followed, saying nothing more until they paused outside the room she was using. Then as she turned the door handle he put his hand on hers.

"Just a minute, Sara. I'm sorry our very pleasant lunch had to end like this. And you didn't answer my question. Will you come out with me some evening?"

She smiled at him.

"Yes, I will. Thanks, Terry," she said, then looked around quickly as Céleste's cold voice said,

"Mrs. David called you, Miss Blake. She wants you to go home at once."

"Why? What's happened?"

"She didn't tell me, but she seemed very upset. I could hardly make out what she said, she was crying so much."

Sara looked at Terry, the worry back in her eyes again.

"I must go to her, Terry. I can't think what can have gone wrong...."

"I'll call a taxi for you. Go down to the main door and wait there, Sara. It'll be quicker that way."

"Thank you. I'll do that," she said gratefully, and hurried back down the stairs. The other two stood together and watched her until she was out of sight.

CHAPTER FIVE

Sara had not been waiting long when the taxi drew up, and she spent the next 20 minutes until she reached the apartment worrying about her sister-in-law and imagining all kinds of calamities, so that Val's trouble seemed almost an anticlimax at first.

"Here you are at last!" Val said peevishly when she hurried into the apartment. "You've taken your time. I thought you'd never come."

"Terry took me out to lunch and I only got your message when I got back to the store. What happened, Val? What's gone wrong?"

"Terry took you out to lunch? Well, I must say that's rich after all he's. . . ." She broke off, pressing her lips together as if sorry she had said so much, and with a dramatic gesture held out an envelope to Sara.

Sara took out the letter it contained and read it, her heart sinking as she did so.

"Val," she said at last, "is this really the rent of the apartment? But it's extortionate," she went on as her sister-in-law nodded. "We can't possibly afford to go on living here. No wonder it's six months overdue. You should never have let David come here."

"I knew you'd blame me," Val said shrilly. "As if I could have stopped him! He never told me anything. I had no idea how much it cost and he always said we had plenty of money."

"But this much for rent!"

Val moved impatiently. "It's not as bad as that, Sara. I'm sure your apartment in the United States cost a lot more."

"Yes, but it was furnished."

"And so is this, partly. Of course, we brought some furniture of our own, too."

Sara looked at her, the worry in her eyes deepening.

"You mean if we have to leave here we've got to refurnish as well?"

"Yes, but I don't want to leave. I like it here."

"That may be, but we simply can't afford it. Don't you understand, Val? Everything's different now."

She saw the tears gather in Valerie's eyes and knew a momentary impatience as she wailed, "Why did this have to happen to me! I'm sure I've never done anything to deserve it. I won't leave here and go to live in some little hole of a place. It's not fair to me or to Jamie."

"It needn't be a hole. Don't you see, Val. . . ." Sara began, then stopped, realizing it was useless to try and make her sister-in-law see reason at that moment. Perhaps later, when she had had time to get used to the idea, she might be more willing to consider it rationally and favorably. "Never mind. Let's forget it, shall we?" she went on. "I'll go and make some tea for us. We both need it, don't we?"

She went into the kitchen, glad to get away from Val for a few minutes, and as she made the tea the worried frown was back between her eyes.

It had been bad enough coming home to find the family business on the point of bankruptcy. It made things even worse to discover that even in his private life David had managed to involve himself and his family in debts and difficulties.

What other things was she going to find out, what other shocks might be in store for her, she wondered unhappily as she carried the tray into the living room.

The tea and perhaps the knowledge that she had sloughed off her worries on to Sara's shoulders seemed to revive Val, and she was chatting quite amiably to Sara when the doorbell rang. She stiffened in her chair, the fear back in her eyes.

"Who can that be? Do you think it's the police? Or a bill collector?" Then as Sara got up to answer the bell, she clutched at her desperately. "Don't go, Sara. Let them ring."

Sara released herself from that convulsive grip and said gently, "Nonsense, Val. It's no one like that. Why should it be? It's probably somebody who's come to the wrong apartment."

But when she opened the door she found that they were both wrong.

"You!" she said. "What do you want?"

"To see you," Brent Maxwell replied with equal brevity. "I'll come in if I may."

He did not wait for her to agree but stepped into the small hall, closing the door behind him.

"How dare you force yourself in here!" Sara said fiercely. "I don't want to see you. . . ."

"Who is it, Sara?"

"It's Brent Maxwell."

She looked around as Val came hesitantly into the hall, then sighed in exasperation as her sister-in-law took one look at the tall man standing just inside the door and burst into tears, rushing to her bedroom without another word.

Brent looked after her in surprise. "What's wrong with her? It's the first time the sight of me has made anyone cry!"

"You astonish me. The way you talked to me this afternoon, I should think you're used to reducing everyone to nervous wrecks."

He smiled. "But evidently not you, Sara. You're made of sterner stuff, aren't you?"

"Never mind that! What have you come here for?"

"To apologize to you," he answered, to her complete astonishment.

"To apologize? You?"

"Yes. I think I did you an injustice, but at the time I was too annoyed to accept the fact that you didn't expect me. You didn't ask me to call, did you?"

"No," she said briefly, so taken aback by an apology from this arrogant man that she was quite incapable of saying any of the cutting things she had thought of.

He frowned. "Someone did, however, and it was a woman's voice. It certainly sounded like you, yet. . . ." He stopped, his eyes intent, then went on abruptly, "I want to talk to you, Sara."

"You'd better come in here, then," she said reluctantly, and led the way into the living room. "Sit down, won't you."

"Thank you. What's the matter with Mrs. David?"

"She's a bit upset."

"So I noticed, not being stupid. Does she always dissolve into tears when somebody unexpected calls?"

"No, of course not." Sara frowned worriedly, forgetting for a moment how much she disliked this man and succumbing to the urge to share her troubles with somebody else. "We've had a letter from the agents today telling us that unless we pay the back rent we'll have to leave this apartment. Naturally she's upset about that."

"Because you can't pay?"

"Partly, and partly because this seems to be the last link she has with David."

She stopped, vexed with herself because of the tremor in her voice that she had been unable to control.

He looked at her sharply. "What else is bothering you? You may as well tell me," he added as she made a gesture of negation. "If you don't, I'll find out some other way."

"It's nothing . . . just that I wish I was sure this was the only debt we'll have to face. And while I don't mind leaving here, it's a furnished apartment and it won't be so easy to find another one at a price we can afford."

"I see. If you like, Sara, I'll pay off the rent until you can find somewhere suitable and cheaper."

She got quickly to her feet, the color rushing into her face.

"You will not! We owe you too much already."

He flicked the letter he had picked up disparagingly. "This amount will make very little difference to the total."

"Suppose we never manage to repay you?" she countered.

"You will," he answered calmly. "One way or another."

She looked at him suspiciously. "You mean you'll force us into bankruptcy if we don't?"

"I didn't say that, but if you like to think it, that suits me. It should suit you, too, because if I do intend to push things to that extreme, you shouldn't mind adding a few more pounds to the bill."

She took an angry turn around the room, then came to stand in front of him, looking him fearlessly in the eyes.

"No, I won't do it."

He frowned.

"I can't see what your objection is, unless of course you've made up your mind not to accept any favors from me. And if that is really your reason," he added with devastating candor, "then I think it's a stupid one, considering you've already begged me to grant you a favor already."

"Oh, you . . ." she began, then stopped, feeling completely helpless, knowing there was nothing she could say.

What he said was quite true, but that knowledge only made her dislike him all the more.

He laughed suddenly, though without mirth.

"I see I'm to have the usual reward of the person to whom someone is beholden," he said grimly.

She colored, acknowledging to herself the truth of his words, but denying it hotly to him. "That isn't why I dislike you."

He raised his eyebrows.

"You have some other reason? May I know what it is?"

"Yes . . . no. . . . Oh, why do you always try to put me in the wrong?"

"I wasn't aware that I did. You're too sensitive, Sara. You need to grow another skin. How did you get on at the store today?"

She blinked at him, taken aback by the sudden change of subject.

"Get on? In what way?"

"You said you were going to start examining the books. Did you have any trouble getting them?" he explained patiently.

"Oh, I see. No. They were already in the office when I arrived."

He seemed surprised but did not say anything, and after a moment she asked, "Why? Did you think I would have?"

He nodded. "I thought it possible. I'm glad for your sake I was wrong. How far did you get?"

She hesitated, then said reluctantly, "I didn't even begin. Terry came in before I started. He wanted to take me around the store to show me all the alterations that have been made. We talked to some of the staff and that took up quite a bit of time."

She stopped, remembering the impression of unrest, almost of antagonism she had sensed, and wondered if she ought to mention it to this man, then decided not to.

There was nothing she could really put her finger on, nothing but a vague impression which possibly had no foundation in fact but might be an extension of her own feeling of insecurity.

She was aroused from her thoughts by his sudden question.

"What is it, Sara? What's troubling you?"

"Nothing," she said quickly. "Nothing at all."

He looked at her penetratingly, and she said hurriedly, "Afterward Terry took me out to lunch and when we came back there was a message from Val asking me to come home at once."

"I see," he said slowly, then sat silently, staring in front of him as if he had forgotten she was there. He roused himself at last. "So even though the books were there you were effectively stopped from working on them."

"I'm sure that wasn't Terry's reason. . . ."

"Are you? Anyway, thank you for being so frank with me, Sara. I'll take this letter with me, if I may, and see if I can stave this particular creditor off for a little while. If I hear of anywhere suitable for you to live, I'll let you know."

"That's kind of you, but I'd rather you didn't bother," she began, then was relieved when the telephone rang.

She didn't really know what to say to him, this man whom she was so determined to dislike and who repaid her by being so thoughtful and so kind.

As she lifted the receiver she was almost tempted to apologize to him for the way she had treated him, then as the operator said, "I have a call for Miss Sara Blake from New York. Is she available?" everything else was forgotten in the happiness of knowing that she was going to talk to Johnnie.

"Johnnie!" she said as she heard his voice, as clear as if he was in the same room. "It's lovely to hear from you. How are you getting on without me?"

"Terrible, honey. Say, what's the idea, sending me a telegram like that? Fourteen days is all I allowed you, and I reckon to see you back here at the end of that."

She laughed ruefully. "I can't do it, Johnnie. Everything's in such a mess over here, you've no idea. I've got to stay because there isn't anyone else to see to things."

"And what about me? What about our job?"

"I wish I could fly right back to you, Johnnie, but I can't. You'll have to let me have three months. . . ."

"I will not. If you don't come back here I'll come over and get you."

"I wish you would! I'd love to see you come walking in through the door. I miss you and, oh, Johnnie, I need you. You don't know how much!"

When they had said goodbye she cradled the receiver, her eyes bright with the happiness of talking to Johnnie, of hearing from him how much she was wanted after the unhappy experiences she had had since coming to England.

In the excitement of talking to him she had completely forgotten Brent Maxwell, and she jumped when he said coldly, "A friend of yours, Sara?"

"Oh! I'd forgotten you were there. Yes, it was Johnnie, Johnnie Acton, my boss."

"Your boss? I'm sorry. I must have misunderstood."

She colored at his caustic tone. "I suppose you mean

you think we're too friendly. Well, let me tell you something, Brent Maxwell. There's none of this boss-employee nonsense about Johnnie and me."

"So I noticed! I didn't mean to denigrate American informality. On the contrary, I admire it."

She could feel the color mounting hotly into her face under his steady gaze and turned away, walking over to the door and opening it.

"I know exactly what you mean," she said quietly. "Now, if you'll excuse me, I have a meal to prepare."

"Certainly I will. I can tell when I'm not wanted." He went over to her and before she could move, took her chin in his fingers, tilting up her face toward him. "Your trouble is that you take offense too easily. You have to watch that temper of yours."

For a moment he smiled down into her angry eyes, then let go of her chin and brought his finger gently down her cheek.

"*Au revoir*, Sara. Until tomorrow," he said, and was gone before she had time to tell him exactly what she thought of him and his opinions.

She stood where he had left her, one hand against the cheek he had touched, angry with herself because she had allowed him to have the final word.

He was opinionated and arrogant, she told herself fiercely, as she slammed in and out of cupboards and refrigerator, assembling the food for their evening meal. He badly needed putting in his place, that was for sure, and she hoped one day before very long she would have the opportunity to do it.

She touched her face, feeling again his finger as it had gently stroked it, then snatched up the dish towel and angrily scrubbed her cheek with it, as if by doing so she could remove him from her mind.

CHAPTER SIX

When the meal was ready Sara called Val, who came out of her bedroom wearing a very lovely pale pink negligée which, to Sara's eyes, looked as if it had cost a great deal of money. *But then who would wear expensive clothes, if not the wife of the owner of the store,* she asked herself, trying to forget the niggling worry that perhaps this, as well as many other things, was not paid for.

"Has he gone? What did he want, Sara?" Val asked as soon as she came into the dining alcove.

"Just to talk about some financial details," Sara replied easily. "That's a gorgeous outfit, Val. It suits you."

Her sister-in-law looked down at herself complacently.

"Yes, isn't it? David brought it back with him from Paris a few months ago."

Sara looked at her quickly, noting that for the first time Val had spoken of David without her eyes filling with tears and hoping that this meant she was beginning to recover from the shock of his death.

"What sort of financial things did he talk about?" Val asked as they began to eat.

"All kinds." Sara hesitated, wondering if she should tell Val of Brent's offer to help them. She decided that now, when Val seemed to be in a fairly placid mood, might be the right moment. "He's taken the letter from the agent and says he'll see to it for us."

Val's eyes brightened.

"Oh, good! Then we can stay here. How clever of you to get him to do that, Sara."

"He's only going to see if he can get us time to pay."

"Pooh, nonsense! I don't believe that."

Sara stared at her. "You mean . . . he's going to pay the bill?"

"Of course."

"But we can't let him do that." She pushed back her chair. "I'll phone him up and stop him. . . ."

"Don't be silly, Sara. Why shouldn't he pay it?"

"Because he's got nothing to do with us, that's why. And we already owe him enough without adding to it."

Val shrugged. "He'll get paid one day, and if it means we can stay here. . . ."

"It doesn't. It's just another reason why we should find somewhere else quickly."

"If we do that, it'll bring all our creditors down on us. We've got to keep up appearances, Sara. Anyway, if you'd only see reason we wouldn't need to worry. If the people we owe money to knew we were selling out, they'd be content to wait."

Sara stared at her, surprised to find her so knowledgeable, so determined to sacrifice the business which had been so important to her husband.

"I can't help that, and all Brent's doing is getting us time to pay."

"Is it? I wouldn't have thought even he would be so mean, with all his money."

"He isn't, Val. It was me who refused to let him pay, but he has promised to look out for a cheaper apartment for us, so we can get rid of this burden."

"That's big of him, but he needn't bother. I don't want to leave here. I'm surprised at you, Sara. I'd have thought you'd have more pride than to keep running to him for help."

That was something Sara herself wondered about, because it was completely against her nature. Yet what alternative had she? Everything she had done, no matter how difficult she had found it and how alien to her, had been done for Jamie, so that if he wanted his inheritance it would be there waiting for him. Only she knew how much it had cost her to take the steps necessary to insure that, and Brent had made it possible for her to try. Val had called him mean, but in that moment of truth Sara admitted that she had been wrong.

Whatever Brent Maxwell's faults were, meanness was not among them, and perhaps one day Val, too, might acknowledge that.

The next few days were quiet ones for Sara. When she went to the store the day after talking to Brent in the apartment, she learned from Céleste that Terry had gone to Paris early that morning.

"To Paris? But he didn't say anything about it yesterday," she exclaimed.

"Didn't he? It was pretty sudden, I suppose. Of course he knew he'd have to go soon, but he discovered yesterday afternoon that he'd be needed earlier."

"I see. Thanks for telling me," Sara said, and settled down again to her work.

Meticulously in the days that followed she checked through the books and, when she needed a rest from that, walked through the store in an effort to become accustomed to the routine and to get to know the staff.

But it was not an easy task, as she said to Mollie when she met her for coffee in the staff dining room.

"I can't make them out. They're so impersonal with me. You'd think they'd be glad one of the family was taking an interest in them and in the store."

Mollie shook her head. "They've heard rumors, Sara, and they're worried about the future. I think they'd feel better if there was a new owner with plenty of money to spend."

"You mean they know there's been an offer? Who told them about it?"

"These things get around," Mollie said evasively.

"Only because somebody makes it his business to do that, surely?"

"Perhaps." Mollie looked at her obliquely. "How are you getting on with your research? Have you found anything yet?"

"Not really. There are a few things I don't understand, but apart from them. . . ."

"Some of those who used to work here could tell you a few things," Mollie said suddenly, then covered her mouth with her hands, looking pleadingly at Sara. "I shouldn't have said that. Forget it! Promise you will."

Sara shook her head.

"I can't forget it, but I won't tell anyone what you said, Mollie." She sighed. "I feel as if there's a conspiracy of silence everywhere. I can't understand it. When we undertake this kind of investigation in the States, everybody tries to help, but here. . . ."

"Here you've got. . . ." Mollie stopped and closed her lips firmly. "No, I won't say it. My job is too important to me to jeopardize it."

Sara looked at her earnestly.

"Mollie, believe me, you needn't worry. Nothing you tell me will be held against you. I promise you that."

"I know you mean it, Sara, but I don't dare risk it. I've seen it happen too often. People have been here one day, then gone the next. I've got Mother to think of, not just myself." She got up and leaned against the table, looking apologetically at Sara. "Remember that, won't you, and don't think too badly of me."

Sara watched her walk quickly out of the dining room, then followed more slowly, trying to understand what she had heard.

It seemed clear that Mollie knew something of what had been going on, and that others had also known and had been fired because of that knowledge. Yet how could it have happened while David had been in control?

She was still frowning over the problem when she walked into her office, to stop short in surprise as Brent Maxwell got up from the visitor's chair in front of the desk.

"What are you doing here?" she asked.

"I called to tell you I've found an apartment. Can you come and look at it?"

"Now? But. . . ."

"Yes, while I've got the key."

"But I've so much to do."

He sighed. "As if that matters! It can wait, surely, for an hour or so. I thought a cheaper apartment was important to you."

She glared at him, this man who always had to have his own way, who rode roughshod over everyone's feelings. She doubted if it ever occurred to him that anyone had feelings which might be hurt.

"That's where you're wrong. I'm just at a crucial point. It's too bad you've made these arrangements. Perhaps next time you'll find out first if it's convenient."

She could hear her voice rising and clamped her lips together, trying to hold on to her control.

"Now what's wrong?" he asked in a long-suffering voice. She felt a choking sensation in her throat and knew that in spite of all her efforts she was not going to be able to do it.

She took a deep calming breath, clenching her hands tightly together preparatory to telling him exactly what she thought of him. But before she could say anything, he added, "If you're not the most contrary girl I've ever known! I did try to telephone you, or at least my secretary did, but although you're so busy, you weren't in your office and no one seemed to know where you were. You seem to have forgotten you asked me to do what I could to help you. However, if you've changed your mind, please tell me. That's all you need to do, you know. Then I won't bother you any more."

She didn't look directly at him, her innate sense of fair play telling her that every word he said was the truth. Not that this endeared him to her in the least. On the contrary, it only increased her dislike of him, especially as she knew she couldn't do as he suggested. It was impossible for her to look him straight in the eye and tell him to go away, that she was quite capable of dealing with everything herself.

She did not have enough time for that. This man had given her three months to get the finances of the store in some sort of order. If she was to succeed at all, she needed every moment she could snatch, so how could she at the same time look for an apartment?

She swallowed hard, knowing she must accept his help no matter how much she hated to do so, and said coldly, "I'm sorry. Of course I'll come and look over the apartment now. It's most kind of you to take all this trouble for us."

"Kind!" he mocked. "You've suddenly found your party manners, haven't you? I'm not sure I like them, Sara."

"Then you'll have to lump them," she flashed. "It's evident that nothing I do will ever suit you, so you'll just have to put up with it."

"That's better! I was beginning to think you were getting sick. No, peace!" he laughed as her eyes flashed fire at him. "I take it all back. Come and look at the apartment before you make up your mind that nothing I recommend will suit you!"

This was so near to the truth that she found herself unable to answer, and when he put his hand under her elbow, she went with him meekly down the stairs and out of the store.

He stopped at a low sports car parked nearby and opened the door for her. "Jump in. It's not far away, but we may as well drive there."

She got in without answering and was surprised in spite of what he had said, when after a very few minutes he stopped in a narrow street of high row houses.

She looked at them, her heart sinking, her thoughts mirrored in her expressive face.

"Don't look like that," he said. "The outside may not be wonderful, but I think you'll find the inside much more to your taste."

She did not really believe him but allowed him to lead her up the steps of the house. Brent opened the front door with the key and stood aside to allow her to go in.

Sara did so, then stopped in astonishment, looking around her. The spacious hall contained a beautiful curving staircase to the upper floor, the stairs were bright and shining with yellow paint and made the hall look as if it was full of sunbeams.

"This hall was once the ground floor of two houses. The whole row had been converted into apartments and the ground floor one on this side is empty."

He inserted the key and pushed the door open. Sara went hesitantly inside, finding herself in a narrow lobby with doors leading off it. He opened them in turn.

"This is the living room and next to it is a good sized kitchen with a dining alcove. Then there's the bathroom with a shower, and three bedrooms."

Sara followed him from room to room, admitting, though not yet willingly, that he had been right. It was the ideal apartment for them—spacious, light and airy. The big windows caught the sunshine, the central heating was unobtrusive, the decorations were fresh and bright, and the furnishings were good.

"Well?" he asked when she didn't speak. "Will it do?"

"Yes," she said, and then was annoyed with herself for the brevity of her answer.

Just because she disliked him and thought him autocratic was no excuse for her to be bad-mannered and ungrateful.

"You were quite right, Brent." She spoke quickly and gratefully. "It's exactly the kind of apartment we need. Thank you for finding it."

"You think Val will like it, too?"

"She'll have to," Sara answered with decision. "She can't stay where she is and. . . ." She looked at him as a worrying idea occurred to her. "If we can afford it. Is it very expensive?"

"No, quite reasonable for a furnished apartment." He named an amount which to her, accustomed to the high rents of American apartments and compared with that charged for the one Val and David had occupied, seemed ridiculously cheap.

"Are you sure?" she asked, putting her doubt into words. "You haven't made a mistake?"

"Of course not. Can you afford it?"

"Oh, yes. Thanks again, Brent, I'm sorry if I seemed ungrateful, but. . . ."

"I know exactly how you felt," he said, and the hot color flooded into her cheeks at the implied rebuke that she knew was well deserved. "If you're really sure, then we may as well go and clinch the deal. Unless you want Val to see it first?"

"No. She must accept my word that it's suitable," Sara said with decision.

His deep blue eyes crinkled into laughter. "I knew you for an autocrat the moment I saw you! Come along, then, and we'll get everything fixed up."

The hot color was still burning in her cheeks as she went with him to his car. It was not until she was seated in the agent's office and was signing the lease he produced that she recovered her usual spirit.

"You're sure the rent is correct?" she asked, her pen poised over the document.

The agent smiled, flicking a glance at Brent.

"Yes, quite right. It's as agreed, isn't it, Mr. Maxwell?"

"Exactly as agreed." He looked at his watch. "There's just time for us to have lunch, Sara, before I go to another appointment. I know just the place where we'll be served quickly with excellent food. Come along."

She went with him, not wanting to argue about it in the agent's office, but as soon as they were outside she said sharply, "There's no need to think you have to treat me to lunch, you know."

He put his hands on her shoulders and gave her a little shake.

"When will you learn to accept an invitation gracefully, Sara? I want to treat you to lunch, so come along and don't argue."

"I wasn't going to. . . ." she began.

"Good. That makes a change. Do one thing for me, will you?"

She looked at him, suspicion in her dark eyes. "Such as what?"

"Give me the pleasure of your company for an hour or so without trying to fight me every minute."

She was so taken aback by his words that she got meekly into the car, and had barely recovered from them when they were being ushered to a table in the window of the restaurant he had chosen.

"This is my club," he said as they sat down. "You can always be sure of a good meal here, even at short notice."

The waiter shook out the table napkin and placed it over her knees, then whisked away the card from the center of the table. It was only then that she realized it spelled "Reserved."

She clenched her hands together, understanding at once that he must have taken it for granted that she would have lunch with him. But he was already consulting with the wine waiter and she was being handed a menu.

This was no time to have a showdown with him, and anyway she had recklessly promised that she would not fight with him while they ate. But as she looked at the menu she vowed to herself that one day, before very long, she would teach this man a lesson.

She would make it clear to him that she would not tolerate his arrogant ways, though she did not know how she was going to do it.

CHAPTER SEVEN

The lunch was all that Brent had said it would be, and as she went into her office later, Sara admitted to herself that nobody could have been a more charming companion during that hour of truce.

Looking back, she could hardly believe she had been with the same man. Then she smiled at herself wryly. Just because he had shown so much interest in her work with Johnnie and had asked so many intelligent questions, she was imagining that this particular leopard had changed his spots.

Of course he had not, she told herself sharply. He had promised her an excellent lunch in congenial company and it was in keeping with his character that he had so meticulously carried out what he had promised.

In spite of that thought, as she pulled the ledger toward her and picked up her pencil she was aware of a warm feeling of comfort within her.

Because in spite of his annoying assumption of omnipotence he had proved one thing, that he had remembered her and her problems and had acted at once to produce the ideal answer to them. And for that she must always be grateful to him.

She didn't know why he had done so, and though she thought about it for a long time, she could find no answer to the mystery. It was not easy to forget about it and concentrate on the work she had to do, but she made a determined effort.

After a while the familiar task engrossed her completely as she searched for the answer to the question that had troubled her for days, the question of what had happened to the money from the sale of her brother's home.

She had just convinced herself that there was no entry to cover it when the door opened and Terry came in.

She looked up with a start, dragging her mind back to the present.

"Hi, Sara," he said. "How are things going?"

"All right. Why did you go to Paris? It was a very sudden decision, wasn't it?"

"Not really. I knew I'd have to go sooner or later to try to pick up the threads. It just happened to become necessary earlier than I expected, that's all. I came in before to ask you to have lunch with me again, but you were out."

"Yes. Brent Maxwell called and I had lunch with him."

He raised his eyebrows. "Did you? That's a surprise."

"Why should it be?"

"Well, after his display of temper in the store, I'd have thought you'd never have spoken to him again."

He spoke lightly enough, but Sara could sense a sharpness under the words which was at variance with his off-hand attitude, and she asked probingly, "Did you expect that to happen?"

He laughed shortly.

"Oh, come now, Sara, that's putting a meaning into what I said that wasn't intended. Knowing you, I must say it wouldn't have surprised me in the slightest if you had quarreled permanently with him after the way he spoke to you. In front of the staff, too."

"I might have done that," she agreed, "if he hadn't come to see me later, to apologize."

"Maxwell apologized? I don't believe it."

"It's true, though. He realized afterward that I knew nothing about the phone call. Who do you think made it, Terry?"

"How should I know? Maybe he dreamed the whole thing up."

"Why on earth would he do that?"

He shrugged. "Who knows what his motives may be? For instance, why should he call and take you out to lunch today?"

She was unreasonably irritated by his words. "What do you mean by that?"

"Oh, I didn't mean to suggest he took you out for any other reason than to sit and look at you, my lovely Sara. I wouldn't be so uncomplimentary."

"Don't be ridiculous. If you must know, he's found a cheaper apartment for us and he took me to see it."

"That was quick work, but then he's got a lot of irons in the fire."

"You mean it'd be one of his apartments?"

He lifted his hands expressively. "Who knows? But I can tell you one thing, you haven't got his measure yet, Sara."

"Perhaps not, but at least I can be grateful for the trouble he's taken," she said with asperity.

"Oh, certainly." He came around the desk and looked at the columns of figures she had written down. "How are you getting on? Have you found anything yet?"

"It's what I can't find that's worrying me. Do you think David used the money from the sale of the house to pay off mortgages?"

He moved away from her and she sensed a moment's indecision as if he was making up his mind what to say. When he did answer, however, his voice was confident.

"Definitely not," he answered smoothly. "He thought at first that he might raise a mortgage, but he found he could get a lot more money by selling, so he did."

"Then what can have happened to it?"

"I've told you that already."

She looked at him, her dark eyes bright with annoyance, resenting the implication behind his words with a depth of feeling which surprised her.

"I know you have, and I don't believe it. I asked Brent if he'd had the money and he said he didn't."

Terry sat down on the corner of the desk.

"Of course he did, my dear. He's hardly likely to admit it, is he?"

"I believe him, Terry."

"Which means that you don't believe me? I'm hurt, Sara."

She made an impatient movement.

"I don't mean it like that at all. . . ."

"Don't you?" He got up and went toward the door, turning when he reached it, his hand on the knob. "Are you sure?" he asked, and in one movement opened the door and went out.

She sat and stared in front of her, acknowledging that he had some grounds for the reproach in his voice. What he said was true. She did believe Brent Maxwell and, having acknowledged that, it followed that she did not believe Terry. How could she when she definitely suspected him of deliberately misleading her about so many things?

She sighed, pushing the honey gold hair back from her hot forehead. Never had she felt so confused about anything as she did at that moment. She had always prided herself on the clarity of her mind, and Johnnie had always called her his "clear-thinking" woman.

Her mouth twisted wryly. He would certainly change his ideas if he could only see the turmoil in her brain now!

She pulled the stock ledger toward her, determined that she would concentrate on one of the most obvious sources of loss in a business and forget about the exasperating Brent Maxwell. Before long she was immersed in the work to the exclusion of everything else.

A very definite picture began to emerge as she checked the purchase of materials against the entries in the stores ledger, finding again and again that expensive consignments of cloth of all kinds were not entered. Carefully she noted down the discrepancies, then took one item, an outrageously expensive gold embroidered silk, and checked through the whole ledger, looking for an entry. There was nothing at all to be found, and she sat back in her chair, looking frowningly in front of her and wondering who she should approach first about it. Then her brow cleared.

How stupid of her! Of course, Mollie was in charge of stores. She would know, if anyone did, what had happened to the missing stock.

She pulled the internal telephone toward her and dialed the stock room number. When Mollie's voice answered her, she said crisply, "Sara here. Can you spare the time to come to my office, Mollie?"

"Yes. In about ten minutes, if that's all right."

"Yes, fine. See you then."

Sara cradled the receiver, trying to work out the best way in which to approach this woman whom she had known so long. By the time Mollie came, she had made up her mind. Only the truth would serve. That would be the way Mollie would prefer it, she was sure.

"Sorry to keep you waiting," Mollie apologized as she came in.

"That's all right. I want you to help me, if you can. Come and look at this item, bought about four months ago. Have you any idea what happened to it?"

Mollie looked down at the entry in the purchase ledger and shook her head.

"I don't remember it, but the stores ledger will tell you what happened to it."

"But it doesn't," Sara said quietly.

Mollie's forehead creased into worried lines. "Are you sure?"

"Yes, and it's not the only one. Quite a number of very expensive items are missing. Could they have gone straight out to the departments, do you think?"

Mollie shook her head decisively. "No. Everything should go into stores first, especially the expensive materials. They're only used for the model clothes and wouldn't be issued until they were required. I can't understand it." She stopped, her usually ruddy cheeks whitening. "They're my responsibility, but I've never seen them. Honestly, Sara. You've got to believe me."

Sara put out her hand and touched Mollie's arm gently.

"Of course I believe you, Mollie. Only . . . what can have happened to them, do you think?"

"I don't know. There are a lot of queer things going on, only I can't talk about them, Sara. You see, those who talked lost their jobs, and I don't dare lose mine. My mother's very old and frail now and dependent on me. . . ."

"Don't worry, Mollie. I'll see you're all right, you know that."

"But you won't always be here."

Sara was silent for a moment, acknowledging the truth of what Mollie had said.

"Think about it, anyway," she said at last. "I won't force you to tell me anything you don't want to."

"Thanks, Sara. I'll have to go now. People will be wanting me, and if they find me here with you. . . ."

Sara sat quite still after Mollie had gone, hurrying out of the room on the heels of her words. She felt shocked and worried by what she had heard.

In her father's time old employees particularly had been looked after and valued. Now it seemed they were dismissed if they knew too much and were not afraid to speak up about things which they thought were wrong. She could hardly believe it was true, yet the fact remained that of the people she had known practically all her life, only Mollie was left.

She had not blamed anybody for what had happened, but Sara knew with a slightly sick feeling that the fault must lie with David, who apparently had not cared about the old employees.

The first closing bell, shrilling through the building, roused her from her unhappy thoughts with a jolt, and she quickly gathered the books together and pushed them into a cupboard.

She had intended to go home earlier, to tell Val about the new apartment. The news that they would be leaving the old one within a week she knew would not be at all acceptable to her sister-in-law. And she was right.

"You mean we'll have to go next week? But that's ridiculous! It'll take weeks to sort everything out. And I haven't seen the apartment yet. What's all the hurry, Sara?"

"Brent Maxwell's arranged it that way, to save us money. The new apartment's much cheaper than this one. I don't know how he managed to get the agents to give us time to pay, but he must have guaranteed us himself in some way."

"And why not? He's got plenty of money. David always said he was rolling in wealth."

"That isn't the point—"

"Nonsense. It wouldn't hurt him to be responsible for a few more pounds. I won't go to some poky little place in a rush—"

"It isn't poky." Sara heard her voice rising with irritation and tried to take a hold on her temper. "It's quite big. You'll like it, Val."

"Is it like this one?"

"Well, no. It's—"

"There you are, then! I tell you, I won't go there."

Sara sighed. "You've no option, Val. Don't you understand, we can't stay here because we can't pay the high rent. It's no use crying," she added quickly as the easy tears began to stream down Val's cheeks. "That solves nothing."

"You're absolutely heartless, Sara. And what about Jamie? It's his school break next weekend and he won't have anywhere to go."

"I didn't know that, but I can't see that it matters. He can help us to move if he's home in time. If not, he'll come to the new apartment instead of the old one, that's all."

"Poor boy! To lose his father and now to have no proper home either. I don't understand you, Sara. Living in the States has changed you. You're not the same girl I used to know."

With an effort Sara controlled the stinging reply she would have liked to make, acknowledging that Val had suffered more than one severe shock in the past few weeks.

"I'm sorry, Val," she said instead. "I haven't really changed, you know. It's just that as things are, we can't go on living as we have. Jamie's a sensible boy. He'll understand."

Val twisted her handkerchief between her fingers. "I hope you're right. Oh, why did David have to die like that and cause me all this trouble?"

Sara put a comforting arm around her. "I don't know, love, but stop worrying. Everything will turn out right one of these days."

"I hope so." Val looked forlornly at Sara. "It doesn't seem possible that it will. I think I'll go and lie down."

"Yes, do that, and I'll bring you a cup of tea and some aspirin to help you to sleep."

Sara watched her sister-in-law trail lethargically into her bedroom before going into the kitchen to plug in the kettle, a worried frown between her eyes.

If only Val would try to accept that everything must change, but it was probably too much to expect of her. Perhaps when Jamie came home she would feel better because he, Sara was sure, would take any changes in his stride. If he was still the placid boy she remembered, he would be too occupied with his own interests to bother about external things. All he had needed was a roof over his head and plenty of food at regular intervals. She saw no reason to doubt that he was still the same, if his letters to her were any indication.

No, it was not the thought of Jamie which brought that worried frown to her forehead, a frown that was still there when she took the tea to Valerie.

CHAPTER EIGHT

Contrary to Sara's expectations, Val made no more protests about leaving the apartment, and over the next few days seemed to recover from her almost hysterical opposition to the plan although she steadfastly refused to see the new apartment.

Sara was glad that at home everything seemed to be comparatively peaceful, because as her investigations at the store proceeded, she was becoming more and more worried.

Always when she walked through, all departments appeared to be very busy, yet although the floor managers assured her that there was a marked increase in trading, cash receipts were considerably down from the previous year. Doggedly she checked and cross-checked, working out costs against receipts, and all the while her concern for the future deepened as the first of the three months allowed her inexorably ticked away.

Perhaps things might not have seemed so dismal if she had had somebody to share her difficulties, as she had done with Johnnie. But at the store there was always the suspicion that the people who could have helped her might be concerned in the discrepancies, and she did not feel she could approach them.

She was so very much alone in the difficult task she had undertaken so lightly. Days had gone by since Brent had smiled at her and said, "*Au revoir*, Sara. See you soon," but he had not come near. And, strangely enough, it was this which caused her the most concern, as though she had lost something of value to her.

It was ridiculous, she told herself fiercely. Three weeks

earlier she had not known of his existence, and from the first he had annoyed her by his arrogance and impatience. Yet in spite of it all, she could not help feeling deserted, as if he had abandoned her when she most needed help.

She looked up as the door opened, her pulses leaping hopefully, but it was Terry who came in, and the depression clamped down again.

"Still busy, Sara? How are things working out?" he asked.

"It's too early to be sure yet," she answered evasively, reluctant to talk to him about her suspicions. There would be time enough for that when she was sure about what had been taking place. "These things can't be hurried."

"I suppose not, but if there's anything I can do to help, you only have to ask me."

"Thanks, Terry, I'll remember that. Oh, by the way, we'll be moving into the new apartment next week and I'll have to take a couple of days off. Will it be all right if I keep the books in here until I'm back again?"

He frowned. "It's not terribly convenient, Sara, because there's work to be done on them. If you're not using them I'd rather they went back to the office."

"Just as you like. I don't want to make things difficult for you."

"You won't do that, I know. If you'll tell me the date you're moving, I'll have them picked up then and brought back when you return."

"I don't know it yet."

"Don't you? I thought from the way you spoke that you'd got it all fixed up."

She hesitated, then said quietly,

"Brent was to let me know when he'd arranged it, but I haven't heard from him yet."

"Was he? He's being very busy on your behalf. Still,

it's not surprising that he hasn't let you know. I heard he'd gone away. He often does for a week or so. He says it's business, but we think he goes to see a rather special girlfriend."

He laughed, though the eyes that watched Sara so closely did not change their expression.

"It would be very odd if he'd got to his age without having a girlfriend," she replied, and was relieved to see the suspicion leave his eyes. "I ought to have made the arrangements myself. It's entirely my own fault."

"Well, take as much time as you need, my dear. How does Val like the new apartment?"

"She hasn't seen it. She says she won't go near it until she's forced to."

Terry shook his head. "You should have left her where she was happy, Sara. Poor Val! Bad enough to lose David without having all her life disrupted as well."

Sara's eyes flashed in sudden anger.

"That's the silliest thing I've heard you say yet! You of all people know how we're placed. Val has no income from the store and the proceeds from David's life insurance will have to be used to pay off his bank loan. She doesn't want to understand, but you should. She's destitute, and you know it."

"All right, I know it," he said sharply. "I also know it's your fault, Sara, because you won't accept the offer that's been made for the business. It's still open, by the way," he added.

"That only solves things in the short term, Terry," she said wearily. "What I'm trying to do is make Val's and Jamie's future secure."

"And Sara Blake's, too, I think."

"Perhaps, but if I'm all right, so are they. Don't forget that, Terry."

"I won't." He smiled suddenly, making a complete

reverse. "That's quite true, Sara. I admire you for sticking to your guns and you know I'll help you in any way I can."

"Thank you."

He turned to go, then came back again and said, "Oh, you'll be glad to know that we think we've found a designer . . . a young woman who's been in Paris for the past two years and seems to be on her toes and have plenty of bright ideas."

"Good. I'm glad. When's she coming?"

"As soon as she's released by her present firm. It's a relief to have found somebody so quickly. We could certainly do with a boost, that's for sure."

She looked at him quickly.

"Is trade as bad as it seems, Terry? I know takings are down on last year, but the store seems to be very busy."

He shrugged.

"Plenty of people walking around, but not many buying."

"I wouldn't have said that, and Mollie tells me the model gown department and the sewing rooms are fantastically busy."

He frowned.

"Does she? That shows all she knows about it. There may be a lot of orders in, but costs have risen so steeply over the past few months that we'll be lucky if we make a profit in those departments."

"You'll have to increase prices, won't you?"

"Yes, as soon as we can. New models will help, and that's what I hope we'll get as soon as this new girl comes. Wish me luck, Sara."

"I do, of course."

"Thanks. See you," and before she knew it, he bent and kissed her firmly, then was gone.

Sara sat where he had left her, automatically trying to rub from her lips the impression of his kiss, feeling unreasonably angry at his action. It was not the first time in her life that Terry had kissed her, only now she didn't want his kisses. Judas kisses, she told herself sadly, because she was becoming more and more sure that Terry was behind all the troubles that had overtaken Blake's store.

If only she did not feel so alone! Even Brent Maxwell, irritating as he was with his firm conviction that he was always right, would have been welcome because he at least, whatever his own opinions were, was actively supporting her in her effort to pull the business around.

But he was off on his own, visiting his girlfriend instead of making the arrangements he had promised he would. He was as unreliable as everyone else. One day, she told herself sadly, she would learn her lesson . . . that nothing was done which she did not do herself.

Only somehow she had thought Brent Maxwell was different, that he understood and sympathized with her. Well, she had been wrong. Tomorrow she would make her own arrangements, and tonight, as soon as she had eaten supper, she would begin to pack in readiness for the move. Perhaps Val could be persuaded to help her.

But when she reached home the apartment was empty. There was no note from Val saying where she had gone, though Sara was glad that her sister-in-law, who had spent the past few days alternately in bed or lying on the sofa had actually roused herself enough to go out.

That must be a good sign, she thought optimistically as she prepared and ate a scratch meal, because it must mean that Val was beginning to accept the situation with good grace.

After she had eaten she changed into jeans and a tee shirt, then turned on the record player before beginning to take the books off the shelves in David's study. She had hardly begun when the doorbell rang.

She went to answer it, wondering who could be calling at that time of night, then stood staring at the last person she had expected to see.

"Good evening, Sara," Brent Maxwell said. "Aren't you going to ask me in?"

"What do you want?" she demanded.

"To see you, of course. What else?"

"That's very good of you, but as you've managed to live so many days without getting in touch with me, I don't think it matters. . . ."

"Now what are you talking about?" He pushed the door wide open and stepped into the hall. She backed away from him.

"I wasn't aware that I'd asked you to come in," she said militantly.

"I know you didn't, but I thought you'd probably just forgotten your manners." He looked down at her with the sudden unexpected smile that lit up his eyes so magically. "Aren't you glad to see me, Sara?"

"Only so that I can tell you what I think of you for not doing what you promised. Though, naturally, I can hardly expect you to give up your pleasures for me."

"Certainly not." He walked past her, taking her arm in his hand and leading her inexorably into the living room. "Suppose we sit down comfortably while you tell me about these pleasures I haven't given up."

She shrugged her arm away from his hand but did not sit down as he suggested. Instead she walked across to the record player and turned it off.

"It's no business of mine," she said coldly, "what you do. You're perfectly at liberty to visit your girlfriend if you want to, only I think you might have—"

"Certainly I am," he interrupted. "How did you know where I'd gone?"

"Terry told me," she said, trying not to let him irritate her, though the strange attitude he was adopting was making it difficult for her to achieve.

"Did he? He's very knowledgeable about my affairs."

"Oh, stop fencing with me! It's nothing to me who you go and see, but—"

He moved suddenly, looking down at her with a half smile, taking her shoulders in his hands. She could feel them burning through the thin cloth of her tee shirt and was acutely aware of his nearness, feeling the pulse in her throat begin to beat strongly.

She saw as if through a mist the deep blue eyes smiling at her and felt a surge of emotion burn through her, so that only the greatest strength of will prevented her from swaying toward him and losing herself in those bright, hypnotic eyes.

She gasped and pulled away from him, breaking his hold on her, and moved over to the window, trying to control the wild beating of her heart, to hide from him the agitation his nearness had raised in her.

What was the matter with her? Why should he, whom she did not even like, who annoyed her by his arbitrary, arrogant treatment of her, affect her like this? As though she had drunk heady champagne and all the joy bells in the world were ringing?

She realized thankfully that he had not moved, and after a moment she was able to turn toward him and say in a casual voice that pleased her, "What did you come for?"

He did not answer immediately but stood looking down, the deep lines of his face very much in evidence.

"To see if the arrangements I've made were suitable," he said at last.

"What arrangements?"

He looked at her then in surprise.

"Didn't Jane, my secretary, phone you?"

"No. Should she have?"

"Yes. I was called away suddenly . . . not to visit my girlfriend, as you apparently thought, but to go to my grandmother who is very dear to me. I asked Jane to phone you about the arrangements I'd made. You're sure she didn't?"

"Well, honestly! I'm not quite out of my mind yet. Of course she didn't," Sara said indignantly.

"I'm sorry, but it's not like Jane to forget anything."

"She's slipped up this time. You didn't mention it to her when you got back?"

"I haven't seen her yet. I only arrived about an hour ago and I came straight here. I thought you'd be expecting me."

She was disarmed by his answer and ashamed of herself because she had misjudged him so badly. Underneath she was aware of a warm feeling of comfort which she could find no reason for, except the relief of knowing that after all he had not neglected her for some mythical girlfriend.

"What arrangements have you made?" she asked at last.

He told her, adding anxiously, "It's very short notice now, Sara, for the day after tomorrow. Can you manage it, do you think?"

"I'll have to. I've started to stack all the books and maybe I'll finish them tonight. Then. . . ."

"I'd hoped you'd come to dinner with me."

She was conscious again of the breathlessness which had seized her earlier, and it was an effort to say calmly,

"Now? Tonight? I'm afraid I can't. There's so much to do if I'm to be ready in time."

"Leave it," he said masterfully. "My men will do everything for you, if you'll direct them."

She hesitated, "If that's all right . . . it would certainly save me a lot of work," she said slowly.

"I wouldn't offer if it wasn't. You'll come, then?"

"Yes. Thank you. If you'll give me a few minutes to change. . . ."

"As long as you like, Sara. Take your time."

But she did not keep him waiting long, coming in to him in less than 20 minutes wearing one of her favorite outfits, a blue green dress of wild silk covered by a loose matching coat. The neckline trimming of thick embroidery was interspersed with sparkling beads which caught the light as she moved. It had been a real extravagance when she had bought it, but now she was glad, wanting in some obscure way to look her very best while she was out with this man.

"You look very lovely, Sara," he said when she came in. "That's a gorgeous color and it suits you."

She felt the pleased color deepen in her cheeks.

"Thank you. I'm glad you approve," she said provocatively. "I think we make a handsome couple, don't you?"

He laughed. "Though unlike the birds, where it's the male who wears the brilliant feathers while the female looks pretty drab!"

That laughing remark seemed to set the tone for the rest of the evening. Brent took her to a quiet but elegant restaurant with tables set in alcoves, where the food was excellent and the service unobtrusive and efficient. For the remainder of the evening Sara forgot all the troubles which had been piling onto her during the past weeks.

The time passed very quickly and happily and Sara was

very sorry when the time came to go home. Brent drove her to the block of apartments and went with her to the elevator doors.

He pressed the button, then as they waited took her hands in his, smiling at her in a way that made her legs feel as if all the bones had been removed from them.

"Thank you for a perfect evening, Sara," he said as the elevator doors opened silently behind her. "I won't come up to the apartment with you in case Val is there, but I'll see you tomorrow."

"Tomorrow?" she repeated in surprise.

"Yes. It's nearly one o'clock in the morning. Sleep well, Sara. Take care of yourself."

He bent his head and she felt his lips against hers for a brief moment, then he was gone, striding across the foyer to the front doors. She waited until he reached them, and raised an unsteady hand in farewell as he turned to look back at her before going out.

Then she went into the elevator and was carried up to the apartment, aware only of the turbulent emotions which surged through her, making her feel weak and breathless.

What was there about this man that he should have such an effect on her? Certainly she had spent an enjoyable evening with him, but that did not alter the fact that their characters were totally at variance. Yet Johnnie, whom she was so fond of, had never raised such feelings in her when he kissed her, had never made her think she was floating on a golden cloud of happiness.

CHAPTER NINE

The apartment was in darkness when Sara let herself in, and she went quietly into the living room so that she wouldn't disturb Val. She switched on a table lamp and sat down in the nearest chair, feeling drained of all strength and glad that there was nobody around to see how disturbed she was.

Then she heard Val's voice calling to her from her bedroom and she got up quickly, going to the door to answer in case her sister-in-law should get up and come in to her.

"What is it, Val? What's wrong?"

"Nothing. I wondered what had happened to you. You're very late. Where've you been?"

"I might ask you the same question."

"I came in ages ago. I've been in bed for hours. Come and talk to me, Sara. There's no point in standing in the hall.

"All right." Reluctantly she crossed to Val's room and went in, glad to find she had switched on a rose-shaded bedside lamp which shed a low, diffused light across the bed, leaving the remainder of the room in semidarkness. Val's eyes were too sharp to risk being seen by her in a bright light, Sara thought, as she walked across to the dressing table and sat down on the stool in front of it. "I tried not to wake you, Val. I've been out to dinner with Brent Maxwell."

"That man? Poor you!"

"I had a very pleasant time. Where did you go, Val?"

"Terry phoned me and asked me to have dinner with

him, so I thought I might as well go," she said defensively.

"Why not? You've got to start going out sometime. Did you enjoy it?"

"Yes, thoroughly. It's ages since I went anywhere. Oh, by the way, I've heard from Jamie. He's coming home on the weekend."

"Oh, good. We'll have to meet him at the station. We'll be in the new apartment by then."

Val sat up quickly.

"In the new apartment? What do you mean?"

"We're moving tomorrow. Brent arranged it and asked his secretary to let us know, but she must have forgotten. But it doesn't really matter. He says his men will see to everything for us, so there's no harm done."

"That's a matter of opinion! How dare you make all these arrangements without consulting me? You take too much on yourself, Sara!"

"I'm sorry, Val. It's just unfortunate that we weren't told earlier, but we knew we'd have to move quickly and once we'd found somewhere to live. . . ."

"Once you found it, you mean. My wishes weren't regarded, that's for sure."

Sara sighed, feeling too tired to go on arguing with her sister-in-law, all the happiness she had been filled with gone as if it had never been.

"You know we have no alternative, Val. Anyway, it's all arranged now and there's nothing to be done about it."

Val's lips thinned and her face looked suddenly sharp and pinched, no longer pretty.

"If you'd done as Terry wanted you to, none of this would have happened."

"Don't start that again, Val," Sara answered wearily. "I know Terry's convinced you that if we'd sold the business everything would have been all right, but I know it wouldn't. I did what seemed right for us all."

"Well, I don't think it was. I'm sure Terry knows more about the store than you do."

"Perhaps he does, but it's too late to change our plans now. This apartment has been given up and we've got to go."

Val hunched her smooth shoulders pettishly.

"I'll be out all that day, so don't expect me to do anything to help."

"I won't. Brent's men will see to everything. You'll only have to get into a taxi when you're ready and drive over to the new place."

"It sounds to me as if that man's got far too much influence over you," Val said sharply. "Why don't you think for yourself for a change? Can't you see he's got his own ax to grind?"

Sara took a deep calming breath.

"No, I can't, and I don't agree that I'm influenced by Brent Maxwell. I don't even like him. Anyway, I'm too tired to argue with you, Val. I'm going to bed."

"Suit yourself," Val said, and switched off the light, leaving Sara to grope her way in darkness to her own room. But it was a long time before she went to sleep. Whether it was because of the emotional upheaval she had experienced earlier that night or her final clash with Val, she couldn't rest, and the dawn was breaking before she finally fell asleep.

It was late when she woke and she was annoyed with herself for wasting valuable time. Although Brent had said to leave it all to him, she knew she couldn't. Everything would have to be sorted out carefully before it was packed.

She phoned Terry as soon as she got up to tell him she

wouldn't be in for a while, then began the task of clearing out closets, cupboards and chests, sorting and dusting the books in David's study, gathering the household linen together and collecting all the china and crockery into one place.

As she had promised, Val did nothing to help, but spent the day in her bedroom, coming out only to eat the meals that Sara got ready.

She was worn out by the time evening came and went early to bed. She fell at once into a deep sleep from which she awoke the next morning feeling much more rested but not looking forward to the day which stretched before her.

Long before Brent came with his workmen to pack everything into the cartons they brought, Val had gone out.

When Sara told him, Brent said nothing, but smiled rather grimly. And when she began to help the workmen he said peremptorily, "There's no need for you to do anything. You can leave it all to us."

"I suppose you'll allow me to make some tea or coffee for you?" she asked with deceptive sweetness.

He smiled, not deceived by her tone.

"Sorry! There I go again, saying the wrong thing. You've done enough, Sara. It doesn't need much intelligence to know you must have spent the whole of yesterday clearing up. But we'll be grateful if you make us some tea. Thank you."

"I simply can't win!" Sara thought as she went into the kitchen and plugged in the coffee percolator and the electric kettle. Was Val right in what she said? Was she allowing Brent Maxwell to assume too much importance in her life, letting him rule her and think for her?

Then she shrugged off the suspicion. It was easy for Val to tell her she should not accept the help Brent had given her so willingly. If she did not, then who was there in the whole world whom she could rely on?

She was right to accept with gratitude, in spite of anything Val might say. Once today was over she would have little or no contact with him, apart from a limited and purely business one.

She didn't know at that moment just how soon she would be proven wrong.

Brent and his men worked quickly and well, so that by the time the moving van came everything was ready. He came into the kitchen where Sara was putting the dishes they had used into her basket and said, "That's the lot, Sara. My foreman will stay and see everything gets out. Are you ready to go now?"

"Yes. Shouldn't we check everything? There's a repair clause in the lease, isn't there?"

"I believe so. I've looked around and made a few notes. The agents are bound to find something which needs doing, but we can come to an agreement about that later. There's no need for you to worry about it."

"But there is. You've done enough for us, Brent. I can't let you do any more. I wouldn't ask it of you."

"I wasn't aware that you had," he said brusquely. "Anything I do is because I want to."

"But you're doing so much, and we haven't even thanked you properly."

"I don't want your thanks. Come along, Sara. It's time we were going, otherwise the van will arrive before we do."

"All right."

Automatically she picked up her coat and the basket and went with him out of the apartment, wondering what he had meant by the heavy stress on the word "your" when he had said, "I don't want your thanks."

She stole a look at his face, as though she could find the

answer to that question in it, but it was dark and expressionless.

He hardly spoke as they drove through the heavy noon-hour traffic and drew up at last behind Brent's van which had preceded them.

"I'll let the men in, Sara, and they can have their lunch here. Then we'll go and have ours and be ready when the removal van arrives."

"I can't do that. Jamie is coming in at two o'clock and I've got to meet him. He doesn't know the new address. I'm sorry, Brent...."

"Stop panicking, Sara. I thought you were a level-headed person. I'll take you to the station, then we can all go and have lunch together. I have no doubt Jamie will be hungry even if he's had sandwiches on the train, if I know anything about boys."

"It's very kind of you, Brent. You must be quite tired of us. You're always having to pull us out of some difficulty or another. If it isn't too much trouble...."

"I wouldn't offer if it was," he said coolly. "Come along then, or the train will be in before we get there."

But they arrived just as it was pulling in and Sara waited with a beating heart, hoping that she would recognize the nephew she had not seen for three years.

She needn't have worried about that. She knew him at once, coming through the barrier with his duffle bag over his shoulder, looking so like David that a stab of pain shot through her.

"Jamie!" she called, and he turned quickly, his face breaking into a wide grin as he recognized her.

"Aunt Sara! Mom said you'd come home. Where is she?"

Sara heard the note of uncertainty in his voice and said gaily, "She's busy today because we're moving. That's why we came to meet you. This is Brent Maxwell, Jamie."

"Hi," Jamie said, and Brent smiled down at him.

"Had a good trip?"

"Okay. Is Mom at home, then?"

"No, not yet, though she may be by the time we get back. We thought we'd have lunch first, if you feel like it."

"Great, I'm famished!"

They had walked toward the car while they were talking and when they stopped beside it, Jamie said admiringly, "What a super job, Aunt Sara. Is it yours?"

She laughed.

"No such luck! It's Mr. Maxwell's."

Brent smiled.

"Get in and we'll go have lunch somewhere."

"When they were seated in the restaurant and Jamie was giving a demonstration of his claim to be famished, Sara said diffidently, "I hope you'll like the new apartment, Jamie. It's not as big as the other one, but. . . ."

"It'll be okay, I suppose. Do I have a room of my own?"

"Oh, yes. I hope you'll like it. The walls are plain white so that you can stick anything you want on them."

He put down his knife and fork and looked at her eagerly.

"You mean I can put up posters and photos? That'll be great! In the other apartment I wasn't allowed to do anything like that in case it spoiled the walls."

Sara breathed a sigh of relief, knowing that one hurdle that she had dreaded was past. Now it was only Val whom she had to worry about. She crossed her fingers, hoping for Jamie's sake, she wouldn't delay too long in coming to the new apartment. She knew that although Jamie was presenting a happy-go-lucky picture to the world, underneath he was unsure and worried in case he should lose his mother as suddenly and irrevocably as he had lost his father.

They went back to the apartment to find that the moving van was already there, and after that Sara saw very little of Jamie as he helped the men tramping in and out of the house.

The next couple of hours were busy ones, but at the end of that time all their furniture was in place and Brent's men were putting up the curtains and unpacking the crates again.

Sara went quietly from room to room, already feeling more at home in this new apartment than she ever had in the old one. Surely even Val would have to admit that she liked its homey and warm atmosphere far better than the modern, almost clinical one they had left.

"Sara!"

She started as Brent called her name and went back into the living room.

"I was just looking around. . . ."

"Everything's unpacked, but I'm afraid you'll have to put most of the stuff away yourself. Only you know where it will go. You can have the men to help, if you wish. . . ."

"No, you've done enough, Brent," she interrupted. "I'm not sure where to put everything yet. I'll have to do some thinking and planning, and there's no point in having them all hanging around. Will you give them this and say how much I appreciate all they've done?"

He made no attempt to take the money she held out to him.

"They don't want that, Sara. They're not expecting it."

"Nevertheless, please give it to them," she said quietly. "I want them to have it."

He smiled then. "Oh, very well. I suppose I must let you have your own way over this."

"It'll be a change if you do," she could not help saying tartly.

He looked at her in surprise. "What do you mean by that?"

"What I say. I think it'll be the very first time you've ever let me do as I want. Mostly you spend your time making sure everybody does exactly as you want."

He seemed thunderstruck by her accusation. "I do? I can't imagine what gives you that idea, Sara."

She laughed. "I was beginning to suspect you didn't even start to know just how autocratic you are, Brent Maxwell."

"That accusation from you! Pot calling the kettle black!" he said.

"Let's not quarrel over who's the worst because we'll never agree. Just let me say how much I appreciate all you've done for us, Brent."

His eyes smiled down at her.

"If you only knew, Sara . . ." he said, then stopped as Jamie came bouncing in.

"My room's super, Aunt Sara. Has Mom come yet?"

"Not yet, but she shouldn't be long. Say goodbye to Mr. Maxwell. He's going now."

"So long," Jamie said. "I'll come with you to the door. You won't forget what you promised, will you?" Sara heard him say as they went out of the room.

She waited for him to come back and said at once, "What did Brent promise?"

"To take me through his mill tomorrow. I remember Dad telling me how super it was, so I asked him. I've got to write an essay, too, so I can do it about that. If you don't want me for anything, I'll go and put a few things up on my bedroom walls."

"You do that, Jamie," Sara said, smiling affectionately.

He paused at the door. "You'll let me know when
Mom arrives?"

"Of course. Anyway, you're bound to hear her, you
know."

"Just in case I don't, that's all," he said in an offhand
way which did not deceive Sara. She wished with all her
heart that Val would come quickly, and that when she did
she wouldn't unsettle him by being openly unhappy about
their new home.

Val came earlier than Sara had expected and Jamie,
hearing her voice in the hall, came flying out of his room,
full of enthusiasm for the new house and anxious to show
her what he had already done in his room.

Whether it was her son's obvious happiness or not Sara
didn't know, but certainly her sister-in-law accepted the
move much more gracefully than Sara had expected.
When she left Val and Jamie together in the living room
and went into the kitchen to prepare supper, she felt more
cheerful and lighthearted than she had since she came
home.

CHAPTER TEN

Sara was still feeling happy when she went to the store a few mornings later. Val had settled down in the apartment quite well, and she and Jamie had thoroughly enjoyed their short time together.

It really seemed, Sara thought optimistically, as though everything was beginning to improve for them, that she was right to feel more hopeful about the future. As a consequence, the blow she received almost as soon as she arrived in her office was the harder to accept.

Terry came in just as she was hanging her coat in the cupboard, and she greeted him cheerfully.

"Hello. I hope I didn't stay away too long, Terry, but there was so much to be done and Jamie was on his school break. How have things been going here?"

"I don't know, Sara. I haven't had time to find out yet."

She looked at him enquiringly. "What do you mean?"

He walked over to the window and stood looking out.

"I don't know how to tell you this, Sara. The day you moved I had a letter from Paris, and as a result of that, I went over there the same day."

"To Paris again? Why, Terry?"

"Because . . . Sara, something awful has happened."

Her eyes widened in apprehension. "What are you talking about?"

"Sit down and I'll tell you." He waited until she was seated, but did not follow suit himself, prowling about the room as he talked. "This letter was from somebody who signed herself Yvonne Blake."

"Yvonne Blake?" Sara echoed.

"Yes. Sara, she said she was David's widow and wanted to claim his estate on behalf of her three sons."

Sara gazed at him in horror. "I don't believe it! It can't be true!"

"But it is. I thought about it, then I decided the best thing to do was to go to Paris and see her. She'd given a telephone number, so when I arrived I phoned her and asked her to come and see me."

"And did she?"

He nodded. "Yes. She told me she and David were married 16 years ago and have three sons aged 15, 12 and 10."

"I'll never believe it, Terry," Sara said obstinately. "She must be making it up."

He came over to her and put his hands on her shoulders.

"I felt that way, too. I told her so, and then she showed me her marriage certificate and the children's birth certificates. It's true enough, Sara."

"But that means . . . what about Val? And Jamie?"

He lifted his hands helplessly. "I don't know, but it looks as if this woman has a prior claim."

Sara stared at him, only slowly assimilating what he had told her.

"You say 16 years ago? But David wasn't going to Paris then. He wasn't even in the firm. He's only done that for the past eight or nine years."

"You're forgetting," Terry answered softly. "I know he didn't come into the business until after he married Val, but before that he was travelling all over the continent, buying for resale, to Blake's as well as to other firms."

She was silent, looking down at the shabby desk through eyes which saw nothing.

"But that means Val and Jamie . . ." she began at last,

then stopped, unable to put the rest of her thoughts into words.

"I'm afraid so. If what this woman says is really true, and I see no reason now to doubt her, then she and her eldest son inherit. The will definitely states that your father's shares are to be left in trust for David's eldest son. We thought it was Jamie, but now it could be this French boy."

"I'll never believe it of David." Her voice was strong now, all the indecision gone from it, and there was a fighting look in her eyes. "He would never have married Val bigamously, which is what you're saying!"

He shrugged. "You don't really have any option, Sara. Remember I've seen the proofs. And it alters the whole situation, doesn't it? That is if your real reason for not selling the business was the one you gave . . . to make sure of Val's and Jamie's future."

She was wary immediately.

"What do you mean?"

"Yvonne Blake says she's practically destitute. She's anxious to get some money, but she isn't vindictive. Naturally she was horrified to hear about Val, but at our second meeting she said she was sorry for her and Jamie and would like them to share in any proceeds."

"I see," Sara said slowly. "You mean, don't you, that if this woman's claim holds and I still don't agree to sell, Val will get nothing?"

"That's putting it the wrong way around. I'd rather say that if you agree, she won't be left destitute."

"A distinction without a difference," she answered drily.

He moved toward the door, turning when he reached it and saying quietly, "Perhaps, but think about it, Sara. It's a tricky position you're in, isn't it?"

It was certainly a very tricky position, as Sara

320

acknowledged honestly to herself as soon as she was
alone, and one which she steadfastly refused to accept.

She had never been very close to her half-brother. He
had been grown up before she was born, yet she was quite
certain that he would not have done such a thing. He had
always been kind and loving to her, and although the
difference in their ages had been great, she had loved him
dearly and could not believe that it was in his nature to
deceive two women in such a way.

She looked back down the years, remembering his
marriage to Val 12 years earlier, at which she had been
the youngest bridesmaid, a proud nine-year-old. Surely
he would never have allowed such a wedding to take
place—Val in a model gown with a full train and two
other bridesmaids as well as Sara. The big affair had cost
hundreds of pounds and everybody who was anybody in
their and Val's circle had been invited.

The David she had known would never have consented
to such a display if at the time he had already been
married and was the father of two sons. Nor would he
afterward have had two more sons, Jamie and this
unknown boy.

She clenched her hands into fists, her mind made up.
She would never accept this marriage, not until she had
proved it to her own satisfaction, and the only way to do
that was to go to France and talk to this woman herself.
To meet the children, too, and see if there was any likeness to David about them.

Until she had done that she would make no further
move, would not agree to anything. She would tell Terry
that and ask him for the woman's address so that she
could begin her inquiries.

But the prospect filled her with a sick feeling of dismay,
because in spite of her championship of David, she was

afraid. Terry's story, supported as it seemed to be by proof, was so final.

She knew that unless she proved it conclusively to herself, she would never be able to accept it as fact. How could David have hidden such a thing from everybody? From their father, from Val, from the old employees at the store? Surely they would have heard rumors! If only she had the courage to ask them!

Then she remembered. None of the old staff were left except Mollie. Her mind flinched away from the implications behind that fact. Was this the reason why no attempt had been made to keep them? Then she pushed that suspicion resolutely from her.

It could not be true, and the easiest way to find out was to see Mollie and ask her, relying on her discretion to make sure that no hint of the story leaked out.

She got up and went to the stock room, walking through the sewing rooms without seeing anyone, her mind fixed on what she was going to say.

She went in without knocking, then stopped in surprise, the words she had been about to speak dying on her lips. The person behind the long desk was a complete stranger to her.

She looked up and smiled at Sara, saying chattily, "Hello. You're Miss Blake, aren't you? I've seen you in the store. Can I get you anything?"

"I'm looking for Mollie Ingham."

"Mollie? She left a couple of days ago."

"Are you sure?"

"I should be. I've been given her job. Céleste said she'd walked out saying she couldn't stand it another minute, and I can't say I blame her. I'm sorry I said I'd take it on. It's too much like hard work."

"I see," Sara said slowly. "Thank you for telling me."

She was back in her own office before the real meaning of what she had been told occurred to her. Then she heard again Mollie's voice saying to her, "I can't afford to lose my job. Mother's very old and frail now and she's dependent on me."

Surely Mollie had never left of her own accord, thrown up her job as Céleste had said she did, after saying that. Something must have happened during the few days she had been away from the store. If, as she suspected, Mollie had been dismissed without notice, then she must do something quickly to set matters right for her.

Barely half an hour after she had made that decision Sara was knocking on the door of the house in which Mollie had lived all her life. It was Mollie herself who opened the door to her.

"Sara!" she exclaimed with pleasure. "I'm so glad to see you. Come in, won't you?"

"Thanks, Mollie. I just heard you'd gone and I must know the truth. Did you walk out of your job?"

Mollie smiled wryly and shook her head. "No, I didn't. I was sacked without notice."

"Then it was my fault," Sara said in distress.

"It doesn't matter whose fault it was now, Sara, because I'm not sorry it happened."

"But you told me you couldn't afford to lose your job."

"I can't, but it was really a blessing in disguise. You'll never believe this, Sara, but after Céleste sacked me, I walked about a bit wondering what to do and ran right into Ralph Martin. Do you remember him?"

"Dad's confidential secretary? Yes, of course."

"Well, he's personnel manager at Jones's, the big store in the center of town. When I told him what had happened he offered me a job right away. It seems they'd been looking for an older, reliable person. I start next Monday. Isn't that great?"

"It certainly is," Sara answered with relief. "I'm glad for you, Mollie, though I'm going to miss you. You were the last of the old staff who knew Dad."

She sighed, and Mollie said quickly, "Don't worry so much, Sara. Things will work out for you, I'm sure they will."

"I wish I was as sure. Can I talk to you about something very confidential, and will you promise you won't speak about it to anyone? Anyone at all."

"You know you can, and that I won't tell a soul."

Sara told her the story Terry had brought back from France with him, and Mollie's reaction was all she had hoped for.

"It's nothing but a pack of lies," she said scornfully. "Fancy expecting us to believe that Mr. David was living a double life for 16 years and none of us guessed! It's ridiculous. Anyway, he wasn't the type, not Mr. David."

Sara breathed a sigh of relief. "That's what I felt, too, only the evidence Terry talked about seemed so conclusive, I began to have doubts. But now you've helped to clear them away again."

"What are you going to do?"

"I'll go to Paris and see this woman, then try to check if the marriage really took place. If only my French was a bit better! It's going to be murder trying to communicate with everyone."

"You'll manage, I'm sure, and I'll be glad to know how you get on. Will you come and have a cup of tea with Mother? She often talks about you and she'll love to see you. You needn't be afraid. Her mind's razor sharp still, but she can't get about as she used to," she added, seeing Sara's momentary hesitation.

"That's not what's worrying me. I was wondering if I'd have time, that's all. I've got to see Terry again to get this woman's address, then make plane reservations. . . ."

"There's time enough for that. A sit down and a cup of tea will do you good. Come along now."

When Sara finally left Mollie's she had to admit that she had been right. The quiet interlude spent talking to Mrs. Ingham about the old times had had a calming effect on her and had helped to put the news Terry had given her into its proper perspective.

She was quite sure now of what she must do in order to prove David's innocence of the charge Terry had brought against him. How she was going to do it was, she knew, a different matter.

For the first time she regretted that she had not taken more interest in the French lessons she had had at school. Then perhaps she would have been able to talk intelligently to this Frenchwoman and understand what she was saying. She was determined not to allow that difficulty to stand in the way of her finding out the truth, however.

She pushed open the door of her office and walked in, then stopped, feeling the hot color rush into her cheeks as Brent Maxwell turned from his contemplation of the yard and said, "Hello, Sara. I hope you don't mind me coming in to wait. White said you wouldn't be long and because you'd left the books open on your desk, I thought he was probably correct."

She sat down, the annoyance she had felt at his words hardening into anger.

"They're all right! I don't expect people to walk in and out of my office examining everything on the desk. Anyway, there aren't many who could interpret them properly," she said defensively.

"I wasn't criticizing you, Sara. I'm sure you're very careful. I'm sorry if you're annoyed because I came in to wait."

She moved impatiently. "Of course I'm not annoyed. What did you come for?"

"Just to ask how you're getting on. Have you talked to Mollie again about the missing stock?"

"No. She isn't here any longer." Briefly she told him what had happened. "I've just been to see her. That's where I was when you came. Thank goodness she's found another job. I'd have felt very guilty if she hadn't, because it's all my fault for telling Terry what she said."

He frowned. "You think that's why she was dismissed?"

"Yes, definitely."

"And she's got another job?"

"Yes. Isn't that lucky? What a relief!"

"It must be, so why are you looking so bothered, Sara?"

She was taken aback by his words, thinking how little those deep-set eyes of his missed, suddenly wanting to tell him what had happened, to ask for his advice and help. Yet how could she? He had done so much for her, for them. It was hardly fair to expect him to come to her aid once again.

"What's troubling you, Sara? Won't you tell me?" he asked, so kindly that all her defences disintegrated in a moment.

"I don't see why you should be bothered with my worries, Brent. It isn't fair."

"Let me be the judge of that. What is it, Sara?"

She leaned back wearily in her chair, and brushed her hands over her face, closing her eyes so that she did not see him take a step toward her, his hand stretched out. By the time she looked up again, he was sitting on the edge of the desk, looking gravely at her, and she began hesitantly to tell him the story Terry had brought back from Paris.

He listened without interruption until she said at last, "I can't accept that without seeing this woman myself, and her children, too. But if she doesn't speak any

English, I know it'll be hopeless. I'll never be able to understand what she's saying."

"You feel this is something she and Terry have cooked up between them?"

"I don't know. I only know it can't be true," she replied helplessly.

"Why should he do that?"

"Because it changes the whole situation. You see, I won't sell because of Val and Jamie, but if this woman's eldest son is the heir, then selling's the best thing for them."

He frowned. "Why is that?"

"Because she says she'll give them part of the proceeds."

He looked at her compassionately.

"Did you know your brother very well?"

"I thought I did. Oh, I know he was years and years older than me, but he was always very good to me, Brent, and to other people as well. He'd never have treated Val and Jamie like this. Mollie agrees with me. It's completely out of character."

"And you intend to prove you're right?"

"Yes. I want to see these proofs she says she has and follow them up. . . ."

She stopped, realizing suddenly the magnitude of the task she had set herself, and he said quickly, "Would you like me to come with you?"

Her face lit up with relief. "Would you? Oh, I'd be so glad!" Then the light died away again. "But I can't expect you to drop everything and go to France with me. It may take weeks to get at the real truth."

"That's my problem, isn't it? And unlike you, Sara, I speak French fluently. I have to in my job. You'll be much more likely to get to the bottom of things quickly if I'm there to interpret for you."

"I know that. It's just . . . I know I shouldn't take advantage of your generosity, Brent, but I'm going to. Thank you for offering. I—"

"There's no need to thank me," he interrupted. "I'm as keen as you are to find out what's been going on. Don't forget I've got a vested interest in the outcome."

Some of the pleasure she had felt in his offer of help died away at his words and she knew a deep sense of disappointment. She had thought he was doing this solely to help her, though why she should she didn't know, when she had been nothing but a nuisance and a hindrance to him right from the first moment they had met.

At least, she told herself sadly, he was honest about it and didn't pretend to have an interest which he didn't feel. And, whatever his reasons, he had solved her most pressing problem of how to communicate intelligently with the woman who claimed to be David's legal wife.

But even that knowledge didn't lessen the depression that hung over her like a dark cloud.

CHAPTER ELEVEN

When Brent had left to make arrangements for their journey to France, Sara went to see Terry. He was not in his office and she found him after a while in the salon with Céleste. As she walked toward them they stopped talking and turned to look at her, waiting in silence for her to reach them.

"I'm sorry to interrupt, Terry, but I must talk to you."

"That's all right, Sara. What is it?"

Sara waited for a moment, then as Céleste didn't move, she said pointedly, "I'd like to speak to Mr. White privately, Céleste."

She didn't answer, but turned on her heel and walked away, her back rigid with anger.

Terry frowned. "Was that necessary, Sara? You've offended Céleste."

"I'm sorry, but I didn't want her to hear what I've got to say."

"Why ever not? I don't have any secrets from her."

"Maybe you haven't, but I don't want her here when I talk about David."

"I don't think there's anything else to be said, Sara."

"Oh, but there is. I want that woman's address, Terry, so that I can go and talk to her."

He frowned, his face suddenly becoming sharp and his eyes wary, "What good will that do you? Unless of course you're a good French linguist. Are you?"

"No, I'm not, but. . . ."

"Then what's the point in going all that way? I've seen all the papers she has and I'm convinced she's telling the truth."

"Well, I'm not," Sara said definitely, "and I've got to be before I accept what you've told me. Surely you can understand that, Terry?"

He made a sudden movement and she stepped back, thinking for a second that he was about to strike her. Then he controlled himself with an obvious effort and his mouth twisted into a smile.

"I do, of course, my dear. This must have been a real blow to your plans. All I'm afraid of is that you'll be wasting your time and your money. I don't think Yvonne Blake will want to see you."

"Why not?"

"Well, apparently David told her you and your father were bitterly opposed to his marriage and refused to see either her or the children. That's why she didn't get in touch when David died. Why she wrote to me instead."

"But that's ridiculous!"

He shrugged. "But understandable. So you see, there's no point in going all that way."

She didn't reply, but stood frowning into space, trying to assess this new information. On the surface it seemed reasonable enough, yet there was something in the way Terry had looked at her out of the corners of his eyes, in a faint nuance in his voice, which made her doubt the truth of what he said.

"That's a risk I must take," she said at last. "If she won't see me, then I'll have to find some other way. Employ a lawyer or something like that. But I've got to go, Terry."

His lips thinned angrily. "Are you being deliberately insulting, Sara?"

"Of course not. What do you mean?"

"I don't like being called a liar any more than the next man," he said sharply.

"I'm sorry if you think that," she said wearily. "It's just that I've got to be sure. Otherwise I'll have to ignore this woman's claim and carry on as I've been doing."

"You mean you'd still refuse to sell? Even though Yvonne wants money for herself and your brother's children?"

"I've got to be convinced first that they are David's children, and she's got to convince me herself," she said steadily.

He gnawed at his lower lip, his face a picture of indecision.

"In that case, there's nothing else to be done. I'll write the address out for you and an introduction telling Yvonne who you are and asking her to see you as a favor to me."

"Thank you. Can I have it today, because I want to go over as soon as traveling arrangements can be made."

"Very well." He looked at her cautiously. "You say you don't speak French? Then perhaps I'd better go with you to interpret, otherwise you'll get nowhere fast."

"Thank you, but Brent Maxwell is coming with me," she said, knowing that under no circumstances would she have allowed Terry to accompany her and glad that she could refuse his help so easily.

She saw an angry glitter in his eyes and it seemed as if she was looking at a complete stranger, a stranger who made her feel very afraid.

Then, as quickly as it had come, the impression was gone and he was smiling at her again in his usual charming way, his voice rueful as he said quietly, "I'm sorry you don't trust me, Sara. It hurts to know that you'd rather go to a complete stranger for help than to me whom you've known for so long. But I suppose I can't expect anything else. You've been away from us too long."

Against her will she felt guilty, which was completely irrational but nonetheless very real, and she heard herself apologizing in what she realized was a very weak way.

"Then won't you change your plans and let me come with you instead?" he asked persuasively.

Sara shook her head. "I can't do that. Brent's already making the plane reservations for us both. I'm sorry, Terry."

"I know just how much that means," he said sharply. "You can keep your apologies. I know their real value."

He turned angrily and she called after his retreating back, "Don't forget to let me have the address," but as she went back to her office was still not sure whether he would now implement his promise. And if he didn't, how could she force him to?

She need not have worried. Perhaps the threat to ignore the Frenchwoman's claim had been enough to make him do as she wished. Whatever the reason, before the store closed that night an envelope was brought to her with the address on the outside and apparently the promised letter of introduction within.

She sat with it in her hand for a long time, looking down at the name and thinking how strange and alien it looked. For the first time she wondered how she was going to explain her unexpected trip to Val.

All the way home she worried over that problem, but she needn't have. As soon as Val knew who was accompanying Sara she asked no further questions.

"You're so lucky," she said enviously. "I wish I could come too, but he wouldn't want me. I used to ask David to take me with him sometimes, but he never would. There was always some excuse why I couldn't go."

Sara's heart sank at those words because perhaps they meant that Terry was right. There seemed no other reason why now and again David shouldn't have taken his wife with him to Paris, unless it was because he already had another wife and family there.

But she still couldn't believe it was true. The real answer must be that he had gone to work, and having Val with him would have meant that he wouldn't have accomplished anything. Val would have insisted on him accompanying her wherever she wanted to go.

She got up and moved around her bedroom restlessly, wishing she knew the truth and wondering whether or not Brent had been able to make the reservations. She didn't think she could have borne another day of this suspense if he hadn't.

When the telephone rang at last she was almost afraid to answer it, yet was relieved to hear Brent's decisive voice.

"Sara? I've got seats on the plane leaving mid-morning tomorrow. I'll call for you at eight o'clock. Be ready."

"Oh, good! Thank you, Brent. Will you have breakfast here?"

"All right, you'd better make it seven-thirty, then. You've got the address?"

"Yes, and a letter to this woman."

"What does it say?"

"I don't know. The envelope's sealed."

He was silent for a while, then said abruptly, "I think you should open it."

"I can't do that."

"Why not?"

"It isn't addressed to me."

She heard the amusement in his voice, although all he said was, "All right, I'll see you in the morning, then. Goodbye, Sara."

She put the receiver down, feeling all the old annoyance

returning. She was foolish to have worried. Brent Maxwell never failed. She might have known he would get exactly the seats he wanted, just as she should have expected him to be as autocratic and dictatorial as he had been.

"Who was that?" Val asked, interrupting her disturbed thoughts.

"Brent Maxwell. He's reserved the plane seats and we're. . . ."

"I don't know how you do it, Sara!" Val shook her head. "First your Johnnie in the States and now Brent Maxwell. But maybe Brent doesn't know about Johnnie, so he won't be jealous."

"Don't talk nonsense, Val. There's no question of that," Sara answered shortly, and went into her room before Val could say anything else.

She sat down on the bed, wondering why she should suddenly feel so depressed. Maybe it was because Val had reminded her that apart from sending Johnnie her new address and telephone number, she hadn't thought about him for days.

She was ready when Brent came next morning. They ate breakfast in the little dining alcove off the kitchen and didn't talk much until they had eaten. Then he leaned back in his chair and said, "Have you decided what you're going to say to this woman?"

"No. I thought I'd wait until she comes. . . ."

"I see." Thoughtfully he stirred his coffee and for the first time since she had known him, Sara studied his face.

Why had she never noticed before how strong and steadfast he looked, how kind the curve of his mobile lips was?

He looked up and held her gaze without speaking, and

she felt the blood begin to pound through her veins. She was incapable of turning away, almost mesmerized by him.

Then he smiled, his whole face lighting up.

"We'd better go, Sara, if we're to be at the airport in good time," he said.

She got up quickly, still feeling disturbed and shaken. "Yes. I won't be a moment."

She hurried out of the kitchen, glad of the opportunity to be alone to try to control the hurried beat of her heart. By the time she came back she had regained control of herself and was able to meet him quite calmly.

He took her suitcase from her and carried it to his car. Soon they were on their way, starting what she knew could be a fateful journey with this man who so short a time before she had not even known, but on whom she was relying without any doubt that he would do everything he could to help her.

It was not until they were on the plane and airborne that he asked her for the letter Terry had given her. She handed it to him and he looked at it frowningly, turning it over in his strong, shapely hands.

"Did he tell you what he was going to write, Sara?"

"Yes. He said it was an introduction to me, telling her who I am and asking her to let me see all the papers she had shown to him."

"It's odd he bothered to seal it if that's all it says."

"You think there's more in it than that?"

"Could be. I feel we ought to read it."

She shook her head. "I wouldn't like to do that—"

He laughed and put his hand over hers, and she was conscious of a thrill like an electric shock which leaped up her arm at his touch. Her hand stiffened under his and at the movement he took his own away quickly.

"You can't have those kind of scruples in a case like this. If this story is really a fabrication cooked up by White to make you sell out, then this letter may contain the proof."

She didn't reply at once, fighting an intense desire to take hold of his hand again and deriding herself for her stupidity.

"I know I suspected that," she answered at last, "but when I thought about it, I couldn't believe it was true. Terry was anxious for me to accept this offer, but that's a bit different from going to all this trouble to force me to. Why should he? It makes no difference to him who owns the store."

"That's true, and he'd be more likely to lose his job under new ownership. Change almost always put executive positions in jeopardy."

"I suppose so."

"So there can be only one explanation. He's the person making the offer."

She swung around toward him, her eyes wide with amazement. "Terry is? I don't believe that. Where on earth would he get the money from?"

"A bank or a finance house, perhaps."

She was silent as she considered that suggestion in the light of her own experience in the States, then shook her head decisively.

"He'd never get enough backing, Brent. Oh, I realize the offer wasn't nearly as good as it should have been, but we'd have improved it during negotiation. He must have known that no financier would back an unknown risk like he is."

"Then he must have managed to get money from some other source. Any ideas about that?"

Unbidden, there came into her mind the discrepancies

she found in the stocks, the sharp drop in store takings
even though the staff said they were busier than they had
ever been. All of which was followed by the dismissal of
Mollie, who had confirmed some of her suspicions.

But she didn't mention them to Brent, because at that
moment the instruction was given to fasten seat belts, and
in the bustle of landing there was no opportunity to tell
him.

CHAPTER TWELVE

It wasn't until they were on the way from the airport that Brent mentioned the letter again.

Then he said casually, "On second thoughts, Sara, I think this letter says exactly what White said it does. It'd be too risky for him to put anything else in it, in case it was opened and read. If he had any instructions for this woman, I imagine he'd have telephoned her today."

"I think so, too. I'd have hated to open it, Brent. I'd much rather wait until we've got in touch with her, then give it to her intact."

But when they reached their hotel they found everything taken out of their hands.

"Miss Blake?" the reception clerk said. "Ah, yes. I have a message for you here."

He handed her a typewritten card and she took it, slowly translating it before giving it to Brent.

"She's coming this evening? Isn't that what it says?"

"Yes."

"Before we've contacted her. How would she know where we were?"

"I imagine White must have told her. I always stay here when I come to Paris, and he'd only have to phone my office to confirm where we'd be."

"I see," Sara said quietly, and for the first time began to feel afraid.

Afraid of meeting this Frenchwoman, of being shown, perhaps, irrefutable proofs. Of having to accept them and go back to England to break the news to Val that she had never been married to David. That Jamie was illegitimate.

Afraid, too, of the heavy responsibility she had assumed.

Because if what Terry had said was true, and the woman was prepared to settle some money on them both, then might not she, by her actions, have jeopardized even this assistance which was being offered to them?

Even as she thought it, she knew she had done the only possible thing. She could never have accepted this terrible accusation against her half-brother tamely.

Those fears were mirrored in her expressive face and Brent looked at her keenly, then put a comforting arm around her.

"What's wrong, Sara?" he asked anxiously. "Aren't you feeling well?"

She leaned against him gratefully, drawing strength from his nearness, even above her fears aware of him with every part of her body.

"I'm all right." She drew away from him, pushing back the thick, honey gold hair shakily. "I . . . I suddenly realized that I might have to accept this woman as David's wife, then go back and have to break the news to Val."

His lips tightened. "It's damnable that you should be subjected to all this worry. I wish. . . ."

He stopped, and after a moment she said, "What do you wish?"

"Nothing," he said brusquely. "It's too soon for that."

She looked down, confused by his words. What could he mean by them? Too soon? Too soon for what?

But she knew she wouldn't be given an answer to those questions because the familiar closed look was back on his face and it was set in the uncompromising lines she had known when she first met him.

"No use crossing that bridge till we come to it," he

said, breaking the silence between them. "Let's go out and do the town, Sara. Enjoy ourselves and see as much as we can. Shall we?"

She smiled up at him. "Yes, let's. I've never been to Paris before, so it's all new to me."

"Good. Then I can take you to all my favorite places. Go and pretty yourself up, my dear, and I'll meet you here in 20 minutes. Not a moment longer, mind."

"I'll be here," she said, and crossed to the elevator, feeling a surge of happiness which made her want to laugh out loud. She was going to be shown Paris by a man to whom it was familiar and loved.

No wonder she was excited as she applied a light make-up with fingers that trembled with anticipation. Brent was right. She must enjoy this break while she could and forget about the ordeal which faced her when evening came.

He was already in the foyer when she came down. He held out his hand to her and she put hers into it, finding the action quite natural. It seemed to be part of the mood of golden anticipation which filled her.

That was the beginning of a halcyon time, during which she was shown a facet of Brent Maxwell's character which until then she had not known existed. It was a happy, almost boyish side which enjoyed the small things that mean so much.

They were both very gay and lighthearted. They went down into the Metro and found their way to the Sacré Coeur, climbing the steps and looking over Paris spread below them.

Then they walked around Montmartre, sitting at a table in the Place du Tertre, watching the students and artists. They drank coffee, and imbibed the atmosphere, so different from anything Sara had ever known.

During that day Sara lost her heart to Paris and was blessed with a greater happiness than she had ever experienced before in her 21 years.

It was not until they were coming to the end of their evening meal that she came down to earth again. Brent looked at his watch and said with a sigh, "Our freedom's nearly over, Sara. We must go back to the hotel. It's almost time for our appointment."

She stared at him without understanding, the real reason why they had come to Paris so far forgotten that it was a physical jolt to be reminded of it. For a moment she felt as if she could not bear to face the woman she had come to see.

Then she pulled herself together and picked up her handbag.

"Is it nearly time?" she asked, and when he nodded, said, "Let's go quickly. We mustn't keep her waiting."

"I'll see about a taxi for us," he said, and while they waited they were silent and serious for the first time in many hours.

It was as though somebody had drawn a thick curtain, Sara thought, shutting off the golden hours they had spent together, a curtain which would shed gloom and darkness over them for the next few hours.

In the taxi she twisted her hands together until they were taken in Brent's hard clasp and he held them until they arrived at the hotel, bringing her warmth and comfort, and a lessening of the tension which had been steadily building up within her.

"I hope she isn't late, Brent." The breath caught in her throat as they went into the hotel. "I don't think I can stand the waiting."

"Yes, you can," he said, and pulled her closely against him.

She relaxed, gaining strength from his nearness as she had done before, from the faint male scent of his jacket against her face. Gradually the blood stopped pounding through her head.

She moved away from him and he smiled down at her.

"All right, Sara?"

"Yes, Brent. Thank you."

They went together to the desk, but before they could ask if there had been a visitor for them, the clerk said, "Mademoiselle Blake? A visitor has come for you. She sits over there."

Sara turned slowly and looked across at the lone figure dressed in funereal black, sitting very upright in an easy chair.

For a moment her legs refused to move, then she felt Brent's hand under her elbow and heard his voice say authoritatively, "Come along, Sara," and went with him to where the woman was waiting.

She looked up as they approached and Sara thought she saw a flicker of uneasiness in her narrowed eyes, but when she spoke her voice was firm enough, "*Bonsoir, mademoiselle, m'sieur.*"

"*Bonsoir*. This is Miss Blake," Brent said in his fluent French. "You are the person she's come to meet?"

"*Oui*. I am Madame David Blake."

"Then let's talk together. Sit here, Sara." He waited until she had seated herself, then sat down opposite the Frenchwoman and continued, "Miss Blake wants to see the proofs you have of this marriage with her half-brother. Have you brought them?"

"*Oui*, but first I must see the letter."

Silently Sara handed it to her and she ripped it open and read it carefully.

"*Merci*." She unzipped the briefcase that was on a low

table beside her and took out some papers. "Here is the certificate of our marriage, and these are the photographs of our children . . . David's children," she emphasized with a challenging look at Sara.

Sara looked helplessly at Brent. "She's speaking much too quickly for me. I can't make out a word of it. What's she saying?"

He told her briefly, looking with a frown at the Frenchwoman, who sat without expression as if she was not remotely interested in what he and Sara were saying. Even if she couldn't understand it, there should have been the same look of strain on her face as there had been on Sara's as she struggled to follow the conversation.

He picked up the marriage certificate and translated it to Sara before putting it down again on the arm of his chair, then held out his hand for the photographs.

"These are the children?"

"*Oui.* Our three sons. Antoine, Emile and Georges. Are they not like their father? It was he who took them. He was so proud of his boys."

Brent passed the photos to Sara. "Are they like David, do you think?"

She spread them out in front of her, looking at them carefully. They showed three nice-looking boys, very French in appearance, and Sara noticed that the middle one had a vaguely familiar look about him.

"This one . . . Emile, is it? He reminds me of somebody, but it isn't David. Jamie is like him, very like the snapshots we have of his father at the same age, but these . . . no!"

"You're sure, Sara?"

"Sure? How can I be? If they were in color . . . David's hair was so bright, like guinea gold. They all look dark, very dark-haired." She pointed to the photos. "These two are like their mother."

Brent looked across at the Frenchwoman. "Have you any color photographs of the children, *madame*?"

Her eyes narrowed. "*Non*, I haven't. Only these that I show you."

"Have you then a picture of yourself and David? On your wedding day perhaps? Or one of him taken with your children?"

"I told you, it was he who took the pictures. Of course he isn't in them. How could he be?"

"*Quel dommage!*" Brent said dryly, and Sara looked at him, recognizing that phrase easily enough.

"What is a pity? What does she say, Brent?"

He told her and her eyes brightened. "You think that's important?"

"I think it significant that she shouldn't have any pictures of David. I'd like to keep this certificate and have it verified."

He looked at Sara, seeing the strain in her face, and said, "Would you like something to drink, my dear? And you, *madame*? Can I order you anything?"

"No, I want nothing," she said sharply. "Only my rights for my children. That is all."

He shrugged. "Very well. She won't have anything, Sara. What about you?"

"I won't either, Brent. Let's get this over as soon as we can. Please!"

He patted her gently on the arm. "Relax, Sara. Everything's going to be all right. I'm becoming more and more convinced of it." He took the certificate in his hand and looked across at the other woman. "I'd like to borrow this for a day or two, *madame*, if you've no objection."

She started up from the chair and put out her hand to snatch the paper from him, but he was too quick for her, holding it out of her reach.

"You can't have it," she panted. "It's all I have to prove my marriage. Give it back to me!"

He shook his head.

"Not yet. As soon as I've been able to make some inquiries about it, you'll get it back, I promise you."

"You're a thief! You steal it from me. I'll call the police. . . ."

"Don't be silly," he said coldly. "Look, I'll write you a receipt for it." He watched her with alert blue eyes. "In any case, even if it is lost you can always get a copy, can't you?"

"That costs money. I have no money for copies."

"But if your claim holds, you're expecting to have plenty of money?"

"Only for my children, not for myself. Never for myself," she said quickly.

"Well, there's no need for you to worry. You'll get it back as soon as possible." He got up and added, "I think that's as much as we can usefully do now, *madame*. Thank you for coming. It was most kind of you."

Under his compelling gaze she got up slowly, her face set and sullen. "And I get nothing for my trouble? Nothing at all?"

"Not until everything is proved to our satisfaction, *madame*. How could it be otherwise?"

She flashed him a look of such hatred that Sara was startled.

"Oh, you English!" the woman said bitterly. "Always so smooth. But I will see I get my deserts."

"You can be sure of that," he replied with emphasis. "*Bonsoir, madame.*"

For a moment she stood irresolute, then turned and flounced out of the hotel. Brent sat down again beside Sara.

"Well, my dear? What do you think of all this now?"
She shook her head.

"I don't know. There's the certificate, and one of the boys looks like somebody I know, but. . . ." She shook her head again. "What can we do now?"

"I'm going to take this to a lawyer friend of mine and ask him about it." He frowned. "You're right about that likeness. I noticed it, too."

"But it's not David. We should have kept one of those pictures, Brent."

He laughed. "We weren't given the opportunity. They were snatched away as soon as we'd looked at them. That's suspicious. You'd think she'd be glad for you to keep a picture of your nephews, if they are your nephews."

"That's true."

"Still, let's not worry. We'll get to the bottom of this without them," he said cheerfully. "Now I'm going to get you a drink to revive you, then we're going out again for the rest of the evening."

"Brent, I don't think I could. . . ."

"You're coming out with me whether you want to or not. We'll see a show and then I'll take you to a place I know where we can eat and enjoy ourselves. Now come and have that drink, then go and get changed, ready for our night out."

She got up, smiling at him mistily. "All right, I knew you for an autocrat the minute I saw you, Brent Maxwell."

CHAPTER THIRTEEN

It was very late when they returned to the hotel. The night porter was on duty, but Sara hardly noticed him as they walked over to the elevator. She was still wrapped up in the golden happiness of the hours she had spent with Brent, hours that had filled her with an excitement which pulsed through her like waves of electricity.

He smiled down at her as they waited for the elevator to arrive. "Thank you for a very wonderful evening, Sara," he said quietly.

"I'm the one who should thank you. Oh, Brent. . . ."

She stopped as the elevator doors opened and he put his hand in the crook of her elbow, holding her arm against him as the elevator moved silently upward.

He didn't speak, yet Sara was sharply aware of him and in a strange way, of his innermost thoughts, as if he was telling them to her.

When they stopped outside her door and his hands slid up her arms to her shoulders, it seemed the most natural thing in the world for him to draw her to him.

"Sara," he said softly, then his arms went around her, holding her gently yet firmly as he kissed her. He embraced her lightly at first, then with an increasing passion that brought forth an answering response from her.

When at last he let her go she was aware of him as she had never been aware of any man, feeling his heart hammering against her, her own pulses beating in reply.

For a while longer they stood close together, not speaking or moving. Then he kissed her again, very gently.

"Good night, my little love," he whispered, so quietly that afterward she could not be sure she had heard him right. "If only all my dreams and hopes could come true!"

He opened the door for her and she went in, feeling bereft and very much alone as he closed it behind her. She ached for him in a way that came as a shock to her, so she turned quickly and opened the door again, going into the corridor and looking eagerly for him.

But he had gone. Only the long expanse of golden carpet stretched before her, empty and forlorn.

She was still in a bemused state as she got ready for bed, and for a while she lay awake, savoring those blissful moments until at last she drifted into a deep sleep.

She was awakened in the morning by the chambermaid bringing her breakfast and she sat up in bed, responding automatically to her greeting.

"*Un billet, mademoiselle,*" the maid said, indicating the envelope on the tray. There was all the wisdom of the ages in her smiling glance.

"*Merci bien,*" Sara said, feeling the color rise to her cheeks. She didn't open the envelope until the chambermaid had gone.

Then she tore it open with suddenly trembling fingers. It was headed 8:30 a.m.

"Sara," she read, "I'm going to see my friend now, but will be back in time to take you out to lunch. I'll be in the foyer from 12:30 p.m. Please be ready and waiting. Brent."

She looked down at the note, aware of a deep stab of disappointment. What she had expected she didn't know. Certainly not this cool and casual information about his plans, that read as if it was from a complete stranger. Not after last night.

She felt tears of disappointment sting her eyes, and fought them back with determination. She might have known how it would be, that the moments which had been

so precious to her had been for him merely the satisfaction of a whim.

In addition to everything else, in his usual high-handed
and arrogant way he had calmly taken everything into his
own hands without consulting her, without even bothering
to find out whether or not she wanted to go with him to
see this lawyer. Then he had finished up by ordering her
to be in the foyer to meet him at half past twelve, "ready
and waiting."

Well, this time, she told herself angrily, he was going to
be disappointed, because she had no intention of waiting
tamely in the hotel until he decided to come and take her
out to lunch. She would have lunch by herself and go back
to the hotel when and if it suited her.

Quickly she ate her breakfast, then dressed and left the
hotel, determined to stay away until she was sure Brent
would have become tired of waiting for her and would
have left.

But the shops held no interest for her and she walked
past them and through them unseeingly, hardly able to
believe that the time was passing so slowly. She was able
to think of nothing except what Brent was doing, how he
was faring in his quest for the truth she was so anxious to
discover.

It was a long while before that thought really became
meaningful to her, but when it did she stopped, heedless
of the people in whose way she was standing.

The truth she was so anxious to discover. She said the
words over and over again to herself, the anger she had
felt against Brent disappearing in her own self-analysis.

The truth that, in such an unselfish way, he had left his
own concerns and traveled with her to France to discover.
He was, that morning, without complaint, seeing his
friend in order to ask him to examine this supposed
marriage certificate.

In addition he had taken her around, had entertained her royally, had shown her the Paris he loved, and had himself been a charming and wonderful companion.

Then, because she was angry with him, because she had thought his note cool and offhand, she intended to leave him waiting for her in the hotel foyer while she deliberately stayed away.

She felt shame surge through her as she acknowledged that it was not Brent who needed to be taught a lesson but herself . . . a lesson on how to be grateful for the help he had given so freely to her.

She moved then, hurrying back to the hotel against a clock which now seemed to be rushing ahead wildly. She saw him as soon as she walked through the doors, sitting, relaxed and handsome in one of the chairs in the foyer.

Sara stood just inside the door, feeling suddenly afraid and fighting the urge to turn and run away in case the news he brought would confirm her worst fears.

Then he looked up and saw her standing there. He got up and came to her, holding out both hands and smiling in a way which twisted her heart.

She put her hands into his, feeling confused and shy, acutely aware of him, of his deep-set eyes with their smiling look.

"Hello, Sara. Come and sit down while I tell you all I've found out before we go in to lunch. I ordered a dry sherry for you," he added as the waiter put the glasses on the table. "All right?"

"Yes, thank you," she said breathlessly. "Tell me what your friend said."

"There's no doubt about it! That certificate has been forged, Sara."

"Brent, is it true? Really true? But that's the most wonderful news!"

"Yes, isn't it? Someone has very carefully erased the man's signature and substituted David's."

"You're sure? It seemed . . . I've been afraid to acknowledge it even to myself, but it seemed very like his writing."

"It may have, but nevertheless it's a forgery! I saw it under a microscope and there's no doubt about it."

Sara put down the glass she had been holding, her hands trembling. "I can't believe it. I didn't notice anything really wrong with the signature."

"Neither did I, but then it's obvious we weren't meant to have the chance to examine it properly. That's why madame was so livid when I refused to give it back to her."

Sara looked bewildered. "But why should she do such a thing?"

"Not her," he answered quietly. "White."

"Terry? It doesn't seem possible!"

He leaned forward, clasping his hands together. "Doesn't it? Think, Sara. Who told you he'd had a good offer for the store but couldn't or wouldn't tell you the name of the intended buyer? Who has always tried to force you to sell, even enlisting Val's help?"

"Terry," she said slowly.

He nodded. "Now think again, Sara. You said there was a likeness between one of the boys and somebody you couldn't put a name to. Who was he like? Not David."

"No, not David, but not Terry either." She stopped, a frown between her brows as she concentrated on that problem. Then with dawning comprehension she breathed, "Of course! Céleste! That's who he reminded me of."

"That's right . . . Céleste Durand. My lawyer friend checked up and found that the original certificate was of a marriage between Maurice d'Islay and Yvonne Durand."

"Is she . . . Céleste's sister, then?"

"Yes."

Sara was silent, struggling to accept this knowledge and finding it almost impossible to believe. How could Terry, who had known her almost all her life, whom her father and David had trusted, have been so dishonest?

She was not misled by Céleste's involvement in the plot. She knew perfectly well that it was Terry who must be behind it.

"It doesn't make sense!" she burst out at last.

He smiled compassionately. "Yes, it does, Sara. Remember, he's been with Blake's almost all his working life, 30 years or more. Don't you see, he would gradually begin to look on the firm as his own, to identify himself with it."

"Perhaps he might, only. . . ."

"When your father died he probably expected to take his place. Instead David took over and Terry was still playing second fiddle. When David was killed it must have seemed as if fate was taking a hand. Here was his big chance, if he could buy the business cheaply enough. He thought Val would be in control and had talked her into it when you came home, and then he discovered just how wrong he was."

"Yes, I can understand that," she said slowly. "But this way of trying to force my hand. This woman, Yvonne Durand, would have had to be paid, and then there was Val. She was going to benefit, too."

"He would only have had to pay Val, wouldn't he? Yvonne would no doubt have received something for her trouble, but think of the advantages to Terry. You'd have been outvoted and he'd have got the business even more cheaply than he expected to."

"But why pay Val? Why didn't he try to get away with that as well?"

"Because that was part of the bargain, I imagine."

She stared at him in disbelief. "You mean Val was a party to this . . . this fraud? Oh, no. I don't believe that!"

"Maybe she didn't actually know the method by which Terry hoped to force your hand, Sara, but I think she must have been aware of the intent, don't you?"

Sara frowned, looking back over the past weeks. She remembered the way Val had shrugged off any serious talk about the store while all the time supporting Terry, and though it hurt her to do so, she had to acknowledge that he might be right.

"What shall we do now, Brent?" she asked, all the pain she felt at this tale of duplicity mirrored in her expressive face.

"I think we ought to go back home. I've reserved seats on the afternoon plane. Is that all right?"

She nodded. "And Yvonne?"

"My friend will return the marriage certificate to her and point out the penalty for forgery. We'll wait and see what happens after that."

"I see. Brent. . . ."

He smiled. "What's troubling you, Sara?"

"Your friend . . . he won't do anything to Yvonne? I don't want her and her sons to suffer because of Terry."

He patted her hand gently. "He isn't going to do anything except warn her of the consequences if she should be involved in that kind of fraud again."

She breathed a sigh of relief. "I'm glad about that. The boys looked so bright and friendly. Such nice boys."

He laughed then. "You're much too soft-hearted to be an American business tycoon, Sara, though I'm not saying that's a bad thing." He got up, then took her hands in his and pulled her to her feet, smiling down at her in a way which made her forget her resolutions about this man. "Come and have lunch. Afterward we'll have to pack and get to the airport."

He was still holding her hand when they went into the restaurant and released it only when the waiter showed them to a table for two in one of the long windows.

All the way through lunch, and afterward, when they were driving to the airport, she could feel that strong, hard clasp, and drew comfort from that memory against the inevitable moment when she would have to face Val and Terry and tell them what she had found out.

CHAPTER FOURTEEN

It was early evening when the plane landed and they got into Brent's car, which he had left at the airport on the way to Paris. Sara felt weary and travel-stained, as though she had been traveling for days instead of only hours, when they finally arrived at the apartment.

"Will you come in with me?" she asked Brent, looking at him with pleading eyes. "It's going to be awful meeting Val, and not letting her see that I suspect. . . ."

"Of course, Sara," he said at once. "Don't worry so much. It'll be all right, I'm sure. Are you going to tell her tonight why you went to Paris?"

"Yes. I want to get it over with. I don't think I could stand the suspense if I didn't."

"Are you sure that's the best thing to do? Wouldn't it be better to wait until after we've spoken to Terry tomorrow?"

"No, I'd rather tell Val first. I think it'll be easier that way. I don't want to quarrel with her, Brent, and this way I'll make sure I don't."

"Just as you like," he said. But in the end all her good intentions were wasted, because when they walked into the apartment the first person she saw was a tall, fair-haired man who bounced out of an easy chair and held out his arms to her.

"Sara, honey! At last! Where've you been? I thought you were never coming."

"Johnnie!" Her face lit up in happy surprise and she ran to him, feeling his arms close around her in a bear-like hug. "Where did you spring from?"

He laughed down at her, his hair lying thick and untidy as always on his forehead.

"I had a couple of days to spare, so I thought I'd better take a flip over and look you up. Say, what are you doing, honey? When are you coming back to me? It's murder at the office without you."

"Soon now, Johnnie, I hope." She became aware of Brent standing silently in the doorway and turned toward him. "I'm sorry, Brent, but I never expected to find Johnnie here. He's my boss in the United States. This is Brent Maxwell, Johnnie, who has helped me so much since I came home."

Johnnie held out his hand. "I certainly appreciate that," he said. "I know Sara always thinks she can do everything for herself and I'm not daring to say she's wrong, but it's great she found someone to help her, just the same."

"Johnnie Acton! I thought you were my friend! Brent will be thinking the very worst about me after that!"

Brent looked at her, his eyes crinkling into a smile. "Nothing anyone says will ever alter what I think of you, Sara," he said. "I was glad to do what I could to help."

"That's the idea!" Johnnie put his arm around Sara's shoulders and hugged her to him. "He's a man after my own heart, honey!"

"Well, Sara, I'd better go. You won't want to talk business now that your friend has come over to see you."

Sara pulled away from Johnnie's arm, feeling suddenly anxious, as she saw the old closed expression back on Brent's face again.

"But you'll come tomorrow? I have to see Terry, and you did say you'd come with me."

"If you still want me to."

"Of course I do. You must know that. You will come?" He nodded. "Very well."

"At ten o'clock as we arranged?"

"Yes. Shall I meet you at the store?"

"No, call for me here. You said you would. . . ."

"But things are a bit different now," he replied enigmatically. "However, as you wish. I'll see you then, Sara."

He turned to go, but she stopped him, putting her hand urgently on his arm. "You're sure you won't stay?"

"Yes, why not do that?" Johnnie broke in. "Val . . . Mrs. Blake, I mean . . . she's got dinner almost ready for us. I know that because I've been helping with it. It'll stretch to one more."

Brent shook his head. "No, thanks. I have a pile of work waiting for me and I ought to go and do some of it. Good night, Acton. See you tomorrow, Sara."

He moved toward the door and after a moment's hesitation Sara followed him.

"I'll see you out, Brent," she said, and added shyly as he opened the front door, "I'm sorry our journey had to end like this. I wanted to talk to Val tonight before we saw Terry, but now we can't."

"Of course not. I wouldn't expect you to when your friend's arrived to visit you," he said coldly. "You'll have other things to think about and talk about now. Much pleasanter things, that's for sure."

"Yes. Yes, I suppose so," she answered, and watched until he left the house.

She stood in the hall for a few minutes, trying to fight the depression that filled her. She couldn't understand her feeling. Surely she should be on top of the world now. To come home and find Johnnie there, to see him again after the past few weeks of strain, with his infectious grin and pleasant drawling voice. Not so long ago that would have been all she wanted. Yet now that it had happened she felt none of the excitement and relief it should have brought her.

When she went back into the living room Johnnie said, "So that's the Maxwell fellow! Val was telling me about him. Queer fish, isn't he? Not very friendly."

"You're wrong!" Sara flared up in defence of him quickly. "He's quite the opposite. No one could have been a better friend to me."

He shrugged. "Maybe you're right, hon, but—"

"I am," she interrupted earnestly. "He's not easy to get to know, Johnnie, but when you do I'm sure you'll like him."

"I'm not likely to stay long enough to find out. I've got to fly back the day after tomorrow. I only came to find out what's been happening to you, Sara. Why you hadn't come back as you promised."

She looked at him guiltily. "I'm sorry, I ought to have written to you, but there's been so much happening, so many things to do. . . ."

"Don't think about it, honey. Now that I've seen you I know the answers."

She frowned, puzzled by his words, but before she could ask him what he meant Val came in, stopping in the doorway when she saw Sara there.

"You're back! I didn't hear you come in."

"She came with that Maxwell fellow," Johnnie said easily, "but he's left now. What about supper, Val? Is it nearly ready? Sara and I are starving, aren't we, honey?"

"Yes. Thirsty, too."

"Everything's ready." Val burst into rapid speech. "Wasn't it wonderful, Johnnie turning up like this? We've had quite a day together and he's been helping me with supper. He's certainly well trained. He can do anything in the kitchen."

"That's no thanks to me," Sara laughed. "It must be his mother's training."

"You're babbling, Val, honey." He put an arm around each of them and hustled them through to the kitchen where the table was already spread in the dining alcove. "Let's eat, before we all fall by the wayside."

"I'll serve," Sara said, "as my contribution to this feast."

"You'll do no such thing. You'll both sit down and be waited on. Though I'll probably allow you to wash up afterward. Now, Sara, tell me all about this spot of bother that's kept you from coming back to me."

Afterward Sara looked back on the next two hours and tried to sort out her impressions, but without a great deal of success.

She was aware of Johnnie and Val, on the best of terms with each other, laughing and talking together, but she felt too tired, both physically and emotionally, to do more than try to eat. She took only a minor part in the conversation.

She was glad when she could admit to being worn out and could go to her own room. The sudden and unheralded appearance of Johnnie, dear as he was to her, after the strain of the past few days, had exhausted her, and the thought of the difficult task that had to be done next day seemed only bearable because Brent had promised to go with her and support her.

Before then she would have to decide how she was going to tackle this interview with Terry, yet as she got into bed, hearing vaguely the others still talking together in the living room, she was not thinking of the morrow.

Instead she was remembering that although Brent had said in his usual kind way that he would go with her to see Terry, he had left her quickly, although he had been pressed to stay. And he had had that cold, closed look on his face again. She felt deeply worried and hurt. He had been such a wonderful companion in France that even while the fear of the Frenchwoman's claim had hung over her, she had been happy.

She had thought that at last Brent had come to accept her as a friend and not as a nuisance whose problems he had to solve whether he wanted to or not. The knowledge that she had been wrong made her feel miserable and sick at heart, so that even the coming of Johnnie did not raise her spirits.

She turned over restlessly, closing her eyes and trying to woo the sleep which would not come. But all she could see was Brent Maxwell as she had slowly come to know him, as she had learned to love him in spite of herself. Honestly now she acknowledged that without reservation, without denying the truth any longer.

She could feel again his lips on hers as he had kissed her that night in the hotel. She knew now why he had disturbed her so deeply, when a kiss from Johnnie had been something that merely gave her surface enjoyment. Poor Johnnie, who had come such a long way to see her. She knew now that she would never marry him, no matter what happened in the future.

Not that she had ever said she would. When he had asked her she had always said, "Not yet, Johnnie. I'm not ready to get married yet," and he had always accepted her refusal without any obvious signs of despair. Now she, who had been unable to give herself any good reason for refusing him, knew that she had been waiting for a deeper feeling—for the love that sacrifices everything for the loved one, a love that follows the loved one to the end of the earth without complaint.

Well, she had found it. She had fallen in love with a man who saw her only as a person he had to help against his will. Although he had done so with the kindness and thoughtfulness that were so much a part of him, she was not deceived.

During that night as she lay sleepless she faced up to the knowledge that the years that stretched before her might be barren and loveless. She knew herself too well: for her there could never be a second best. If Brent did not want her, then no one else would do. Not Johnnie, not anyone. But she also made her mind up to accept what she was given and make the most of it while she could. Then perhaps in the lonely years when she no longer had Brent with her, she might have some happy memories to look back on.

She was waiting for him when he came at ten o'clock as he had promised.

"Are you sure you want to see White this morning, Sara?" he asked when he came in. "Wouldn't you rather wait until Acton goes back so that you can be with him?"

She shook her head. "No, I'd rather get it over. Anyway, it's too late. He and Val have gone out for the day already," she said, her voice after the sleepless night sounding flat and despondent even to her own ears.

He looked at her with concern. "You should have gone with them. You could easily have telephoned me. I would have seen White for you."

"As if I'd let you do that! You've done enough for me, Brent, over the past few weeks. Though I may have seemed ungrateful, I'm not."

"I don't want thanks from you," he said briefly.

"Maybe not, but even though I've taken so much advantage of your kindness, I'm not really the ungrateful type who would push off all my responsibilities on you."

He took a step toward her.

"I know that, Sara. I think you're . . . oh, what's the use? When are you going back to the States?"

She was surprised by the sudden change of subject and didn't know how to reply. She knew very well what the truthful answer was—that she didn't want to go anywhere that wasn't near to him—but she couldn't tell him that. Once she might have done so, when he was the eager and wonderful companion who had made her stay in France so magical. Not now, when he appeared to have forgotten those happy hours.

"We'd better go," she said abruptly, and walked past him through the door.

He put out his hand as if to stop her, then let it drop back to his side and followed her out of the house to his car.

They didn't speak as he drove to the store nor as they walked from the car park and through the store toward the escalator. But before they reached it they were stopped by the floor manager in a state of great agitation.

"Miss Blake! Thank goodness you've come! I've been trying to contact you all morning, but there was no reply from your home."

"But I've been in . . ." Sara began, then recollected the recent move and knew she ought to have given the operator the new telephone number. "I'm very sorry, Mr. Lewis. We moved a few days ago. What's happened? Has anything gone wrong?"

"It's Mr. White. He hasn't been in this morning and his secretary says his office has been completely cleared out. And Céleste hasn't come in either."

She looked quickly at Brent, seeing the same look of awareness in his eyes as she knew was in her own.

"Don't worry," she said quickly. "We'll probably hear something from them during the day. In the meantime, carry on as usual. I know I can rely on you."

"Of course you can, Miss Blake," he said in gratified

tones, and she moved across to the escalator with Brent. They didn't comment on the new situation until they were standing in Terry's office and had pulled open some of the drawers in the big desk, finding them empty as the manager had said.

"So we're too late," she said at last, aware of a surge of relief at the words. "He must have found out that we knew, and he and Céleste have gone before we could tackle them about it."

"Yes. I'm sorry, Sara. That must be my fault. I should have told my friend not to send the papers and the warning to Yvonne until today. She must have got in touch with him as soon as she received them. I've made a real botch of it, haven't I?"

She took an impulsive step toward him. "You can say that after all you've done for me? I'd have gotten nowhere at all if you hadn't come to Paris with me. I'm glad it's happened this way, Brent. Really glad."

"Even though they've probably been defrauding you, Sara? Making away systematically with the firm's money?"

She nodded. "That makes no difference, not as far as Terry's concerned. You see, I've known him practically all my life. When I was a little girl I used to come in here to see my father and Terry was always so kind to me. In those days I hero-worshipped him. I thought there was nobody like him. I'm glad he's gone. Dad would have been too, I'm sure of that."

"Then I'm glad too," he said simply. "Sara. . . ."

He stopped, looking at her silently, and after a moment she asked, "Yes, Brent. What is it?"

He went closer to her and put out his hand, and without hesitation she put hers into it.

"Sara, I want to ask you something. Will you promise

to answer truthfully, no matter what the answer may be?"

Her eyes widened and she could feel the blood begin to throb through her as his hand tightened on hers, willing herself not to let him see how much his touch disturbed her.

"I promise," she said breathlessly.

"I know I've got no right to ask you this, Sara, but I've got to know the answer. Are you in love with Johnnie? Are you going back to the States to marry him?"

She did not reply, but stood looking at him, trying to read in his eyes the reason behind those questions.

"Sara!" he said urgently. "You must answer me. Please!"

"First tell me . . . why do you want to know?" she asked softly.

"Because until I do I won't have a minute's peace of mind."

She felt a surge of happiness thrill through her at his words and saw his face alight with emotion and desire. She swayed toward him, her eyes bright with love and hope.

"No, Brent, I'm not in love with Johnnie, I know that now, and I'm not going back to the States with him."

His hands moved up her arms and she felt their clasp, warm and urgent, through the coat she was wearing.

"Does that mean I've got a chance, Sara? You must have realized long ago how much I love and want you. Have I, Sara? Have I?"

She put her arms around him and turned her lips up to his. "Yes, I know now, Brent, and that's my answer. Yes, my dearest love. Yes," she said, and then there was only silence as his mouth came down demandingly on hers.

BEYOND THE SUNSET

Beyond the Sunset

Flora Kidd

Penelope Jones didn't look like a nanny: her youth and prettiness belied her experience. But she was infuriated when Tearlach Gunn refused to consider her just because she wasn't middle-aged and shapeless!

Their meeting was stormy and his sudden acquiescence surprising.

"All right, Miss Jones," he said. "I still think you're not suitable for the job, but I'm willing to give you a trial. If at the end of four weeks you can cope satisfactorily with the children and you don't give me any problems, I'll let you stay."

Penelope accepted his condition. In a month, she vowed, Tearlach Gunn would eat humble pie!

. . , My purpose holds
To sail beyond the sunset, and the baths
Of all the western stars, until I die.
It may be that the gulfs will wash us down;
It may be we shall touch the Happy Isles.

TENNYSON: Ulysses

CHAPTER ONE

Penelope Jones arrived at Mallaig, a fishing port on the northwest coast of Scotland, on a day bright with the sunshine of mid-August. Not a breath of air stirred as she stood on the quayside and looked about her in delighted fascination at a scene strange to her eyes.

The fishing fleet was in and the sturdy boats, some varnished, some painted green or black, with high bows and spiky radio masts, jostled each other beside the stone wall of the quay. Derricks swung and creaked as the catches were lifted out of deep holds. Seagulls and terns swooped and screeched, tormented by the sight and smell of so many silvery, netted fish.

Beyond the boats the water of the harbor was a deep blue, reflecting the serene cloudless sky, which arched above grayish green curves of treeless hills. Several sailing yachts, on their anchor chains, nodded in narcissistic admiration of their reflections on the smooth water. The air was tangy with the smell of herrings being kippered in nearby sheds, where wood chippings, used in the fires, were piled on the floor like heaps of golden cereal.

Turning away from the kippering sheds Penelope caught her breath as she saw for the first time, across an expanse of glittering sea, the dark serrated peaks of the mountains of Skye, those magical, mysterious heaps of rock; they had dominated the stories told by her grandmother, who had been born on an island called Torvaig, one of the Inner Hebrides, lying farther to the north of Skye.

Suddenly excitement flared through Penelope. The

feeling was unusual because she was normally a calm person, who prided herself on being able to keep her cool in most situations, as befitted a children's nanny. But this was the first time she had been in the Highlands of Scotland and, since she considered them to be her spiritual home, a little excitement was to be expected.

As she swung around again to look at the harbor, her eyes were caught by the glitter of chromium-plated fittings on a big, two-masted yacht anchored near the entrance to the harbor. It seemed to her to be as flagrant an example of affluence as anything she had seen during her journey north that morning, and she wondered who owned it.

But instead of standing and staring she should be looking for the person who had come to meet her. Slim and neat in her navy blue pantsuit, she turned and walked briskly to the white building where the harbormaster had his office.

She was just about to turn the handle of the door when it opened and a young man walked out, almost knocking her down. Big hands grasped her shoulders to prevent her from falling, and a pair of roguish brown eyes laughed down at her.

"Well now, I wasn't expecting to walk into someone like you. I hope I didn't hurt you?"

His voice was deep and lilting. His red-gold hair was long enough to lap the neck of his sweater. He was also wearing sailcloth trousers tucked into short rubber boots. He was big and handsome and she judged his age to be the same as her own. She decided he must be a fisherman off one of the boats.

"I'm all right, thank you," she replied, rather primly, very conscious of his hands still on her shoulders. The roguish glint in his eyes had increased, as his glance wandered over her flushed cheeks, shining dark hair and trim figure.

"I've just arrived here and I'm expecting to be met at this office," she explained.

His eyes widened incredulously and his hands slid from her shoulders. He folded his arms across his wide chest and stared down at her.

"You can't be Miss Jones from London?" he said in awed tones.

"Yes, my name is Penelope Jones," she answered. "I'm on my way to Torvaig."

"And I'm the one sent to meet you at the harbormaster's office," he murmured, obviously still incredulous. He held out one of his big hands. "Hugh Drummond at your service, Miss Jones. You can't possibly be a nanny. Nannies are middle-aged and shapeless. They wear awful frumpy clothes and funny hats with round brims, and they nearly always carry umbrellas."

"Not these days," replied Penelope with a grin that made her eyes sparkle and produced two dimples in her soft cheeks. "I'm pleased to meet you, Mr. Drummond. My luggage is over there. Where is your car?"

He gave her piled luggage a cursory glance and then looked at her. Mischief began to dance in his eyes again.

"I haven't a car here," he said.

"Then how will we get to Torvaig?" she demanded. Being very efficient herself she sometimes grew a little impatient with what she considered to be inefficiency in others.

"By sailing yacht. Have you ever been in one before?" he asked.

"Never."

"Then it's just as well the weather is calm." He put back his head and let out a crack of laughter. "I can hardly wait to see Tearlach's face when he sees you."

"Tearlach?" she repeated questioningly. The name sounded strange, almost foreign, to her ears.

"It's the Gaelic name for Charles; but he's Tearlach to his people, some of whom still speak Gaelic."

"His people!" exclaimed Penelope. "Who is he? You make him sound like a feudal lord."

"Which is the last thing he would claim to be," murmured Hugh. "He's the head of our section of the Gunn clan, and on Torvaig his word is law because he owns the island."

"Then who is Mrs. Drummond, who wrote to me?" asked Penelope, thoroughly mystified by her new acquaintance's statements. "I thought she must be the owner of the island."

"She would like to be and thought she would be for a time. But Tearlach turned up, the long-lost son of Magnus Gunn, laird of Torvaig. Murdoch inherited the island from his great-uncle, but never had the guts or the money to do anything for the island. Anyway, after 18 years of wandering about the world Tearlach turned up to claim his paltry inheritance."

"I wouldn't call an island paltry," objected Penelope.

"You would if you'd seen it when Tearlach took it over. Houses were in ruins, the land was unfarmed and the big house was falling down. It's very different now."

Penelope had heard of islands being bought by wealthy industrialists and being restored to life. Already she was building in her mind the image of a rotund, kindly eyed, middle-aged philanthropist who had used his wealth to improve the island of her dreams.

"He came back, like Ulysses, to claim what was rightly

his," she murmured dreamily, and Hugh threw her a surprised glance.

"I didn't know nannies went in for classical education," he remarked.

"I don't know Greek or Latin, but I've read the tales of the Greek heroes in translations."

"And being called Penelope you'd naturally be interested in Ulysses," teased Hugh. "All the more reason why I should warn you about my cousin Tearlach."

"Cousin?" repeated Penelope, thinking she was falling into a habit of repeating everything he said. But she was puzzled by his oblique references to the owner of Torvaig, whom she had never before heard of and she had to use some means to make him stop and explain.

"Sort of cousin," he amended. "Cousin umpteen times removed. My mother's father and Tearlach's father were second cousins and so that makes me and Tearlach—"

"All right," interrupted Penelope, laughing. "I understand. In some way you and he are related. And your mother is the Mrs. Drummond who wrote to me."

"Yes. Now, as I was saying, don't make the mistake of thinking Tearlach is a classical hero. He's very much of the twentieth century, and he's been a bit of a ruffian in his time. His father was a no account and did nothing to uphold the good name of Gunn. Tearlach grew up in one of the poorer areas of Glasgow and learned at an early age to hold his own against all comers. Although he's acquired a veneer of civilization, there are times when the veneer cracks and the roughness shows both in his speech and his behavior."

"Well, whose children am I coming to look after? His?" asked Penelope.

"Ach, no. His sister's. After the car crash my mother found a nanny for them, a Miss Swan from Inverness.

But as far as Tearlach is concerned, she's blotted her copybook in several ways. She's not been able to control wee Davy and she's talked too much around the island about Tearlach's affairs. Anyway, when Mother was visiting Torvaig recently, Swannie said she'd had enough and gave notice. Tearlach said he'd have to find another nanny, one who wouldn't twitter at him like Swannie does when he roars at her, and Mother took it upon herself to find someone sensible and responsible. But I'm afraid when he sees you Tearlach is going to be more than surprised. You're not what he had in mind at all."

"I'm sensible and responsible; I don't gossip and I don't get the twitters when some arrogant man roars at me," replied Penelope coolly. "Neither you nor your cousin seem to have the slightest knowledge about trained nannies. Do you think they're all born middle-aged? I can assure you I'm properly trained and I have a diploma. I've already held a similar position to a very important person in London. I have excellent references, which your mother must have seen before she recommended me to Mr. Gunn—your cousin."

Hugh held his arms above his head in a mocking gesture of surrender.

"I give in," he said with a laugh. "Please don't misunderstand me. I'm glad you're young and pretty. I live on Torvaig, too, and it's nice to know that someone like yourself is coming there. Still, Tearlach won't be pleased when he sees how young you are. His reception might be somewhat hostile and cool."

"Don't worry about me, Mr. Drummond. I won't let him put me off. I'm used to dealing with cool customers," replied Penelope confidently, straightening her slim shoulders and tilting her rounded chin. The sunlight picked out glints of blue and gold in her smooth, shoulder-length dark hair, and a gleam of admiration twinkled in Hugh's eyes as he surveyed her.

"I'm thinking you're a cool customer yourself," he said. "We won't waste any more time. I'll just tell the harbormaster I've found you, and then we'll load the luggage into the dinghy and be away to the yacht.

The dinghy was a sturdy clinker boat, painted white, with an outboard engine. Quelling her fear of the water and hiding it under her habitual mask of composure, Penelope climbed slowly down the iron ladder set into the stone wall of the quay and stepped into the slightly rocking boat. She sat in the bow, as instructed by Hugh, and soon she was having a different entrancing view of the harbor and town.

Handling the dinghy with the careless ease of one used to messing about in boats most of his life, Hugh steered it toward the big two-masted yacht Penelope had noticed earlier. He took the dinghy alongside the yacht and stopped beside a small ladder.

Looking up at the gleaming white hull of the yacht, Penelope once more felt the surge of excitement she had felt on shore. Hugh stopped the engine and when all was quiet he yelled, "Tearlach? We're here!"

Penelope's spurt of excitement changed to a feeling of apprehension. She had not realized she was to meet the "cool customer" quite so soon. Collecting all her hard-won poise about her, she followed Hugh's instructions on how to get out of the dinghy and onto the ladder and then climbed carefully onto the deck. There she waited and watched Hugh heave her luggage up before he came aboard himself to tie the dinghy to the stern of the yacht.

Uncertain as to what to do next, she stood on the side-deck holding on with one hand to a stiff wire, which seemed to be part of the rigging of the main mast. The deck was made of strips of teak laid closely together and was scrubbed so clean it was almost white. The other woodwork, she could see, was also teak, but was golden in color, in marked contrast to the white paintwork of the yacht. The chromium-plated fittings, which she had noticed glittering in the sunlight, were dazzlingly bright at close quarters.

"Sit down," invited Hugh, pointing to the cushioned bench seats around the cockpit, and feeling a little strange, she did as he suggested. Yachts and all their equipment were completely new to her. Slender and upright, her hands folded on her knees, she betrayed her uncertainty and curiosity by her quick glances at the steering wheel in the centre of the cockpit, at the sturdy gleaming winches, and at the taut white ropes coiled around cleats.

She was about to ask Hugh a question when a man appeared in the open hatchway. The surprise that flashed in his eyes when he saw her was replaced by an expression of annoyance as he climbed into the cockpit and glanced inquiringly at Hugh, who was sitting precariously balanced on the cockpit coaming.

"Miss Penelope Jones, Tearlach. She's fully trained as a children's nanny and has a diploma to say so," Hugh introduced her mockingly.

Tearlach Gunn, owner of the island of Torvaig, turned slowly to look again at Penelope. He was as much a surprise to her as she was to him. Her image of a plump fatherly philanthropist had been far from the truth. This man was not much more than ten or 12 years older than herself; he must have set out on his wanderings while in his midteens.

Not as tall as Hugh, he possessed, nevertheless, a tough muscular physique, and she had the impression that he was no stranger to hard physical labor. He was wearing faded denim pants and a shirt to match, and the rough clothing emphasized the impression of tough masculinity.

As a child he must have had blond hair, thought Penelope, because his longish, untidy brown hair was still streaked with blond. The morning's sunshine had put a reddish glow in his lean square-chinned face. There was a touch of wildness to that face and the measured glance of his narrowed gleaming eyes and the calm politeness of his manner when he spoke to her only seemed to underline the wildness. The spirit of the man was as untamed as that of the original Highland chieftains from whom he was descended.

"How do you do, Miss Jones," he said in a deep vibrant voice. "I think a mistake has been made. I asked specifically for an older woman. I have no use for a fledgling nanny."

Penelope returned his impersonal gaze with one she hoped was as impersonal as his own, while her insides quaked a little as she recognized that she was up against a formidable personality.

"I was available and I have had experience with hyperactive children, which was requested. Mrs. Bennet of the agency seemed to think I would be highly suitable for the job and recommended me to Mrs. Drummond," she said evenly, thinking rather guiltily of the way she had pleaded with Mrs. Bennet to recommend her for the position on Torvaig, far away from London and the memories of her disastrous affair with Brian Hewitt. "I'm quite competent," she added coolly as he lifted his eyebrows skeptically.

"I'm not doubting your competency. I'm sure you're most efficient and that the children might benefit from being in your charge," he replied suavely. "My request for someone older to look after them is related to the fact that there's no other woman living in my house."

"But surely you have a housekeeper," said Penelope, not understanding the implication behind his words.

"I have, but she doesn't live in the house. Also, should I have to go away on business, which happens often, I'd like to think I would be leaving the children with someone mature and responsible. Young women are often easily distracted from their work."

"I am responsible," she objected hotly. Something about his attitude was getting beneath her skin. She had a miserable feeling that this was a battle of wills she might not win. "And I'm not a bit worried about being left alone in the house. In my last position I was often left to take full responsibility when my employers went away," she added.

"That may have been so," he conceded, still polite, "but the situation at Torvaig House is different. Your last employers were a married couple. I'm a bachelor."

Still blind to the point he was making, completely bewildered by his attitude, Penelope exploded into speech again.

"I can't see why that should prevent *you* from employing *me*."

He looked over her head at Hugh, and the curl of his mouth and the slight shrug of his shoulders conveyed, more clearly than words, his contemptuous opinion of her. She felt her temper rising steadily.

"I'm surprised you've been able to hold a position that has put you in the care of young children," he said in the same quietly insolent drawl. "Your disregard for the usual proprieties is, to say the least, reckless."

Behind her Hugh sputtered with laughter. As she fully

understood for the first time what Tearlach Gunn was implying her cheeks flushed a becoming dusky pink and she looked away from him.

"Apart from that," he continued, "I find you unsuitable for the job, no matter what Mrs. Bennet or my cousin, Mrs. Drummond, think."

Her flush having subsided and her temporarily scattered wits having been collected once more she was able to glare at him, all her indignation and her disappointment revealed in her blue eyes.

"Oh, this is ridiculous!" she stormed, pricked beyond endurance by his insolence. "Just because you remember your nanny as being middle-aged and possibly dowdy, you think all nannies should be like that. I may seem too young to you, but probably I'm better trained and more adaptable than an older woman would be. If you refuse to employ me, I doubt very much if you'll find anyone else willing to come and live on your island, which is far away from the amenities most nannies are in a position to demand today. There aren't many of us, you know."

Slightly unnerved by his unwavering gaze, she paused, aware that her voice was shaking. Taking a deep breath of air, she continued, determined to point out to him that he was wrong in his assumption that she had no regard for the proprieties. "As for your thinking that I have no respect for correct moral conduct just because I have no objection to being employed by a bachelor, I'd like you to know that it never occurred to me that I might be violating any proprieties. You must have a very low opinion of women, if you believe that because I'm willing to work in your house it should be assumed that my morals are lax. Your remark reeks of prejudice!"

Her voice shook so much that she had to stop speaking. Never before had she spoken her mind in such a way to a prospective employer. All her hopes of going to Torvaig were ruined now by her own plain speaking, and not even Hugh's softly spoken, "Up the Joneses," could console her.

"I never had a nanny," said Tearlach Gunn quietly, and she remembered, rather belatedly, Hugh's telling her that his cousin had grown up in one of the poorer parts of Glasgow. "Take Miss Jones ashore and book a room for her in one of the hotels," he went on in a brisk cold voice. "Then buy a ticket for her journey to London." He glanced down at Penelope again. "The train leaves early in the morning, so make sure you're up in time to catch it. Please accept my apologies for any inconvenience caused you for having had to travel so far north unnecessarily."

The expression in his narrowed gleaming eyes belied his politely spoken apology. He looked as if he would have liked to have wrung her neck, she thought with a shiver. Then he turned to go down into the cabin.

"Wait, Tearlach," said Hugh in his softly persuasive voice. "She's probably right. An older woman wouldn't accept the position. Why don't you give her a chance to show her mettle? After all the trouble she's taken to come this far it seems mean to send her back untried. And if you send her back, who's going to look after the bairns? I'm pretty sure Kath won't, and Swannie will throw a fit when she finds we've returned to Torvaig without anyone to relieve her."

Tearlach's heavy shoulders stiffened, and for a moment he stood perfectly still as if considering Hugh's suggestion. Then he swung around to look over Penelope's head at his cousin.

"You know the situation and what might be said," he murmured.

"Yes, I do. But it isn't like you to be so careful of public opinion."

"What do you mean by that?" asked Tearlach, his eyes gleaming dangerously.

"You've never seemed to mind who stayed in your house before, male or female."

"That was before I had the responsibility of young children thrust upon me," retorted Tearlach.

"You're taking that responsibility very seriously," commented Hugh.

"How can I do otherwise? Avis asked me to look after them and I've never refused responsibility yet. At the moment it looks as if I'm the only relative willing to provide for them, and that means employing someone to look after them, whether I like it or not," replied Tearlach shortly, as if the whole business irritated him.

"You could get married and then your wife could take care of them. I know of at least one young woman who would like to marry you," said Hugh, with a touch of flippancy.

"Then you know more than I do," was the curt answer. "And you're talking too much as usual."

In the slightly uncomfortable silence that followed the sharp exchange, Tearlach looked at Penelope again and a faint smile curved his mouth.

"Sometimes Hugh talks sense," he said. "If we return to Torvaig without you, Miss Swan, who has been the children's nanny until now, is likely to have apoplexy at the thought of having to stay with them and with me a day longer than necessary. I'm still of the opinion that you're not suitable for the job, but I could be wrong. I'm willing to give you a trial. If at the end of four weeks from now I find you can cope satisfactorily with Davy and Isa and that you don't give me any problems, I'll eat humble pie and let you stay."

He should have been a psychologist, thought Penelope, because challenge was implicit in his offer. Without having backed down one step he had changed course. By raising a mental picture of an elderly lady struggling to deal with two lively youngsters as well as a difficult employer, he had engaged her sympathy and then had implied that she herself could do no better and would be unable to last more than a month in the position. The desire to show him that she was more than equal to the task was all-powerful, sweeping aside any other consideration, and she let it have its way.

"I accept your condition, Mr. Gunn, and you'll be eating humble pie," she replied with a lift of her chin.

"We shall see, we shall see, Miss Jones," he drawled, with a sudden suspicious glance at her. "The immediate task is to relieve Miss Gunn from a duty she is finding too onerous."

"Thank heaven you've seen the light," said Hugh gaily, and in his turn he was regarded with suspicion by Tearlach. "If you're really worried about the propriety of having a young single woman living in your house, I suggest you ask Mrs. Guthrie to live in. There should be enough room."

"I'm not worried about it, but I'm pretty sure some of the islanders will be. And it's just possible Mrs. Guthrie won't agree. For all I know she might be on the side of the puritans too," remarked Tearlach, with a wry twist to his mouth. "Now, pull up the anchor, while I start the engine. We'll need all the power we have if we want to reach Torvaig before nightfall in this calm."

Her immediate future settled in this surprising manner,

Penelope was determined to enjoy her voyage. The idea of approaching Torvaig by sailboat appealed to her liking for the unusual, and although she was slightly disappointed because there was no wind, she realized she could not have had a better day for seeing the scenery.

Once he had carried out the orders issued to him by Tearlach, Hugh came to sit beside her. He showed her on a chart, which he brought from the cabin, the route they would take through the Sound of Sleat into Lock Alsh, then through the narrows at the Kyle of Lochalsh to the Inner Sound, a stretch of water separating Skye from the mainland farther north. They would pass the islands of Raasay and Rona and would eventually come to Torvaig, a lobster-shaped piece of land lying at the opening to one of the great sea-lochs that faced the Minch, a wide expanse of water between the Outer Hebridean Islands and the mainland.

"When the weather is bad, the Minch is as wicked a piece of water as you could wish to know," said Hugh, as he rolled up the chart. "How about something to eat, Tearlach? It's a long time since breakfast and I'm sure Miss Jones is famished."

"If you'd like to steer I'll make some sandwiches and something to drink," replied Tearlach obligingly. He had steered the yacht out of the harbor and now the craft was moving swiftly northwards through the water to where the Sound of Sleat narrowed as rocky spurs of land encroached upon the glittering sea.

Hugh stood up willingly and moved aft to take his place at the wheel.

"Can I help?" offered Penelope, as her new employer stepped past her on his way to the cabin.

His answer was brief to the point of rudeness.

"No."

Then he was gone and she was glancing ruefully at Hugh.

"I suppose I shouldn't have been so outspoken," she said.

"You both lost your cool," he replied with a grin. "It was like seeing two flints come together and strike sparks off each other. But you got your own way in the end."

"Thanks to you."

"I have my uses; anyway, I was thinking solely of myself," he said with that roguish twinkle in his eyes. "Although I intend to stay a bachelor, I don't mind having a few special women friends on the side, and you could be one. But tell me, why were you so angry with him?"

"Oh, I suppose it was because he was obviously against *me*. I thought, perhaps, that he was one of those men who think that because a woman is young and presentable she must automatically be regarded as a sex object, good for nothing else."

Hugh blinked his bewilderment.

"I hope you aren't one of those fervent feminists I've read about," he said anxiously.

"Not fervent. I don't go in for bra-burning, if that's what you mean," she said with a laugh. "But I've always believed a woman should be recognized for her intelligence and her ability to do a job and not for her sex appeal."

"That's all right, then," said Hugh with relief. "I think you'll find Tearlach agrees with that point of view. He's no male chauvinist, nor is he a misogynist. Quite the contrary, he enjoys the company of women, and I've a feeling there are a few females here and there in the world who were sorry when he left them behind and continued his odyssey."

His eyes twinkled as he made deliberate reference to the voyages of Ulysses and the hero's stay with various nymphs and princesses before he eventually returned to his homeland and his wife Penelope. Meeting his amused glance Penelope could not help laughing.

Sunshine, blue sea, green slopes, purple mountains. A sleek efficient yacht and a pleasant young man with a sense of humor, for company. What more could she want? Here was peace and timelessness it would be easy to get hooked on. She wondered if the owner of Torvaig knew how lucky he was to possess the yacht and live among such wonderful scenery.

"This is a lovely yacht," she said to Hugh.

"It is. The hallmark of a successful man," he replied. "Tearlach sailed it back from the West Indies when he returned from his wanderings."

"Alone?" she queried, wide-eyed.

"No, but he's the type who could have done a single-handed crossing of the Atlantic. He had a crew of ruffians who wanted to get back to Britain somehow and were willing to help him bring his latest acquisition here."

"You said he was away for 18 years. He must have been only a boy when he left."

"He was almost 16. He ran away from home. He couldn't stand living in the poverty to which his father's bad management had reduced the family. He was determined to make his fortune before he came back."

"Did he?"

"Judge for yourself," said Hugh, waving his hand at the yacht. "He has money and he knows how to spend it."

"How did he make his fortune?"

"First of all he went to South America and, by lying about his age, managed to find work in the oil fields of Venezuela—rough tough work that pays well. Then, with money in his pocket, he began to speculate, buying and then selling at a profit—shares, land, anything. He's a real financial wizard, is Tearlach, and a far cry from the rundown poverty-stricken absentee landlord his father was. And all because he had the courage to kick over the traces and bolt. A school dropout with the Midas touch."

"You sound envious."

"I am. I wish I had half his daring and a little of his energy. I have to admit that if he hadn't come back with the idea of developing Torvaig into a viable economic community again, I wouldn't have been able to give up teaching in order to paint and fish for lobsters."

"Does he subsidize you?"

"Only to the extent of letting me have a croft for a small rent. That almost free house with its bit of farmland is one of the reasons why my mother puts up with what she calls his rough behavior and his strange friends."

"In what way are they strange?"

"They're not really. They're just different from the usual run of people my mother prefers to know. And then some of the younger women have obviously been the fortune-seeking type."

"Oh, I see. Then that's why there's been talk."

Hugh flashed her a warning glance. She stopped talking and turned to see Tearlach appear at the hatchway with a plate piled high with sandwiches, two cans of beer and a mug of hot coffee. He handed her the coffee, helped himself to a handful of sandwiches and, with one of the cans of beer in his other hand, he walked off along the side-deck to the bow of the boat, without a word to herself or Hugh.

The sandwiches and the coffee were delicious and Penelope's opinion of her employer rose slightly. By the time she had finished them, the yacht had been sucked into a narrow strait of water and was being swept along rapidly by the swirling current.

"If we didn't have enough power to beat the whirlpools we'd be helpless and would be tossed about like a cork," explained Hugh, noting her interest. "I've sailed through here only once or twice, and then the wind was strong and fair and we were able to keep going. But to be caught here in a calm without an engine is asking for trouble."

Soon they had passed the whirlpools and were in the calm waters of Loch Alsh. To the east Penelope saw five mountain peaks, soaring majestically against the sky in pastel-shaded folds of rock. The lower slopes were cleft by deep glens and at the shoreline, where they swept down to the loch, they were edged by the deep green of forests.

"The Five Sisters of Kintail," said Hugh, "and over there you can see the silhouette of that most romantic of castles, Eilean Donan." Glancing toward the bow to make sure his cousin was out of earshot, added confidentially, "You were right about the talk. Swannie has spread lurid tales about the behavior of some of Tearlach's guests this summer, with the result that some of the older, more old-fashioned islanders will have nothing to do with him and will not work in the house. That's why he couldn't find anyone on the island to take Swannie's place."

"Oh, now I understand why he didn't want me," said Penelope.

"Naturally he's a little bitter about it because he's done his best for the island. By going to live there himself he's encouraged others to do so. Already many younger people have gone there to farm and fish because they know that the island has an interested owner. Ach, now, where are you going?"

Penelope had stood up and was carefully stepping out of the cockpit onto the side-deck.

"I must go and apologize for being rude to him."

"No. If you do that he'll know I've been talking too much, and I've been reminded already today that I talk too much."

"You're afraid of him," accused Penelope.

"A little," he admitted with a grin. "I'm afraid he'll throw me off Torvaig if I don't dance to his tune."

"That isn't very nice of you," she reproached him. "But no matter what you say, I must apologize. I can't work for him if I don't."

Holding carefully to the lifelines, she walked along the side-deck. As she moved forward the sound of the engine became muffled and she could hear a rushing sound, caused by the forefoot of the yacht as it cleaved the water. A thin spiral of tobacco smoke gave her a clue as to where she would find her employer. He was sitting on the deck in front of the cabin roof, leaning back against it. His arms were folded across his chest and between the fingers of one hand he was holding a cheroot. He was staring blankly ahead of him and between his eyebrows frown lines furrowed.

As she studied his profile Penelope felt her urge to apologize dying. He appeared invulnerable and completely self-contained. His mind was far away and was probably not concerned with any criticism she had thrown at him.

At that moment the yacht hit a wave, made by the wake of a fishing boat that had just passed; it bounced gently up and down, causing Penelope, who had not yet acquired her sea legs, to lurch forward. Wildly she grabbed at the lifeline, missed it and fell right across the man sitting on the deck.

Shaken, she stared at the laid teak deck inches below her nose. Then she felt a hand on her arm.

"Are you hurt?" asked Tearlach, and she felt his legs move beneath her.

Suppressing a desire to giggle at her ridiculous position, she shook her head and managed to crawl backward off his legs. Not wishing to risk losing her balance a second time, she stayed sitting on the deck facing him, her legs curled under her.

"I'm sorry, I didn't mean to throw myself at you," she said.

He considered her from behind a gray screen of smoke before he answered.

"You mean that remark in its literal sense, I suppose," he commented dryly, and then watched curiously as the dusky pink color washed over her face.

"Of course," she replied crisply. "I was on my way to apologize for losing my temper and for saying what I did."

"You said what you felt. Why apologize for that? Now that I know how you feel about some subjects, I know how to deal with you," he said coolly, enigmatically.

He raised the cheroot to his mouth and drew on it, his eyes narrowed against the bright sunlight as he looked ahead again.

Not quite sure how to take his cool reception of her apology, Penelope felt she had been dismissed and was about to stand up and make her way back to the cockpit when he surprised her by saying, "Why are you so keen to go to Torvaig?"

"How do you know I am?" she parried.

"The disappointment expressed on your face when I

told Hugh to take you ashore indicated how much you were set on this particular job. What is it about Torvaig that attracts you? Is Hugh the attraction?"

"Oh no, never! My reason for wanting to go there has nothing to do with him," she answered vehemently, annoyed that he should suspect that she and Hugh had a secret understanding of some sort. "Nor has it anything to do with knowing you're wealthy. I'm not a fortune-seeking female. I wanted to get away from London, that's all."

"Hugh has been talking too much again," he murmured. "Why did you want to leave London?"

"That's my business."

"Then you must be on the run from something. My guess is that you're on the run from an unsuccessful love affair," he drawled.

Unprepared for that, Penelope gasped, and he turned to give her a sardonic glance.

"Do I have to be on the run from anything?" she countered.

"If you're not hunting then you must be escaping," he said provocatively. "Women are usually doing one or the other, and I can think of no other reason for someone as young and as attractive as yourself wanting to come to Torvaig."

"I have a perfectly good reason for wanting to go to Torvaig," she flung at him angrily. "My grandmother on my father's side was born there. She used to tell me many stories about Torvaig and the other islands. The Happy Isles of the West, she always called them. Ever since I can remember I've wanted to come, to see the seals basking on the rocks and to watch the sunset. When the chance came in the form of work for which I'm trained, naturally I seized it."

"And bullied the agency into recommending you even

though you know that an older woman was wanted," he insinuated softly, and her eyes fell before his shrewd glance. "What was your grandmother's maiden name?"

She could tell he was skeptical, and it gave her great pleasure to look him in the eye once again and announce the old name her grandmother had been so proud of.

"Sandison," she said defiantly, watching for surprise to change his expression, but not by the flicker of an eyelid or the twitch of an eyebrow did he show any emotion.

"A common enough name, hereabouts," he conceded coolly. "The Sandisons are a branch of the Gunn clan, as any book on Scottish clans would inform you."

He didn't believe her! She clenched her hands and, with a great effort, repressed a desire to return to the cockpit and ask Hugh to alter the course of the yacht to take her back to Mallaig, because she did not think she could work for such an obdurate cynic as Tearlach Gunn.

She tried vainly to think of something to tell him about Torvaig that would convince him that her grandmother had lived there for a while, and a name sprang into her mind.

"She lived in a house called Achmore," she persisted hopefully.

"There's no house on Torvaig of that name, although there are the ruined shells of many houses scattered here and there among the bracken and the heather," he replied. Then, picking up the empty beer can from the deck beside him, he rose lazily to his feet and balanced easily on the swaying deck. "You've thought up an ingenious reason for wishing to come to Torvaig, but I doubt the truth of your story. Like Sandison, Achmore is another name common to this part of the country. If you consulted a map before you came, which I'm quite sure you did, you'd find it mentioned often."

He turned and made his way back to the cockpit. Penelope blinked furiously at the glitter of sunlight on the sea as the yacht nosed its way through a narrow passage of water at the Kyle of Lochalsh. A wide ferryboat crammed with cars and holidaymakers crossed in front of the yacht. Soon a small lighthouse, perched on a tiny rocky island, appeared on the right. A red navigation buoy loomed on the left. The land retreated on all sides and a wider expanse of water was before her, blandly blue, dotted with the dark humps of islands and edged by the majestic sweep of high mountain as it stretched north to a faint horizon.

That path of scintillating blue water led to Torvaig, and suddenly Penelope felt very close to her grandmother's spirit.

"I'm going home, Grannie," she whispered. "Home, beyond the sunset, to the happy isle of Torvaig, because it is home, no matter what Mr. Gunn says."

"Do you make a habit of talking to yourself, Penelope Jones?" asked Hugh mockingly, approaching her quietly.

She glanced up at him, a little embarrassed at having been found muttering to herself.

"Not often," she said.

He lowered himself to the deck, easing into the place his cousin had just left, and like him, stared with narrowed eyes at the sea.

"You were cursing Tearlach, perhaps," he suggested, with that touch of mischief never absent for long from his eyes and his speech. "Did you apologize to him?"

"As much as he would let me. Is he always so skeptical?"

"What makes you ask?"

"He wouldn't believe anything I told him about my grandmother."

"Your grandmother?" exclaimed Hugh, puzzled in his turn. "Where does she come into the picture?"

"She was born on Torvaig and lived there until she was 14. She used to tell me about it. I promised her before she died that I would visit the island when I could and look for the house where she was born, but Mr. Gunn tells me many of the houses are in ruins, and that I could have found the name of my grandmother's family in a book about the clans. He thinks I've made the whole thing up. Oh, if I wasn't so determined to reach Torvaig, now that I'm near to it, I'd ask him to put me ashore at that ferry landing back there, and I'd find my own way back to London," asserted Penelope, her anger with her new employer making her voice shake.

"You'd be playing right into his hands if you did," chuckled Hugh, amused by her righteous indignation. "He doesn't want you on Torvaig, but he's in a difficult position because he has to have someone to look after the children; and because you dared to set your will against his back there in Mallaig, he's likely to make life as uncomfortable as he can for you during the next four weeks."

"He's not my idea of a Highlander. I thought they were renowned for their good manners and hospitality," said Penelope.

"I warned you that sometimes the roughness shows. Tearlach is not Highland-bred, nor born, and you must remember that for 18 years he was away from this country, making his way in the world alone. Of course he's hard and sometimes rude. He is also very shrewd and businesslike, but make no mistake, he can be generous and hospitable when he wants to be," replied Hugh. "But let's talk about something else. Tell me more about your grandmother. I'm not in the least skeptical. Perhaps I'll be able to find the house where she was born for you. I've a good knowledge of the island."

Comforted by his offer, she told him all she knew about her grandmother's family and their reason for leaving Torvaig.

"That fits in with the general pattern of some of these islands. After the First World War many of the inhabitants left and went to live on the mainland," he remarked. "Although Torvaig is fairly big and has much fertile land, life was never easy in the past and cultivation was done manually. When the younger men returned from the war they were promised new houses and agricultural equipment by old Magnus Gunn, the laird of the time. But he never fulfilled his promises, and soon only elderly people were left. Then Magnus died, and Tearlach's father inherited and did nothing."

"Whereabouts do you live on the island?" asked Penelope.

"In a little cottage on a croft. It's on the shore of a wee cove facing the Minch along with several other crofts. One has recently been taken by a friend of my family, Ian McTaggart. He's a silversmith. When he heard of Tearlach's aim to revive Torvaig, he jumped at the chance to come here. Like many of us he'd been struggling along in a humdrum job, unable to get started in his own business through lack of capital and contacts. This summer, with Tearlach's financial support, he's been able to set up his own workshop and now he's designing and making filigree jewelry. My sister Kathleen is a jeweler too. She collects and polishes stones. She came over to Torvaig to stay with me for a holiday and went into partnership with Ian," explained Hugh, then added with a sidelong glance in her direction, "You and Ian have something in common. His family came originally from Torvaig, too, but left to settle on the mainland."

"Are there farms as well as crofts?" asked Penelope.

"Seven, including the home farm, which belongs to the Gunn estate and is managed for Tearlach by a Guthrie, a member of another Torvaig family who returned to the island. Dairy cattle do well. The place is green and favored with mild weather because it's protected from the east by a great bank of mountains. In the past the mountains created a problem because they made access to the island from the mainland difficult. But Tearlach is negotiating with the local country council to have the road improved, so that dairy produce can be transported faster than it is now."

"Does your mother live on Torvaig?" she asked. Hugh's obvious enthusiasm for life on the island was soothing her ruffled feelings. Her grandmother had not been wrong when she had described it as a lost paradise.

"Not she," he said with a grin. "She lives in Inverness with my father, who is a doctor. It's better if she and Tearlach don't meet often. She looks down on him because his father was no good and because his mother wasn't a Highlander but came from somewhere in England."

"You mentioned a car crash earlier," said Penelope. "Were both the children's parents killed in it?"

"Their father was killed outright. Avis lingered for about a month afterward. It was a great shock when she died as we had every hope she would survive."

"How sad! Poor little souls," said Penelope sympathetically, for she knew what it was like to lose both parents at once.

"Not as poor as you would think," replied Hugh. "They have a wonderful place to live in and, if you stay, they're going to have a pretty nanny to look after them. Now that you know all about my relatives, let's return to yours. One way you could find out if there were really any Sandisons on Torvaig would be to visit the old grave-yards. There is one near my croft. Ian is always poking about in it. Anything to do with early settlement of the island fascinates him—he fancies himself as an amateur archeologist. You know, if you could prove that your grandmother's family once owned a croft here, you could claim it and have every right to stay on Torvaig."

Vaguely excited by this suggestion, Penelope continued to question Hugh about the island. The yacht motored steadily north, and the long island of Raasay and the small island of Rona slipped by, while the mighty Cuillins dominated the scene. Occasionally Hugh pointed out an interesting landmark, and sometimes Penelope wondered whether they should both return to the cockpit to keep the man at the wheel company. But it was too pleasant sitting on the foredeck in the warm sunshine of late afternoon, listening to the bow wave as it sang its merry song. She felt she could have sat like that for ever, and she began to understand why people loved to sail among these isles.

Gradually the view changed and soon only the sea was between them and the dark outline of the Outer Hebrides. Beneath the smooth surface of the water there was a noticeable rolling swell that affected the motion of the yacht.

"Look," said Hugh, pointing. "There's Torvaig, over there."

Penelope looked and could see only a dark shape beyond the glitter of sunlight on the sea.

"How long will it take us to get there?" she asked.

"We should reach it just before sundown. There's wind

on the water. Can you see it? Maybe we'll be able to sail now."

Rising to his feet, Hugh went back to the cockpit presumably to tell his cousin, and realizing that her pleasant time alone with him was over for the day, Penelope followed him.

When the wind reached them it was no more than a faint fanning of cooler air against her cheek and a dark shirring of the pale blue satin of the water. But it was enough for Tearlach, who ordered Hugh to set the foresail and then the sail on the small aft mast. As the wind increased and thin feathery wisps of cloud streaked the western sky, the big billowing mainsail hoisted and the engine stopped. The yacht bounded forward like a hound released from a leash.

Now the only noises were the sound of water, rippling along the hull, and the occasional creaking of the masts and the boom, which carried the mainsail. Sitting in the cockpit again, Penelope noticed the difference the act of sailing made to the two men.

Hugh was smiling to himself as he leaned out of the cockpit and watched the foresail. He turned to his cousin and said, "You were right. This is the only way to approach Torvaig."

"There's none better," replied Tearlach. The note of deep conviction in his voice caused Penelope to look at him. His eyes were alight with excitement as he watched the mainsail and corrected the wheel occasionally with his lean, muscular hands. His legs braced against the movement of the yacht, his blond-brown hair tossed by the wind, his lean cheeks bronzed by the sun, he looked intensely alive, in love with the wind and the sea and at one with them.

Acutely disturbed by this discovery, Penelope looked away. The sea was building up now, under the onslaught of the steady wind. It deepened to cool greenish hollows and rose to crisp white crests. To the south of them the islands had lost their warm welcoming colors and had become coolly, distantly blue. Ahead, across the turbulent water towered a cliff turned golden by the light of the setting sun. On top of it stood a lighthouse, gleaming and graceful.

Rudh nan Torvaig. Torvaig Point. Penelope felt again a leap of excitement and recognition. She had never been to this place in her life before, but she knew it and had known it long before the lighthouse had been built.

She was almost home, had almost reached the island beyond the sunset.

Home! But that was how Hugh Drummond and Tearlach Gunn must regard Torvaig, and it was really much more their home than hers.

She glanced at Hugh, wanting to share her thoughts with him. He turned to smile at her and she smiled back. A crisp order from Tearlach interrupted their moment of silent communication. Hugh obeyed it, unwinding a rope from a winch and pulling on it. The yacht heeled suddenly. Water creamed along the teak edge of the deck. Thrilled by the burst of speed, Penelope leaned back against the coaming, tossing the hair back from her face, and encountered the shrewd, narrowed gaze of her employer.

On meeting that searching glance her nerves quivered, but refusing to be disconcerted she returned it frankly. Then she noticed the slightly cynical twist to the corner of his mouth. He must have noticed Hugh smiling at her. He thought she had come to Torvaig because she was a friend of Hugh's, and now, having seen them smiling at each other, he would be more than ever convinced that they had known one another previously.

Annoyed by his cynicism, she looked away over the heaving glinting sea to the island and immediately was swept by the most alarming sensation.

She had been here before. Long ago, in the mists of time, she had sat in the company of two men and had sailed to Torvaig. But the boat had been different. It had been square, striped red and gold. There had been other men, sitting on benches, rowing with long oars. She had sat at the stern near the helmsman and her wrists had been bound together with a rough, leathery rope.

The feeling of déjà vu frightened her. She shook her head to clear it and looked around. Everything was as it had been. Hugh was sprawled on the other side of the cockpit. Tearlach was steering and watching the mainsail. Glancing almost furtively at her hands she saw with relief that they were as usual, smooth-skinned and long-fingered, resting casually on her lap.

Hugh spoke suddenly, making her jump.

"The first Gunn came to Torvaig by sea. He was a Viking trader on his way back to Norway with cloth and metal, as well as slaves, from Ireland. The story goes that a storm blew up and he had to take shelter in Cladach Bay, where I live now. He and his fellow seamen liked the place so well they decided to settle there. He took one of the female slaves to be his wife. It's said that her hair was as dark as a blackbird's wing and her eyes were as blue as a wee lochan on a fine day in spring."

"All that heady romantic stuff appeals to Miss Jones, I'm sure," scoffed Tearlach. His sudden grin was an attractive curving of his long upper lip over even white teeth. "You'll be saying next that you believe she's the reincarnation of the lass from Ireland, just because she has similar coloring, and then casting yourself in the part of the first Magnus Gunn of Torvaig. But probably she knows the story already because her grandmother, who told her so much about Torvaig, included it in her own personal tales of the Hebrides."

His mockery was designed to needle her. Still tingling in reaction to her strange experience, Penelope flung a furious glance at him, hating him suddenly for his sarcasm.

"No, she didn't," she retorted. "But I felt it just now before Hugh spoke."

"Felt it?" Hugh sounded excited. He leaned forward, his tawny eyes ablaze.

"Have you ever had the feeling that you've done something before even though you *know* that you haven't in this lifetime?" she asked, guessing that he would be sympathetic and understanding.

"You mean as if you'd done it in your other time on earth?" he queried.

"That's right. Well, when I looked at Torvaig just now, I felt I'd done this before. I was in an open boat and there were men rowing it."

"And was Hugh there, wearing a winged helmet and carrying an ax?" Tearlach's voice throbbed with sarcasm.

She stared at him, trying to recall the two men of whom she had been aware in her flashback. One of them had been the steersman. The other had stood near her, hovering over her, and now, looking at Tearlach's square-chinned face, glinting eyes, derisive mouth, and sun-bleached hair, she recognized him. A description of a Viking she had once read in a history book at school flashed throught her mind:

"Blond his hair and bright his cheeks
Eyes as fierce as a young serpent's."

She was about to blurt out, "No, but you were," when she realized that such an admission on her part would only give him another chance to make fun of her.

"You may scoff, Tearlach," put in Hugh seriously, as if he'd noticed her hesitation and wanted to help her out in an awkward situation, "but such flashbacks are not uncommon. It's the inherited memory trying to tell us something. It's possible that Penelope really is the reincarnation of the first Magnus Gunn's slave-wife. One of us could be the reincarnation of him. I've been practising yoga, which is the union of the individual soul with the universal spirit, for some time. It helps me to paint, and reincarnation is a tenet of yoga. The soul travels through several lives and has a memory of previous lives."

Tearlach studied his cousin's serious face for a moment and then burst out laughing. His laughter was a spontaneous full-throated sound. Clearly he had no use for fairy-tales or religious theories.

"Well, I don't practise yoga and I don't believe in reincarnation," he retorted forcibly. "And the legends about the islands were made up by the inhabitants to pass the time in the long winter, based on the truth perhaps, but exaggerated and changed so much that there's now little truth left in them. As for Miss Jones's flashback, it was nothing more than the overworking of a powerful imagination, which has been fed by the romancings of her grandmother. She's imagined coming to Torvaig so often she's reached the point when she believes she's actually done it. Now that's enough of your nonsense. Go and take that mainsail down. With the wind like this we can run into An Tigh Camus under the other two sails."

Hugh flashed a sympathetic smile in Penelope's direction and left the cockpit. Soon the white triangle of the mainsail came swishing down. He rolled it around the boom and tied it. The yacht altered course a little as Tearlach freed the foresail and it billowed out.

Looking ahead Penelope could see the rocky shore in front of the cliff. To the left of the cliff a bay was opening, a pool of crimson water reflecting the sunset. The yacht was steered toward the entrance of the bay, and as the sun prepared to slip below the horizon, Penelope had her first glimpse of the house where she would be living for the next four weeks. It was set back from the water at the top of a sweeping lawn and she had no memory of having seen it before.

The yacht swept around almost in a complete circle toward a red mooring buoy bobbing on the water in the shelter of a headland that protected the bay at its north-western end. Hugh caught the buoy with a boathook and Tearlach left the wheel to run up on the foredeck to help his cousin make the mooring line fast to the kingpost on the boat; then he came back to take down the mizzen sail.

Wishing she could help with the stowing of sails and other equipment, yet reluctant to offer help to the man who had refused her help earlier and had recently made fun of her, Penelope sat and looked about her. Dark jagged rocks protected the entrance to the bay making it almost landlocked. A curve of golden sand glinted at the foot of the green sweep of lawn in front of the house. Bare, gently rolling hills were rose-tinted by the last rays of the setting sun. The place possessed a magical quality, tranquility plus mystery, ancient yet untouched by time, a happy isle beyond the sunset.

Yet, her future there was uncertain, complicated by the attitudes and personalities of the people she had already met and had yet to meet. Somehow during the next few weeks she had to prove her employer wrong and, in his own words, make him "eat humble pie."

CHAPTER TWO

In the clear light of the afterglow of the Hebridean sunset, Hugh took Penelope ashore in the dinghy, having been told to do so by a terse Tearlach, who stayed behind to make sure his yacht was secured for the night.

Sitting in the bow of the dinghy, Penelope watched him moving about the deck of the yacht as it bobbed at the mooring on the swell of the evening-pale water, and she wondered if "things" such as boats meant more than people to the tough, realistic owner of Torvaig.

She said as much to Hugh and he grinned at her, pushing the longish red-gold hair back from his forehead in a boyish gesture that made him seem more attractive than ever.

"Hating him, aren't you?" he shouted about the roar of the outboard engine. "I'm not surprised. You're the type to hate him."

"Oh. What type is that?" Penelope shouted back, intrigued by his comment.

"Independent in outlook, yet romantic at heart. Refusing to admit that any man could be your master, yet secretly nursing a hope that one day someone you respect will turn up so that you can give him all the love you have stored up inside you," he yelled back at her. "It's the romantic in you who hates Tearlach for his uncompromisingly realistic attitude to life. You could rip him apart, right now, for making fun of your flashback and your grandmother's stories, which obviously have meant a great deal to you. But you see he has no time for fairytales and legends. He's the sort of person who makes his own legend, and has done so already, by living vigorously and sometimes uproariously."

She was a little alarmed that this young man, whom she had met for the first time only a few hours ago, could read her so well. There had been a time in her life when she had thought Brian Hewitt, the nephew of her employers in London who had often been a visitor at the house where she had been nanny, was the person she respected and could love.

For a while theirs had been a joyous, if clandestine, relationship—clandestine because of the nature of her position in his uncle's household. Then, one day, she discovered that Brian, who was a student of political science and still at university, had had similar relationships with other young women, as he had gone about making the most of permissiveness. He had thought that she, like those others, was prepared to live with him without going through the formality of marriage.

She had refused, her own inner fastidiousness dictating that she should not follow the trend. But deep depression had set in culminating in her resignation from a position she had been so happy and comfortable in and then in her search for another job, away from the sights and sounds of London, which had been the background for her unsuccessful love affair.

On the run from an unsuccessful love affair. Tearlach Gunn's jeer returned to mock her. Hateful man! He had probably never known what it was like to be in love in his life!

With an effort she pushed Brian to the back of her mind. She had come to Torvaig to forget him, and now that she had come, she wasn't going to let her employer's jibes stop her from staying.

A stone jetty loomed up on her right and Hugh maneuvered the dinghy alongside it, cut the engine and jumped ashore. Making the boat fast, he helped her to get out and then took her cases.

"There's Swannie waiting on the front doorstep and wringing her hands," said Hugh, as they walked along the jetty and onto the fine springy turf of the lawn. "I wonder what sort of day she's had with Davy? He tends to run wild at times. It's because of the shock of his parents' death."

"What about the little girl?"

"Ach, Isa is fine. A plump cushion of a bairn with a stolid down-to-earth outlook on life. But she likes to wander off and Swannie gets into a tizzy when that happens and runs around in circles."

Miss Swan fitted Hugh's description of a nanny exactly. She was of medium height, thin and shapeless, and was wearing a midcalf tweed skirt and a fine wool sweater. Her hair was the color of pale sand and her anxious blue eyes were fringed by almost white eyelashes. As soon as Hugh and Penelope were within earshot she began to complain, all the time clasping and unclasping her thin ringless hands.

"Ach, it's a terrible day I've been having with the bairns. Davy hasn't stopped whining since you left."

"Why?" asked Hugh, as he placed two of Penelope's cases on the step in front of the porticoed front door and gazed down at the distressed nanny with an air of mild resignation.

"He wanted to go with his uncle. I did everything to pacify him, and then Isa ran away while I was seeing to him. I was fairly out of my mind with worry, wondering where she'd gone and what Mr. Gunn would say to me if she was still missing when he came back. You've been an awful long time."

"There wasn't much wind," replied Hugh. "Where's Isa now?"

"They're both in bed, praise be. Your sister is reading to them. Ach, I can't think what I'd have done without her and Mr. McTaggart today. They found Isa for me and brought her back. Miss Drummond is a dear lass and very fond of the bairns."

"Very fond of someone else too, I'm thinking," said Hugh in a low voice, with a wink at Penelope. She widened her eyes questioningly at him and he mouthed "Tearlach" at her, over the unsuspecting Swannie's head.

"Where is Miss Jones?" asked Miss Swan, gazing at Penelope vaguely and then looking out at the bay as if expecting a person similar to herself to materialize. "Didn't she come with you? Ach, I had a feeling she wouldn't. I told Mr. Gunn he should go by car to fetch her. Not everyone wants to sail, I said. But he wouldn't listen to me. It's quicker by boat, he said. Ach, what will I do?"

The woman wailed like a banshee, that spirit peculiar to Scots and Irish mythology whose wail portends death in the house. Afraid that she might go into hysterics, Penelope stepped forward, smiled comfortingly, and introduced herself.

"I'm Penelope Jones, and I didn't mind coming by boat one little bit. In fact I enjoyed the experience. I've come to relieve you."

For once Miss Swan was incapable of speech. She could only blink at Penelope with a flutter of pale eyelashes.

"You're not a nanny," she exclaimed at last. "You're too young."

"I was the only one on Mrs. Bennet's books who would come to a place as remote as Torvaig," replied Penelope.

"Aye, I can imagine that. It's not a place anyone in their senses would want to come. It's certainly not what I've been used to. If I'd known what sort of a man I was coming to work for I'd never have come, not even for your mother's sake, Hugh. The things your cousin has said to me don't bear repeating. And the way some of his friends, young women too, have behaved in this house . . . ach, it's a wonder the old lairds of Torvaig haven't turned over in their graves!"

"Now, Swannie," cautioned Hugh, trying hard not to laugh, "you're letting your feelings get the better of you. You'll have Miss Jones thinking my cousin is a fiend out of hell, or a twentieth-century Marquis de Sade."

"I don't know about yon marquis or what he did, but I do know I've always been used to working for gentlemen who know how to treat an employee. I'm sure Miss Jones is welcome to work for him, and good luck to her, for she'll be needing it," continued the agitated little woman.

"Miss Jones is quite able to take care of herself as far as I can tell, after knowing her for only a few hours," said Hugh comfortingly. The sound of a horn being blown carried across the water from the yacht, making a plaintive sound in the long-lingering twilight. An expression of relief passed across Hugh's face. He was obviously glad of the interruption.

"That's Tearlach wanting to be brought ashore," he explained. "Please take Miss Jones into the house. I expect she'd like to wash before having a meal. Leave the cases. I'll take them upstairs when I come back."

He sprang down the steps and made his way across the lawn to the jetty. A rather wintry smile on her thin face, Miss Swan turned to Penelope.

"I'm afraid I didn't give you much of a welcome," she said. "Come into the house and I'll show you your room.

I've moved out already and I'll be staying the night with a friend in the village of Strathnish, on the other side of the island."

Suddenly realizing how hungry she was, Penelope followed Miss Swan into the house through the big paneled front door, stepping into a wide hallway with a high ceiling from which hung several carved oak Jacobean chandeliers. On the floor a priceless Persian rug glowed, red and blue, surrounded by the sheen of highly polished parquet. The walls were stark white, an excellent background for the few pieces of dark antique furniture and the numerous framed paintings and engravings.

From the hall they went up three shallow steps into a narrow passage with doors that opened into rooms she could not see. Turning left, they went down another passage to a narrow stairway that, Penelope guessed, was the old servants' staircase. At the top of two flights of stairs was a square landing onto which six doors opened.

"This is the attic," explained Miss Swan. "Give him his dues, Mr. Gunn has spared no expense in having the rooms tastefully furnished and arranged for the children. Your room is here between the children's rooms. On that side of the landing is the bathroom, the kitchen and the playroom."

She turned the handle of a door painted a soft shade of green. Once in the room she closed the door firmly behind her.

Penelope was delighted by the bedsitting room allotted for her use. Some antique furniture, as well as some of more functional modern design, had been entrusted to her care. The dainty walnut chest of drawers had a genuine Chippendale mirror over it and beside it, in the corner, was a Chippendale chair of Chinese design. The simple divan bed was covered in brightly colored folkweave material and was scattered with several cushions covered in solid jewellike colors. Two big armchairs were set on either side of the window and a long walnut coffee table set between them. The floor was covered with fluffy pale green carpeting and folkweave curtains hung at the window.

Peering through the window, she could just make out the moorland, stretching away to a loch whose surface shone with the last pale light of evening. Beyond the loch the rugged outline of hills was carved dark against the sky.

"Do you like the room?" asked Miss Swan anxiously.

"Oh yes, it's lovely," said Penelope, turning to smile at her. "I like the old furniture particularly."

"You'll find many other pieces like it throughout the house. It was all here moldering away when Mr. Gunn took over the house. He let Miss Drummond have the run of the place to redecorate and refurnish it. This suite was designed for his sister and her husband and the children so that they could come and stay whenever they liked. There's no television yet, but it should be installed soon."

"Who wants television in a place like this with views like that?" said Penelope, waving her hand toward the window.

"I'm glad you appreciate the beauty of the place, because I'm afraid that otherwise someone as young as yourself might find living here dull, especially during the winter. Mrs. Drummond asked for a television because the agency told her most nannies won't take positions these days unless they can have their own private sitting room complete with television and radio. Very different from my day, not that I ever lacked for anything," said Miss Swan with a superior sniff.

"Where were you before you came here, Miss Swan?" asked Penelope.

"Well, I'd been retired for more than a year, but before that I was with the Hope-Sinclairs in Inverness. It was Mrs. Hope-Sinclair who gave my name to Mrs. Drummond when she was looking for someone to mind the bairns. Since I had known her and her family for many years I didn't mind obliging." Miss Swan sounded as if she had conferred a great honor on Tearlach Gunn by coming to Torvaig to care for his nephew and niece.

Penelope could see now that the woman was much older than she had first thought and that she was extremely upset about something. With a surge of sympathy, knowing how uncomfortable the position of a nanny in a household could be at times, she decided to try to put her mind at rest.

"I realize, Miss Swan, that I'm a disappointment to you. Mr. Gunn has already pointed out that he also thinks I'm too young and incapable of holding this job," she said earnestly. "In fact he wanted me to go back to London, but Mr. Drummond intervened."

Surprise replaced the anxious expression on Miss Swan's face.

"Now why did Hugh do that?" she asked.

"He was thinking of you. He knows you've been unhappy here and want to leave, but he knew you couldn't go unless there was someone here to take care of the children."

Miss Swan's face softened and tears brimmed in her eyes.

"Ach, Hugh's a good lad. It's quite true, I have been unhappy here. I'm getting too old to deal with young children and the wee laddie is difficult. He throws tantrums and cries a lot in the night. Some nights it's been three and four o'clock before I've been able to get to sleep. When I told Mr. Gunn that I thought the child should see a specialist, he just laughed and said I wasn't firm enough, and that he paid me to settle the child."

"I believe he lost his parents in an accident. Maybe he hasn't recovered from the shock of that yet," suggested Penelope. "Could you please tell me a little about the children's backgrounds before you go? It might help me to understand."

Miss Swan studied the pretty face of the young woman standing before her and, letting out a sigh, sat down suddenly in one of the armchairs.

"I can see now that you're not what I thought you were," she said apologetically. "You must forgive me, Miss Jones, but you see there have been some young women staying in this house this summer whose behavior I can only call loose. Now, I know young women are much easier in their relationships with men today than they were when I was young, but I find it difficult to accept. Ach, it's a great load off my mind to see you're not one of those flighty pieces and that you'll have the welfare of the bairns at heart. Now, what is it you want to know?"

"I'd like to know more about the accident in which the children's parents were killed."

"They were staying here for a wee holiday and they decided to go to the mainland. Coming back, they took one of those awful bends too fast. The car went out of control and plunged down an embankment."

"Were the children with them?"

"No. They were left here with Mrs. Guthrie, who is the housekeeper."

"And what were they told when their mother didn't come back for them?" asked Penelope.

"I believe Mr. Gunn told them that their mother had died and wouldn't be coming any more. Ach, he didn't soften it one little bit. He has no interest in children and I think their mother made a grave mistake when she put them in his care before she died. They'd have been far better off with their father's relatives."

"Where are they?"

"In Spain, I suppose. He was a Spaniard who worked for the Spanish Embassy in London, I believe. When you see Davy you'll see that he's no Scot. The wee lass is more like her mother, so I'm told. Their surname is Usted. It's really a lot longer than that, but Mr. Gunn said not to bother with the rest of it. Is there anything else you'd like to know?"

"No, that will do for a start. I expect Mr. Gunn will tell me anything else I want to know."

"He might, if he's in the mood," said Miss Swan tartly. "You'll learn more from young Hugh or from his sister. And now I must be going. My friend from the village has been waiting for me down in the kitchen for more than an hour. You'll find a cold buffet supper has been left in the dining room for you to help yourself. Mrs. Guthrie couldn't wait to see you."

After wishing Penelope more luck, Miss Swan left. Finding her cases outside the door of the room, Penelope lugged them into the room. She decided to unpack after she had eaten.

As she washed her face and hands and combed her hair in the small bathroom, she reflected quietly on everything that had happened to her that day. From the moment she had walked into Hugh Drummond at the harbormaster's office, life had taken on a magical hue. Until then it had been blurred, almost impressionistic. Now it was sharply etched and painted in bright colors; and the people who moved about her appeared larger than life-size, like those seen on a movie screen.

What had made her suddenly more aware, not only of the beautiful scenery through which she had come that day but also of the people she had met? Dominating her thoughts was Hugh with his Viking good looks, his sunny smile and his soft, persuasive voice. Then there was Tearlach Gunn, a close second—never would she be able to think of him as Charles. He was cool, self-contained, *nouveau riche*, and was looked down upon not only by some of his relatives but also by the woman he had employed as nanny. He had roused her own temper so easily on the yacht that it was not difficult to imagine him upsetting the thin-skinned Miss Swan.

But there were more people for her to meet that night. As she left the room, closing the door behind her, she came face to face with a woman a few years older than herself, who was quietly closing the door to the right.

She's beautiful, quite beautiful, thought Penelope, as she noted smoothly braided bronze hair, fine white skin, high cheekbones and wide, dark-fringed golden eyes. A tall elegant woman dressed in a long tartan skirt, topped by a finely ribbed, pale green sweater, which accentuated the sumptuous lines of her figure.

As she sensed the other woman's shyness, Penelope took the initiative and spoke first.

"I'm Penelope Jones. I've come to work here."

The golden eyes widened even more and Penelope braced herself for the inevitable, incredulous reaction to her own appearance.

"You are never saying you're the new nanny come to look after Davy and Isa?" said the woman in a softly lilting voice.

"Yes, I am. You're Kathleen Drummond, aren't you? Miss Swan told me you were reading to David."

"Davy," corrected the other. "He doesn't like being called David. He's asleep now, poor wee lamb. He was very upset today because his uncle went away on the boat without him."

They moved together toward the stairs. Standing back at the top of them, Penelope let Kathleen go first. Watching the other woman move so gracefully in her simple, yet obviously homemade clothes, she felt at a slight disadvantage in her pantsuit and wished she had changed into a dress.

When they reached the lower floor Kathleen turned toward the wide hallway and Penelope hurried after her.

"Miss Swan said I was to go to the dining room for my supper," she said, "but I'm afraid I've no idea where it is."

Kathleen looked over her shoulder, a regal movement of a long white neck.

"It's the room to the right of the front door," she replied, a touch of condescension in her manner. "I don't suppose you'll be coming to that part of the house normally, since you have your own room in the nursery suite."

"No, I don't suppose I shall," murmured Penelope, as she followed the gracefully swaying figure down the three shallow steps, thinking to herself that Kathleen Drummond had none of her brother Hugh's frank friendliness.

Still in the wake of the other woman she approached the dining room and heard the sound of men's voices and laughter coming from within. The door swung wide and Tearlach Gunn came out of the room. He was still dressed in his sailing clothes and his sunburned face glowed under the forward-falling blond-streaked hair.

He held a glass half full of pale gold liquor in one hand, and as Kathleen approached him he smiled and said, "I've suggested that you all stay for supper. Mrs. Guthrie has left enough to feed me and several other people."

"Welcome home, Tearlach," said Kathleen softly, smiling back at him. "I'd love to stay and eat with you."

Over Kathleen's shoulder he glanced at Penelope briefly, impersonally, then looked down again at the smiling face of his cousin.

"To receive a welcome like that when I return to Torvaig makes going away seem worthwhile," he said, with surprising gallantry. "Come in."

He turned and as Kathleen moved forward he slipped a casual arm around her shoulders to guide her onward.

Gazing at their backs Penelope thought with a grin that she had been very subtly put in her place and followed meekly behind.

The dining room was in keeping with the rest of the house that she had seen so far. It was cool and formally furnished with an oval regency table, which was covered with a white lace tablecloth and set with silver candelabra and cutlery.

There the formality ended, because the meal was a help-yourself buffet set out on a long sideboard at which Hugh was already helping himself to slices of roast beef and salad. He glanced up briefly as Kathleen and Tearlach approached the buffet, scowling at them before moving away to sit at the table. Another man was already sitting there. He had brown hair and a thick brown beard, and Penelope could only assume that he was Ian McTaggart.

Taking her cue from the others, who completely ignored her, Penelope helped herself to food. She noted with pleasure that someone had thought to provide a pot of tea and wondered whether it was Hugh or Miss Swan who had given a thought to the new nanny. She realized that she was being allowed to eat in the dining room this evening because it was a convenient way of providing her with a necessary meal, and she was glad that Hugh and his sister and Ian McTaggart were there, for otherwise she would have been forced to eat alone with her employer. And being alone with him was something she wished to avoid.

Her plate full, she went to sit at the end of the table farthest away from him. He was lounging indolently in a beautifully carved Jacobean chair talking to Ian who sat on his left. On the other side Kathleen sat next to her brother, who was opposite Penelope.

Looking at Hugh she had the feeling that he was deliberately avoiding her glance. Perhaps he had been warned not to associate with the new nanny, she thought. He looked rather sulky, like a small boy who had been sharply reprimanded by an adult.

Accustomed as she was, in her position as nanny, to being poised between two worlds, that of the kitchen and that of the drawing room, she did not feel ill at ease as she sat slightly apart from the others. She attacked her food with a good appetite, half listening to the conversation of the others.

It seemed that Ian had been digging on his land that afternoon and had found some articles buried in the soil that, he was convinced, were tools once used by the Viking settlers. He was sure, he said, that the crofts where he lived were built on the site of the original Viking settlement on Torvaig and he wanted Tearlach's permission to continue digging in the hope of discovering more artifacts and possibly the remains of a building.

As he listened, Tearlach regarded the silversmith with a

tolerant smile and then said easily, "If it pleases you you can dig up the whole of your land searching for tools and walls. I can't see that you'll offend anyone as long as you keep within your own boundaries. But you won't get much other work done while you're doing that sort of digging. What else do you hope to find?"

"There may be the remains of a Viking house such as the ones that have been excavated at Borsay in the Orkney Islands and at Jarlshof in the Shetlands," replied Ian in his deep singsong voice.

"And supposing there is, what good will that do any of us?" asked the practical Tearlach.

"It will prove once and for all that the first settlers on Torvaig were Vikings, as legend tells us," put in Hugh, shaking off his sulks and joining in the conversation enthusiastically. "I'll help with the digging, Ian. I once helped with a dig at Stirling. We found some Roman nails."

"Do you share all this preoccupation with the past of Torvaig, Kathleen?" drawled Tearlach. "Perhaps you have visions, like our new nanny, Miss Jones. This afternoon she 'felt,' so she says, that she had sailed across the sea to Torvaig in a Viking ship."

There was no mistaking the jeer in his voice. Penelope's head jerked up in reaction, and she sent an angry glance in his direction. Her cheeks went pink as she realized that both Ian and Kathleen had turned to stare curiously at her.

Tearlach returned her glare coolly, a faintly mocking smile hovering about his mouth, and she knew suddenly and instinctively that the battle between them was joined. He was going to make her life as unpleasant as he could for the next four weeks, using every weapon available to him.

Kathleen laughed, a delicious musical sound.

"How silly of Miss Jones," she remarked. "No, I'm not at all fascinated by the past. I'm strictly a woman of the present, gathering rosebuds while I may."

Tearlach slanted her a narrowed speculative glance while he selected a cheroot.

"And what does that mean?" he murmured.

"It means I'm not going to waste any time delving into the past when the present is all too brief and I have so much living to do," replied Kathleen, and it seemed to Penelope that there was subtle invitation in the way the woman looked at Tearlach. "Don't you know the poem by Robert Herrick in which he advised young virgins to make good use of their time?"

"No. I haven't read much poetry," said Tearlach, with a grin. "I've been too busy living. How does it go?"

"Like this:

'Gather ye rosebuds while ye may,
   Old Time is still a-flying:
And this same flower that smiles today,
   Tomorrow will be dying.' "

quoted Kathleen softly, smiling at him.

"An interesting philosophy, much like my own," said Tearlach, and again his glance lingered assessingly on his cousin's lovely face, which seemed to gleam with a radiance of its own.

Gritting her teeth so as not to show how irritated she was by Kathleen's amusement at her expense, Penelope drank her tea. The warm sweet liquid was as comforting as ever. As she replaced the cup on the saucer her eyes encountered those of Ian McTaggart. He was gazing thoughtfully at her. He looked away quickly, obviously shy.

The conversation continued on more general terms and Penelope closed her ears to it, finished her meal and decided to have another cup of tea. At the sideboard she poured milk into her cup and was about to add sugar when a lean hand appeared and took the sugar bowl from her. She looked up into eyes that were narrowed against a spiral of gray smoke rising from a cheroot. Tearlach raised a hand and removed the cheroot from his mouth to speak to her with smooth politeness.

"You must be tired after your journey, Miss Jones."

"No, not at all, thank you, Mr. Gunn," she replied cheerfully and turned to pick up the teapot. But the same lean hand that had taken the sugar bowl was there again, setting the pot just beyond her reach.

"I believe Miss Swan showed you to your room and that Hugh has taken your luggage up there," he said.

"Yes. The room is very pleasant," she replied, refusing to be disconcerted.

"I'm glad you think so. Davy wakes up in the night crying for his mother, sometimes, and Isa is an early riser, so I advise you to go to bed early. Sleep seems to be an essential part of a nanny's life if she is to keep up and give the right amount of attention to such active youngsters," he added, still smooth. "Good night, Miss Jones."

He was really telling her that she was no longer welcome in the dining room. He had allowed her to take a meal with him and his guests, but that did not entitle her to linger and listen to the conversation.

Penelope felt again the faint stirring of rebellion as her gaze clashed with his. She longed to treat him with the smooth insolence he showed to her. Then she remembered he had said she would not last a month in this job. She must not play into his hands by giving him the chance to dismiss her, so she bowed her head and murmured, "Good night, Mr. Gunn."

Crossing to the chair she had sat in, she collected her handbag and walked to the door. As she left her eyes met those of Kathleen, who had obviously been very interested in the short verbal exchange at the sideboard. Mockery gleamed in the clear golden eyes before they turned away to look at Ian, who was talking.

Infuriated by that mockery, Penelope tilted her chin and said loudly, "Good night, everyone," then, turning on her heel, she marched out of the room.

She had reached the nursery before she had calmed down. As she closed the door of her room and switched on the light she heard the unmistakable sound of a child sobbing. Instantly she forgot her own bruised feelings. The sound was coming from the right, from the room where Davy slept.

Going to the communicating door, she opened it quietly and stepped into the other room. It was full of shadows cast by the night light glowing on the chest of drawers. She could see quite clearly the small bed in which a figure was hunched over the clothes.

She went over and sat on the side of the bed. Speaking his name softly, she touched the little boy. He stopped sobbing and raised his head to look at her. She could see that he was thin and that he had a mop of dark hair and great dark eyes.

"Hello," she said. "I'm your new nanny."

"Go away!" he howled in disappointment. "Don't want you! Want Uncle Tear. Kathy said she would ask him to come and see me and he hasn't come. Go away! Don't want new nanny!"

Sobs shook him afresh, as he buried his head in the

pillow, and for the next half hour Penelope's training and ingenuity were put to the test as she tried every method she could think of to calm him. But nothing worked and eventually she rose quietly to her feet and left the room.

She intended to undress and go to bed, thinking that the child's crying would subside and he would fall asleep through sheer exhaustion. Although it went against the grain to allow that to happen, it was also quite obvious that there was nothing a stranger like herself could do to make up for the neglect of the child by his uncle. But standing there listening to the sobs, she realized she could not rest either, knowing that a child was disturbed. She had to take action, and the only action left was to go and find Tearlach Gunn and tell him his nephew wanted to see him.

Leaving her room to go downstairs, she wondered if Kathleen Drummond had kept her promise and had told Tearlach that he was needed by Davy. Or had the lovely Highlander conveniently forgotten to tell him because she had not wanted to share the attention he gave to her with a small motherless boy?

There was certainly something special going on between the forceful, arrogant owner of Torvaig and his beautiful cousin, thought Penelope, and, if ever she had seen two of a kind together, she had seen them tonight, both of them confident in their ability to attract the opposite sex, both intent on grasping any pleasure the present offered, two believers in the cult of "now."

The stairs were dark and the house was quiet. As she reached the hall she realized she had no idea where to look for her employer. For all she knew he could have gone out with his supper guests to walk in the perfect moonlit night.

Temporarily nonplussed, she stood quietly in the middle of the hall, listening. No sound came from the dining room although the light still blazed there. On the other side of the hall a door stood partially open revealing the moon-dappled darkness of another room.

"In here, Miss Jones."

The sound of Tearlach's voice from behind her made her jump. Swinging around, she saw another door wide open. She advanced toward it and on entering saw him lounging in a big leather chair behind a wide desk. His feet were on the desk and he was holding a sheaf of papers in his hand.

"I gather you're looking for me," he said coolly.

"Yes. Davy keeps crying and won't go to sleep."

His thick dark eyebrows rose a fraction.

"Defeated already, Miss Jones?" he jeered.

"No," she snapped. "Miss Drummond promised him that she would tell you he wanted to see you before he went to sleep, and nothing else will satisfy him. He was sobbing when I went to my room, and although I've tried every way I can think of to comfort him, he still insists on seeing you."

"And you, judging by the disgust in your voice and the expression on your face, are thinking I'm a monster for not having been to see him," he remarked dryly. He swung his feet down from the desk, threw the papers down, stood up and came toward her. "Kathleen didn't tell me," he said.

"Probably she had other and more interesting things to tell you," replied Penelope stiffly. "Little children are often forgotten when they're out of sight and there are more important people around. Will you come now and see Davy?"

"Yes, I will. But first I'd like to warn you, Miss Jones,

that catty remarks on your part about my guests are not welcome," he said freezingly. "You will keep your opinion of them to yourself in future."

Remembering rather belatedly that she must not give him any chance to sack her, she once more bowed her head with reluctant meekness, her long dark eyelashes fanning out on her cheeks as they covered her eyes.

"Yes, Mr. Gunn," she muttered.

"Meekness suits you, Miss Jones," he said softly. "Perhaps if you remember that you will not be so tempted to twist the lion's tail."

He turned and walked out of the room. Slightly disconcerted by his last remark, Penelope followed, thinking that with his shaggy golden-brown hair, deceptively sleepy eyes and big bulky shoulders he reminded her of a lion.

He took the narrow stairs two at a time and by the time she arrived, slightly out of breath, he was sitting on Davy's bed talking to him. He glanced at her when she entered the room and, pausing in what he was saying, jerked his head in the direction of her room. Taking that as a hint that he did not want an audience while he talked to the boy, she retreated.

In her room she stood by the window looking out at the moonlit countryside, wondering what she should do next. Should she go to bed or should she stay and wait for her employer to tell her he had finished talking to his nephew? She was still rather surprised that he had come so willingly to talk to the little boy. Going by Miss Swan's opinion of him, she had expected to have a hard time persuading him to leave his papers to give some time to the child. He was really rather a disconcerting person, and he had no hesitation in speaking his mind, as his reprimand concerning her remark about Kathleen had shown. Of course, she should never have made such a remark in the first place. In doing so she had acted completely out of character. She knew full well that a person in her position had no right to make remarks about her employer's guests.

But then she had acted peculiarly all day, almost as if she *were* another person. The reincarnation of the first Magnus Gunn's slave wife, perhaps?

Irritated by her wayward thoughts, she tiptoed to the communicating door and opened it. The room beyond was quiet except for the sound of a child's breathing, occasionally interrupted by sobs. There was no one sitting on the bed. Davy was asleep and Tearlach had gone back to his study.

With a sigh Penelope turned back to her own room leaving the door slightly ajar. She went over to the other communicating door that she assumed, led to Isa's room. In there a night light also glowed, revealing the little girl comfortably asleep in her crib, her plump cheeks rosy and her gold-streaked brown hair fanned out on the pillow.

Satisfied that her new charges were settled for the night, Penelope unpacked a few articles of clothing for the next day and prepared for bed. Once again she was aware of the silence, not only in the house, but also outside. Here, on Torvaig there was no noisy traffic to pollute the fresh air that wafted in through the open window.

Contentedly she snuggled down in the comfortable bed. It was not until she was drifting off to sleep that she remembered that, apart from the two children, there were only herself and Tearlach Gunn in the house that night.

The next day, her first in Torvaig House, was extremely tiring and exacting, partly because, being conscientious about her work, she made it so and partly because of the demands made upon her by the two children.

As Tearlach had pointed out, the two-year-old Isa was an early riser. She was on the go in her room from six o'clock onward, chattering to herself as she sat in her crib. Listening to the little girl's voice, Penelope decided that she might as well get up and make her acquaintance before Davy awoke. If he had behavior problems it was possible he would require a great deal of attention and then the little girl would suffer. Time must be set aside during the day for Isa to receive attention on her own.

Fortunately Isa had a happy disposition and accepted her new nanny without question, showing off her teddy bear and the other soft toys she had taken to bed with her. She showed a certain amount of feminine independence by insisting on dressing herself in a T-shirt and jeans, socks and shoes, but she allowed Penelope to brush her long, sun-bleached brown hair and tie it up with a red ribbon.

In the small kitchen Penelope found everything she required to cook simple meals, including well-stocked cupboards and a small refrigerator. Under the window was a table with four chairs where meals could be taken.

Isa chattered all the time, repeating herself many times in the manner of a two-year-old, while Penelope prepared her cereal, to be followed by a soft-boiled egg; then Penelope drank tea and ate toast for her own breakfast.

They were still eating when Davy burst into the room. He was still wearing his pajamas. He snatched Isa's orange juice from her and poured it all over the table and then threw the plastic mug across the room, in a fine display of jealousy. His black eyes glowing, he began to stamp around the room, screaming at the top of his voice.

Thrown a little off balance by this startling behavior,

Penelope stared at him for a moment, wondering if he were deranged. Then she caught his sidelong glance in her direction and knew it was a deliberate attempt on his part to upset her as, presumably, he had been able to upset Miss Swan.

Hiding a grin with a severe frown, she looked at him coldly and told him sharply to stop screaming and to go to his room and dress. He took not the slightest notice, so she grabbed him the next time he stamped past her, picked him up, smacked his bottom lightly, carried him to his room and, setting him down just inside the door, left him there with a final sharp instruction to get dressed or he wouldn't have any breakfast.

Glaring at her with rather surprised black eyes, he retaliated by banging the door closed. Ignoring his action, Penelope began to mop up the mess he had made. She was still wiping juice from the table, while Isa reiterated over and over again, "Davy naughty boy, Davy naughty boy," when there was a knock at the door. It opened and a small plump woman whose black hair was snatched up into a bun on top of her head and who was wearing an apron over her flowered print dress, came into the room and introduced herself as Bessie Guthrie, the housekeeper.

"Ach, you are young, an' no mistake. I can see now what himself is getting at," she said, going straight to the reason for her visit. Behind her glasses her brown eyes twinkled as she sized up the young woman who was carefully wiping the table. "From London, too, I've been told. Then you should be able to take care of yourself, well enough."

"Have done most of my life," replied Penelope with a grin.

"Aye, I can see there's no nonsense about you and that you're here to do a job—which is more than I could be saying for the last nanny we had. We weren't good enough for her and Mr. Gunn hadn't been to the right schools and didn't have the sort of manners she was used to," said Mrs. Guthrie, mimicking Miss Swan's soft complaining voice. Then peering over her glasses at Penelope she added in her own voice, "Spread tales about him, she did, and there are some folks on this island who believed her, just because yon man is a wee bit different from the usual run of lairds Torvaig has had!"

"Oh. How is he different?" asked Penelope.

"Well, for one thing he doesn't think of the place just as his country estate, a place to bring his friends to hunt and fish, as the others did. He's made it his home. Then he holds to the principle that charity with no strings attached leads to apathy, so he only offers aid to those who are willing to help themselves with the result the farms are farmed properly and the crofts are being worked. The owners know that if they produce they'll receive aid in the way of new equipment and buildings," asserted the plump woman.

"Since you have such a high opinion of Mr. Gunn, I suppose you are willing to agree to his request that you should come and live in while I'm here, to prevent any further damage to his reputation," said Penelope, untying Isa's bib and lifting her down from her chair.

"Ach, well now, it isn't as easy as all that. You see Alec and I have our own wee cottage on the estate which we like well enough, and it's really up to him to decide. A man likes his own fireside, especially when he's getting older, and he may not take kindly to moving into the two rooms downstairs that Mr. Gunn says we could have," explained Mrs. Guthrie.

Presuming that Alec was Mrs. Guthrie's husband, Penelope asked if he worked on the estate.

"Aye, he's the head gardener. Gardening is his love and

his work and always has been," replied the housekeeper. "We were over on the mainland on the Falkland estate, but when Jimmy, my eldest son, came here to manage the home farm and learned that Mr. Gunn wanted someone to rescue the garden of the house from the wilderness it had become, Alec came right over and asked for the job. He was born here on the island, you see, and lived here until he was called up into the army during the last war. He didn't come back because there was nothing to come back to, but all the years I've known him he's wanted to come back."

"I wonder if he ever knew anyone called Sandison on Torvaig?" asked Penelope.

"You can ask him yourself, lass, when he comes in for his elevenses. Come into the kitchen and have something yourself. Bring the bairns with you. They're as much at home there now as they are anywhere because Miss Hoity-Toity Swan often used to leave them with me. I'd like Alec to meet you, anyway, because then he'll understand the need for us to move into the house to stop the tongues from wagging, and he might be more agreeable to the idea."

Pleased and relieved to find Mrs. Guthrie was a friendly sensible woman, Penelope promised she would go down later to have a cup of tea with the head gardener. When the housekeeper left Penelope went to Davy's room. He was lying on his bed sobbing again.

"Go away!" he shouted at her. "Don't want you. Want Uncle Tear."

"Well, you can't have him, so you'll have to put up with me," she replied cheerfully.

He was really a very beautiful child, she thought, with his black waving hair, golden skin and elegantly chiseled features, but he required firm handling and she guessed he got it from his uncle and responded to it, so she intended to use the same methods. It was just possible that Miss Swan had found him exhausting and demanding because she allowed her compassion for him to get out of hand and had consequently been too soft with him. Davy, she decided, would use his very obvious masculine charm to get his own way and then, when he saw that failing, would resort to tempers and tantrums.

It was a fight to make him sit down and eat his breakfast, but it was the first fight and Penelope was determined to win it. After that he seemed more disposed to do as she asked and occasionally gave her the benefit of his brilliant smile. Like most four-year-olds, he wanted to do much more than he was capable of and possessed a great deal of energy that needed direction.

At 11 o'clock Penelope found she was quite glad to take advantage of Mrs. Guthrie's suggestion and go down to the kitchen for a cup of tea.

As she entered the big room a short stocky man in his middle fifties stood up politely and held out a square, rough-skinned, work-gnarled hand to her.

"I'm thinking you're the lassie from London," he said, in a lilting Hebridean drawl. "I'm Alec Guthrie."

His shy smile seemed to split his long face in two and his Celtic blue eyes twinkled under the dark bushy eyebrows, which threatened to hide them from view.

"Sit down, Miss Jones," said Mrs. Guthrie, "and tell me how you like your tea. Here, put the wee lassie on this stool. She'll be liking a glass of milk and a biscuit, I shouldn't wonder, and the same for Davy. Ach, there he goes to his favorite place."

As Alec Guthrie sat down again Davy went straight to him and climbed up onto his knees, happily sure of his welcome. He placed his two small hands around Alec's big mug of tea and, with some help, lifted it to his mouth and took a sip of tea.

"Now you can be asking your question about the Sandison family," prompted Mrs. Guthrie, as she passed a cup of tea to Penelope. "Did you say they lived on Torvaig at one time?"

"Yes, my grandmother was a Sandison and she was born here, but her father decided to leave the island when she was in her teens and she went with him."

"He would be Hector Sandison," said Alec. "The Sandisons held crofts over Cladach way for many generations. Your grandmother's father was a lively, rebellious sort of man, but intelligent too. He led several deputations of crofters to the old laird, Magnus, to try and persuade him to make improvements to the island, by helping the crofters to buy modern farm machinery and by reallocating some of the land. But Magnus wouldn't listen. He preferred to think of the whole of Torvaig as his country estate and he even encouraged islanders to leave, so that he could have the place to himself and his hunting and fishing friends. In disgust Hector Sandison left and went to the south of England to work. So your grandmother was Heather Sandison? She was a friend of my mother's. Have you told Mr. Gunn?"

"Yes, but he didn't believe me. I'm afraid he's very suspicious of me because I'm not his idea of a nanny."

Alec Guthrie chuckled, a warm infectious sound.

"I can't say you're my idea of a nanny either. I can see why he wants Bessie and me to live in the house here. When it gets round the island that there's a pretty young woman living at the big house there'll be a great blethering." He turned and looked at his wife. "When did you say he wanted to know our decision?"

"By this afternoon. Ach, having the care of these

bairns put upon him has put him in a difficult position, there's no doubt of that," sighed Mrs. Guthrie. "Before, he didn't need a housekeeper who lived in and that suited him and us fine. And it was all right when Miss Swan was here because with her being older, no one cast aspersions on either her or him."

"I'm thinking that Miss Swan made his position difficult," mused Alec, staring down into his mug. "If she hadn't carried tales about that young woman who was staying in the house earlier this summer, he wouldn't be worrying about what might be said about Miss Jones here."

"Aye, but it's himself he's protecting too," said Mrs. Guthrie.

"Then what do you think we should do?" asked her husband.

"You know how I feel about Tearlach Gunn. I'd do anything to help him because of what he's done for the people of Torvaig."

"I thought that would be the way of it," said Alec with a grin and a wink in Penelope's direction. "Then you'd better be telling him we'll do as he asks and we'll start moving in today. I daresay young Wilson who has just come to work on the home farm will be glad to move into our cottage while he's waiting for his own to be built. He and his wife are lodging with the Browns in the village, but she's expecting a bairn and would be glad to be on her own."

The problem of providing her—or was it her employer?—with a chaperone solved, Penelope spent the rest of the morning going for a walk with the children. It was not a very long walk, only down to the jetty and back. Then they had lunch in the kitchenette and Isa was put down for her afternoon's rest. For the next hour Penelope spent the time getting to know Davy better. She discovered that he knew his alphabet and some numbers and that he had several games using letters and numbers, which he could play with her. He also enjoyed doing simple jigsaw puzzles, which he had quite a collection of.

When Isa awoke they went for another walk. This time they walked a little farther along the shore and tossed pebbles into the calm water of the bay. As she returned slowly to the house holding the hands of both children, Penelope realized she was going to be severly restricted as to movement on the island because neither of the children could walk very far. The chances of her exploring the place were limited while she had to stay with them. Some time in the near future, when she felt more secure, she would have to ask her employer about free time. He could not expect her to stay with the children all day every day. Even nannies were entitled to a few hours off to attend to their own needs.

A tug at her right hand made her look down. Davy was doing his best to escape from her grasp.

"Uncle Tear, Uncle Tear!" he shrieked in his piercingly shrill voice. "Wait for me!"

Looking toward the house she saw a sleek black car parked on the driveway. Tearlach Gunn was just about to open a door and get into it. He turned when he heard his name being called.

"Hello, Davy," he said, and leaving the car, came toward them. He was dressed in a dark brown tweed sports jacket and fawn-colored trousers. A green paisley patterned neckerchief was knotted around his neck inside the open collar of his fawn-colored shirt. The sunburn of the day before had toned down to a uniform bronze color, emphasizing the clear-cut angles of his face and contrasting attractively with his blond-streaked hair and the whiteness of his teeth when he smiled at Davy and Isa. The full force of his aggressive masculinity hit Penelope hard, putting her immediately on the defensive.

"Look what I've found, Uncle Tear," said Davy, encouraged by the smile and holding up a shell he had found.

"Flowers, pink flowers, pretty flowers," sang Isa, holding up a posy of sea pinks she had gathered. "Uncle have pink flowers."

"Thank you, Isa," he said gravely, taking the proffered posy, and then, to Penelope's surprise, he bent and picked the little girl up in his arms. Holding her high against his shoulder, he said. "How do you like your new nanny?"

"Nice nanny, pretty nanny," said Isa magnanimously, leaning forward to pat Penelope's smooth shining hair with a chubby hand.

"How about you, Davy?" asked Tearlach. "Miss Jones suit you as a nanny?"

"She's all right," conceded Davy. "I want to go for a ride in your car. Please, Uncle Tear."

An impatient frown twitched Tearlach's eyebrows together and he glanced at his watch. Sensing his reluctance to give in to the little boy's request, Penelope supposed this was a time when she should step in and remove the children from his sight. But that faint flutter of rebellion she always felt when in the presence of this self-confident man kept her quiet and stationary. Let him get out of his predicament himself, she thought.

"Not just now, Davy," said Tearlach smoothly, allowing Isa to slide to the ground. Immediately both children burst into tears.

"It's the least you could do for them," Penelope found herself hissing at him.

"And give you a much-needed rest from them, I

suppose," he retorted. "Oh, no. I may have helped to settle Davy for you last night, but don't count on me to relieve you from your work by taking him for drives around the island."

"Unlike you, I'm not thinking of myself all the time," she retaliated, casting caution aside. "I'm thinking of him. You must know how he adores you. You are his mother's brother and so you represent security to him in her place. Is it any wonder he wants to be with you more than with me? He hardly knows me yet. Don't you realize you're in a position to make or break that boy's faith in others?"

That unpleasant expression was back in his eyes and she stepped back, afraid that he might do what his eyes threatened—wring her neck. But the wild look faded and he laughed good-humoredly. Hands on his hips, he looked down at her almost tolerantly, while he ordered Davy and Isa to be quiet.

"In exchanging Miss Swan for you I seem to have exchanged a twitterer for a termagant," he scoffed. "Where did you learn to brawl with your employer, Penelope Jones? It isn't done, you know, if you want to keep your job. Don't forget, you're walking a tightrope here at Torvaig House. One false move and you fall, at the end of four weeks."

"That doesn't mean I'm going to sit by and watch you destroy a child's faith in you," she answered. "You have the care of these children and it's up to you to take the place of their father. Giving them toys and every comfort isn't enough. You have to give something of yourself and your time."

The humor fled from his face, leaving it hard and cold. She had the impression she had touched a sensitive spot.

"Quite finished?" he asked harshly. Taking herself in

hand, she nodded dumbly. "Then I shall do as Davy asks. I'll take him and Isa for a drive. But don't think you're going to have some free time. You can sit in the back of the car with Isa and keep an eye on her. We'll go to the ferry, and that way it's just possible I'll be able to kill two birds with one stone, without putting myself to too much inconvenience. Come on, Davy lad, in you get."

The little boy needed no second bidding and scrambled into the front seat beside the driver's when Tearlach opened the door for him.

Slightly dubious about her employer's sudden change of mind, Penelope helped Isa climb into the back seat of the car and sat down beside her, keeping behind Tearlach's broad shoulders so that he could not see her without having to turn right around.

Yet in spite of her turbulent state of mind she could not help being excited at this first opportunity to see more of the island.

From the front of the house they followed a winding road through the mixed woodland that lay to the east of the house. Then leaving the shadow of the trees they joined another wider road that curved over the moorland around the head of the small loch that Penelope could see from her bedroom window.

Striking across the wild moorland country, where the feathery fronds of emerald bracken alternated with a purplish haze created by heather just coming into bloom, the road twisted in a series of hairpin bends between drystone walls, rising gradually to the top of the rocky ridge of hills forming the spine of the island.

Once over that ridge it began to descend again to flatter land where lush meadows were dotted with thoroughbred dairy cattle whose golden coats glistened in the sunlight. A white-gabled farmhouse appeared and a man driving a red tractor along the road raised his hand in greeting as they passed. Tearlach responded with a wave of his hand and, after a slight hesitation, Davy gravely imitated him with a slow, unconsciously regal salute—just like a young prince, thought Penelope with a grin.

The road wound eastward toward the coast, past fields where barley and oats waved under the summer wind, past the ruins of old cottages overgrown with tall grasses among which red poppies blazed.

Her annoyance with Tearlach forgotten, her interest in the island revived by all she could see, Penelope asked a question.

"How big is Torvaig?"

"I thought you'd know. Didn't your grandmother tell you?" was the mocking reply, making her grit her teeth and clench her hands.

"Grandmother? What's that?" asked Davy, before she could think of a retort.

"Who, not what," corrected Tearlach lazily. "Your nanny has a grandmother, so she says. Why not ask her?"

Davy leaned over the back of his seat to gaze at Penelope with intelligent dark eyes.

"What's grandmother?" he demanded.

Swallowing the acid remark she had intended to fling at her employer, she said instead, "The mother of your mother or father. You usually have two." Satisfied with her answer, Davy slid back into his seat.

"Do I have a grandmother?" he asked Tearlach.

"Yes, you have one."

"Where is she?"

"In Spain. She's your daddy's mother."

"I want to see her."

"Perhaps one day you will."

"I want to see her now," stated Davy with his usual determination to get his own way.

"Can't be done, Davy," replied Tearlach cheerfully. "Look over there. You can see the ferry coming across from the mainland."

He was really very good with the boy, thought Penelope, as she also looked and saw sunlight glinting on the dimpling blue water of a narrow strait. Beyond the water, rolling moorland, purple and black, sloped upward to cliffs of rock with pointed peaks, silvery gray and rose, cleft by deep, shadowed gullies.

Soon they were passing down a village street, past a row of semidetached houses of modern design, past the low, squat original cottages. Flowers blazed in neatly kept gardens. Some children ran by, laughing and shouting. They waved to the black car and receive the usual careless wave from Tearlach and the more sedate salute from Davy.

Then they were turning down a rough road toward the ferry terminus. No others cars were waiting, but there was one person standing alone, a tall woman with glowing bronze colored hair. She was wearing a simple green dress and around her shoulders was draped a wide plaid of scarlet and green tartan.

There was only one woman she knew who could wear a plaid like that in this day and age, thought Penelope, as she watched Kathleen Drummond turn at the sound of the car and wave. There was no doubt that she was expecting Tearlach, and she must be the reason why he had been reluctant to take his nephew for a drive.

CHAPTER THREE

Tearlach did not take the car right down to where the ferry docked, but parked off the road to the slipway and sat watching the ferry approach. He did not seem to have seen Kathleen or, if he had, he did not acknowledge her wave; when she saw that he had company in the car, Kathleen turned away and also watched the ferry.

"I'd no idea the island was so near to the mainland," exclaimed Penelope.

Tearlach turned in his seat and aimed a sardonic glance over his shoulder.

"Something else your grandmother didn't tell you?" he mocked. "Distances are deceptive. The strait is five miles wide, wide enough to have made transporting goods and people a problem in the past. The road through the mountains on the other side is in poor shape and takes only single line traffic. It was on that road that the accident took place that killed Davy's father and my sister."

Penelope felt she should show some sympathy, so she said softly, "It must have been very sad for you when she died after lingering so long."

A strangely dour expression flitted across his face making him look older.

"If she'd lived she would have been no more than a vegetable," he murmured, then added more crisply, "Don't waste too much sympathy on me, Miss Jones. I hardly knew my sister. She wasn't much older than Davy is now when I left home. My biggest regret concerning her untimely death is that it has left me in charge of two young children."

While Penelope was recovering from the effect of this abrupt, hard speech, he opened the door and stepped out of the car. Davy scrambled after him. As soon as she saw Davy go, Isa wanted to get out too, and soon they were all standing beside the car watching the ferry dock.

A small green car, very new and very shiny, trundled off the ferry. It was driven by a young man who brought it to a stop just ahead of the black car, opened the door and stepped out.

"Everything all right, Donald?" asked Tearlach, who began to walk around the Mini, examining it carefully.

"Fine, just fine. I had no trouble at all," replied the young man.

"Good. Give me the keys."

Donald handed over the keys and glanced curiously at Penelope as Tearlach walked back to her and said brusquely, "Hold out your hand, Miss Jones."

Releasing Isa's hand, she held out her right hand obediently, and he dropped the car keys into it.

"It's for your use," he said. "Like the television, it was supposed to be here before you arrived, but there was some difficulty about delivery. It's important to me that you and the children should be as independent as possible. Now Davy can have as many rides as he likes without having to ask me and you won't feel so restricted."

She stared in amazement at the keys in her hand. He said another few words to the interested Donald, called goodbye to the children, swung behind the wheel of the black car and let it drift slowly down to the ferry. He stopped beside Kathleen, who put her case on the back seat and sat down beside Tearlach, before the black car moved forward onto the ferry.

Still startled by her employer's latest move, Penelope put the excited children into the back seat of the little two-door car and then offered a lift to the young man who have driven it up from the factory. He turned out to be Donald Lang, a crofter who was also a motor mechanic and who looked after the agricultural machinery used on the farms. He accepted a lift as far as Torvaig House, where he said he had left his own van. On the way he told her that he and his wife Molly had their croft on the shores of Cladach Bay, where Hugh Drummond also lived, and invited her to call in any time she was over that way.

In the days that followed Penelope found the green Mini car a great help and wished that she had been able to show her appreciation to her employer for his thoughtfulness in providing it for her use. That was not possible, however, because, as Mrs. Guthrie informed her, having learned that the Guthries had agreed to live in the big house, Tearlach had gone to the mainland on business and would not be back until the following week, and then he would be bringing guests with him.

Penelope soon worked out a routine for herself and the children. She kept to it closely, knowing that the consistency of behavior on her part would develop a sense of security in them. She took them for drives every day to a different part of the island, and discovered that it was much bigger than she had realized. Its scenery varied considerably. In the north end there was a high flat-topped mountain, Ben Luran, where it was said that witches used to dance on May Day eve and on Hallowe'en. The whole of the northern area possessed a wild romantic beauty, having many small lochs and steep-sided glens through which burns rushed down to the sea. It was a great contrast to the serene farm fields of the east and the gentle slopes of the barren green hills of the west and the south.

It was not until the day before Tearlach was due to return to Torvaig that Penelope went to Cladach Bay. It was a dull day, which was threatened by rain from blowsy gray clouds chasing one another across the perpetually moving pewter-colored sea.

A perfect sickle of pale yellow sand edged the gray water. Several small cottages were scattered on the land behind the shore and behind them, set on the bare hillside, was a small graveyard surrounded by a drystone wall.

Each cottage was separated from the next by fields where the usual crops of barley, oats and rye were growing. As Penelope drove slowly down the road she noticed a young woman taking in washing from a line strung between a cottage wall and a barn. She stopped the car, helped the children out and crossed the road to speak to the woman. As she had hoped, the woman was Molly Lang. She was about the same age as herself, had orange-red hair, wide sea-green eyes and a friendly grin.

When she introduced herself, Molly nodded and said, "Aye, Donald told me all about ye. Would ye like to be coming in for a cuppa?" She spoke in a thick Scottish brogue that did not have its origin in the Highlands. "Bring the wains in, too. I've a wee lass myself, but she's asleep just now. Do ye mind if I call ye Penny? I find Penelope a bit of a mouthful."

Drinking tea in the homey, rumpled living room of the four-room cottage, while Isa and Davy played with wee Sheila's toys, Penelope learned that Molly and her husband had lived 18 months on the croft and liked it fine.

"We were both working in Glasgow, but we were tired of the city. Then Donald, whose people came from Torvaig, saw the croft that had once belonged to his family being advertised. He wrote after it, had an interview with Mr. Gunn, who was wanting to attract people back to the island, and we came here to live. I look after the animals and help in the fields at harvest time and in the spring, and Don has plenty of mechanical work to do because he's the only mechanic living on the island just now. Ach, there's no life like it and wee Sheila is growing up healthy and bonny. Do ye think ye're going to like working at the big house?"

"I'm on probation for a month. You see, Mr. Gunn wanted someone older and wasn't pleased when he saw me," replied Penelope.

"Aye, I can imagine ye were a bit of a surprise to him," said Molly with a grin.

"Anyway, he says that if I'm not satisfactory I'll have to go at the end of four weeks."

"Ach, he says that to everyone. It's his way to keep people on the hop, so that they'll do their best. He said the same to us. Gave us 12 months to show willing. He said the same to his own cousin Hugh. If at the end of 12 months Hugh hasn't worked his croft properly and hasn't made any income from his fishing and his painting, he'll have to go too."

"Mr. Gunn is a hard man."

"So he is, but he's fair too. I'd rather have him than one of those soft-spoken types who say one thing and do another. Ye know where ye are with him," said Molly, pouring more tea. "Have ye met Hugh?"

"Yes, I have, and his sister," replied Penelope. "I was thinking I'd call in to see them while I'm over this way. Which croft is his?"

"He lives at the other side of the bay where the road ends. He's a blithe laddie, and we've had some great evenings with him. Ye should hear him sing and play the guitar. But yon Kathleen is a different matter. I suppose it takes all sorts to make a world, but between you and me, she fancies herself a wee bit above the rest of us. She has her eye on Mr. Gunn, ye ken."

"I had noticed. Does he have his eye on her?"

"I dinna ken, but I'm thinking he'd be a hard nut for any woman to crack."

Later Penelope drove around the bay to the other side and called at Hugh's cottage. There was no answer to her knock. Glancing about her, she noticed a narrow road winding up the hillside to the graveyard and remembered what Hugh had said about the possibility that members of the Sandison family might have been buried there, so she decided to leave the car by Hugh's cottage and walk up the lane.

On the way she passed another house. Its walls, which had been newly painted white, gleamed in the pale sunlight that had just broken through the clouds. In the garden she could see heaps of earth beside a shallow trench and she realized that it must be Ian McTaggart's house. Driven by a sudden impulse, she went up to the plain black front door and knocked.

Ian McTaggart's clear gray eyes widened with surprise when he opened the door and saw Penelope and the children standing there.

"We came to visit Hugh, but he isn't in," she explained. "He told me that his sister is in partnership with you, so I thought she might be working here and would tell us where Hugh is."

"Hugh is away to sea collecting his lobster pots," replied Ian in his slow singsong voice. "Kathleen is away also, with Tearlach to Edinburgh. She's been gone this past week."

And I had thought he had merely been giving her a lift

the day I saw her get into his car at the ferry, thought Penelope.

Aloud she said, "Oh," feeling slightly nonplussed, not wanting to leave, yet not sure how to stay. Ian seemed to sense her hesitancy, for he smiled and explained a little further.

"Kathleen and I are looking for new markets for our jewelry, and Tearlach, with his usual generosity, said he'd introduce us to people he knows who might be interested. Kathleen is much better at public relations than I am, so she went with him to meet them. Now that you're here, perhaps you'd like to come and see some of our work. You're Miss Jones, aren't you?"

"Yes. I'd like very much to see how you make your jewelry. I've often admired Scottish jewelry and I've a cairngorm brooch that used to be my grandmother's."

In the house they were greeted excitedly by a lovely red setter called Duff. The interior was quite different from Molly's homey place and Penelope though she could see the imprint of Kathleen's sense of design. In the living room, which was two rooms made into one, beautiful antique oak furniture was shown off to good effect against pale blue walls. Hand-woven curtains hung at the windows. Above the fireplace in the long room, simple wooden shelves were decorated with antique pewter jugs and hand-thrown pieces of pottery.

Ian led them from the main part of the house into a wing he had added to the original building. When she entered this big barnlike room it seemed to Penelope that she had walked into the workshop of a small light engineering firm—several work benches and numerous tools sat about. Ian was soon showing her examples of his fine workmanship, pendants, brooches and rings made not only from silver but also from gold and pewter.

"Most of my designs come from plant forms or natural

objects I find washed up on the shores," he said in answer
to a question. "Don't be surprised if you'see me roaming
along the coast of the island looking for driftwood,
seaweed or bits of cork. I also look at cross-sections of
plants and leaf-cells through a microscope and try to
reproduce the shapes in silver and their colors in enamel
work, which I enjoy doing too."

He showed her some of the enamel pieces, explaining
the various techniques he used. Limoges was the simplest,
but least durable. In cloisonné the silver was built up into
retaining walls to keep the colors of the enamel separate,
whereas the pliqué à jour could be compared to stained
glass, with the light showing through the enamel.

"I like to think I've inherited my talent directly from
my Pictish forebears. They really knew how to deal with
metal," said Ian with his pleasant, diffident smile. "There
were many living here, who originally came from Ireland
and were expert at this sort of thing, but then so were the
Vikings, and much of the old jewelry, which has been
found buried in the ground is Pictish in inspiration but
executed by Viking craftsmen, pointing to the fusion of
two cultures. Kathleen scoffs at me for being so interested
in the past, but I can't help myself."

"Neither can I," confided Penelope.

"Then perhaps you wouldn't mind telling me about
that strange experience you had on your way here. Were
you able to see the other people who were on the ship with
you? Could you describe any of them?"

"I'm not sure. When I told Hugh and Mr. Gunn about
it Mr. Gunn made fun of me and asked me if Hugh had
been in my . . . I don't know what to call it?"

"Why not call it a dream? It was obviously your
subconscious trying to tell you something," suggested Ian
gently. "What was your answer to his question?"

"I tried to think back to it, as you do try to remember

dreams, and I could only remember one of the men. He was like Mr. Gunn. So I decided that was because I'd been watching him just before I had the dream."

"It could mean, you know, that when you came to Torvaig in a previous life, you were with him. Have you ever been *here* before?" asked Ian seriously.

She stared at him in bewilderment. His bearded face was familiar, but she could not be sure whether it was because she had seen him that afternoon or because she had sat like this with him another lifetime.

But then, she remembered, he had worn the long habit of a monk and had sandals on his feet. She had seen him through the window of a small cell into which the sunlight had slanted, lending a glow to the pinkish stone it had been built of.

Penelope blinked rapidly. How could she remember such an incident when as far as she knew it had never happened to her?

"I haven't been to Torvaig, but my grandmother was born here," she said quickly.

"Maybe that is the explanation," said Ian. "Was her family here a long time?"

"I don't know. Mr. Guthrie says that the Sandison family held crofts for generations in Cladach, and Hugh has suggested that I should look in the old graveyard here for a headstone that would show where the family grave is."

"Let's go there now," said Ian. "Your young charges are getting a little restless and they might enjoy a walk with Duff, my dog."

The setter shook its plumed tail with joy in anticipation of the walk with young companions, and they all set off up the lane as the pale sun slide from under a cloud again and bathed the hillside with yellow light.

The graveyard followed the slope of the land and was overgrown with tall grasses and bracken. A clump of rowan trees crowded in one corner beside the gate, planted there to keep the witches away. On the other side was a small broken-down chapel whose walls were covered in wild roses. As the two of them peered in at the narrow window, Penelope recognized, with a shock the cell she had just seen in her "dream."

She glanced quickly at Ian to see if he had recognized it too, and she noticed for the first time the fine bones of nose and jaw, the creamy pallor of the skin, the dreaminess of his gray eyes. Truly it was the face of an ascetic.

He became aware of her stare and turned to look at her.

"Well? Do you recognize the place?" he said.

"Yes. Do you?"

"I've visited it before, but not until now have I felt so strongly that I might have known it in another lifetime. I feel today that once, a long time ago, I lived here in Achmore."

"Did you say Achmore?" asked Penelope excitedly.

"I did. This group of crofts, I've discovered recently, once had the name Achmore to distinguish it from the group nearer the shore, known as Cladach, which is the Gaelic name for shore."

"Then that proves it," said Penelope with a smile of satisfaction. "My grandmother wasn't romancing. She did come from Torvaig and she lived in a place called Achmore. I can hardly wait to tell Mr. Gunn."

At that point Isa, who had wandered off, fell among some brambles and rose briars. She let out a shrill shriek and had to be rescued by Ian.

"It will take time to clear this place," he said when he returned to Penelope's side. "It's impossible to search for a headstone while everything is overgrown. Shall we come back another day?"

Penelope agreed and they began to walk down the lane.

"Why is it necessary to prove to Tearlach that your grandmother wasn't romancing?" asked Ian.

"He refused to believe anything I told him about her," she said, with more vehemence than she realized, and Ian gave her an amused sidelong glance, noting the pink flush on her cheeks and the sparkle in her misty blue eyes.

"And he infuriated you," he commented. "He has a knack for doing that. I get the impression that you don't like him very much."

"Let's say I have difficulty in understanding him," said Penelope carefully. After all, she did not know Ian very well and he might relay anything she said about her employer to Kathleen, who might relay it in her turn to Tearlach.

"Do nannies take a course in diplomacy these days?" asked Ian teasingly. "You can be frank with me, Penelope. I won't betray you to anyone."

Flushing slightly at this gently phrased rebuke, she tried to put her feelings regarding her employer into words.

"I know he has done a great deal for Torvaig and the people. Davy and Isa lack nothing in the way of material goods, but I can't help feeling he's cold and hard, almost heartless. He doesn't seem to love them."

"Or anyone else, for that matter, or so it seems," added Ian soberly, nodding his head. "I know what you mean. There's an inner wall he has built up over the years to prevent anyone from knowing his real feelings. Behind that wall none of us are allowed to penetrate. Yet on the surface he's friendly, outgoing. I have my own theory about that inner wall."

"What is that?"

"It's based on what Kathleen has told me about Tearlach. His mother died when he was only eight, soon after his sister was born. His father married again, more for convenience than anything else, and from the first Tearlach loathed his stepmother. It was she who drove him to the desperate action of running away from home before he had finished school."

"He doesn't seem to have had any affection for his sister, either," said Penelope, and she told him what Tearlach had said about Avis when she had offered him sympathy.

"Yes she asked him to take care of her children. She knew, of course, that they would benefit," mused Ian.

"They are benefiting, materialistically speaking."

"But not in the way you think they should. Yet why should you worry about them?" asked Ian.

"I'm just made that way, I suppose. I can't bear to see children rejected."

"Then you'd have felt sorry for Tearlach when he was a boy, ignored by his father, rejected by his stepmother and with no one to turn to. Maybe that's why he finds it difficult to love or show love in the way you mean. He's very lucky at cards, you know; it doesn't do to play with him for money for he invariably wins, as Hugh and I well know," Ian replied with a laugh.

"I see. He's lucky at cards but unlucky in love."

"It seems to be that way. Do you know, Penelope, I've a curious feeling that you and I have discussed someone in this way before?"

"I've the same feeling," she said seriously. "Only then you were wearing a monk's habit."

"Are you sure?" he exclaimed.

"Quite sure."

"This is very exciting. My name, McTaggart, means 'son of a priest,' and I have a theory that there were some

Pictish priests already living on Torvaig when the Vikings came," he said in awed tones. "They were hermits and their settlement was here at Achmore. I base my theory on the artefacts Hugh and I have found when we've been excavating."

"Have you found more tools?"

"Yes, made of slate and stone, such as the Picts used. We've also found the remains of a building, but its masonry technique is like that used by the Picts in Ireland, and I think that possibly the Vikings used the dispossessed Picts as their slaves to build their dwellings."

"But couldn't Magnus Gunn have brought them from Ireland as he brought his wife?"

"That's possible too." Ian glanced thoughtfully toward the bay. "There's Hugh coming back," he said, pointing to an open fishing boat chugging into the bay. "Let's go down and tell him about your most recent flashback. I know he's interested in your experience too."

Ian's excitement was infectious, and by the time they had reached the jetty as Hugh brought his fishing boat alongside, Penelope felt just as excited. She was getting high on history, she thought, and wondered when her next flashback would take place.

Hugh stepped ashore, seeming bigger than ever in his glistening oilskins. Beyond him in the boat Penelope could see the openwork lobster pots that held the mottled blue lobsters.

"How did you get here?" he greeted her. Briefly she explained about the car and he whistled. "Makes me think that perhaps someone is doing his best to encourage you to stay rather than drive you away. Are you still on probation?"

"Yes, I'm afraid so. Tearlach hasn't been here all week, so I haven't had a chance to blot my copy book again, although I did blot it rather badly, more than once, before he left."

"Why? What did you do?" asked Hugh, his eyes gleaming inquisitively.

"I just told him what I thought about his attitude to the children and how material goods, like toys and games, can never take the place of real love and attention."

Again Hugh whistled, and then with a touch of mockery, murmured, "What are you trying to do, Penelope? Are you hoping to make the old lion change his ways by behaving like Mary Poppins? Better take care. You can be sure he's adding up those blots, and when the end of your probationary period comes he'll be balancing them against your credit side and deducting them. He's doing the same with me. That's why I haven't been over to see you."

"I wondered why."

"I was warned off," said Hugh, with a slightly sheepish grin.

"By Mr. Gunn?" Penelope's eyes were wide.

"Yes. You see, Miss Jones, you and I are here to work and we needn't think we can play together during working hours. Get the message?"

"Yes. I had an impression he was suspicious of us on the yacht," murmured Penelope, seething inwardly at Tearlach Gunn's assumption that she was involved with Hugh.

Davy was showing an interest in the lobsters and Hugh squatted down beside him to tell him about them.

"Isn't this one a beauty?" he said and, glancing up at Penelope, added, "Stay and have tea with Ian and me. I can offer you lobster thermidor à la Drummond."

"I'd love to, but I think I'd better go back. The children are tired."

"Then come back later this evening, when they've gone to bed," suggested Ian.

Regretfully thinking how much she would have enjoyed spending the evening with this quiet, shy and yet interesting man, Penelope declined again.

"I'm sorry, but I have to stay with them. Davy sometimes wakes up and someone has to be there," she explained.

"Surely Tearlach isn't slave driving." Ian murmured, and she glanced at him sharply. Once more he was the hermit priest of her earlier vision and she was the slave girl brought to Torvaig by the first Magnus Gunn so long ago. "Don't you have any free time?" he added.

"I forgot to ask him before he left. If I do have time off, it means someone else will have to look after Davy and Isa, and I can't imagine Mr. Gunn doing that," she replied.

"When is he coming back?" asked Hugh.

"Tomorrow."

"Then I suggest that the mice should play while the big cat is away. Ian and I will come and see you as you can't come and see us. Will eight o'clock this evening be suitable?"

Penelope agreed, pleased at the thought of having visitors, and drove back to Torvaig House happily having enjoyed her afternoon. She felt quite at home on the hillside at Achmore, which was to be expected since her grandmother's ancestors had lived there for such a long time. She and Ian McTaggart had known each other very well in that other life, she thought, when he had been a priest and she had been in thrall to a Viking.

She shook her head vigorously. She must stop having these strange feelings. She remembered her grandmother talking about Gaelic women who had possessed the second sight and had been able to foretell the future, but she had never heard of anyone whose visions had been of the past! If she wasn't careful she would be living her life as the unnamed slave girl whose coloring had been like her own, and that would never do!

After she had put the children to bed that evening she went down to the kitchen to tell Mrs. Guthrie that Ian and Hugh were coming over later. She found the housekeeper busy baking in preparation for the invasion of guests the next day.

"Then we'll have a wee *ceilidh* in our sitting room down here," said Mrs. Guthrie. "Ach, I love to hear Hugh playing his guitar and singing those saucy Scottish songs he picked up when he was a student."

"There's something else I want to ask you," said Penelope, a little diffidently.

"Ask away, lass," replied the kindly woman as she rolled pastry with a few deft strokes of her rolling pin.

"It's a ticklish subject. Did Mr. Gunn say anything to you about my having any time off?"

"I suppose you'd like to be going somewhere with Hugh?" said Mrs. Guthrie with a knowing twinkle in her eyes. "Well, that's natural enough with you both being about the same age. And I'm thinking you should be entitled to a few hours off. I'd be more than willing to keep an eye on the bairns for you."

Penelope shook her head negatively.

"Oh no. I don't want to do anything unless it has Mr. Gunn's approval, and I just wondered if he'd said anything to you about my free time."

"No, but then I didn't expect him to. I suppose he went away in such a hurry he forgot to mention it to you. You can ask him about it tomorrow when he comes home," said Mrs. Guthrie practically.

Penelope looked down at her hands and then up again, a faintly rueful grin curving her lips.

"I was hoping to avoid having to do that and that's why I'm asking you. You see, every time Mr. Gunn and I meet we seem to strike sparks off each other, and since I'm only here on probation for a month I'd like to avoid the risk of annoying him and so losing my job," she explained.

Mrs. Guthrie cocked a shrewd eye in Penelope's direction. "Striking sparks, eh? And how would you be doing that?" she asked.

"I don't know. It just happens. He says something and I overreact, and before I know it I've said things I shouldn't say to an employer," explained Penelope.

"Humph. Well, that's something only you can sort out for yourself, lass. But if it's any help I don't mind asking him about you having free time, because it stands to reason you should have it. I'm only surprised he didn't say anything to you before he went away. He's usually very particular about such things."

Grateful for and relieved by Mrs. Guthrie's offer to ask Tearlach Gunn about her time off, Penelope was able to relax and enjoy the visit of Ian and Hugh. The Guthries made the two young men welcome as only Highlanders can, and when their eldest son and his wife arrived bringing with them another young couple, who lived on the island, the wee *ceilidh* that Mrs. Guthrie had promised turned out to be a much larger one. Hugh played his guitar and Aileen Guthrie sang; Alec Guthrie, after much persuasion from the others, brought out his bagpipes and played a *pibroch*—a series of variations composed especially for the bagpipes.

Thinking she had seldom enjoyed an evening so much, Penelope went to bed happy and lay thinking for a while about Ian and Hugh. For the first time in her life she knew what it was to be friendly with two young men on an equal footing. Neither of them expected anything from her other than her friendship, she was sure. The only other man she had ever known well was Brian, and he had expected too much! When she had said good night to them, they had made her promise to go over to Cladach as soon as she had some free time, and together they would take her to the old graveyard to search for a head-stone bearing the name Sandison.

If she hadn't come to Torvaig she would never have known what it was like to have such friends, she thought sleepily, and she must not let anyone drive her away from her home, now that she had found it.

Next day, in the late afternoon, Tearlach returned to Torvaig House, closely followed by two other cars carrying his guests. Penelope did not see them arrive, but knew they had come because Mrs. Guthrie came upstairs to tell her, and to say that Miss Drummond was also in the house acting as hostess for the laird.

Both children were in bed and Penelope was about to sit down at the small writing desk in her room to write to an old school friend who was also a nanny, when a wail from Davy's room sent her scurrying in there. He started to complain that his uncle hadn't come to see him, and with a sigh Penelope began the usual efforts to distract him. She was just coming to the end of a story when the door opened and Tearlach came in. Davy greeted him with a shriek of delight and flung himself out of bed to clutch him around the legs. Coolly disengaging himself from this ecstatic embrace, Tearlach bade him sternly to get back into bed and told Penelope to finish reading the story.

Rather embarrassed by his presence while she was reading, she finished the story in a monotonous voice, most unlike the usual dramatic one she usually used, and was aware that her employer, who was standing by the window looking out, was listening to every word. When she had finished, she closed the book, kissed Davy on the cheek as he snuggled down in bed, and then went through the communicating door into her room, closing the door behind her.

She had only been in the room a few seconds when the door was wrenched open again and Tearlach stepped through it, closing it rather violently behind him.

"I came to talk to you, not to get involved in a good-night session with my nephew," he grated. "What's all this about your wanting time off?"

Sometimes the roughness shows, Hugh had said, and this was one of the times. Obviously, Mrs. Guthrie had lost no time in informing him of the nanny's request for time off, and the effect seemed to be disastrous, thought Penelope ruefully as she noted the unpleasant twist to his mouth and the anger flickering in his narrowed eyes.

She swallowed hard, rubbed the palms of her hands against her skirt, a sure sign she was nervous, and squared up to him.

"I asked Mrs. Guthrie if any arrangements had been made for me to have time off and she said she'd ask you about it," she said.

"Why couldn't you ask me yourself?" he rapped back.

"You weren't here," she replied sweetly, and to her alarm he swore and interrupted her rudely.

"Don't play the innocent with me! I know I haven't been here. What I meant was you should have asked me when I was here, or now that I've come back."

She wondered if he had guessed she had wanted to

avoid another run-in with him and was annoyed with her about that for some reason, but she had no answer to his question other than the one that she had wanted to avoid him, so she said nothing.

Her silence seemed to irritate him even more. Advancing toward her he stood with his hands on his hips and glared down at her.

"Come on, out with it. Why couldn't you ask me yourself?"

"Shush!" she murmured, putting a finger to her lips. "You'll wake Isa."

His straight white teeth snapped together audibly as he gritted them and refrained from swearing at her again.

"Since you won't answer my question I'll answer it for you. You didn't ask me for time off yourself because you were afraid you'd lose your temper again and say what you feel, and that might lead you to being sacked before the end of the month. Isn't that so?"

She nodded dumbly. The anger seeped out of his face leaving it strangely tired-looking. He swung away from her and went over to the window. When he spoke again his usually vibrant voice was flat and dreary.

"I'd thought better of *you*," he muttered obscurely; then there was a little silence. As she stood in the middle of the room looking at his broad hunched shoulders and shaggy mane of hair, Penelope wondered what to say.

"Anyone on this island will tell you I've no time for the oblique approach," he went on slowly. "I'm your employer, not Mrs. Guthrie. If you want to know anything about the children or about the conditions of your employment here, you come straight to me. You don't go behind my back. Is that clear?" He turned to look at her.

"Yes, Mr. Gunn," she said with a touch of breathlessness as understanding dawned. He preferred it when she bearded him in his den. She should have remembered he had said to her at their first meeting that she should never apologize for saying what she felt to him. "Please could you tell me how much free time I'm allowed in this job?" she added hurriedly.

His glance was enigmatic.

"That's better," he murmured. "How much time off did you get in your last job? I hope you're not going to tell me that there's a nannies' union and that I've been breaking the regulations."

"No, as far as I know, there isn't," replied Penelope seriously. "In my last job I had two half days each week and a full weekend once a month, but that was a different situation from the one here because the children were with their parents when I was off."

He nodded his understanding and turned to look out of the window again as if giving her statement some thought.

"If I allow you time off what will you do with it? Where will you go?" he asked.

"I shall attend to personal necessities such as shopping and mending, and I shall explore the island, although I don't really think I have to account to you for those hours of freedom, even if you are my employer," she replied crisply.

His head turned sharply at that and he gave her one of those unnerving, narrow-eyed stares.

"That's true, you don't. I'm just trying to make sure that you don't intend to make mischief at my expense as your predecessor did," he said coldly. "Then you shall have, for the time being, a half day and one whole day off every alternate week, starting with a half day this coming Wednesday. The following week it will be all of Satur-

day. Whether you will ever get any more free time is
entirely up to you, as it's just possible you'll be packing
your bags when your four-week probation period is up
and leaving Torvaig for good. Will that suit you?"

"Yes, thank you. And I shan't be leaving Torvaig, Mr.
Gunn."

He came across and stood in front of her and grinned
down at her. The tired look had gone and the vibrancy
was back in his voice.

"I wouldn't be too sure about that, Miss Jones," he
said softly. "Did you invite Hugh and Ian here last night
or did they invite themselves?"

"Hugh invited himself and Ian. I met them yesterday
when I was over at Achmore," she replied, wondering a
little uneasily what lay behind his question and deciding
that since he didn't like what he called an "oblique"
approach she had better be scrupulously honest with him
at all times.

"When you were where?" he demanded, making no
effort to hide his surprise.

"Achmore." She couldn't help sounding smug. "That's
the name of the group of crofts up on the hill at Cladach
Bay. You told me there was no place with that name on
Torvaig."

"Because I didn't know. This is the first I've heard of
it. Why did you go there?"

"I wanted to see the graveyard Hugh had told me
about. I called on Molly Lang and then went on to find
Hugh. He was fishing, so I walked up to the graveyard
and called on Mr. McTaggart, thinking I might find Miss
Drummond there. But she was away too, with you in
Edinburgh." His quick frown came. Obviously he did not
like her reference to Kathleen. "Mr. McTaggart went
with me to the graveyard and it was there that he told me

the name of the group of crofts. And it may interest you to know that Mr. Guthrie has already told me that my grandmother's father, Hector Sandison, left Torvaig and went to live in England because the old laird wouldn't make improvements on the island."

He stared at her for a moment and then burst out laughing.

"How you enjoyed telling me all that!" he remarked. "Very well, I'll concede that round to you. I really don't know much about Torvaig's past or about the people who used to live here. All I'm interested in is its present and future, and the people who live here now. There's been too much looking over the shoulder at the past in this part of the country and it hasn't done anyone any good at all."

"Do you accept, then, that my reason for coming here was to see where my grandmother was born?" persisted Penelope.

"I do now. When you told me on the boat coming here it seemed a little far-fetched and I admit to being suspicious of you. Even so I'm sure it wasn't your only reason. You're on the run from something. What happened? What did he do to you? Did he find another woman?"

Her resolve not to let him rouse her anger was almost destroyed by his abrupt, rather crude way of describing Brian's behavior. She went pink with pain. He had no right to probe so carelessly in a wound she had hoped was well on the way to being healed.

"Supposing he did; what has it to do with you?" she hissed.

"Nothing really. I'm just curious to find out if my hunch about you is correct. You've a bruised look about you that young women sometimes get when they think they've been defeated in the game they call love," he replied, his shrewd gaze never leaving her face.

"How can you possibly tell? What do you know about love?" she flung at him wildly, hoping to make a hit somewhere.

"Again, nothing," he replied. "At least I know nothing about that romantic mushy feeling women often confuse with love, which puts a man on a pedestal and dehumanizes him. I deal in realities, not in romances."

"Oh yes, anyone can see that," she flared. "You heap material goods on two little children, thinking that gifts will make up for your lack of real affection for them."

"Are we back in that groove again?" he mocked. "You're getting monotonous, Miss Jones."

"I daresay you've done the same to women in your time," she rushed on, heedless now of the danger in saying too much. "Buying them with gifts, but making sure they get nothing of you."

"And to think you once accused me of being prejudiced!" he jibed.

Why didn't he go? thought Penelope wildly. Why was he here in her room tormenting her, trying to make her lose her temper and tell him home truths about himself so that he could accuse her of rudeness and sack her? Why didn't he go back downstairs to his guests and to Kathleen Drummond?

She raised her head and said in a quivering voice, "This is my room, Mr. Gunn, given to me for my private use. Would you mind leaving? I have a letter to write before I go to bed."

"To your grandmother, to tell her you've found the place where she was born?" he taunted, not moving an inch.

"My grandmother died two years ago," she said patiently, although her heart was beating so hard she thought it would burst.

"To your parents, then?" he persisted.

"My parents died when I was very young."

"So now you're all alone in the world, pining for the man who got away," he jeered. "Heartbreaking," he added.

For the first time in her life Penelope literally saw red. Of its own will, or so it seemed, her right hand swung up, aiming for the handsome, sun-tanned face inches above her own. It was halfway there when common sense asserted itself. If she hit him he would have good cause to dismiss her, and judging by the expectant mocking gleam in his eyes he was waiting for her to make a wrong move.

With a great effort she forced her arm to change direction and crossing it with her left arm, she took a deep steadying breath and said, as coolly as she could, "But that's impossible, Mr. Gunn. You haven't a heart to break."

He smiled, and she was watching him so closely that she was able to see that his smile began in his eyes as a distinct twinkle before it spread to his mouth. A person who could smile like that must have a heart, she thought contrarily.

"That was a very close thing," he murmured, and then glanced at his watch. "But I've no more time for brawling, much as I enjoy it. About your time off, make it every Wednesday afternoon until midnight instead of every other Wednesday and every alternate Saturday from nine in the morning until midnight, and be sure to be back by midnight or you'll be in trouble. Don't get lost when you're exploring, and beware of getting too entangled with red-haired Viking types or you might get hurt again. Good night, Nanny."

With another tantalizing grin he turned and left the room. Penelope let out a long shuddering breath, flopped down on the divan and pounded one of the cushions with her fists.

Hateful, tormenting man, prodding at her, rousing a temper she had not known she possessed until she met him, then retreating behind a charming, yet strangely indulgent smile. How dared he warn her against Hugh and then call her Nanny! Oh, how she wished she could have slapped him! There was certainly no danger of her ever putting *him* on a pedestal!

She punched the cushion with all the force she could muster; then to her surprise, she burst into tears and cried, something she had not done for years, not even when she had learned about Brian's deception. After a while she sat up, blew her nose and wiped her eyes. She felt much better, as if the storm of tears had released an inner tension.

For a while she sat in the gloaming, considering her violent reaction to her employer's remarks. Was it possible that with his own brand of mockery he had cauterized the wound inflicted on her sensibility by Brian's treatment of her? Perhaps now she would really begin to forget that for two whole years she had been taken in by a handsome philanderer who had duped her into believing he was in love with her. One thing was sure, she would never allow herself to be duped again. Mr. Gunn need have no fear; she would never become too entangled with his cousin Hugh or with any other man, if she could help it. From now on all her friendships with the opposite sex were going to be completely platonic.

During the next few days squally weather hit the island, but the wind and rain did not prevent the guests from going out of doors. Every day Penelope saw them leaving the house on their way to fish the island's numerous lochs and burns. Usually, but not always, they were accompanied by Tearlach, and sometimes by Kathleen.

From Mrs. Guthrie, Penelope learned that the guests were two married couples and that they were interested in the jewelry Ian and Kathleen were making.

"That's why Miss Drummond has been over here, helping to entertain them, acting as hostess, you might say. Ach, the house needs a mistress, so it does, and I wouldn't be surprised if they didn't make a match of it one of these days," said the plump jolly housekeeper one day, when Penelope had joined her and her husband for elevenses in the kitchen. She loved to speculate about Tearlach and was always looking forward to the day when he would settle down and marry.

"But I thought Miss Drummond and Mr. Gunn were cousins, and that he was a confirmed bachelor," said Penelope, who loved to tease Mrs. Guthrie, in the kindest, gentlest way.

"So was I until I met Bessie," put in Alec Guthrie, following her lead. "But I was no proof against a determined woman and look at me now, 35 years married."

"Any regrets?" asked Penelope.

"Not I. Ach, we've had our disagreements, but we've always been able to compromise. We've always needed each other."

"Then you've been very fortunate," said Penelope. "What makes you think Miss Drummond will be able to change Mr. Gunn's attitude, Mrs. Guthrie?"

"Well, it stands to reason a man in his position should have a wife, now that he has a home. It was different when he was knocking about the world. And they're not close cousins and they get on very well together. Then you can't deny she's a beautiful woman. If he'd been married he wouldn't have had to ask Alec and me to live in when you came to work here, and he wouldn't have to invite a single woman to act as hostess to his guests," replied Mrs. Guthrie.

"Maybe he prefers it that way," said Alec musingly. "If Miss Drummond or Miss Jones do anything to displease him he can tell them to leave. It's not so easy to get rid of a wife. And then it's not every young woman that wants to get married these days. They're an independent lot, if what I read in the newspapers is true."

"Aye, I've read all that nonsense about women wanting the same freedom as men," growled Mrs. Guthrie. "A lot of rubbish, I call it. Any woman who believes that marriage makes a slave of her, or a second class citizen, needs her head seeing to. Marriage is the best career there is for a woman, and I haven't noticed our daughter thinking any differently from me. What about you, Penelope? Wouldn't you like to get married and have children?"

"Only if I could find someone who would respect me and treat me as an equal. As for children, I would just as soon look after other people's. There are so many children in the world who don't get the proper attention and treatment, even from their own parents, that I think there's a need for men and women who don't have children to help look after the rejected and the parentless."

"Aye, I can see your point there, lass," said Mrs. Guthrie accommodatingly, "but I wouldn't mind betting that in a year or so you'll have found the man who respects you and treats you right and you'll be wanting to have his children. You won't be able to help yourself. And now, miss, I'm told you're to have this afternoon off and I'm to mind the bairns for you. So I'd be much obliged to you if you'd bring young Davy down here after lunch. He can help me with the baking. He likes nothing better than to cut pastry shapes and make gingerbread men."

After doing her much-needed washing and mending, Penelope set off soon after two o'clock to walk to Cladach Bay. She had learned from Alec Guthrie that it was possible to walk there by way of a path running across the headland that jutted into the sea north of An Tigh Camus, the Gaelic name for the Bay of the House where Torvaig House was situated.

As she was leaving she noticed Tearlach Gunn's black car sweep up to the front door. It was driven by Donald Lang who sometimes acted as a chauffeur when he wasn't repairing machinery. Pausing on her way across the lawn, she turned back to see who had arrived and was not surprised to see Kathleen Drummond step out of the car. She was wearing blue jeans and a white high-necked sweater, and she was carrying a canvas bag. As she went up the steps to the house the front door opened and Tearlach came out to greet her. He held out a hand to her and when she reached his side, she reached up and kissed him on the cheek.

Penelope lingered only to see him guide his cousin into the house. It looked very much as if Mrs. Guthrie had been right in her prediction that the laird and his beautiful cousin might make a match of it, if indeed they hadn't already, she thought, as she followed the path from the sandy shore over the headland. She could imagine both of them ignoring the conventions and carrying on a fairly torrid affair without blessing it with the name of love or the dignity of marriage.

"Why so sour, Penelope?" she whispered to herself, as she scrambled up the rocky incline. "Just because you didn't have the courage to throw convention to the winds and indulge in that sort of relationship with Brian, why be critical of others? Anyway, it isn't any business of yours. You're here to do a job, to look after two motherless children, and you're jolly lucky to be able to do your job in such a lovely place, among such pleasant people as Bessie and Alec Guthrie, and all the others you've met since you came here."

Having put herself in her place, she lifted her head to the sky and smelled the clear fresh air. Beneath her feet the grass was short and springy, starred with sea-thrift and small Scottish bluebells. The clouds of morning were lifting slowly as a faint breath of wind from the north blew them away. Blue sky appeared and pale sunlight glinted on the gray sea, changing its color to gold-shot green. As she mounted to the top of the headland she could see the distant Outer Hebrides showing blue black against a backcloth of eggshell-green sky. Nearer, the dark points of the Shiant Isles loomed, spectacular cones of rock rearing out of the sea.

Suddenly she felt again the feeling that she had been there before. She had stood on that spot and had looked out to sea. But then there had been longing in her heart as she had searched the wide expanse of water for the shape of a ship returning home to Torvaig; that same Viking ship in which she had come.

Shaking her head to clear it of the fantasy, she glanced down into An Tigh Camus, to the white two-masted boat swinging at its mooring. On the water to the right of it there was movement. The dinghy was speeding across the bay, its wake a white furrow of churned up water. It slowed down as it approached the yacht, and swung around to go alongside.

The sun, bursting forth in full strength, glinted on the chromium-plated fittings of the yacht, swaying slightly as someone climbed aboard. It glinted also on Tearlach

Gunn's blond-streaked hair as he turned to help someone else aboard. He was helping Kathleen, of course, and behind her came one of the guests. Then the dinghy, steered by Hugh, whose red-gold hair also caught the sun's light, was off, roaring back to the jetty to pick up the rest of the party.

Green serpents of envy coiled within Penelope's mind as she watched Kathleen step down into the cockpit and then disappear into the cabin. They were all going for a cruise and she longed to go too. In fact she felt it was her right to be going, not Kathleen's.

Disconcerted by the strength of her jealousy and unable to account for it, she turned and ran until she could no longer see An Tigh Camus, and Cladach Bay was in sight. Steadfastly keeping her thoughts away from the scene she had just witnessed, she scrambled down the rocky path that led to the shore. By the time she reached the road that curved round the bay, envy was banished and she was in control of her feelings again.

Reaching the end of the lane leading to Achmore, she turned into it and went toward the house of Ian McTaggart.

CHAPTER FOUR

Penelope found Ian in his workshop. He was leaning over a delicately twisted piece of silver, clamped in a vise on the bench, and he was using a small coping saw to cut shapes in the fine metal. He showed he was aware of her presence by glancing at her and smiling, then turned to concentrate on the intricate work.

Waiting for him to finish before she talked to him, she had time to study his face. His neatly trimmed mustache and beard combined to draw attention to the sensitivity of his mouth. Above his wide-set gray eyes his fine dark eyebrows arched intelligently making three horizontal creases in his high forehead, partially hidden by his brushed-forward hair.

He was, she thought, a man of gentle disposition whose emotions were well disciplined. She could not imagine him hurting anyone, yet judging by his face she guessed he was very vulnerable to hurt inflicted on him by other people.

At last he laid the small saw aside, released the piece of silver from the vise and held it out to her.

"What is it?" she asked, turning it over between her fingers and marveling at the workmanship. It was triangular in shape, a fine web of filigree silver.

"It's a pendant."

"It makes me think of the skeleton of a leaf."

"You're right," he replied. "It's intended to represent the shape of a birch leaf. Is this your day off?"

She looked up to answer the smile in his eyes with a smile of her own.

"It is. I'm free until midnight, and every other Saturday too. You look as if you're very busy."

"I have been. The other day I was visited by the guests staying in the big house. One of them is a buyer from a big jewelry house in London, which has branches all over Britain. The other is a well-known Scottish businessman. The buyer wanted to buy Kathleen's and my entire stock, the other ordered several pieces to be made for his wife and his daughter."

In spite of the orders he had received he did not seem to be particularly happy, thought Penelope, noticing lines of strain around his eyes and mouth.

"Aren't you pleased?" she asked, handing the pendant back to him.

"Of course. An artist likes to have his work appreciated," he replied rather drearily. "I'm grateful to Tearlach. Without his interest this wouldn't have happened. He has contacts and influence."

"Because he has money," said Penelope shortly.

"Sometimes it can be a blessing, you know," Ian reproved her gently. "People like myself and Hugh, and even you, would not be able to put our talents to good use if there were not people like Tearlach, who has the heart of a lion and is quite fearless when it comes to taking chances with money. With the support of the London jeweler he's willing to finance an exhibition of Kathleen's and my work in London in December."

"I suppose you're right," she admitted. "He's taken them all sailing. I saw them going aboard as I came over to the headland."

"A cruise, I believe, to the Outer Hebrides, to the islands of Barra and Uist," said Ian, a rather troubled frown darkening his face. "Was Kathleen with them?"

"Yes, and Hugh. Didn't they tell you they were going?"

"I knew about Hugh, but Kathleen was not sure whether or not there would be room for her." His frown was deeper and his sensitive mouth looked taut as if he was having difficulty in hiding his feelings. "She's been at the big house a lot recently!"

"Yes. She's been acting as hostess for Mr. Gunn. Mrs. Guthrie says she would be surprised if Mr. Gunn doesn't marry her," replied Penelope. She watched the color drain out of Ian's face.

"I suppose that's possible," he said huskily. "You're at the big house all the time. Have you noticed anything between them? No, don't bother to answer. I can see by your face that you have."

He turned away ostensibly to tidy the tools on the bench, and Penelope stared at him, not knowing what to say as understanding dawned and she realized that he was in love with Kathleen. She wanted to question him about his feelings, but hesitated because she guessed, like most of his countrymen, he was reticent about discussing such matters.

While she hesitated he turned back and, making an effort to throw off his melancholy, smiled at her again and said, "I've done enough work for today and it's your day off. Outside the sun is shining at last. Shall we go and look at the headstones in the graveyard? Hugh and I have cleared away some of the undergrowth."

"I was hoping you would come with me. That's why I called on you, and I must tell you that on my way here I had another of those strange flashbacks," she said, touched by his interest and wishing to distract him from his obviously unhappy thoughts. "Do you think there's something wrong with me? Am I going out of my mind?"

He laughed a little and put an arm across her shoulders to guide her to the door.

"Not at all, Penelope. You strike me as being one of the sanest people I've ever met. No, I think that, like me, you're wholly Gael and as a result have one foot in the past and one foot in the present, and that coming back here, where your forebears lived for so long, has awakened your inherited memory. You're responding to the spirits of the people who once lived here. It isn't unusual for that to happen."

"I hope you're right. But Mr. Gunn's forebears lived here too and he doesn't have any flashbacks. In fact he told me he had no time for the past of Torvaig, that it was only its present and future that interest him."

"But then Tearlach, for all his name, is no Gael really. He was brought up in the city of Glasgow and his mother was English. It seems as if he has inherited her practical realistic attitude to life, which is just as well for Torvaig when you come to think about it seriously. Torvaig needed Tearlach as much as he needed Torvaig."

"What do you mean by that?"

"I have the impression he was tired of wandering and that he wanted a home. Torvaig provides both that and a challenge as well, something very necessary to a man of his temperament."

It was strange, thought Penelope, how often they talked about the laird. It wasn't only she who found him a powerful and dominating personality, but as none of them would have been there on Torvaig if he had not returned to the island, it was only natural that he should loom large in their conversation.

She had never thought of a graveyard as being a pleasant place to spend a sunny afternoon, but the one at Achmore was so pretty with its rose-entwined chapel, peaceful and scented in the warm mild air, that she forgot Ian's unhappiness and her own dark primitive feelings when she had watched Kathleen going aboard Tearlach's yacht. Wandering around with Ian she felt closer than ever to the past life of the island, as she peered at the names and dates on the headstones, some of which were so old and moss-covered, that it was difficult to make out the carved letters.

At last they found one bearing the name Sandison. On it were listed several Hectors and their wives and other members of their families. The last date was the mid-nineteenth century, and Penelope assumed that the Hector who had been buried then had been the father of her grandmother's father.

"I wish that Grandmother could have come here just once before she died," she whispered, looking down the hill at the sea. Far away sunlight glinted briefly on white sails. Then the gleam was lost and she wondered if she had imagined that there was a sailing boat out there on the wide expanse of glittering water.

"Wasn't it possible for her to come?" asked Ian.

"I imagine that when she was young she didn't think about it, being too busy bringing up my father and his two sisters. Then later, after my parents were both killed in a train crash, she was too busy working to keep me."

His glance was keen as he watched her looking at the distant smudge on the water—the big yacht, which he had also seen.

"Like the laird, you're one of the lonely ones," he murmured and took one of her hands in his.

Surprised by his words as well as by his warm sympathetic gesture, she could not help comparing him to the absent Tearlach. He offered gentleness instead of jibing sarcasm, soothing her instead of rousing her.

"Come and have tea with me," he said, "and then afterward we'll talk about Torvaig's past and I'll show you the excavation and the few artifacts Hugh and I have uncovered."

And so the rest of the afternoon and the evening passed in a pleasant blur. When the long Hebridean twilight touched hill and sea with mysterious shadows, Ian walked back with Penelope over the headland and along the shore. He left her where the lawn swept down from the house to touch the pale sand, and she stood for a while watching him return along the shore, stopping now and again to pick up a shell or some other piece of flotsam that had caught his observant artist's eye.

"Come to Achmore again, on your day off," he had invited when he had left her, and she knew she would, not only because she was attracted by the quiet sensitive man but also because she felt she could ease in some way the heartache she guessed he was suffering.

She turned to cross the lawn to the house and immediately her tranquil mood was shattered, as smooth glass is shattered by a stone. In turning her glance was caught by the mooring buoy bobbing on the water. Devoid of color in the twilight, it looked dark and lonely, giving the bay a desolate appearance. The big yawl was not there, and she was shaken suddenly by a feeling of forlornness as if someone she loved dearly had gone from her.

Frightened by the feeling, she whirled and turned her back on the empty bay, hurried up to the house, which, pale and ghostly, was silent and without light among the dark trees. Here, too, was an atmosphere of desolation, of emptiness, as if the owner had left the house and would never return.

Her heart thumping madly, Penelope walked quickly around the side of the house and saw, to her relief, a light shining from the Guthries' sitting room. Quietly she let herself in through the side door and went upstairs to her room.

The yawl was gone from the bay for ten days. Each time Penelope looked out at the bobbing red buoy, alone on the shimmering water, she experienced that strange aching feeling, as if she had been bereft, and she would look away quickly.

Most of the time, however, she was too busy to question the feeling and wonder whether it was her own or an inherited one. The spell of fine weather made getting about easy, and she and the children visited most of the island's little coves and beaches in turn. Once, much to Davy's delight, they went to the mainland on the ferry.

Wednesday came around again and she used her time off to call on Molly Lang. Then she walked up to the old graveyard. As a matter of course, she called on Ian to find him still working on the jewelry he had promised to have ready for Tearlach's guests, when they returned from their cruise. Once more Penelope stayed for tea, and when she walked back to Torvaig House she enjoyed the golden afterglow of the sunset.

She was beginning to feel very much at home and was surprised to find that only three and a half weeks had passed since she had first set foot on the island. Next Monday her four weeks' probation would be ended. She knew that she was coping satisfactorily with the children. Although Davy still showed signs of having a nervous temperament, she was becoming more and more convinced that it was caused by the influence of his Spanish father, and that it was nothing to do with him having lost both parents. He was naturally volatile, swinging from fierce passionate tempers to happy gaiety. He did not like the rain or the wind and would obstinately refuse to go out on such days, but when the sun shone he responded to its warmth like a flower.

On the other hand, Isa was a placid, complacent child, happy wherever she was, as long as there was enough to eat and toys to play with. She would sit for hours building with wooden bricks, and she never cried when Davy knocked her castles and churches flying with one kick of his foot; she would just start building them again.

One afternoon when they were all down on the shore of An Tigh Camus, the big white yawl appeared around the southern point of the bay. It was moving slowly in the light breeze from the south, pulled forward by a red and yellow striped spinnaker.

The sight of the striped sail had a peculiar effect on Penelope. She stood up, heedless of Davy's excited chatter. Her heart was beating faster than normally and her cheeks glowed with a strange heat as she watched the graceful yacht enter the bay. Its spinnaker was taken down and the other sails were trimmed as it altered course, and making a curve of deeper blue on the surface of the water it swept around the bay and approached the red buoy. Its white sails shimmered and shook as the helmsman brought its bow into the wind.

Standing in a sort of trance, Penelope watched the sails being lowered and stowed away. Then the dinghy was launched, and it was when she saw the bright sheen of Hugh's hair as he stepped into the dinghy that she moved. Although every part of her clamored to stay on the shore and greet the homecomers, she knew that she must not be found there waiting. In that other life she had waited and had held out her arms to a tall man whose hair had been blond, whose cheeks had been bright and whose eyes had gleamed like the serpent's.

Swiftly she swooped on Isa and lifted her in her arms.

"Come along, Davy," she called. "Time for tea!"

As she expected, he howled, but she paid no attention, knowing that he would follow eventually. He could not bear to stay alone for long. By the time she reached the lawn in front of the house he was close behind her, wailing that he wanted to see Uncle Tearlach and Hugh.

She stopped walking to tell him that probably his uncle would come to see him later when he was in bed, but by the time she had read three stories and Davy's long black eyelashes were fluttering sleepily on his cheeks, Tearlach Gunn had not come to the nursery and she guessed they would not see him that evening. She felt relieved that this was so because she intended to keep well clear of her employer until Monday and her probationary period were over. She was pretty sure that he would not find her unsatisfactory and that she would have the pleasure of seeing him eat humble pie.

Next day, from a window in the front of the house, she watched the guests leaving. It was the first time she had really had any chance to see them at close range because Tearlach had not considered it necessary to introduce his young relatives to them. One of the men was putting cases into the boot of a car. He turned to say something to someone who was closer to the house and out of her line of vision. Then two women appeared with Kathleen followed by Tearlach. They all stood together with the man laughing and joking obviously facing an unseen photographer. When the photograph was taken one of the women looked up at the front of the house, apparently saying something about it. Kathleen looked up, and before Penelope could duck out of sight, she had been seen and recognized.

Wishing she hadn't lingered to watch, she scurried away to her own part of the house, not wishing to be caught peeping. On no account must she blot her copybook this weekend! But where should she go? It being the alternate Saturday, she had the whole day off. She decided that she would find Hugh and ask him about the cruise.

He must have been thinking about her at the same time because half an hour later he arrived at the house to see her.

"I've been hearing from Ian that you have today off," he said with his inimitable grin. "So I came over thinking you might like to come to Inverness with me. I'm going to see my mother. Leaving here now, we should be there by one o'clock. We'll have the whole afternoon there and be back on the other side of the strait in time to catch the last ferry at 11:30."

"I'd love to come," said Penelope, thinking it was as good a way as any of keeping out of Tearlach's way, as well as an opportunity to see something of the Highlands.

Soon she was sitting beside Hugh in his old van, which rattled around the bends of the road across the island in the pleasant mellow September sunshine. Everywhere fields were showing signs of being ready for harvesting, shimmering with golden light as a faint breeze ruffled the ripened oats and barley. On the moors the bracken was turning brown, but the heather still blazed purple and the rowan trees were aglow, hung with clusters of orange red berries.

Across the strait of Torvaig the lavender-tinted mountains beckoned beneath a pale blue sky streaked with white cirrus, and Penelope felt a stirring of excitement as she realized that at last she was going to penetrate behind that barrier of rock through the deep glens that delved inland.

As they approached the sheltered fields of the eastern part of the island she noticed that the reaping had already begun. She asked Hugh when he was going to start harvesting his fields.

"I should be starting today," he replied, "but I thought to myself that it's also a fine day for driving through the mountains, and there's a young sassenach at the big house with the day off and she hasn't seen much of the Highlands, so I decided the fields could wait another day or two."

"Supposing it rains?" said Penelope.

"That'll be my bad luck," he answered with a grin. "You'll not be saying you're sorry I asked you to come with me?"

"No, I'm glad. Did you enjoy your cruise?"

"It was fine, and an education in more ways than one. I saw the islands of the Outer Hebrides I've always wanted to visit. We went to the Uists, Benebecula and Barra, and now I know not only how to handle a big yawl but also how to keep at arm's length a woman who has her heart set on matrimony without offending her."

"Who on earth are you talking about?" demanded Penelope, thoroughly mystified, as usual, by his odd way of referring to events and people.

"My dear sister and the old lion of Torvaig, of course. Who else?" he replied with his wicked grin.

"You mean Mr. Gunn? Why do you call him that? He isn't all that old, although I must say I can see why you call him a lion."

"He's 37 next birthday, which makes him older than you or I," retorted Hugh. "And I call him the lion of Torvaig because the Gunns of Torvaig used a lion's head in their family crest, which you may have noticed is carved over the front door of the big house. And after these past ten days in his company I've another reason for calling him old lion."

Laughter rippled through Hugh's voice and she turned to glance at him. He was really very attractive, she thought, and she was very pleased to see him again, but sometimes his sense of humor could get out of hand.

"What is your reason?" she asked cautiously.

"I read a story recently in a newspaper. It was about a zoo. The owners of it were having no luck in getting their lionesses to breed, even though they had some handsome young lions. The lionesses wouldn't look at the lions or have anything to do with them. Then one day an old lion was brought from a circus. After years of performing in the ring he had been retired and was going to spend the rest of his life in the zoo. Handsome, yet battered by his life in the circus, he possessed a *je ne sais quoi*, an elusive magnetic attraction that the young lions didn't have, and in no time the lionesses were all over him. Soon the zoo was boasting several litters of lion cubs. After seeing my sister making up to Tearlach during the past few weeks and then watching the two other women on the cruise licking their chops every time he spoke or sat next to them, in spite of the fact that they were both married, I think he's like that old lion. He attracts the opposite sex without any effort at all."

Penelope couldn't help laughing, although she remonstrated with him.

"That isn't a very nice thing to say about him," she objected, and he gave her a sharp glance. "After all, he did ask your sister to act as his hostess."

"Did he? That's the first I've heard of it. Well, whether he asked her or not she's certainly been trying to turn it to advantage. But his handling of her was very clever and I doubt very much if she knows just where she stands with him now."

"Mrs. Guthrie is sure they'll make a match of it,"

murmured Penelope, who was finding she did not like Hugh's references to his sister's behavior toward Tearlach.

"I doubt it," replied Hugh. "Although Tearlach is probably willing to engage in an affair with Kathleen, I can't see his marrying her. That's why I can't help feeling worried. Just lately I've sensed a desperation in her. She's just turned 30 and she has an almost feverish tendency to take anything that might be offered as a substitute for love in the hopes it will be the real thing. I wish I could persuade her to leave Torvaig."

"Why?"

"I'm afraid she's going to make a fool of herself. As you know Tearlach doesn't suffer fools gladly, and if she throws herself too much at him he might be tempted to discard the kid gloves and teach her a hard lesson in his own rough way. Being very proud and sensitive, she might do something awful as a result. But I didn't bring you with me just to talk about them. Have you blotted any copybooks lately?"

"No, because Mr. Gunn hasn't been near me or his relatives. In fact Davy and Isa might be nonexistent as far as he's concerned!" replied Penelope tartly.

"Better keep it that way if it means not making any more blots," said Hugh with a grin. "Are you managing the bairns satisfactorily?"

"Of course I am. Davy is still a little difficult. He's so highly emotional."

"Does he still cry for his mother?"

"Not now. He cries for his uncle instead," she said dryly. "Did you ever meet Davy's father?"

"Only once. Davy looks a lot like him. He was handsome and knew it. He had a wonderful physique and he showed it off whenever he could, which wasn't often in our climate. But he seemed very fond of Avis, for all she was a bit of a mouse," murmured Hugh. "Good, the ferry is in, which means we won't be wasting time waiting for it to come back from the other side."

The conversation lapsed when they reached the ferry and Hugh had to concentrate on maneuvering the van across the gangway into the narrow space left by the one other vehicle that was using the ferry at that time. When they started to talk again it was about the sale Ian had made of his entire stock of jewelry to the London buyer and from there it was an easy step to Hugh's own plans to sell paintings he hoped to make of the things he had seen during the cruise.

On the mainland they took the road leading straight from the ferry into the heart of the mountains, following a burn winding through a narrow glen. Soon they were edging along the shore of Loch Maree, a lovely stretch of fresh water over which the forbidding slopes of Beinn Eighe towered.

The loch was dotted with many islands and Hugh told her that each one had its legend. One of them, known as Eilean Maree, was supposed to be the home of St. Maelrubha, who had founded the church of Applecross, a village on the coast, and the name of Maree was in fact a corruption of his name. But in spite of the Christian influence, bulls had been sacrificed in pagan rites as late as the seventeenth century, and a well on the island was credited with curing insanity.

Hugh had many such stories to tell her about the rugged countryside the road wound through and the time passed quickly. Enthralled as she had been by the wildness of the scenery, Penelope came back to the amenities offered by modern civilization with a slight sense of shock as they came down from the mountains to a fertile plain and onto a wider faster road, which took them to the capital of the Highlands, the town of Inverness.

The town was bigger than she had expected, a place of sturdy Victorian villas, many shops and the usual Saturday afternoon traffic. They crossed the bridge over the River Ness, curving away, Hugh said, to the Moray Firth and the North Sea. The steeples of two churches dominated the scene, soaring against a background of houses, factories and the distant hills, tinted ochre by the autumnal sun.

Hugh's parents lived on the outskirts of the town in a gabled granite house. Mrs. Drummond had obviously been on the lookout for them because they had hardly stopped the car in the driveway when a tall slender woman with graying hair appeared at the front door. She came down the steps to greet them and Penelope could see the strong likeness to Kathleen in the lovely lines of cheek and chin and in the amber color of her eyes. Likeness was also there in the unconsciously regal pose of her head and in the slightly condescending way she greeted the nanny employed by her cousin.

"I must say you are as much a surprise to me as I hear you were to Charles," she said. Her speech was clear and uncluttered by any accent, and Penelope remembered being told once that the people of Inverness spoke the best English in the British Isles. "I realize now," continued Mrs. Drummond, "that Josie Bennet didn't mention your age and I just assumed that she would send an older woman, as I requested. No wonder Charles was annoyed."

"Penelope looks young and defenseless, but she's well able to take care of herself, and she seems to be doing a better job than Swannie," said Hugh. "From all accounts she stands her ground when the lion growls at her and gives back as good as she gets. Today is her day off and I thought you'd like to meet her and see for yourself that Davy and Isa are in good hands."

"I'm very pleased to meet you, Miss Jones," said Helen Drummond politely. "I'm also glad to see you safe and sound, back from your cruise, Hugh. But where is Kathleen?"

Hugh looked slightly uncomfortable as if he didn't care much for having to tell his mother why Kathleen hadn't come with him.

"She wouldn't come. I'll tell you why while we're having lunch. Is Dad home?" he said.

"No. He and Neil have both gone to play golf at Nairn, so unless you stay the night and return tomorrow, you won't see him. It's the closing tournament and of course they didn't want to miss it. Come in. I'll take you up to Kathleen's room, Miss Jones, and you can tidy your hair there. You'll find the bathroom on the same floor. The meal is all ready and only needs serving."

By the time she was halfway through the first course of her lunch, Penelope was very much aware that her hostess was an extremely proud and austere woman and that her pride lay in her Highland heritage. Her home was immaculately kept and every piece of the furniture, some of it antique, was highly polished. The meal was perfect in every way, excellently cooked and properly presented, with all the right cutlery. It was served in a gracious dining room whose window overlooked Culloden Moor, the old battlefield where the way of the life of the Highland clans had died in a savage fight. Knowing that her own table manners and her whole behavior were being assessed by those sharp, amber-colored eyes, Penelope could not help thinking of the meal she had taken in the dining room at

Torvaig House on the night of her arrival there and contrasting its casualness with the formality of this meal. No wonder Helen Drummond disapproved of her cousin's way of doing everything. His casual attitude to meals and his disregard for etiquette must have irritated her greatly.

Politely, but insistently, Mrs. Drummond questioned Penelope about her upbringing and her previous job. Penelope answered her coolly and honestly because she had nothing in her past to be ashamed of. She thought she detected a softening in the other woman's face when she mentioned that her grandmother had been born on Torvaig.

"Then you have a wee drop of Highland blood in your veins, Miss Jones. I'm glad to hear that," she said with a faint smile.

"More than a little is my guess," said Hugh, with a wink in Penelope's direction. "Ian says Penelope is a true Gael because she has one foot in the past and one in the present, just like you."

Although Mrs. Drummond raised her shapely eyebrows in mild surprise at her son's use of the nanny's first name, she seemed satisfied by Penelope's credentials and behavior and turned to the subject that was obviously uppermost in her mind.

"Why didn't Kathleen come with you? I wanted to talk to her."

Hugh ate several mouthfuls of roast Aberdeen Angus beef before he replied carefully, "She and Ian are very busy. They are going to hold an exhibition of their work in London in December, thanks to Tearlach."

"Why thanks to him?" asked Mrs. Drummond.

"He found a buyer for their stuff and is also financing the exhibition. Kathleen came on the cruise with us, but I

486

tell you, Mother, you'll have to do something about her. Either write to her, telling her she must come here for some reason, or go to Torvaig yourself and bring her back here."

Mrs. Drummond's stiff facade cracked and for a moment she looked thoroughly bewildered.

"I don't mind writing and I'd like to see her, but I'm not going to Torvaig unless Charles invites me, and after our last meeting I don't think he'll be doing that for a long time," she said with a touch of outraged sensibility.

"Ach, he isn't like that, Mother. He doesn't bear grudges. He says what he thinks, then it's over and he's ready to be friendly again."

"Well, I'm not like that," said Mrs. Drummond haughtily. "I shall never forget the fun he made of all the things I hold dear, the traditions of the Gunn family, handed down through the generations, things I've tried to preserve because there was no one else to do so."

"He was only trying to point out that the preservation of those traditions hadn't done him or Avis much good. His father may have been a gentleman like all the other lairds of Torvaig, but that didn't prevent him from not caring a hang for his wife or his children," argued Hugh. Then noticing the stiffening of his mother's face, he changed his attitude. "But I'm not here to defend Tearlach. He can do that better for himself. I'm here to tell you that your dear daughter is in danger of making a fool of herself by throwing herself at him. And I think that as her mother, you should do something about it."

"I shall do nothing of the sort. Kathleen is a grown woman with a mind of her own. She wouldn't like any interference. I don't like Charles, I admit, but if she can get him to marry her, I shall do nothing to stop the marriage from taking place," said Helen Drummond firmly, and her eyes gleamed between narrowed lids reminding Penelope suddenly of Tearlach Gunn. "And I hope to see my grandchildren bearing the name Gunn and inheriting the island of Torvaig."

"Mother, Mother, come out of your tartan twilight," laughed Hugh. "The days of arranged marriages between members of the same clan to keep property in the family are over. This is the second half of the twentieth century and to get what they want from each other neither Kathleen nor Tearlach have to marry. There's a distinct possibility that she'll become his mistress. How do you like that?"

This time Mrs. Drummond's expression was one of distaste.

"Really, Hugh, do you have to be so crude? It must come of associating too much with Charles," she complained.

"I'm not being crude. I'm being frank, as my generation always is about such matters. On the cruise I had the opportunity of watching them at close quarters. Give Tearlach his due, he kept his distance, but the more he plays hard to get the more fascinated and infatuated Kath is becoming. She's at a vulnerable age, Mother, and is just ripe for the picking."

"Hugh," remonstrated Mrs. Drummond, "must we discuss this in such an offensive way in front of Miss Jones? I can scarcely think she is interested in our family affairs." Then turning to Penelope, she said with a faint smile, "Let me take your plate. There's pie and fresh cream for dessert. Apples, blackberries and plums all cooked together and placed in the same crust. I hope you like it?"

Penelope said she did and offered to help to carry the dishes out to the kitchen, but her offer was refused politely yet abruptly, reminding her of the way Tearlach had refused her help when they had been leaving Mallaig in the yacht. In some ways Mrs. Drummond was like him. Both had strong aggressive personalities, but they had grown up in different worlds. The same metal was in both of them, but the manner of forging had been different. She wished suddenly she could see them together, and said so to Hugh.

He shook his head, and said quite seriously, "You wouldn't like it. Ever heard of blood antagonism? Well, it's there between them. She dislikes him because he's the head of the Gunn family and owns Gunn property, and she doesn't think he's fit to do so. He dislikes her because she wants to preserve all that he hates about the Gunns. You know, she doesn't believe a word I've told her about the possibility of Kath becoming his mistress rather than his wife. She can't accept that a daughter of hers could be so lacking in moral fiber. Talk about a generation gap! I can see it widening every minute. You've seen Kath and Tearlach together. You must have noticed the calculating way he looks at her sometimes."

"Yes, I have," said Penelope.

"Then you can tell Mother and back me up," he suggested.

"Oh, I couldn't," she objected. "I couldn't tell tales about my employer. That's what Miss Swan did, even going so far as to make up some tales. Once he learned I'd done that he'd sack me on the spot."

"Ach, I was forgetting your precarious position. But what am I going to do about Kath?" groaned Hugh.

"Why should you do anything? As your mother says, she's an adult and it's her life."

"I know. If she was dealing with anyone other than

Tearlach, I wouldn't worry. I'm afraid she'll do something desperate."

No more was said on the matter because Mrs. Drummond returned to the room to serve the dessert and for the rest of the meal the conversation was mostly about local activities, including news about Hugh's own nieces and nephew, the children of his elder brother, Neil.

Penelope showed such an interest in Culloden that after the meal was over Mrs. Drummond invited her to go for a walk to the moor, while Hugh called on some friends. The moorland, once bleak and wild, was now broken up into fields brilliant with harvest color and patches of neatly planted forest.

Together they stood beside the stone cairn built as a modest memorial to the violent battle, and Mrs. Drummond pointed out the long low mounds in the earth that marked where the bodies of those killed had been buried long ago. Each mound had a headstone bearing the name of the clan buried there and, to Penelope's surprise, Mrs. Drummond placed a small posy of autumn flowers she had brought from her garden on the mound below the rough stone engraved with the name of Drummond.

"There is no record of any Gunns being at Culloden, so I remember the battle by placing the flowers on the mound where members of my husband's clan were buried," she explained to Penelope, and by that single gesture showed more clearly than ever her attachment to the past of the Highlands.

When she told Hugh about his mother placing the flowers on the old grave, he sighed heavily.

"She is one of those who thinks the Highland sun set at Culloden field. She looks back too much. I mean, pride in race and culture are all very well, and I share it to a certain extent, but I'm also aware that you can't stop the clock. Time goes on without you if you do."

"That's your cousin's philosophy, and also your sister's," said Penelope, recalling her first night at Torvaig House. "Maybe that's why they'll gather rose-buds together."

They did not discuss the subject any more, although it stayed in Penelope's mind to trouble her occasionally during the drive through the mountains back to Torvaig. She found herself recalling vividly the distress on Ian's face when she had told him that Kathleen had gone on the cruise and when he had commented on Kathleen's perpetual presence at Torvaig House recently.

Then, quite unexpectedly, she began to wonder about Tearlach's part in all this. Hugh had said his cousin kept Kathleen at arm's length on the yacht, and later had told his mother that Kathleen was becoming infatuated with Tearlach because he kept his distance from her.

Why did he do that? Was it possible he suspected Kathleen's intentions? Did he see the scheming mother behind the daughter, with her eye on his wealth and on his property, that inheritance Mrs. Drummond regarded as hers? In the light of Mrs. Drummond's approval of her daughter marrying the owner of Torvaig, even though she herself didn't like him, it seemed as if he had every right to be suspicious of Kathleen's advances and to keep her at a distance.

But he was only flesh and blood, after all, and in being tempted to have an affair with her, as Hugh was sure he might be, he could be trapped in an age-old manner and find himself having to marry the lovely woman with whom he had allowed himself to gather rosebuds.

But why should she be worrying about him? The old

lion, as Hugh mockingly called him, was wily and worldly-wise, difficult to deceive. Even so she would not like to see him trapped in a loveless marriage, although on the other hand it might serve him right for being so materialistic in his outlook. From all accounts he had not known much love in his life and so possibly he would not know when it was missing from a relationship.

Deep purple gloaming had descended upon the countryside. Here and there a light twinkled from a solitary house, a reminder that there were people living in the apparent wilderness of rock and moorland through which the remnants of the clans had once traveled, hiding from the red-coated soldiers who had hunted them.

With darkness came heavy cloud. By the time they were skirting Loch Maree, the windshield was filmed with fine rain. At times visibility was nil and Hugh had to drive slowly, along a road that sometimes hung dizzily over precipices that plunged to the loch below.

Aware that time was passing, Penelope began to grow anxious. She knew the ferry left Loraig on the mainland at 11:30 p.m. to take islanders back to Torvaig. It did not return until Monday morning because the strictly religious islanders refused to run it on the day of rest.

"Can't you go any faster?" she asked Hugh. "I must be in by midnight."

"Like Cinderella," he replied with a chuckle. "I'm doing my best. This fine rain is as bad as mist, and I don't want to have an accident like the one that killed Avis and Manuel. If we miss the ferry, we can always spend the night in the back of the van."

"I couldn't possibly do that," retorted Penelope, really worried about being late by now. "I must get back to Torvaig tonight. Imagine what your cousin would say if I spent the night in the van with you!"

"Mm, I get the point. He's suspicious enough of you and me. We'll just have to hope that Roy Dermid, who runs the ferry remembers us and holds it back for us."

His hope was in vain. As the van shot down the final incline toward the Kyle of Torvaig, they could see the lights of the ferry as it sidled across the water. In silence they sat in the van and watched the lights become dimmer and dimmer, and then disappear altogether.

"I must get back somehow," said Penelope desperately. "If I'm not back tonight he'll have every reason for giving me the sack. It'll be a blot I'll not be able to erase."

"I didn't realize you were so afraid of him," said Hugh with a touch of flippancy, as if he couldn't take her plight seriously.

"I'm not. But he did warn me that if I didn't get back by midnight on my days off, there'd be trouble. The least I can do is respect his wishes and remember that he pays my wages, and that when I have time off someone else has to take care of Davy and Isa."

Respect! The word seemed to mock her. She wasn't afraid of Tearlach Gunn, but she respected him and she would always do her utmost to abide by his wishes.

"I'm sorry, Penelope," said Hugh contritely, squeezing her arm in the darkness. "I forgot that it's a question of your bread and butter. Let me think. I should be able to borrow a boat. I'll try Fergus Beath. You stay here and keep dry. You're going to get wet enough, crossing the strait."

"I don't mind as long as I can reach Torvaig House before Mr. Gunn realizes I'm late."

Hugh was gone much longer than she expected and by the time he loomed up in the dark beside the van she had given up all hope of them reaching Torvaig before daylight. His grin, when he opened the door and told her to get out, reassured her.

"I've managed to borrow a dinghy. Fergus won't come with us because it's the Sabbath now, so I'll have to bring the boat back on Monday. I've launched it and it's tied up at the end of the ferry pier here," he explained, as they made their way along the pier in the fine seeping rain.

Penelope stepped down into the swaying dinghy after him and sat down in the bow as he had told her to do. The thwart she sat on was cold and wet and she could feel the damp penetrating her thin skirt. Shivering a little with apprehension, she stared out into the murky night and hoped that Hugh knew what he was doing.

Once the outboard engine had started and the boat was thrusting its way through the inky water, conversation became impossible. Screwing up her eyes, Penelope tried to see ahead, but all she could make out was the flat oily water immediately in front of the bow. Several times she thought she saw the dark sinister shape of a rock looming up and she turned to yell at Hugh, but the shape was only a hallucination after all.

They seemed to have been going for about half an hour when the outboard engine suddenly stopped. The silence was dreadful, accentuated by the lazy lap of water against the dinghy's sides and the pat-pat of raindrops on the calm water. Twice Hugh tried to start the engine, pulling vigorously on the cord while the little boat began to turn at the mercy of the current.

"It's no use. I daren't waste any more time trying to start it," he panted. "We'll lose our sense of direction if I do. Can you see any light at all?"

He was getting out the oars and fitting them into the oarlocks as he spoke. Penelope peered around her. She could see nothing and said so.

"Well, we'll just have to chance it," he muttered, and sitting on the middle thwart, he began to row.

After another half hour Penelope thought she could see light glimmering faintly.

"Let's hope it's the end of Torvaig pier," said Hugh breathlessly as he rested for a moment. "The engine should be cool by now. Do you think you could row while I start it?"

Although she had never rowed a boat in her life Penelope could hardly refuse now, when her return to Torvaig depended upon her doing so. The oars felt very heavy and had a disconcerting way of not going in the direction she wanted them to go. After several false starts she managed to get them into the water at the same time, but she had a tendency to "catch crabs," dipping them in too deeply and flinging up spray, which drenched not only herself but Hugh as well.

At last the engine started and with a sigh of relief she slumped on her seat and pulled the oars inboard. Once more the dinghy bounced through the water, and within another 15 minutes they could make out the shape of the ferry boat, which was docked at the end of the pier, white and ghostly, beneath the single light glowing there.

The engine stopped again, but they had sufficient momentum to reach the beach. Hugh leaped ashore and pulled the bow up so that Penelope was at least able to step onto dry land, where she stood shivering and wet. Then Hugh pulled the boat up farther for safety.

"Now to find someone who will lend us a vehicle to take us to Torvaig House," muttered Hugh as they walked up to the road. Not a light showed from any of the houses. It was very early Sunday morning and everyone was asleep.

"Unless," added Hugh, hopefully, as they trudged

along, "you'd let me call up Mrs. Guthrie and ask for someone to come and fetch us."

"Oh, no, don't do that. I'd like to be able to get into the house without anyone knowing I'm late," said Penelope.

"You've got a hope," he remarked ironically. "If only Ian had a phone, we could ask him." He snapped his fingers suddenly. "I know, we'll ask the Griersons to lend us their bicycles. They're a young couple and not as stuffy as some of the older islanders, so they won't mind if we wake them up."

When Jimmy Grierson heard Hugh's story he was so amused that he woke his wife Jean so that she could share in the laughter. They agreed to lend their bicycles and Jean wanted them to stay and have a hot drink before they set off. But Penelope was so horrified when she saw that it was two o'clock in the morning that she declined for herself and Hugh, regretfully.

Riding in the dark along the winding road wasn't easy. The connection on the lamp on the bicycle Penelope was riding wasn't very good and the light kept going out. This meant that she had to depend on the light from the lamp on Hugh's bike, and she had to pedal hard to keep up with him. It was some years since she had ridden, so she tended to wobble all over the road, and when they reached a hill the muscles in the backs of her legs ached.

On the other side of the ridge it was all downhill and they were able to coast. Hugh was finding the whole adventure amusing, and he put his feet up on the handlebars and let out a series of bloodcurdling Highland yells, which split the silence of the wet night, startling the sheep on the hillside and disturbing sleepy birds.

Penelope, who by now was thoroughly irritated with him, managed to persuade him not to come with her to the house, feeling that she could approach it quietly without his help. She left the bicycle under some bushes. Lights were still on in the house, but that was not unusual when the laird was at home because he often left them on all night, forgetting to switch them off when he went to bed.

To her relief the side door was still unlocked and she crept in and along the passage to the back staircase. A light was on there too, and afterward, when she had time to think about it, she realized that the light and the smell of tobacco should have warned her. But at the time she was so eager to reach her room and go to bed that she did not pause.

Her wet shoes squelched as she walked up the stairs and she could not stop shivering. In fact she felt quite faint with hunger and weariness. She reached the pale green door of her room, opened it and looked straight across the room into the narrowed gleaming eyes of Tearlach Gunn.

CHAPTER FIVE

When Penelope saw her employer lounging in one of the armchairs in her room, his feet resting on the coffee table, dismay knocked all the breath out of her and she sank back against the door.

"Oh!" she gasped weakly, as dismay was succeeded by a haze of faintness.

He flung down the book he had been reading, stubbed out his cheroot in the ashtray, stood up and came over to her.

"I ought to give you hell," he said softly and succinctly.

The viciousness of his attack flashed like a shining blade of a sword through the haze, alerting her, bringing everything back into sharp focus again.

"Why? What's happened? Why are you here in my room?" she challenged.

He placed his hands on his hips and leaned nearer. She cringed back against the door, away from the flare of anger in his eyes.

"I'm here because Isa woke up just after midnight and wanted the potty. I'm here because that woke Davy and he cried because *you* weren't here. It took me an hour to settle him. I'm here, Miss Jones, because you have not been here. I've been doing your job for you," he hissed savagely.

"But I thought Mrs. Guthrie was looking after them?"

"At midnight Mrs. Guthrie came to tell me you were not back and to ask me what she should do. I told her to go to bed and I would wait for you and listen for the children in case one of them woke up. I've been waiting for three hours. The arrangement was for you to have every other Saturday off until midnight, I believe. Correct?" he asked with suspicious calm.

"Yes," she agreed miserably.

"Then perhaps you'll explain why you're late," he said. "I know that you don't think it necessary to account to me for what you do with your time off, but I think that when that time off encroaches on my time I can demand an explanation."

The sarcasm in his voice flayed her. She was tired and wet, and still a little shocked at finding him there.

"We missed the ferry," she replied feebly.

"Who are 'we'?"

"Hugh and I. He took me to Inverness."

"Why?" It was rapped out and her head reared up in reaction to the autocratic tone.

"He thought I might like to see something of the Highlands and meet his mother. After all, she is responsible for me being here."

"So she is, blast her," he said between clenched teeth. "She's responsible for a lot more too. What time did you leave Inverness?"

"About seven-thirty."

"Of all the irresponsible, stupid. . . ." She guessed he was going to say something rude about Hugh, but he changed his mind. "He must have known he was cutting it fine," he went on. "The last part of the road is hell on a wet night. If you missed the ferry, how did you get here?"

Fighting off the waves of faintness that were trying to engulf her, bracing herself against the door, she explained in a dull voice what had happened.

When she came to the part of the dinghy's engine stopping, he broke in to sneer, "A likely story!"

That did it. All her resolutions not to let him rouse her

temper faded away. She flung back her head and flared at him, "It's true! You can ask Hugh."

"And how did you get to the house?" he queried.

"We borrowed bicycles from the Griersons in the village."

His eyebrows went up and his glance flickered over her wet hair, soaking clothing, down to her wet shoes, as if he'd only just noticed the state she was in. His glance came back to her face, his expression softening slightly.

"Has it occurred to you that your probationary period is almost over?" he asked.

Penelope nodded, feeling her heart sinking.

"I suppose that's why you made an effort to return to the house before midnight? You hoped to get in unseen so that no one would know you'd stayed out after midnight," he suggested softly.

Again she nodded dumbly in agreement. Her feet felt icy and she longed for a hot bath.

"What's happened to that quick tongue of yours, Miss Jones?" he taunted. "Lost it?"

"Mr. Gunn, I'm tired and wet and I'd be very grateful if we could postpone this discussion about whether I'm to stay in your employ until tomorrow. I'm sorry I was late tonight. I did my best to get back in time," she replied, making an effort to appear calm and collected.

"There's really no reason for any discussion," he said curtly. "I could sack you now."

Still braced against the door, Penelope searched frantically in her mind for a suitable retort.

"And save yourself the trouble of having to eat humble pie and take back what you said to me at our first meeting," she sniped. To her annoyance he laughed quite easily.

"So you remember that first meeting, do you? Quite a

collision, wasn't it?" he said. "Yes, I could sack you now to avoid eating humble pie, but I'm not going to, because I have something in mind for Davy and Isa that might take a few weeks to come to fruition. It hardly seems worthwhile to sack you and find a new nanny for the short time they'll be remaining here."

Her amazement at this announcement had the effect of making Penelope forget her own plight temporarily.

"Oh, you're not going to send them away?" she exclaimed.

"My intentions concerning them are merely a few thoughts at the back of my mind and are dependent upon the attitude of other people," he replied coolly. "Meanwhile, I'd like to take this opportunity of complimenting you on your handling of them. I admit that when I first saw you I didn't think you were any more capable of dealing with them than Miss Swan was. Added to that your youth created a few complications that we seem to have overcome by having the Guthries live in." He paused, and then smiled. "There, that's quite a big piece of humble pie for a not very humble person like myself to eat. Are you satisfied?"

Penelope was never sure what happened next. She was aware of a sensation of relief because he was not going to fire her, which was followed by another feeling of faintness. She remembered thinking that Tearlach Gunn could be very charming when he chose to be and that his smile was enough to make any woman feel faint. Then she was hazily aware that she was being carried to the divan and being placed on it carefully with her head on one of the cushions. Blearily she stared up at him as he leaned over her, an anxious frown between his eyebrows.

"What happened?" she whispered, and in one of those alarming flashbacks she had the impression that he had leaned over her like this once before, only then the room had been lit by flaming torches that cast shadows on the stone walls.

"You fainted," he said tersely, and sitting down on the side of the divan began to remove her soggy shoes. "I'd like to know what Hugh has been up to tonight to let you get into such a state. I thought I'd warned you about him. He's wholly irresponsible and thoughtless about other people. He's been spoiled by his mother."

"He hasn't been up to anything, and I can't agree with you. He isn't entirely thoughtless. He's very worried about his sister."

He gave her a narrowed sidelong glance, but made no comment as he removed the second shoe.

"Anyway, it's your fault I fainted," she continued fretfully. "You kept me standing about when I was wet, cold and hungry."

"You can blame me if it makes you feel any better. My shoulders are broad," he said equably as he placed her shoes on the floor. "Can you sit up?"

"Yes, of course I can," she said with a flash of independence. She sat up and the room whirled around her, and the black gulf of faintness yawned before her again. She felt the divan sink to one side as he sat beside her and put an arm around her shoulders to hold her close.

"Steady," he murmured, and she felt his breath stir her hair. She had a strong desire to stay like that, held against his warm hard body, but his arm slackened and he said impersonally, "Your jacket is soaking wet. Let me help you get it off."

When that was done he touched her blouse, which was also damp. Beneath the thin stuff her skin seemed to burn in reaction to the feel of his fingers.

"This is wet too. Off with it," he ordered brusquely.

Alarm that he might help her to take off the blouse and then proceed to help her take off the rest of her damp clothing cured Penelope temporarily of the faint feeling.

"I can manage, thank you, Mr. Gunn, if only you'll leave the room," she said coldly.

"Very well, I'll go and warm up some soup for you while you have a bath and change. If you feel faint again just yell and I'll come and help you," he offered casually, as if he was accustomed to helping women who had fainted in his company.

He left the room, closing the door behind him, and she heard him crossing the passage to the kitchenette. Her heart beat frantically as she removed her torn stockings, then slipped out of the rest of her clothing. She pretended that the sudden increase in the number of her heartbeats was due to having to move about so soon after fainting, but she feared that wasn't true. Whether she liked it or not, physical contact with Tearlach Gunn had set up a longing within her for more contact, and as she lolled in the warm fragrant bath water, she found herself wishing that she had been conscious when he had carried her to the bed.

She shook her head. What was the matter with her? This crazy light-headed feeling could only be due to lack of food. The sooner she had eaten something and was in bed asleep the better for her. Yet it was pleasant to linger, knowing that someone was finding something for her to eat. He had said he ought to have given her hell for being late, but he hadn't. Oh, he had been brusque and rude, but he hadn't been really angry, and he'd ended up eating humble pie in such a charming manner that all her original antipathy had gone, leaving her with this decidedly odd feeling of wanting to be close to him, to feel his arms around her, his mouth on hers.

The thought shocked her so much that she was up and out of the bath almost before she had realized she had moved. She stood shaking, fighting off the waves of faintness, struggling hard not to give in to the temptation to yell, as Tearlach had told her to do if she felt faint again.

She must be smitten with the same fever as Kathleen Drummond! Hugh had said that his cousin had a way of attracting women without making any effort, and she had thought herself immune!

A loud rap on the door stampeded her into action. She grabbed a towel and draped it around her. She hadn't locked the door and she half expected him to walk in uninvited.

"Are you all right?" he called.

"Yes, oh yes, I'm fine," she stuttered.

"You've been so long I thought perhaps you'd fainted again," he said, and she found herself turning pink at the thought of what he might say if he'd known she'd been wallowing in the bath romanticizing about him, of all people!

"I'm all right, thank you. I'll be out soon," she called out, then heard his footsteps retreating.

Back in her room she wished quite irrationally that she had something more glamorous to wear than her simple blue pajamas and blue woollen dressing gown, suitable for wearing in the night when attending to crying babies. Then she doused the thought with a shower of common sense. He probably wouldn't be interested enough to notice what she was wearing.

Entering the kitchenette, from which came the tantalizing aroma of hot soup, she went to the table and sat down in one of the chairs quickly as grogginess threatened once more to overwhelm her. Tearlach heard her and turned to look at her searchingly.

So much for thinking that he wouldn't notice what she was wearing, she thought, as she braved his narrowed gaze, which took in everything from her tousled dark hair to her serviceable leather slippers.

"This soup smells very good. I think I'll join you in your early morning feast," he murmured. He crossed to the table with two bowls of steaming soup, set them down and sat opposite to her.

She had never known a simple meal of canned soup and toast to taste so good, and she wondered whether her taste was affected by the company she was keeping at that hour. At no time in her life had she shared a meal with a man in the small hours of the morning.

Across from her sat the one who had prepared the meal and who had very recently helped her when she had fainted. In his own way he had been kind and surprisingly gentle. Having had to cope for so long by herself with the few illnesses she had known she appreciated his help. Yet for the past month she had been regarding him as a heartless ruffian incapable of a kind thought, let alone a kind deed. How different he appeared under the present circumstances!

He had finished his soup and was leaning back in his chair seemingly lost in thought. Looking at him, Penelope noticed for the first time that there was humor as well as shrewdness and cynicism in the lines around his mouth and eyes. There was also confidence and strength in his face, and those who are confident and strong can afford to be gentle, she thought.

He looked up suddenly, smiled and said, "Do you feel any better?"

"Yes, thank you. Much better."

"Good. Then perhaps you won't mind if I go back to what I was saying before you fainted," he continued in businesslike tones. "You seem to go over with Davy and Isa and can cope with them satisfactorily. I'd like you to stay on here until their future is settled. Will you do that?"

At this point in time when he looked at her like that she was willing to do anything he asked, thought Penelope dreamily. Anything!

"Yes, of course," she murmured.

"Even though it will mean you'll probably be looking for another job in another household around the end of November?" he queried, casting her a shrewd glance.

She did not like the sharp pang of disappointment that stabbed through her at the thought of having to leave Torvaig so soon, but she covered it up by saying coolly, "Changing jobs is something nannies always have to keep in mind. May I ask what you intend to do with the children?"

"I think you are aware that their father was not British," he said.

"Miss Swan told me that."

"My sister met Manuel when he was attached to the Spanish Embassy in London. She had gone to London to work, and they met at a party. When they decided to marry apparently his family were horrified. She was not considered good enough for him. In spite of their objections, Manuel went ahead and married her, and his father refused to have anything more to do with him."

"How mean of him," murmured Penelope hotly, her eyes sparkling with her dislike of such injustice. "Have you met him?"

"Yes. He came to Manuel's funeral after the crash, but was unable to stay and see the children. Since then I've been in touch with Senora Usted, their grandmother. It seems that she's coming to Britain in a few days' time on her way back from South America. She's traveling with her daughter. I've invited them to come to Torvaig to see Davy and Isa. They should be here by the end of October."

"If they couldn't come when your sister and her husband were alive, how is it they can come now?" demanded Penelope. "They seem very hypocritical to me."

His mouth twisted wryly in appreciation of her remark.

"Let me explain their attitude a little further. As far as they were concerned my sister was a nobody, a typist in an office, like dozens of other girls in London. The Usteds are a very old family as well as wealthy. Honor and pride of family count for everything with them," he said.

"As they do with some Highlanders," commented Penelope, thinking of Helen Drummond.

He grinned at her.

"Now I know you've met Helen," he said. "Anyway, it seems that the Usteds are much more disposed to accept an invitation from Avis's brother, who happens to be the owner of an island in Scotland and is apparently descended from Highland chieftains, and who at the same time holds considerable shares in a certain oil company in Venezuela in which Senor Usted is also involved. Money talks, Miss Jones," he added cynically.

"I'm beginning to realize that. But what has this to do with Davy and Isa?"

"Reading between the lines of the letters I've received from Senora Usted, I have the impression that she was very fond of her elder son and would like to have the upbringing of his children in her hands."

"Will you let her take them to Spain?"

"If I'm satisfied that they'll be well treated and will be given a good home, I shall."

"But you promised your sister that you'd take care of them," objected Penelope.

He looked suddenly very troubled, the lines etched on his face deepening as he rubbed his hand across his forehead, pushing the hair from it. In Hugh the same gesture was boyish, attractive. In Tearlach it was one of weariness of spirit, and it touched Penelope's heart in a way that didn't happen when she saw Hugh do it.

"I know. She didn't know what she was doing. She hardly knew me," he muttered. "I suppose she thought she was doing the best she could for them." He glanced up at her suddenly, his eyes wide and for the first time she saw that they were blue, dark blue. "I can see you don't approve of what I intend to do," he accused harshly.

She straightened in her chair.

"It isn't my place to approve or disapprove of what you wish to do," she said stiffly.

He banged the table with the flat of his hand.

"Come off it, Miss Jones. You've disapproved of me ever since we met because of my materialistic outlook on life, and you haven't hesitated to tell me so. I thought you'd be delighted to think that Davy and Isa might find a home with someone who can give them all the love they're lacking here."

"Would that be your only reason for letting them go to Spain?" she asked.

"What other reason could there be?"

"I thought perhaps that you were considering marriage and that the children would be an inconvenient encumbrance to you and your future wife," she replied.

His face stiffened and his eyes narrowed to those dangerous gleaming slits that always made chills run up and down her spine.

"A good try," he jeered. "Who put you up to it, Helen or Hugh?"

He must think she was prying on behalf of his cousins to find out if he was going to marry Kathleen. Indignation that he should think that brought Penelope to her feet.

"No one did," she snapped at him.

"Then you should remember that whether I intend to marry or not is my affair at the moment and no one else's," he rapped back. "I've discussed the matter of the children's future with you, because as you're employed as their nanny, it naturally involves you. I'd be obliged if you don't mention the possibility of Senora Usted's visit until I'm sure she is coming. As soon as harvesting is over, I shall go down to London to meet her and the senorita and escort them back here if necessary."

Still quivering from the reprimand he had delivered, Penelope bent her head and looked at her hands.

"Yes, Mr. Gunn," she muttered.

He stood up and came over to her. To her surprise he put a hand under her chin and forced her to look up at him.

"I know you look very pretty when you are being meek, but I also realize that it's a pose as unnatural to you as being humble is to me," he scoffed. "I think I prefer you when your cheeks are on fire, your eyes are flashing blue sparks and your tongue is spitting flame at me."

"Oh, you are the most—" she began, and got no further, for his hand moved upward and clamped on her mouth. Over it she glared up into eyes that were suddenly brimful of laughter.

"I agree with you entirely," he said, "but calling me names isn't going to change me. Now, can you make it to bed under your own steam or would you like me to carry you there again?"

Using all her strength, Penelope wrenched free of his

restricting hand, gave him one more glare and then fled from the kitchenette, through the sitting room to the bedroom, and banged the door closed. Her heart thumping loudly, she waited. Nothing happened. He didn't follow her, and as her heartbeats slowed down, she wondered why she had thought that he would.

She heard the door of the kitchenette closing and then the creak of a board on the landing as he went past to the stairs. Only then did she untie the belt of her dressing gown, fling it off and climb gratefully between the cool sheets of the bed to fall asleep almost instantly, exhausted by her nocturnal adventures.

Three weeks later Penelope stood on the headland looking down into the bay. It was empty. No big yawl swung at its mooring on the periwinkle blue of the water. It had gone to the mainland, taken at the beginning of October by Tearlach and Hugh to be laid up in its winter quarters. Even the red buoy had gone.

She sighed a little before turning away to continue her walk across the headland to Cladach. The big house was also empty again. Oh, the children and the Guthries and she were still there, but the laird was away, gone about his business in the city. He had been absent almost a week now and when he returned at the beginning of November he would bring Senora Usted and her daughter with him.

And from the moment of their arrival Penelope's days on Torvaig would be numbered. This recurring thought distressed her far more than it should, because since the night of her return from Inverness she had awakened every morning with a wonderful feeling of contentment. Her period of probation over, she felt settled in the big house on the island of her dreams, close to the place where her grandmother had been born.

She had felt particularly secure while the owner of the

island had been there. She could see him going about the estate consulting with various workers, helping with the harvesting on the home farm and occasionally coming to talk to her and the children.

But now the harvest was over. All had been safely gathered during a spell of fine weather, and the fields lay shorn under the pale skies and slanted sunlight of October. Tearlach Gunn had left the island and so had Kathleen Drummond.

Ian said that Kathleen had gone to London to see the buyer who had bought all their stock of jewelry and who would be organizing the exhibition of their work in December.

Hugh, however, had a slightly different tale to tell when Penelope had called on him and had found him absorbed in his painting, making an effort to record the images of the past summer.

"She may be seeing the jeweler, but you can guess who else she's seeing," he had growled. "She and Tearlach are probably staying at the same hotel in adjoining rooms."

Penelope hadn't liked what he'd said, so she'd pushed it to the back of her mind. It had an unpleasant way of pushing to the front of her mind on afternoons such as this one, when the sea was a placid lavender color and the distant islands were finely etched against the autumnal sky and the Hebridean tranquility gave rise to feelings of nostalgia and yearning.

Afraid of those feelings, Penelope turned from the view and was soon on the road that curved around the edge of Cladach Bay on her way to Achmore and Ian.

He wasn't in, so she walked up the hill to the grave-yard. As usual it was quiet there. Only the occasional bleat of a hillside sheep or the plaintive cry of a whaup winging slowly over the moorland disturbed the peace.

Once again the past came around her as she peered in at the chapel window. She was the slave wife of the first Magnus Gunn waiting to meet the hermit priest to discuss the best way of converting her heathen Viking husband to Christianity.

The priest wasn't there, but she could see him coming up the lane, brown-haired and bearded, with sandals on his feet.

Penelope blinked rapidly and the priest became Ian, just turning toward his house. Shaking off the past, she hurried down the hill and entered the workshop soon after him.

"I've had another flashback," she said. "Between us we converted Magnus Gunn to Christianity."

He smiled at her, his usual warm welcoming smile, but she noticed that his face was drawn and sad. Beneath his eyes were lines, scored by sleeplessness.

"And that's the way it was," he murmured. "The heathen Norsemen soon adopted the Christian faith of those they had conquered. Some of their festivals were absorbed into the church year, just as some of the Celtic festivals were also adapted to Christianity. In fact we shall soon be celebrating the great Celtic fire-festival held in honor of the sun."

"Which is that?" asked Penelope.

"Hallowe'en, on the last night of October. The fire-festival was always held on the last day of the ancient Celtic year. The new year always began in Scotland with the entry of winter on November first. At dusk the Druids lit great fires of sacred wood on the hilltops and offered up sacrifices, partly as a sort of thanksgiving to the benevolent sun that had ripened the crops, and partly for the purification and protection from the powers of evil during the dark winter months to come."

"What form will the celebration take on Torvaig?"

"I expect there'll be the usual dance and children's parties, ducking for apples and so on. I believe Hugh is concocting something with Molly Lang, but he'll tell you all about that himself," said Ian with a touch of weariness, as if he couldn't be bothered with childish amusements. "Let's go over to the house. I have something we found in the dig to show you. We'll put the kettle on and have a wee *strupach* together. I'm glad to see you. I'm tired of working and just lately the days have been long and wearisome."

"Are you missing Kathleen?" asked Penelope. "Have you heard from her?"

"Yes, I do miss her, and I haven't heard from her; neither has Hugh. Any news of the laird?" he replied, opening the door of the house and gesturing to her to enter.

"No, he won't be back until the first of November," she said. Then, made anxious by the stricken look on Ian's face, she rushed on into the kitchen. "I'll make the tea and you find whatever it is you want to show me."

In the small neat kitchen she busied herself taking out crockery, making far too much noise as she did so, humming to herself and occasionally breaking into song, trying to pretend that Ian did not look unhappy. And all the time in her mind she was talking to Kathleen Drummond, telling her what a fool she was for throwing herself at Tearlach Gunn and saying that Ian McTaggart was worth two of the laird, then contradicting herself and saying no, he wasn't, but he was different.

Ian was gentle, idealistic, a bit of a dreamer, with one foot in the past like herself. He needed someone practical and hardheaded to look after him; to see that he ate the right food at the right time and didn't spend too many hours bending over his silver work. Whereas Tearlach was tough and realistic and didn't need anyone to look after him.

When she went into the living room with the tray, Ian had just come downstairs. He had changed his mud-stained clothes and in his hand he was carrying something wrapped carefully in tissue paper. He put the small parcel down on the table and carefully unwrapped the paper. There, gleaming on the white softness, was a brooch. It was circular in design, and made of gold. A pin made of the same metal, which had a carved head, was attached to the brooch.

"It's beautiful!" exclaimed Penelope.

"It is a superb piece of craftsmanship, a pennanular brooch that would be worn by a man to secure his cloak. The inscription on the back is in Norse," said Ian, turning the brooch over and showing her the markings around the circle.

"What does it say?"

"I think it says 'Magnus owns this brooch,' " he replied. "As soon as Tearlach comes back I'm going to ask his permission to let me take it to a museum in Glasgow to have it verified. The carvings on the front of it I'm sure are Celtic in design, not Nordic, and I think it's another example of the fusion of Celtic and Nordic races and culture, which took place not only in the Highlands and the Hebrides but all over the British Isles in the early part of the ninth century."

As he talked some of the weariness left Ian's face and, noting this, Penelope led him on to talk more about the artifacts he had found.

Outside the sun slipped down behind the dark silhouettes of the Outer Isles, and inside they switched on the lights to disperse the gloom as they talked. Penelope made a simple meal and later Ian walked part of the way back with her in the cool October night, which held just a hint of frost.

They came to the other side of the headland and paused to look down at the dark water of the bay in which the sickle of the new moon was admiring its own reflection.

"When the moon is full it will be Hallowe'en," said Ian with a sigh. "The year is going fast, and I had intended to do so much before it ended."

"Such as?" prompted Penelope.

"Such as asking Kathleen to marry me," was the surprising reply. "I hoped that once success came my way I'd be in a position to ask her. Success, to a certain extent, has come. I have more orders for jewelry than I can cope with, but Kathleen seems to be lost to me," said mournfully.

"She's only in London," replied Penelope.

"And probably with Tearlach," he said heavily. "I can't bear to think what he'll do to her, not deliberately because I don't think he's a cruel person, but unwittingly because, being invulnerable himself, he does not understand how easily others can be hurt."

"Why don't you go to London too?" urged Penelope. "After all, you have a perfectly good excuse for going. You could say you wanted to know what was happening about the exhibition."

He turned to her and to her surprise touched her gently on the cheek.

"You are kind, and sensible too, and I value your friendship. This afternoon I was as low-spirited as a man can be and you came, to sing in my kitchen, make my tea and laugh me out of my misery. It's no wonder children love you. I would go to London, but I hate big cities and

I'm afraid of what I might find there. It's better if I stay here and wait. One day Kathleen will have need of a friend and she'll remember and come back to me."

Penelope was about to remonstrate with him, but he touched her cheek again and said, "No, don't tell me I should have more courage and should be prepared to go out and fight for my love. I'm not a knight in armor ready to go and slay dragons. I can only sit and wait. Good night, Penelope. Come and have tea with me again."

The autumn days drifted by. Life went on quietly. Davy and Isa helped Penelope to rake leaves from the lawn and then played in the heaps they had made or helped Alec Guthrie to plant bulbs for the next year's show of spring flowers.

No word came from the laird and no word from Kathleen, as Penelope discovered one day when Hugh turned up to see her. He was sent upstairs by Mrs. Guthrie to the bedsitting room, where it often seemed to her the smell of cheroot smoke still lingered and a small slender book on sailing lay on the coffee table waiting to be returned to its owner.

"I'd no idea you were so well done to," said Hugh, looking around with a grin before he collapsed into an armchair. "It certainly pays to be a nanny these days," he added, reaching out and picking up the book from the table. He glanced at the title, flicked open the cover and stared. Knowing what was written there, Penelope watched him and held her breath.

He whistled softly, cocked an eyebrow at her and read the written words with a questioning lilt in his voice.

"Charles Gunn, eh?"

She met his slightly mocking gaze squarely.

"He left it the last time he was up here," she said coolly.

"And when was that?"

"The night we missed the ferry."

"You mean he was waiting here for you at three o'clock in the morning?" He sounded incredulous as he placed the book back on the table.

To her intense irritation Penelope's memory, over which she seemed to have no control, winged back to the time she had returned to her room, tired, wet and hungry, and had fainted into her employer's arms, and a tide of pink color washed over her face. It was noted by Hugh's mocking eyes.

"I thought you'd managed to get in without being seen and that was why you didn't get the sack," he murmured. "I wonder what it is that Tearlach has that makes such a big impression on women? He hasn't always been pleasant to you, yet the mere thought of him has made you blush and his presence in London has kept my sister Kathleen down there long after she should have finished her business."

"Have you heard from her?" asked Penelope, refusing to let his reference to her blush embarrass her.

"No. Neither has my mother, although of course she isn't at all worried. She thinks her little plan to get her own back on Tearlach for coming back after all those years and claiming what she thought should be hers may work yet, and her daughter might become mistress of Torvaig!"

Penelope moved restlessly about the room, startled by his reference to a definite plan on Mrs. Drummond's part. She did not like to think that Tearlach Gunn might fall a victim to his older cousin's machinations.

"Any news of when Tearlach might return? It would

give me some idea of Kath's movements," asked Hugh casually.

"The first of November."

"Good. Then that means we mice can have another play," he said with a chuckle. "Are you going to come to the Hallowe'en dance in the village hall?"

"How can I? It's on a Friday and you know my time off is on Wednesdays and Saturdays."

"You could swap one Wednesday for a Friday, I'm sure. Mrs. Guthrie would oblige. Will you ask her? It's going to be fun. Molly Lang and I have been thinking that some of us might dress up as witches or ghosts, like we used to do as children, and call on people all over the island before we go on to the dance. At each house we'll sing a song or recite a poem."

"Sounds like fun," said Penelope. "I'd like to come."

"Then be at Molly's house on Wednesday night. We're all going to meet there to make plans."

Penelope did as he had suggested, going first to Ian's house to watch him working in his workshop and then to have tea with him. He didn't mention Kathleen once, and she thought he seemed much more relaxed than the last time she had visited him. She was quite surprised when he told her he was going to the dance and would be taking part in Hugh's and Molly's plans.

They went together to the Langs' house and it wasn't long before the meeting to discuss costumes and masks had turned into a *ceilidh*. Hugh suggested songs and played them on his guitar and they all sang. Disguises presented no problems because the men were all going as ghosts, wearing old sheets, and the women as witches in black paper hats and cloaks. Masks were to be made by the women.

While she was at Molly's house Penelope received an

invitation for Davy and Isa to a children's party that Aileen Guthrie was organizing for little ones on the afternoon of Hallowe'en.

When the last day of October came it was damp and mild, the sea flat and gray, stretching away to a faint horizon. Davy and Isa enjoyed the party at the home farm and Penelope had no trouble in settling them for the night as both children were worn out by their activities.

Penelope had not been to many dances in her life. This was the first time she had ever been sure of having a partner. Ian would be there to escort her and to show her how to do the intricate Scottish dances, so it was with a flutter of excitement that she dressing in a long blue and white patterned skirt, which she teamed with a white lace blouse. The blouse had a low neckline gathered with a drawstring which tied in a bow between her breasts. Over this outfit she wore a short coat and then the black witch's cloak.

Hugh was late coming for her and she was sitting in the kitchen wearing the high black hat on her head and holding the white and red witch's mask, talking to Mrs. Guthrie, when they heard footsteps coming along the passage from the direction of the front hall.

"It must be the laird," exclaimed Mrs. Guthrie, rising to her feet. "He's returned earlier than I expected." She went to the door, opened it and called out, "Is it yourself, Mr. Gunn?"

"It is," came the answer, and Tearlach appeared in the doorway. Above the black high-necked sweater he was wearing under his black and white tweed jacket his face was pale and slightly drawn, and he frowned against the bright lights of the kitchen.

As he saw the small dark form crowned by a tall black

hat holding a hideous mask in front of its face, his eyes narrowed suspiciously.

"Who's that?" he demanded of Mrs. Guthrie.

"A wee witch who dropped in on her way to the Hallowe'en dance being held in the village hall tonight," replied the housekeeper, her eyes twinkling with mischief behind their glasses.

"And how is she going there? By broomstick?" queried Tearlach dryly. He crossed the room and lifted the high hat off Penelope's head.

"I thought so," he murmured, as she looked up at him, her blue eyes wide, her cheeks a dusky pink and her heart knocking against her ribs in reaction to this unexpected encounter.

"I changed my day off so that I could go to the dance," she said defensively.

The smile that always began in his eyes widened his mouth and he dropped the hat back on her head.

"You're going with Hugh, I suppose," he said.

"And Ian and the Langs and the Griersons," she said hurriedly, not wanting him to think she was going alone with Hugh. Quickly she explained what they were going to do. Hands in his pockets, his head slightly bent so that his blond-streaked hair fell forward onto his forehead, he watched her expressive face and listened. When she had finished talking it seemed to her that he looked rather wistful, almost envious, as if he would have liked to have been participating in the evening's fun and merriment.

With a sudden impulsive wish to erase that expression from his face, she said urgently, "Please come to the dance."

For a moment, there in the kitchen, which Mrs. Guthrie had left, they looked at each other as equals. She was no longer his employee. She was a young woman going to a dance and he was the man she had invited to go with her. The differences that had always existed between them created by age, outlook and background were as nothing. Their minds met and were briefly united.

Then the horn of a motor vehicle sounded brashly outside. Mrs. Guthrie bustled into the kitchen to announce Hugh's arrival and the moment of brief union was over. A bland shuttered expression came over Tearlach's face and he turned away, said something to Mrs. Guthrie and went quickly from the room.

The horn sounded again, Penelope grabbed her broom and her mask, and hurried down the passage to the side door, wishing with all her heart that Hugh hadn't come just then and that she wasn't going to the dance with him and the others.

Outside the night air was cold and damp and a hazy moon was peering down out of a black sky. As soon as she was settled in the van beside Hugh, Penelope sensed there was something wrong.

"Where's Ian?" she asked.

"He isn't coming."

"Why?"

"Kathleen came back on Wednesday evening. I tried to persuade her to come with us tonight, but she dismissed the whole idea as childish and wouldn't come. I didn't want to leave her alone, so Ian said he'd stay with her."

Penelope was silent, looking out at the dark shapes of the land, thinking back to the taut tired paleness of Tearlach's face when he had appeared in the kitchen and wondering what had happened between him and Kathleen in London.

"The laird is back too," she said at last.

"I saw his car," murmured Hugh.

"Did he teach Kathleen a lesson?" she asked diffidently.

"Yes, but not in the way I expected. From what I can make out from her rather sparse comments he didn't take much notice of her. They met only once and that meeting was not very pleasant," said Hugh tersely.

Penelope experienced a strange surge of relief.

"Is Kathleen upset?" she asked.

"I think so. Of course, I can only judge by her behavior. I haven't done anything right in her eyes since she came back, and poor Ian has really been suffering from her sharp comments."

"I'm sorry about that," said Penelope. "I know he was hoping she would need him."

"She does, but she won't admit it. As far as she's concerned, all men are now to be regarded as no good, just because Tearlach showed that he couldn't care less about her. You see, he ignored her because he was far more interested in another woman who was staying in the same hotel."

"Oh." Penelope was so surprised she couldn't think of anything else to say.

Somehow after hearing about Tearlach's treatment of Kathleen and his involvement with another woman, she found it difficult to be as gay as the others as they went from farmhouse to farmhouse and croft to croft, singing their songs and accepting their treats offered to them in the old time-honored way of celebrating Hallowe'en. They reached the village hall soon after ten o'clock, but even though the dance was in full swing, Penelope felt slightly out of the gaiety and she spent many of the dances sitting alone and watching.

She told herself that she would have felt differently if Ian had been there. He would have been her partner. She could hardly expect Hugh to stay with her all the time because she knew that, being a naturally gregarious person and fond of dancing, he would want to dance with every woman present.

The odd feeling that she had sat like this and had waited for someone to arrive once before swept over her suddenly, and she turned to glance in the direction of the main entrance to the hall. With a sense of shock, she saw Tearlach standing near the door talking to some of the young men who worked on the estate. He had changed into Highland dress, which accentuated the blondness of his hair and the freshness of his complexion and drew attention to the strong line of his jaw. While she watched, the Scottish country dance band took the stage again and sounded an introductory chord. The master of ceremonies announced a group of dances, and dancers began to form sets on the floor. Tearlach looked around as though searching for someone. His glance alighted on Penelope, sitting in a corner by herself, and he began to shoulder his way through the crowd toward her.

He stood in front of her, an apologetic expression on his face.

"I don't dance," he said bluntly.

"I can't dance this sort of thing either," she replied.

"Then we'll sit out together and watch," he said, promptly sitting down next to her.

"Why have you come?" she asked.

He gave her a long lingering glance that took in her shining dark hair, faintly flushed face, white-skinned neck and shoulders and the blue bow nestling between her breasts.

"If any other woman had asked that question I would conclude that she wanted me to answer 'Because *you* asked me to come, darling,' " he said, with a touch of mockery. "But because it's you who asks I have to tell you I'm not sure why I came, just as I'm not sure whether you invited me to come or whether you were merely making a suggestion that I should come because it's the sort of thing I should do as laird of Torvaig. As a matter of interest, which was it? An invitation or a suggestion?"

He was no longer pale or tired-looking and seemed full of that vibrant energy she would always associate with him.

"I don't know," she answered a little wildly, confused by his nearness. "It just came out. When I was telling you what we intended to do tonight you looked wistful, as if going out guising on Hallowe'en night and then going to a dance was something you'd always wanted to do and had never been able to do, and suddenly I wanted to share the experience with you."

"As Nanny Jones or as the reincarnated wife of the first laird of Torvaig?" he jibed lightly.

"Oh!" She swung on him to retaliate scornfully, saw the glint in his eyes and recognized it as amusement. "I'm beginning to realize that you needle people deliberately to provoke them into retaliating," she snapped.

He laughed outright.

"And I've a feeling you're beginning to get my measure, Penelope Jones, because you're quite right, I do."

"Then you can't have many friends," she said crossly.

"That's true, I haven't, but those I have seem willing to put up with my needling, as you call it. Tell me, have you enjoyed yourself this evening? Has it been an experience worth sharing? It seemed to me you looked a little forlorn sitting here in the corner all alone," he commented.

He must have been watching her before she had seen him, and she wished that she had been in Hugh's arms, dancing with wild abandon, when he had arrived.

"No, I haven't enjoyed it as much as I had expected," she admitted reluctantly.

"Because Ian isn't here?" he asked shrewdly. He leaned back in his chair and placed his arm along the back of her chair in an effort to be more comfortable on the hard narrow seat.

"Partly. He was to have been my partner," she said.

"Why didn't he come?"

"He wanted to stay with Miss Drummond, instead."

"Why did he want to do that?" he asked, with a lilt of surprise.

"I don't suppose *you've* noticed, but he's in love with her."

"No, I hadn't noticed, because, unlike *you*, I haven't a romantic slant on life and don't go round looking for such behavior. Does Kathleen know he's in love with her?"

"He's never told her, but she should know by now, because he preferred to stay with her tonight to comfort her instead of coming here."

"Why does she need comfort?" He asked the question idly as if he were only half-interested in the conversation.

"You should know," she challenged. "I would have thought that you of all people should know why she came scurrying back to Torvaig and why, now, all men are an anathema to her."

He glanced at her sharply.

"That's strong language you're using," he mocked softly. "You sound as if men are anathema to you also and that's why you can sympathize with her. How should I know why she's been behaving oddly? I ran into her a couple of times in London. One night when I'd been out to dinner I returned to find her waiting for me in my room. I had some difficulty explaining her presence to my business associates as well as to Senora Usted, who being Spanish has some very definite views on the way a young unmarried woman should behave. Kathleen could have become an embarrassment, so I had to tell her that although she is my cousin I really didn't have the time to take her out and about, as she seemed to expect."

Penelope looked at him. His face wore a bland expression, but there was an amused twinkle in the depths of his blue eyes.

Exasperated by that twinkle, she sat up straight and said with a touch of acidity, "You know very well why Kathleen is miserable. She's in love with you, and you've encouraged her by letting her supervise the furnishing and decorating of your house, by allowing her to act as a hostess to your guests. She had every right to think you wanted to be more than a cousin."

The twinkle vanished. The eyes that returned her accusing glance were hard and cold.

"I'd always managed without a hostess until she got it into her head that she would look beautiful sitting at the end of the dining table by candlelight, or reclining gracefully on the deck of a yacht," he observed cynically.

"You took her to Edinburgh, too."

"That was her idea, too," he murmured. "You're on the wrong track this time, Miss Romantic Jones. Kathleen is not and has never been in love with me. She has been in love with the idea of herself as the wife of the owner of Torvaig. She has been encouraged in that by her mother, who is convinced her side of the family has more right to the island than I have, and has done her best to poke a finger into my pie ever since I returned to Scotland. She pushed her daughter forward to help me with the doing up of the house and later to act as a hostess when I had guests. She provided me, very conveniently, with an old friend of hers as a nanny for my sister's children when they were left in my charge. And when I managed to get rid of that nanny because I suspected her of spying on me and taking her tales back to Helen, she was only too pleased to offer to find me another nanny."

Penelope flashed him an uncomfortable glance. He was watching her with narrowed eyes.

"Is that why you wanted to send me back to London? You thought I was going to spy on you?"

"Yes, especially when I noticed how friendly you were with Hugh. I'd hoped to put off the new nanny by going for her in a sailing boat, but the weather let me down. Then you stood up to me and answered me back so honestly that I began to think perhaps my suspicions of you were wrong. I let you come on probation and warned Hugh to stay away from you, then waited to see if you were going to spy on me on behalf of Helen. You put yourself completely in the clear the night you returned from Inverness, much to my relief. I wouldn't have liked to have sacked you, when you were obviously very good at your job. As for Kathleen," he added with a slight shrug of his shoulders, "Helen should have known better. I'm not a callow youth to be bowled over by the approaches of a beautiful woman with seduction on her mind."

Penelope sat still and straight. A reel was being performed and the floor was shaking with the beat of many feet. She was glad Tearlach had not been taken in by Helen Drummond's little plot to ensnare him as a husband for Kathleen, but she kept thinking of Ian who had been made extremely unhappy by recent events.

"Ian is welcome to Kathleen," said Tearlach suddenly. "She is cold and proud like her mother, and I can't help thinking he would do better with someone like you, a little impulsive, but sound at heart. Have you fallen in love with him? Is that why you were looking all forlorn a few minutes ago?"

The question surprised her and she sat silent, examining her thoughts on the subject. Was she in love with Ian? Had she fallen in love with him because he was the exact opposite of Brian who had hurt her? Was that why she often went to his house and sat with him and made his tea? Utterly confused by her own feelings, she could find no answer to Tearlach's question.

A hand tugged her hair back hard and kept on holding it.

"Come on, give. Are you in love, as you call it, with Ian?" demanded Tearlach. Although his voice was rough there was laughter in it too, as if the whole idea of people falling in love was highly amusing. His amusement irritated her and she refused to add to it.

"I'm not going to tell you," she retorted, twitching her head so that her hair was pulled from his hand. "You won't torture me into telling you my secret feelings, even if you do pay my wages."

"Fair enough," he replied equably, just as the music ended and groups of laughing, breathless dancers began to make their way to the chairs set round the side of the hall.

He stood up and leaned over her.

"I'm going to take you home," he said firmly. "The way Hugh is carrying on, you'll never get back to the house before midnight. Go and get your coat and I'll see you outside."

Before she had a chance to reply and refuse to go with him, he turned and walked away. She saw him stop and have a few words with Hugh, who glanced across at her and nodded his bright head with a grin and a wink, showing that he had agreed that she should leave the dance with his cousin.

Not sure whether or not she wanted to be taken home by her employer, she went to the cloakroom, slung her coat over her shoulders, put on the tall hat, collected her broomstick and went outside through the back door of the hall.

The sky had cleared and the moon was high, silvering everything with its radiance. In the nearby strait the water glittered and on the mainland she could see the mountains silhouetted against the sky.

On the gray asphalt of the parking lot behind the hall her shadow appeared before her, grotesque and elongated. A witch carrying a broomstick. If only she could really ride it all the way back to Torvaig House and avoid the intimacy of the front seat of a car being driven through the night.

As she walked around the end of the hall to the road, she wondered whether she could find Hugh's van and hide in it until Tearlach gathered that she didn't want to go with him and left without her. But her wild plan was short-lived, because he was standing by the front entrance of the hall, waiting for her, and as soon as he saw her he approached.

"I thought you'd gone by broomstick, little witch," he murmured, taking her arm and guiding her inexorably toward his car.

"I would have if I could," she replied, and he laughed.

"Let this be a lesson to you. Never invite a man to a dance unless you're prepared to let him take you home afterward," he jeered softly, and she stiffened with alarm. "Here, put your broom and hat in the back seat and come and sit in the front with me."

Reluctance showed in every movement she made as she did as he directed. Soon the car was sweeping with a muffled roar along the single village street. Then the open road was before them, a path of ghostly gray leading to the mysterious darkness of the moors.

CHAPTER SIX

In front of Tearlach's car, Penelope sat looking out at the moon-bleached road and thought about Ian and Kathleen, together in Hugh's little cottage on his croft at Cladach Bay. Were they also looking out at the moon? Were they holding hands after Ian had confessed his love? Perhaps they were kissing. She had no doubt that Kathleen would accept and return Ian's love once she had been told about it, and that their story would end happily, as all true love stories should.

"I brought Senora and Senorita Usted back with me today," Tearlach's quiet yet vibrant voice broke into her romancings, bringing her back to reality with a jolt.

"How long will they be staying?" she asked.

"That will depend to a certain extent on the weather. Being used to a warmer climate they won't take kindly to the sort of weather we have up here in November. It will also depend on how the senora takes to Davy and Isa," he replied crisply.

"And how they take to her," she couldn't help saying.

"That too, although it isn't as important because they're both too young to have a say in the matter. They'll do as they're told," he retorted curtly.

"Poor little things," she said softly.

"You needn't be too heavy-handed with the pity," he countered. "Senora Usted is extremely fond of children and apparently doted on Manuel. It was against her wishes that Senor Usted would have nothing to do with his son after his marriage, and she thinks she could have talked her husband into accepting Avis eventually. Unfortunately before that could happen they were killed.

The accident upset Senor Usted very much and now he wants to do all he can to make it up to Manuel's children—a natural enough reaction."

Penelope didn't say anything. What could she say? He didn't want the care of the children and he was doing his utmost to get rid of them.

"It's just possible," he went on, "that Senora Usted will be interested in employing you when she sees how well you handle them."

"I'm sure she'll prefer to employ a Spanish nanny who could manage equally well and would have the advantage of being able to teach them to speak Spanish," she replied shortly.

"It would save you the trouble of having to look for another job. Why not keep it in mind?" he returned practically.

"I've no doubt that it would ease your conscience considerably, Mr. Gunn, if Senora Usted took me away with her as well as them," said Penelope tartly. "You can't wait to be rid of them, can you?"

"It isn't a case of wanting to be rid of them," he answered coldly. "I have to do what I think is best for them and what I think Avis and Manuel would want for them. I'm convinced they will have a much better home with Senora Usted than with me. Also, since Davy is the only son of the Usteds' eldest son, he stands to inherit considerable wealth and property."

"What about love? Will they inherit any of that?" asked Penelope, wondering why she disliked him to talk in this way about the children.

"You are hung up on that word 'love,' aren't you? You've been on about it ever since you came to Torvaig. Tonight it was, 'Ian's in love with Kathleen,' and Kathleen's in love with me. I think it's just another word for sentimentality," he jibed as he swung the car around a bend far too fast for Penelope's comfort.

"That's because no one has ever loved you, and as a result you have never loved anyone," she flung at him, hurt by his mimicry of her. "Do you want Davy and Isa to be as deprived as you have been?"

He was silent, and she guessed, with a feeling of uneasiness, that this time she had scored a hit where it hurt most. She had breached the wall he hid his real feelings behind. But she derived no pleasure from the fact. Instead she was overwhelmed by a desire to apologize. The words formed in her mind, but were never spoken, because fear closed her throat as a dry stone wall loomed in front of the headlights. She was convinced the car was going to hit it.

The wall fell away to the left as the car skidded around the bend and roared through the night down a straight stretch of road. Tense on the edge of her seat, Penelope searched for the safety belt, managed to fasten it, and then leaned back with her eyes closed.

"Do you have to drive so fast?" she objected in a husky voice.

The car slowed down immediately and from then on his careful handling of it as he drove it around the last few bends was a deliberate insult to her.

"Were you frightened?" he asked.

"Yes," she whispered.

"I intended you to be, because there are times when you irritate me so much I come very close to wringing your neck," he said viciously.

"I know, I'm sorry," she quavered. "After the children, I come next on your list of people you'd like to be rid of. I wouldn't be a bit surprised if that isn't why you've thought up this plan to push your responsibility for them on to someone else. Then you won't have to employ any more nannies."

"You never give up, do you, Penelope Jones?" he said through gritted teeth. "All right, have it your way. Although that aspect of letting the children go to live in Spain had never occurred to me, now that you mention it, I agree. The relief in knowing that I won't have to put up with a self-righteous little prig who has spent her time trying to change me will be enormous. A good riddance."

Penelope felt vanquished. Had she really seemed like that to him, a Mary Poppins of a nanny trying to change the ways of her materialistic employer? She had no retort ready and sat slumped in her seat, wishing with all her might that the drive was over; wishing she'd never given in to impulse and invited him to the dance. As Molly Lang had once said, Tearlach Gunn was a hard nut to crack and in trying to crack him a woman could destroy herself. Kathleen Drummond with all her beauty had failed and had returned to Torvaig bruised. Why should Penelope think that she, a plain little nobody of a nanny, had any better chance?

They turned into the driveway and in a few minutes the house appeared, dark and ghostly in the moonlight. Wishing to be ready to leave the car as soon as it stopped, Penelope began to unfasten the safety belt, but by the time the car had stopped in front of the house she was still struggling to release the clasp of the belt, which seemed to be jammed.

Tearlach switched off the engine and the lights, then noticing her furtive, desperate fumblings, he turned toward her.

"What's wrong?" he asked irritably.

"The clasp on the safety belt won't open," she admitted reluctantly.

He leaned toward her and his hand touched one of hers as he felt for the fastening. Already in a highly emotional state, she reacted wildly snatching her hand away and jerking backward as if from a snake bite. In the moonlight slanting in through the windshield she saw anger glinting in his eyes.

"What the hell's the matter with you?" he growled. "I'm only going to try and release the fastening for you. Or would you rather I didn't? I could quite easily leave you to struggle on your own. I don't pretend to be chivalrous, although I don't mind helping people, if I think they need help."

She leaned farther away from him, back against the door, her face chalk white in the light from the moon, her eyes pools of darkness.

"I give you a bad time of it, don't I, Penelope?" he said in a softer voice. "Once I made you faint. Tonight I frightened the wits out of you because I drove too fast, and now I've reduced you to jelly just because my hand happened to touch yours. I think it's high time I gave you something to shake about."

His hands grasped her shoulders and she was pulled roughly against him. His mouth came down on hers in a savage kiss that sent desire shooting through her, flame-like, consuming all resistance. There was silence in the car, broken only by their quickened breathing. It stretched into minutes as, finding so little opposition to his good night kiss, Tearlach settled down to enjoy it, relaxing against the back of the seat and holding Penelope closely. Warmed and comforted by his hold, she responded freely, twining her arms around his neck to keep him close, while the curious moon slid reluctantly down the sky and soon had a view of what was happening in the car, though partially hidden by a discreet and kindly cloud.

It was the opening of the front door and the spilling out of light on to the front steps, followed by the crunch of footsteps on the gravel, that brought them both to their senses. Pushing her away from him, Tearlach sat up, thrusting a hand through his hair to push it back from his forehead, and turned to open the window on his side of the car.

Mrs. Guthrie approached and bent her head to peer in.

"I thought I heard a car. Is it yourself, Mr. Gunn?"

"No one else, Mrs. Guthrie," he replied, with a touch of mockery. "I've brought Miss Jones home from the dance."

"Ach, well now, that's just as well, because Davy is sick, the poor wee soul. He can't stop vomiting and I don't know what to do with him." She looked past Tearlach to Penelope, who was doing her best to tidy her hair and her clothing, hoping that her lipstick wasn't smudged and that she didn't show any other signs of having been kissed. "Perhaps you'll come to him straight away, miss. He'll feel better as soon as he sees you. You know how much he misses you when you're not there. He's had too many green apples at the party this afternoon, I shouldn't wonder."

"I'm coming, Mrs. Guthrie," said Penelope breathlessly. "Good night, Mr. Gunn. Thank you for bringing me home."

"The pleasure was mine, Miss Jones," he replied, not bothering to control the amusement he was feeling. "Wait. You can't go yet. You're still fastened in."

Once again she felt his hands moving against her as he fiddled with the clasp and she held her breath until it was unfastened and he moved away.

"Good night," he said coolly as she opened the door. "I hope Davy will be recovered by morning, because I'll want to see him to tell him about his visitors."

The possibility of Davy being in a fit state to see his uncle the next morning became more and more distant as the night wore on. It seemed to the Penelope that the little boy vomited every half hour, and she gave up lying in bed to go and sit in the armchair in his room, so as to be on hand. Twice she had to change his bedclothes and she soon decided that his sickness wasn't due to green apples as Mrs. Guthrie had suggested, but was caused by a germ. Her experience with that sort of stomach upset had taught her that nothing could be done until the vomiting had stopped.

In a way she was glad to be busy most of the night because she knew that had she been able to go to bed she would have lain awake a long time, wrestling with her thoughts. Even so she still had time to think between Davy's bouts of sickness, although she tried hard to keep her thoughts at bay by reading a novel.

But the events in the car before Mrs. Guthrie had opened the front door were too recent and too real to be obliterated by fiction, and as she relived them Penelope kept wondering what would have happened if Mrs. Guthrie hadn't opened the front door when she had.

Her cheeks suddenly hot with embarrassment, she could not help feeling slightly shocked at her own behavior; the heat in her cheeks increased when she thought of how amused Tearlach must have been by her passionate and easily aroused response. He might not have loved or have been loved, but he certainly knew how to make love. All the time she had known Brian he had never been able to rouse her in that way, and she had thought she had loved him.

At last Davy fell into an uneasy sleep and, curling up in the chair under the eiderdown she had brought from her own bed, Penelope slept too, worn out by the discovery she had made about herself that night.

She was awakened after less than three hours' sleep by Isa crying and vomiting. She hurried to the little girl's room. Feeling jaded and suspiciously squeamish herself, she changed the sheets on the cot, washed the little girl and put her in clean nightclothes, then sat down beside her, all prepared to do for her as she had done for Davy during the night.

Before morning had progressed very far she realized she also had the stomach germ, and leaving Isa during a lull, she crept down the stairs to tell Mrs. Guthrie.

"Ach, you poor soul!" exclaimed the housekeeper, although it seemed to Penelope, who was still feeling guilty and miserable about her behavior in the car the previous night, that there was a reproachful glint in Mrs. Guthrie's eyes. How much had she seen last night before Tearlach had heard her and had moved? How long had she been standing beside the car?

The questions twisted through her mind, unanswered.

"I'd be glad if you could explain to Mr. Gunn," she said. "He was going to come and see Davy and Isa this morning and then bring the visitors to see them, but I think it would be better if they all stayed away from the nursery until we're better."

"I'll tell him. But is there anything you're wanting now?" asked Mrs. Guthrie. "Shall I ask the doctor to come?"

"No, it won't be necessary. Davy is already sleeping it off and I think Isa will be over the worst by midday. If you'll just warn Mr. Gunn, I'd be very grateful."

At that point Penelope had to turn and run, as she felt a wave of nausea sweeping over her.

The morning was one of the worst she had ever known in her life. Between her own bouts of nausea she had to get up and attend to Isa and then to Davy who, although he had slept, was petulant and wanted her to stay with him all the time. She had just ordered him rather weakly to go to sleep again and had lain down on her own bed when the door of her room opened and Tearlach walked in.

"I hear you're not well," he said, coming over to the bed and looking down at her. Conscious of her tousled hair and greenish white cheeks, she stared up at him. He looked full of good health and energy, his cheeks bright, as if he had just enjoyed a walk in the frosty air, and his eyes gleaming between narrowed lids.

"I'll be better soon," she said, and tried to smile, but to her horror tears of self-pity brimmed in her eyes and rolled down her cheeks.

"Not if you keep on having to get up and down to those two, you won't be better soon," he remarked dryly, as Isa screamed to her to come and at the same time Davy let out a fretful bellow that he wanted a story read to him. "I've arranged for the doctor to come," continued Tearlach, "but until he arrives I think you'd be better off in another bedroom away from the kids."

"No," she objected as forcibly as she could.

"Yes," he retorted, with a sudden heart-jolting smile, which made her feel weak, only in a different way. "Now don't argue with me. I know you're very conscientious and all that about your job, but this is one time when Davy and Isa can do without you. Can you manage to walk or shall I carry you?"

He spoke as if carrying her from one room to another was a normal procedure. Penelope could imagine the expression on Mrs. Guthrie's face if she saw the laird carrying the nanny in his arms through the house; she sat up quickly and swung her feet to the floor. She stood up and nausea attacked her immediately.

"No, you mustn't carry me," she managed to mutter, and then added hurriedly, "I think I'm going to be sick again."

"Go ahead, don't mind me," he said mildly. "I'll wait for you and have a word with that abominable nephew of mine, who sounds as if a good spanking wouldn't do him any harm."

When she emerged from the bathroom Davy had stopped yelling and Isa was quiet. Tearlach was waiting in the passageway. He took her by the arm in an impersonal way, although as soon as he touched her all sorts of strange sensations tingled through her, in spite of her feeling ill.

"Come on," he urged. "Mrs. Guthrie has put an electric blanket in the bed, so it should be warm by now, and you're to stay there until I tell you to get up."

"But what about your visitors?" she asked.

"They're no concern of yours," he said curtly.

"But who'll look after the children?" she asked.

"Never mind. For the next few hours you're to think only of yourself and to concentrate on getting well again."

He took her down to the second story of the house where she knew the other bedrooms were. The room he led her into was big and pleasant, decorated in a color scheme of wine-red and gray. Sunlight streamed into it through two windows overlooking the bay.

Penelope stood uncertainly by the inviting-looking double bed, with its freshly laundered striped sheets turned back to reveal firm pillows. She was waiting for

Tearlach to leave the room before she took off her dressing gown. But it seemed he wasn't going, because he stood there waiting, too.

Eventually, with fingers that fumbled, she untied the belt and unbuttoned the shabby gown. As she tried to slip it off he stepped behind her and lifted it from her shoulders so that she had only to pull her arms out of the sleeves. Very conscious of her thin cotton pajamas, she hurried to the bed and slid between the warm sheets while he placed her gown on the chair near the bed.

"Does that feel better?" he asked, looking down at her.

She nodded, suddenly shy of him. Then she said what was uppermost in her mind, faint color creeping into her wan cheeks as she remembered how closely he had held her in the car the previous night.

"I hope you don't get the germ."

"I hope not too," he replied, a suspicion of a smile in his eyes. "The doctor should be here soon. Is the sun bothering you?"

"No. I like to see it, thank you," she said politely. The delicious warmth of the bed was making her feel drowsy already, and she was having difficulty keeping her eyes open.

"I like it too," he murmured. "That's why I have my room on this side of the house." But she hardly heard him, nor did she feel him push the hair back from her brow as he murmured, "Sleep well."

She slept so well that she didn't hear the doctor come into the room. According to Mrs. Guthrie he refused to disturb her from such a sound sleep, deciding that it was a far better cure than any he could offer.

The housekeeper had come into the room in the late afternoon and had awakened Penelope when she had closed the window.

"How are Davy and Isa?" was Penelope's first question.

"Ach, they're getting along fine, just fine."

"Have the visitors seen them?" was the next question.

"Aye, they have that," said Mrs. Guthrie with a touch of enthusiasm. "There's no doubt that the senora is a lovely woman. When the laird told her that perhaps she ought to wait until they were well before she saw them, she overruled him like a true grandmother and went straight to the nursery to give them the gifts she had brought. Wee Davy took to her at once. Ach, you can say what you like, uncles and aunts are all very well, but when you haven't any parents, your grandmother is the next best person, as both you and I should know."

"Yes, I do know," said Penelope, but she could not help her heart from sinking. If Davy liked his grandmother so much he would soon be leaving Torvaig, and so would she.

"What about Senorita Usted? Is she nice too?"

"Aye. She's a wee bit older than yourself, very pretty in a dark sort of way. She's been out all afternoon with Mr. Gunn looking at the island. Alec had a wee crack with her this morning when she was looking around the gardens. He says she's very knowledgeable about plants," enthused Mrs. Guthrie.

"I'm sorry to have been such a nuisance having to stay in bed like this," murmured Penelope. "I think I should get up now."

"Mr. Gunn says you've to stay there until he sees you again," said Mrs. Guthrie firmly. "It wouldn't be so bad if all the spare rooms weren't in use and you could have gone into one of them."

Penelope looked around the room wildly, noting for the first time that it didn't have an unused look that spare rooms usually have.

"Whose room is this?" she demanded weakly.

"Himself's. Whose do you think?" said Mrs. Guthrie, with a glint of disapproval. "I never thought I'd see the day when an employee would be sleeping in the laird's bed. But then I'm learning that Heather Swan was right when she said some funny things went on in this house and that Mr. Gunn was a bit unconventional in his ways."

"I can't stay here," said Penelope urgently. "I must go back to my own room."

She flung back the covers and was about to step onto the floor when Tearlach appeared in the open doorway.

"You'll stay where you are," he ordered brusquely. "The doctor said you wouldn't be fit to work until the day after tomorrow. You've had one of those 24-hour stomach flu germs. Make the most of your time in bed, because you might find yourself having to look after the rest of us."

Realizing there was no point in arguing with him when he spoke like that, Penelope lay back in bed and let Mrs. Guthrie cover her up, which the housekeeper did with much clucking of her tongue and many warning flashes from her bright eyes.

"But what will you do? Where will you sleep?" she managed to ask at last.

"Downstairs in the study. There's a bed-settee down there. I just came to get a few articles I need from the drawers here," he replied. "Do you feel like eating?"

"No, not yet."

"Then that settles it. In bed you stay until tomorrow." He was opening and closing drawers, and when he had found what he wanted, he came to stand by the bed and smile down at her.

"Stop worrying about it," he admonished gently. "It's my reputation that will suffer, not yours. Isn't that right,

Mrs. Guthrie?" He flung a suspicious glance in the direction of the housekeeper.

"Not if I can help it, Mr. Gunn," replied the housekeeper, although she looked rather troubled. "I'll away now to see that the table is laid in the dining room."

She bustled out of the room, leaving the door wide open.

"It was mean of you to say that to her. She's quite upset at the idea of my being in your room," said Penelope. "She thinks the world of you, and now it looks as if you're wilfully destroying her good opinion of you. Couldn't I have gone into another room?"

"Only if I'd asked Senora and Senorita Usted to share a room," he said, "and I wasn't prepared to do that. I suppose as laird I'm expected to turn a blind eye when one of my employees is sick, just because she's a young woman and the rest of the household might get the wrong idea about her morals as well as mine," he added, with a bitter twist to his mouth. "I didn't have the advantage of being brought up a gentleman, like my father, and I know nothing about love, as you do, but I do care when anyone is ill or is in trouble, and I try to do something to help. I do what I feel is best at the time, not what I'm *expected* to do. But I thought you'd understand that, because you usually do and say what you feel instead of what you think, don't you, Miss Jones?"

Was he referring to last night when she had returned his kisses with passionate interest, or was he referring to all the times she had told him what she felt about his attitude to life? She was too confused to tell and could only blink up at him.

"Obviously you're not in form or you'd have come back with some provocative remark designed especially to prick my inflated ego," he murmured with a wicked grin. "I'll leave you to rest now. Don't worry about Davy and Isa. They're having a great time with their granny from Spain."

He left the room, banging the door closed behind him, and Penelope was left alone to reflect on the fact that she was no longer needed at Torvaig House.

Although she felt fully recovered by the next afternoon, she found that the children were quite contented to stay with their grandmother and aunt and did not require her supervision. At loose ends, she decided to have some fresh air and she walked over the headland to Cladach to see Hugh.

She found him in his studio flinging paint at the canvas. She was sure that the mess he was making was the ultimate in self-expression, but she hadn't the slightest idea what the various blobs and swathes of color were supposed to be.

"You could have knocked me down with a feather when I saw Tearlach at the dance the other evening," said Hugh. "Then, when he told me he'd come to take you back to the house, I wondered what was wrong."

"He doubted your ability to take me back before midnight. You have to admit you slipped up the last time you took me anywhere. Hugh, what is this painting of?"

He gave her an exasperated glance and then grinned.

"Do you mean to tell me you don't recognize it? That's Torvaig as we saw it the day you came to the island. Stand back and you'll see the bay, the rocks and the lighthouse. If you try really hard you might even see the spirits of Magnus Gunn and his Irish slave wife."

She stepped back and gazed hard at the picture. In the cold northern light coming through the window all she could make out were wild sweeps of reddish brown she assumed were land, a flat wash of yellowish gray she supposed was the sea, and a stark, upright streak of white, which must be the lighthouse.

"I can't see the spirits," she complained with an impish grin, and he proceeded to chase her around the room with a paintbrush dipped in orange paint. He only stopped threatening to paint her face when she gave in and admitted that the painting did resemble the view of An Tigh Camus from the sea.

"Why all this sudden activity?" she asked, strolling around the studio to peer at other canvases. "Who's this?" she exclaimed, not waiting for an answer to her first question.

"Molly Lang, of course. Who else has hair that color?" he replied.

"But she isn't cross-eyed. She has just a slight cast in one eye."

"That's how she looks to me," replied Hugh serenely. "And the answer to the first question is that the date of my exhibition in Edinburgh has been brought forward and if I don't do some painting I'll have nothing to exhibit."

"Where is Kathleen?" asked Penelope, suddenly aware that his sister wasn't in the house.

"Striding about the moors somewhere, like a tragedy queen. She's all taut, angry and silent. I'm quite afraid she'll do a Lucy of Lammermuir one of these days and start screaming at me," murmured Hugh, sitting on his stool once more and applying paint to his picture.

"Who's Lucy of Lammermuir?"

"Don't you know the story about the girl who went mad at her wedding? One of Sir Walter Scott's best. Donizetti made an opera out of it. A real hair-raiser."

"But why should Kathleen do that? Because your cousin gave her the cold shoulder in London?"

546

"Possibly, although I'm thinking there's something more to it than that. She and Ian aren't speaking to each other at all."

"Oh. I thought he'd have told her he loves her by now," said Penelope, disappointed.

"He might as well have come with us for all the good he did by staying with her on the night of the dance. She went off to bed and he sat here all alone." A thought occurred to him suddenly and he stopped painting to swing around and stare at her. "It isn't Wednesday or Saturday, it's Sunday, so what are you doing here?" he asked.

"We have visitors."

"Ach, yes. Kath recognized them when she saw them with the laird yesterday. The young one is the woman Tearlach showed so much interest in, in London."

"She's Davy's Aunt Rosa and the other woman is his grandmother from Spain. They've come to see the children with a view to taking them back to live in Spain with them."

Hugh whistled soundlessly.

"It's a pity they couldn't have come while Avis and Manuel were alive," he said.

"That's what I think. But never mind, they're here now, and the Senora is more than willing to make amends for what happened in the past."

"How long are they staying?" asked Hugh.

"A week, maybe two. Then I think they'll probably take Davy and Isa with them to Spain."

"Tearlach will be relieved if they do. He never saw himself as a beneficent guardian. But what will you do?"

"I don't know yet. Senora Usted has offered me a position in her home to continue as their nanny, but I'm not sure."

"What does Tearlach say?" Hugh regarded her curiously.

Penelope thought back to the conversation she had had that afternoon with her employer and from which she had not yet recovered.

"*He* thinks it would be the chance of a lifetime for me. The Usteds are wealthy and live in a beautiful place on the shores of the Mediterranean. They know all the *right* people and have all the *right* contacts, whatever that means," she replied scornfully. "*He* thinks I should go with them."

"Then why don't you?"

"Because I don't want to leave Torvaig. I'd like to go on living here. I feel at home here."

"Have you had any more flashbacks?"

"Yes, of when I lived here before I had children. Boys, strong and golden, like young lions."

"Why, Penny Jones, you're becoming quite poetic," he scoffed. "Who was their father? The old lion of Torvaig House?"

"Hugh Drummond, you should be . . ." she began, and then realized there was no mockery in his eyes. He was looking at her quite seriously.

"How do you know?" she demanded.

"The way your face changed when you looked up and saw him at the dance," he replied, applying more paint to his picture. "He brought you here in his boat and you've lived like a servant in his house. At first you hated him, but now you're going through a period of not being sure. That's why you don't want to leave."

In a panic because Hugh with his observant artist's eyes had noticed more than he should, Penelope paced about the room. Hugh merely watched her.

"It's just one of those physical things," she flung at him

by way of explanation. "Women have them just like men. I'll get over it."

"Supposing it is? There's nothing wrong in that. In fact I always think that purely spiritual love between a man and a woman must be damned dull. I know of a way in which you could stay on Torvaig."

"How?" she asked.

"You could claim one of the crofts at Achmore and live on it."

"But I'd have to plough the land and grow crops and look after the animals, and I know nothing about those things," she said slowly, thinking how much she would enjoy owning and working a croft.

"You'd soon learn. Many women in the islands look after the crofts, and you'd be following the tradition of the Viking women who enjoyed good status, owning their own land and managing their own property," replied Hugh. "It would be better than working as a nanny all the time, belonging nowhere and to no one."

His suggestion appealed to Penelope's imagination. Already she could see herself independent and free.

"Where will I find out about the croft?" she asked.

"You'll have to ask Tearlach. He probably knows all the legalities about proving that you're Hector Sandison's only descendant. Of course, these days you don't even have to do that if you really want a croft and one is available, but the fact that you have a right to one here gives you more pull, should he say he doesn't want you to have it."

"Most of the other croft owners do some other sort of work," murmured. Penelope. "There isn't much I can do except look after children."

"You can take in tourists in the summer. There isn't really enough accommodation on the islands for visitors.

Tearlach has often mentioned that it's time there was a hotel or even a youth hostel. Oh, there's plenty of possibilities for anyone who is willing to work," said Hugh.

During the following week, when she was supposed to be considering the position offered to her by Senora Usted, she kept thinking about the last remaining empty house on the hillside above Ian's croft. Maybe it was right that she should go and live there and till the ground, become part of Torvaig's community. She had no ties, no relatives to make claims on her, and during the past few weeks she had made friends she would value all her life. Why leave them when she could stay?

In the end she decided that there was only one person whom she could ask for advice on the matter. She would have to talk to Tearlach himself about it. She would let him make the decision for her. If he said no, he didn't want her to have the croft that was hers by right, she would abide by his decision, knowing that he had meant what he had said on Hallowe'en night—that she was a prig and he would be glad to be rid of her.

His derisive comments still hurt, even though she knew he had been goaded by her criticism of him into flinging such words at her. They hurt almost as much as the memory of his lovemaking in the car. There had been an undercurrent of contempt to the way he had kissed and caressed her, as if he had known the effect he would have on her. He had been able to set other women afire with desire, and he considered she was no better than they had been.

And she had to agree with him. She wasn't any better than Kathleen Drummond, who was beautiful and proud yet had gone chasing after him to London. Nor was she any better than Rosa Usted, who was gay and highly intelligent yet stayed downstairs long after everyone else had gone to bed to talk with Tearlach alone in the lounge or in his study.

One afternoon Rosa, whose English was excellent, brought the two children back to the nursery for their tea and asked if she might stay and have the small meal with them.

She was a shapely young woman of medium height with a mop of waving black hair and a plump olive-skinned face. Her smile was wide and friendly, a curving of full red lips over white, slightly crooked teeth. She wore very little makeup and was dressed that afternoon in a wine-red sweater and beautifully cut tweed skirt.

"I would like to see what you give them to eat," she explained. "It is important, because at first we shall try to give them the food they are accustomed to and then gradually introduce them to Spanish food. We don't want their small tummies to be upset too much."

Penelope showed her how to poach two eggs and serve them with fingers of hot buttered toast. Rosa decided she would also have a poached egg and soon she and Penelope were having tea together in typical British fashion.

"This is very pleasant," said Rosa. "I would like to think you are coming to Spain with us, Miss Jones, but I think that is not so."

Penelope looked up in surprise and met a pair of very shrewd, twinkling black eyes.

"What makes you think that? Senora Usted gave me until Friday to make up my mind, and I haven't decided yet."

"If you really wanted to come to Spain you would not be taking so long to come to a decision. It isn't often the chance comes the way of someone like you, who has to work for her living, to go to Spain to live in the sunshine away from this horrible climate." She glanced with a shudder at the window, which was being lashed with rain and shaken by the wind. Then she looked back at Penelope with an apologetic smile. "You must forgive me," she said, "if I'm critical of the weather, but it is as you say, the end."

Penelope laughed.

"Yes, I'm afraid it must seem like that to someone who isn't used to the damp and the cold."

"Perhaps there are other attractions I don't know about that make you want to stay here?" suggested Rosa with a sly little smile.

"How do you know I want to stay here?" countered Penelope.

"You walk about this house with a confident manner as I do in my parents' home, as if you belong here, and then you talk to Charles as if you had known him a long time and will go on knowing him an even longer time," replied the Spanish woman, still watching Penelope closely.

Alarm shot through Penelope. This intelligent, very pretty girl noticed far too much.

"Possibly it seems like that to you only because he and I are of the same heritage and culture. I've only been here two months and I haven't known him longer than that," she replied cautiously.

The Spanish woman raised her eyebrows in slight surprise.

"One would not think so," she murmured. "But you do want to stay here and not come to Spain. Am I not right?"

Suddenly Penelope found herself confiding to Rosa all about her grandmother and the Sandison croft. Rosa listened with interest and said finally, "I understand about the croft. Charles has taught me much about the

Highlands since I have been here. It is very exciting that you can own your own land. You must talk to Charles soon, before you give my mother your decision. Then if it isn't possible for you to have the croft you will still have the chance to come with us."

Rosa paused and a faint enigmatic smile flitted across her face.

"I hope our return to Spain will not mean the end of our association with Charles," she continued. "He is very charming. He took me about London. I find him much more relaxed than the younger men I usually go out with. But then he is not impressed by my father's wealth and so is not intent in making an impression on me. We deal very well together."

Too well for Kathleen's peace of mind, thought Penelope. She had noticed how attentive Tearlach had been toward the Spanish woman and had occasionally been appalled at the flashes of jealousy she had felt as a result.

When she saw Hugh again the next afternoon, she asked him if he thought his cousin was attracted to Rosa. He had met the Usteds by this time and so was able to pass an opinion.

"After seeing them together the other evening I think there's a possibility that he is attracted to her. After all, his sister and her brother were so attracted that they were willing to defy the Usted family," reflected Hugh. "But then Tearlach is a wily old lion. He gave the impression that he was attracted to Kathleen, too, and deceived all of us. He's not above putting on an act, you know."

"For whose benefit?" snapped Penelope.

"Anyone who happens to be noticing. You, for

instance," he said, with a mischievous grin, "so that you won't get any ideas above your station."

"Oh, if you're in that sort of a mood I'm not staying any longer," retorted Penelope. "I'll go and see Ian and make his tea. At least he's too civilized to make fun of me."

"Yes, do that," replied Hugh, his face suddenly grave. "He's pretty miserable these days and would welcome a visit."

Ian was interested in the possibility that Penelope might stay at Achmore, and he suggested that they walk over to the croft. They found the stone walls of the little house still sound, though they would be improved by being painted white on the outside. The roof was in a bad state and needed recovering.

"If you ask Tearlach he'll get someone to see to that for you," said Ian. "Most of the houses around the bay here were in the same condition, and look at them now."

Inside the house was a different story. There was no doubt in Penelope's mind that a great deal of work would have to be done to the interior of the walls before she could live in the place.

"I shall look forward to having you as my nearest neighbor," said Ian in his deep, slow voice. "If you would like to earn a little extra cash during the winter I'd be glad if you'd come and clean my house once or twice a week and perhaps do some baking for me."

"But what about Kathleen?" asked Penelope.

"She'll be leaving Torvaig," he said with a sigh. "After the exhibition she'll be setting up her own workshop in London nearer to the market."

"Oh, I'm so sorry, Ian. Why didn't you tell her?"

"There was no point. She was looking at me and talking to me, but not seeing me. My little dream concerning her is over just as hers concerning Tearlach is over too. We're both a little sadder and a little wiser."

"I still think you should have told her that you love her," persisted Penelope.

"But she should know how I feel about her by now. It makes no difference to her."

"Rubbish!" flared Penelope.

He looked pained and bewildered by this abrupt comment.

"What do you mean?" he asked.

"It's rubbish your saying that she should know how you feel without you telling her. How can she know?"

"I've shown her in every way I can think of."

"In what ways?"

"I've been sympathetic. I've sat with her when she's been too unhappy to speak to me. I've told you before I'm no knight in shining armor, and that I can't go out and slay dragons for her."

"Couldn't you take her in your arms and kiss her?" demanded Penelope.

"Not unless I thought she wanted me to. I love her too much to make that sort of demand."

By now they were back at his house and they lingered outside in the damp November twilight. The winds rustled a few dry leaves about their feet, and out in the bay the water rippled with silvery light. Someone was coming up the lane, their footsteps crunching on the loose stones.

Penelope, who was trying hard to control an urge to shake Ian because he was so obstinately obtuse, guessed it might be Kathleen coming to do some work in the workshop. Impulsively she took a chance.

"Ian," she whispered.

He looked down at her. At that moment she reached up and putting her arms around his neck planted a smacking kiss on his cheek.

It was as if she had given a much-needed cue to an actor. His reaction caught her unawares. His arms swept around her and he kissed her very thoroughly. Held helpless against him, she heard the footsteps stop and then start again as whoever had been approaching turned and went back down the lane.

"Well, Penelope?" said Ian softly. "Did you get more than you bargained for? You must forgive me. It isn't every day that someone as young and kind-hearted as yourself offers to kiss me, so when it happens I'm likely to explode."

"You're forgiven, Ian," she said with a little laugh. "But why don't you try kissing Kathleen like that? You might find you get results. There's such a thing as being too gentle, you know."

She left him, and going down the lane the feeling of déjà vu was very strong. It persisted all the way back to Torvaig. In another life she had had a secret assignation on the hill behind Achmore with a bearded man who had worn a priestly habit. She had been seen by someone who had turned and had gone back down the lane to tell of what she had seen.

Had Kathleen seen Ian kiss her? If so what was her reaction to the sight of another woman in Ian's arms? Penelope grinned to herself. She hoped it had shaken the lovely proud Highlander.

Later the same night she crept downstairs and along the passage to the room Tearlach called his study, where she hoped to find him alone. The time had come for her to beard the lion in his den again and ask him for the croft at Achmore. In her hand she carried the book he had left in her room the night he had waited for her to return from Inverness.

As she walked through the hallway she was reminded of her first night at Torvaig when she had gone to ask her employer to come and say good night to his nephew. So much had happened since then. She had twisted the lion's tail many times, and he had punished her only once, rather violently and contemptuously, kissing her in a way she would never forget. Otherwise he had been tolerant of her youthful impulsive attacks, and there had been times when he had been very kind.

"Looking for me?" His voice startled her out of her musings.

He was leaning in the doorway of the lounge, a glass of whisky in his hand. He took a sip of it while he waited for her reply.

"Yes."

"What's the matter? Won't Davy go to sleep?" he asked sarcastically.

"I came to return this book to you. You left it in my room. Also I'd like to ask your advice about something, please."

He looked faintly surprised by her request.

"I'm honored," he said with a touch of irony. "Come in here. We may as well be comfortable."

He turned back into the lounge and she followed him. She half expected to find Rosa, dressed in one of her exotic evening dresses, lounging on the big chesterfield, but only the strong fragrance of the Spanish woman's scent lingered in the air, bearing witness to the fact that she had left the room recently.

In a gruff voice Tearlach told her to sit down. She sat in an armchair, while he flung himself down on the chesterfield. He looked dour and moody and she wondered whether he and Rosa had had a disagreement.

"What do you want advice about?" he asked indifferently.

She put the book down on the arm of the chair, took a deep breath, looked at him directly and said, "I want to know if I can have the last remaining croft at Achmore. As the only living descendent of Hector Sandison I believe I can claim it."

He gave her a long level look, leaned back and took a sip of his whisky before replying.

"You can, provided you can prove that you're a descendant," he murmured cautiously.

"I have my grandmother's birth certificate showing she was born here. Is that proof enough?"

His eyes narrowed.

"You've been thinking about this for some time," he accused.

"Ever since I knew you wouldn't be requiring my services as a nanny any longer."

"Why?"

"Because I want to stay on Torvaig."

"And if I refuse to let you have the croft, what will you do? Find some other way of staying?" he rapped.

She hadn't anticipated that question and had no answer ready, so to avoid his searching glance she looked down at her hands.

"Come, Miss Jones, surely you have an alternative plan? You should never put all your eggs in one basket. It doesn't pay," he said softly.

He cut to the quick as usual. He was watching her with that narrow-eyed measuring gaze to which he subjected everybody and everything. He would always have an

alternative plan as well as an alternative woman, she
thought wildly, because it wouldn't pay for him to gamble
on one only. Well, she was different.

"No, I haven't an alternative plan. If I can't have the
croft I won't stay," she said defiantly.

"Will you go to Spain?"

"No."

"Then where will you go?"

"That's none of your business. Once I leave your
employment you're rid of me. That's what you want isn't
it?" she retorted.

This time he didn't have an answer, or if he did, he
didn't say anything. He finished his whisky in one
swallow and set the glass down on the long low table in
front of the fireplace. Then he gave her another level
look.

"All right, you can have a croft," he said suddenly, and
she nearly fell off her chair with surprise. "How will you
pay the rent?"

"I have a little money that my grandmother left me
when she died. I think she would like me to use it in this
way. I can live on it for a while if I'm careful. I can take
in tourists in the summertime and in the winter I think I
can find work," she replied.

"What sort of work?"

"Well, Ian has asked me to do some cleaning for him,
and Hugh—"

He held up his hand and interrupted her. "Wait, wait.
You're going a little too fast for me. You mention Ian
and Hugh. I suppose they know of your intention to claim
a croft?"

"Yes. Really it was Hugh's idea that I should claim
one, and when I told Ian, he said he could do with someone to clean and do a little cooking for him," she replied
frankly.

"Then why doesn't he marry you?" he queried sharply.

"Surely even you know there's more to marriage than a woman just cleaning and cooking for a man," she retaliated, with counterfeit sweetness.

"Is there?" he questioned ironically. "Oh, yes, I'd forgotten. You'd require to be loved too, wouldn't you? Doesn't Ian offer enough of that precious commodity?"

"I've told you before, he's in love with Kathleen, not with me."

"I wouldn't have thought so from the way he was behaving this afternoon," he said slowly, watching her closely.

At first the implication was lost on Penelope and she blinked in puzzlement. Then she noticed the mocking gleam in his eyes and understanding hit her.

"They were your footsteps I heard!" she exclaimed.

"They were. I was coming to call on Ian. Who did you think was coming up the lane?"

"Kathleen."

"I see. Then that little performance was for her benefit, was it, to show her she has competition?"

"Yes . . . I mean no." Penelope's face burned.

"What exactly do you mean?" he drawled, and she had the impression he was enjoying her discomfiture.

"I mean I'm not competing with Kathleen for Ian," she almost shouted at him, irritated by the sardonic curve to his mouth. "Kissing a person doesn't necessarily mean that you're in love with him or her," she added wildly. Immediately the moments in the car when he had kissed her and she had responded were between them, adding to her confusion and making her cheeks glow a hotter, brighter pink as she saw that sardonic curve to his mouth become a sneer.

"I know that about myself, but I didn't realize it was true of you," he said curtly. He leaned forward with his elbows on his knees and rested his head in his hands so that she couldn't see the expression on his face any more. "Let's get back to this business of you having a croft. I suppose you'd like me to tell the senora that you're not taking the position she offered you?"

"Yes, please."

"Now the cottage needs renovating before you can live in it. Where do you intend to live while that's being done?" he asked, turning to look at her. The dour expression was back, making him look older and tired, and making her very aware of the differences between them; differences which they had bridged in so many ways on Hallowe'en.

"I don't know. I hadn't thought about it," she stammered.

"Well, you'd better start thinking fast, because you can't stay here after the end of this week," he said harshly. "I shall be accompanying the Usteds to Edinburgh and then to Spain. This house will be closed while I'm away. Mrs. Guthrie is longing to return to her cottage."

Desolation, gray and arid, was sweeping over her, and she had the utmost difficulty in keeping her head up and hiding her dismay at the thought of him going to Spain. He could only be going for one reason—to be close to Rosa.

"I think Molly Lang will let me stay with her," she managed to say huskily.

"Good. That's fine. I'll ask someone to start work on the cottage before I leave Torvaig," he replied coolly. He smiled briefly, impersonally, and stood up. Penelope knew that the interview was at an end.

"Thank you. Good night," she muttered and left the room.

Through the hall and up the narrow stairway she went, keeping her mind a blank until she reached her room. There she began to prepare dully for bed and remembered the first night when she had dared to twist the lion's tail. Well, the lion was leaving Torvaig and she was staying. One day he might return and bring with him his wife. One day she might be able to use her training as a nanny for his children, who might have dark hair and dark eyes like the little boy who was sleeping peacefully in the next room.

She climbed into bed and lay awake most of the night, her eyes dry, staring into the darkness, and her heart heavy, aching with an indefinable sadness.

CHAPTER SEVEN

On a dank November day, when the sea was flat and gray and the distant islands seemed like mirages floating above the rim of the horizon, Penelope left the house up on the hill at Achmore, which was still being renovated, and walked slowly down the hill toward Ian McTaggart's house.

A week had passed since Davy and Isa had left Torvaig bound for Spain in the company of Senora Usted, her daughter Rosa and Tearlach. During that week Penelope lived with the Langs and every day had walked up to see her own house, to watch the progress of the workmen, three crofters who were also skilled in roofing, plastering and painting.

Although she was pleased with the work that was being done and was enjoying staying with Molly and making the acquaintance of the other crofters who lived in Cladach and Achmore, she was conscious of a flatness of spirit; a flatness that had descended upon her the night she had asked Tearlach for the croft; a flatness that was like the sea that day, stretching gray and empty away to nothing.

She had seen Tearlach several times since that night, before he had left with the Usteds and the children, but she knew she had really said goodbye to him that night when she had said good night. On the day of their departure she had felt no real wrench at parting from Davy and Isa, but the sight of Tearlach's shaggy head disappearing into the interior of the black car as he had taken his seat behind the steering wheel had made her throat go suddenly dry. Unbidden tears had sprung to her eyes and she had hurried away from the window from which she had been watching.

He had gone from the island and once more the big house was empty and desolate. She had the most peculiar feeling that he would never return. The lion had left Torvaig forever.

Penelope sighed and squared her shoulders. Well, she was on Torvaig to stay. She had a house and land. She was free, healthy and strong. No man was her master and she was slave to no one, not even to those strange flashbacks, which had now stopped. How many other young women of her age could say that they were independent in the way she was, as they toiled away in the cities at typewriters, in hairdressing salons or in classrooms?

She decided that she would call on Hugh and ask him if he had any ideas about where she could acquire some furniture for her house, and after that she would go and help Molly with some sewing.

She was just aproaching Ian's house when Kathleen came up the lane from the other direction. They met almost at the door to the workshop. Beneath the hood of her cloak the fine-boned face was sharp and pale, and Penelope was shocked to see how much weight Kathleen had lost since the last time she had seen her.

"I'm told you are going to live on the hills," said Kathleen politely.

"Yes, I should be able to move in soon," replied Penelope.

"Why do you want to stay on Torvaig, of all places?" asked Kathleen curiously.

"Because I feel I belong here," said Penelope coolly.

"Feel you belong?" queried Kathleen with a touch of mockery, and she arched her lovely white neck and laughed. "Oh, yes you've been here before, haven't you?

You *felt* you came here in a Viking ship. How well I remember Tearlach's amusement that night when he told us of your vision of the past. He didn't want you here then, and he went to a lot of trouble to get rid of you, short of sacking you outright. But you're not going after all and so he has had to remove himself."

The color drained out of Penelope's face. Surely she had not looked as if she had been chasing the laird?

"I find it quite ridiculous that a city sparrow like you should feel she belongs on an island in the Hebrides," scoffed Kathleen. Pain and disappointment had turned her into a sneering shrew, thought Penelope, and if she went on like this much longer she would lose all that beauty and grace, which were her inheritance.

"No more ridiculous than I find the idea of you, a country hen, going to settle in the big city," she retorted. "You'll soon be lost."

"Who told you that I'm going to live in the city?" asked Kathleen sharply.

"Ian did. He says that after the exhibition of your work you won't be returning here. You'll be staying in London."

Kathleen's face seemed to go paler and tauter than ever as her pride stepped in to help her conceal her true feelings. Suddenly Penelope felt sorry for her. "He's very worried about you," she said impulsively.

Kathleen's fine eyes flashed with golden fire.

"Who is?" she demanded.

"Ian. He has been ever since you went to Edinburgh with Mr. Gunn. You see, he loves you very much and he was afraid you might be hurt."

"Loves me!" exclaimed Kathleen, a faint pink color touching her cheeks. "But he's never given any sign of loving me. He just sits there more interested in twisting silver than in me. He's always been the same. There was a time in the spring when I thought—" She broke off and bit her lower lip. "You must be mistaken," she added stiffly.

"No, I'm not. Just because he's quiet and patient and can't slay dragons for you, you mustn't think he doesn't love you," persisted Penelope. "His is the sort of love that grows slowly, but lasts forever."

"Why are you telling me all this? I thought you were attracted to him and that's why you want to stay at Achmore. You've spent many hours with him lately, and the day I returned from London I saw you and him in his workshop. You looked well together, and I know you share an interest in the past. I have to admit I was unhappy about the way Tearlach treated me in London. He was so cutting and sarcastic, and oh, so right. You see, I'd been doing what my mother suggested."

"What was that?"

"She suggested that I should make myself indispensable to Tearlach. He had told her when he returned to Scotland that he would like to settle down, that it was time he had a home. She was annoyed with him for coming back and more or less snatching Torvaig from under her nose, and she suggested I seduce him and make him marry me. The idea appealed to me. Tearlach is an attractive man, and I knew that as his wife I would be well treated even if he never loved me. Also at the time I felt I would never know a man's love. Ian seemed disinterested, and I supposed having reached my thirtieth birthday I was getting a bit desperate." Kathleen paused and her eyes narrowed as if she were in pain. "But Tearlach saw through my attempts to inveigle him and I came running home to Ian for comfort, only to find he had a new friend in you."

"So that's why you've been unhappy, stalking about like a tragedy queen," exclaimed Penelope. "How silly of you!"

Kathleen's mouth twisted into a travesty of a smile.

"I once said that to you. Do you remember?" she murmured. "Yes, I have been silly. Oh, the time I've wasted in my life waiting for someone to sweep me off my feet with his love, and all the time Ian has been waiting," she cried, suddenly dropping her pride. "I'm not going to waste any more. Excuse me, please, and thank you."

She opened the door of the workshop and hurried through it, leaving it swinging. Penelope could hear her calling to Ian, and with a smile she closed the door and went on her way down the lane to Hugh's house.

She found him sorting through his canvases, choosing which ones he would take to Edinburgh. Quickly she told him what had just happened.

"A fairy godmother, that's who you are. Now I won't mind leaving Kath here. How is the house?" he said.

"I should be able to move in next week, if I have any furniture by then."

"I'll take you over to Invercol tomorrow. You should be able to pick up some pieces at the weekly auction there. If you find anything we can bring it back in the van," said Hugh, and Penelope thought what a good friend he had been ever since she had come to Torvaig. In fact if it hadn't been for Hugh she might never have come and might not have been able to stay.

"Do you think I'll be able to manage the croft?" she asked him hesitantly, betraying her uncertainty.

"With some help from your neighbors, I think you will," he answered serenely. "That's what's so wonderful about living on Torvaig. We all help one another. It's a

real community. Before Tearlach came back I was thinking of going to live in one of those communes with some
friends of mine in an old house, but Torvaig has been a
much better experience. Do you know what Tearlach said
to me the last time I saw him?"

"How could I know? I wasn't there," she retorted.

"He said he'd decided to let you have your croft
because it had occurred to him that there are far too
many single men on the island to make it a really
balanced community, and that single women would have
to be encouraged to live here. He thought he would make
a start by allowing you to have your croft. He said he
wouldn't be surprised if you weren't married before you'd
been at Achmore 12 months, and that in a couple of years
you'd be acting as nanny to your own baby," said Hugh
with a chuckle. "Hey, Penny, what are you doing with
that paint? Be careful! Tearlach said it, not me. You do
get upset easily, don't you?"

Having chased him around the room with the paintbrush in the way he had once chased her, Penelope
collapsed in a chair and for the next half hour sat
watching Hugh paint while she thought up devastating
retorts to be delivered to Tearlach Gunn the next time she
saw him. Only there might never be a next time, she
realized forlornly.

As she had hoped, she was able to move into her
cottage within three days. There was still much work to
be done, but at least the kitchen and the living room were
habitable. Hugh was there with the few pieces of furniture
they had managed to pick up at Invercol, and he helped
her to carry them in. He was, as usual, very talkative, full
of the good news that Ian and Kathleen had gone to
Inverness to be married.

"In a register office, much to Mother's disgust. She

568

wanted Kath in white with all the trimmings, which is only natural since Kath is her only daughter. But can you imagine Kath in white doing all the right things, or Ian in a morning suit? I hope when I get married Mother will have realized that such conventions are unpopular with me and that she won't even try to persuade the girl I'm going to marry to have a white wedding," he said.

"But I thought marriage was out as far as you're concerned," said Penelope, with an air of sweet innocence. "I thought you were going to be a bachelor all your life with a few special women friends on the side."

He grinned at her and cocked his head to one side.

"Sometimes, when I come across someone like you, I think how pleasant it would be if you didn't have to go back to Torvaig House, or the Langs, or wherever you happen to be staying for the night, when I've plenty of room in my cottage for a lodger," he teased. "And I start thinking how nice it would be if meals were always cooked well and served on time just when a man is needing some food instead of him having to stop work and start scavenging for it."

"You're as bad as your beastly cousin! He thinks that's all wives are for, cleaning and cooking," retorted Penelope, remembering Tearlach asking her why Ian didn't marry her if he wanted her to cook and clean for him.

"I'm thinking he's wishing he had a wife at this very moment," Hugh said casually, giving her a shrewd sidelong glance. She was putting up the curtains she had made for the kitchen on Molly Lang's sewing machine, but at his words she turned, her face expressing a strange feeling of apprehension.

"Didn't I tell you that Tearlach's back?" added Hugh even more casually.

"At Torvaig House?" she whispered.

"Yes. He came yesterday, from the hospital in Edinburgh."

"Hospital? Oh, Hugh, stop tormenting me! What was he doing in hospital?" she demanded, dropping a curtain in the sink thoughtlessly, too worried by what he had said to notice.

"There was an accident," he said curtly, then watched the color fade from her cheeks. "Young Davy ran away down some steps at the Castle. Tearlach went after him, slipped and fell. He cracked a couple of ribs. The Usteds and the children went on to Spain without him. After six days in hospital he came back here to hole up in his den and lick his wounds, like an old lion. I met Mrs. Guthrie in the village and she told me. She's been in to see him, but says he isn't in a very good mood, and she's worried because she can't stay to look after him because. . . , Hey, where do you think you're going?"

Penelope was pulling on her jacket over her blue high-necked sweater, zipping it up and then pushing her hands into blue woollen mitts and cramming a beret on her dark shining hair. Her blue and white checked skirt swirled around her shapely legs, clad in long blue stockings, as she made for the door.

"I'm going to Torvaig House, of course. Where do you think?" she snapped at Hugh, wondering why he should be so obtuse. "Your cousin is hurt and there's no one to help him, so I must."

"Wait a minute!" Hugh's big hands were on her shoulders stopping her, and his bright tawny eyes searched her pale, big-eyed wedge of a face. "There's half a gale blowing and it'll take you hours to walk there."

Penelope tilted her chin and her blue eyes sparkled with determination.

"I'm still going," she said, trying to free herself from his hands.

Seeing that determination Hugh accepted his defeat with a sigh and a faintly rueful grin as he realized that he had never had a chance with this small, impulsive whirlwind of a girl. He released her and, picking up his sheepskin jacket from the chair where he had thrown it, shrugged into it.

"I'll drive you over," he said crisply. "I must say I felt a bit sorry for the old lion myself when I heard he'd been hurt. It's put paid to his courting of Rosa Usted for a while. I wonder if he'll ever marry."

"I wish you wouldn't call him old," said Penelope impatiently. "Hurry up, if you want to take me."

He drove along the road as fast as he dared in his old van. Beside him Penelope sat tense, staring out at the tossing windswept water, her mind and her heart already ahead of her in Torvaig House with Tearlach Gunn.

"Have you done this before, in that other lifetime of yours?" asked Hugh, suddenly flicking a curious glance in her direction.

"No, this is all new," she said slowly, as if she had come back to the van from somewhere far away. "I haven't had a flashback since Mr. Gunn left Torvaig to go to Spain. How strange! In the last one, I felt as if he'd gone away and would never be coming back."

"Who is *he*?"

"Why, my. . . . I mean the slave girl's husband, I suppose," stammered Penelope, her face flushing as she felt confused.

"That fits in with the legend," said Hugh. "He went away on one of his trading expeditions and didn't return. Lost at sea, presumably, or in a fight."

"Yes, it does fit in, doesn't it?" she murmured faintly. "Hugh, how badly hurt is Mr. Gunn?"

"Not badly, or he'd still be in hospital. Have you fallen for the old . . . I mean Tearlach?"

"Am I in love with him? I don't know. I'm all confused. He can be as exasperating and as tantalizing as you," she replied evenly, not really wishing to tell him how she felt.

"Then why are you rushing off to help him?"

"Because he helped me when I fainted, and when I had the flu he was awfully kind. The least I can do is help him when he's down."

"That sounds reasonable enough," murmured Hugh, noting that she had gone pale and tense again, and drawing his own conclusions.

They drove up to the front door of Torvaig House with a rattle, and the van had hardly stopped when Penelope was out of it and running to the side door, clutching her hat with one hand in case the tearing wind pulled it from her head. She ran down the passage to the kitchen and bounced off Mrs. Guthrie's ample bosom as the housekeeper was leaving the room.

"Ach, it's yourself, then," exclaimed Mrs. Guthrie. "What are you wanting here?"

"I've come to look after Mr. Gunn," said Penelope breathlessly, taking off her jacket and throwing it on a kitchen chair. Hats and mitts followed it as she pretended she hadn't noticed the strange look Mrs. Guthrie gave Hugh as he came into the room. "Where is he?" she demanded.

"In bed, where he should be, resting," said Mrs. Guthrie, with a snap. "And the job I had persuading him to go there, him three sheets to the wind, I'm thinking, with all the whisky he's been drinking. To ease the pain in his chest, he said," she grumbled with a scornful growl. "Ach, wait now, Penelope. You can't go up there. It isn't proper for a young woman like you to be visiting a man in his bedroom."

At this point Hugh intervened to offer to take Mrs. Guthrie to the ferry because he knew she wanted to go to the mainland to see her daughter. Not waiting to hear any more cautionary remarks, Penelope sped out of the room to the hall. Up the front stairs she bounded. At the top of them she paused for breath, listening to the pounding of her heart. Then she walked quietly to the door of Tearlach's room. It was open and she could see that a lamp was on, making a warm pool of amber light in the purple gloom of the wild November afternoon.

She stepped into the room and closed the door quietly behind her, then went over to the bed. Tearlach was lying flat on his back. He hadn't bothered to undress and was lying on top of the bedspread. Under the tumble of blond-streaked hair his face was pale and seemed thinner. A frown of pain make a dark line between his eyebrows. His eyes were closed, but she could tell by the firm set of his mouth that he was not asleep.

The sight of him made her heart feel as if it would burst. She longed to fling her arms around him and hold him close, and in that moment she recognized that it was love for him that had sent her hurrying through the bleak wintry day to be by his side.

"Mr. Gunn," she said softly.

He opened one eye, looked at her, closed it again and groaned, turning his head restlessly on the pillow.

"Oh, what is it?" gasped Penelope. "Are you in pain?"

"Yes," he murmured.

"What can I do to help you?"

"Sit down and hold my hand." This time his voice seemed stronger and there was the suspicion of a laugh in it. She eyed him warily as she sat down on the edge of the bed. Immediately one of his hands grasped one of hers. There was nothing wrong with the strength of his grasp, she thought, wincing a little as long muscular fingers closed around hers.

"Where is the pain?" she asked.

"Everywhere," he replied. "Why have you come?"

"I came to help you because Hugh said Mrs. Guthrie was worried about you and couldn't stay to help you."

"But why should you come and look after me?" he asked. His eyes were open now, dark and unfathomable in the subdued lighting.

"Once you looked after me, when I fainted, and then when I had stomach flu you were very kind; so I thought this would be a good chance to repay my debt."

He closed his eyes, groaned again and his fingers lost their grip on hers. Not knowing what to make of his behavior, half-suspicious, thinking that he might be playing on her sympathy for his own amusement, she said agitatedly, "I thought you said the pain would go away if you held my hand."

"I did, but it's come back."

"Did they give you any pills to kill the pain when you left hospital?"

"I suppose they did. I can't remember. I prefer whisky," he murmured.

"So Mrs. Guthrie told me," she commented dryly. "But obviously it isn't having any effect. Where might the pills be? Shall I look for them?"

She tried to withdraw her hand from his, but his fingers

tightened again. Their strength was astonishing in some-one who was supposed to be in pain, rousing her suspicions even more. She remembered Hugh once saying that Tearlach was not above putting on an act when he wanted to deceive someone.

"No, stay where you are," he ordered curtly. "The pain is going away again. It came back only because I didn't like your answer to my question. You don't have to pay any debt to me. I didn't look after you when you fainted and had the flu because I expected repayment. I'm glad you've come, though. I haven't been very good company for myself. I hate being ill."

"Everyone does," she comforted him. "How did it happen?"

"We went to Edinburgh from here. The Usteds wanted to shop in Princes Street and see the castle and Holyrood Palace. The day we went to the castle, Davy behaved abominably. I think he was beginning to realize that he wasn't going to see you again."

He closed his eyes again and the frown line came back.

"He hadn't known me for very long, so why should he be upset?" she asked.

"You know how he used to behave when he couldn't have me dancing attendance on him? Well, he was acting in the same way, only it was you he wanted. Anyway, there we were, Rosa and I, with him in tow, looking at the place. It was the wrong time of the year, damned cold, with the wind off the Pentland Hills doing its usual good job of penetrating even the thickest tweed," he remarked with a wry twist to his mouth. "Rosa kept wishing she was in Spain, and I kept wishing—"

He broke off. The frown deepened, but she was sure that it wasn't produced by physical pain this time. She wondered if he was regretting having taken Rosa to see

the castle in Edinburgh because the visit had led indirectly
to him being separated from her.

"Davy ran off down some steps," he continued tersely.
"I went after him, fell, cracked my ribs and knocked
myself out. It was a damned foolish thing to do."

Self-disgust thickened his voice and he turned his head
restlessly on the pillow again. This time, when his fingers
tightened on her hand, Penelope returned the pressure as
her foolish heart went out to him.

"But why did the Usteds go to Spain without you?" she
asked.

"I asked them to. Rosa wanted to stay, but Davy was
restless and I decided that in the long run it would be
better if the break with me was made then and there, a
clean cutting off of the relationship. So she and the
senora flew to London the next day with the children,
and on to Spain."

"You must have been very disappointed."

He opened his eyes to scowl with puzzlement at her.

"Why should I?"

"Because you couldn't go to Spain."

"I was only going because, in the first place, I had
thought it might be easier for the children if I went."
When he saw disbelief on her face his eyes began to
twinkle. "Oh ho," he said softly, "You had me paired off
with the dark and beautiful Rosa, did you? It looks as if
my little act was too convincing."

Her glance was wide and bewildered.

"Was it an act?" she asked sweetly, and he grinned at
her and squeezed her hand so hard that she cried out.

"Yes, it was, although I have to admit, as in the case of
Kathleen, I was temporarily attracted. Rosa is an intelligent woman, but too amenable for my taste, and she has
an aggravating way of agreeing with everything I say. I

prefer to have a few hot arguments with my women. Argument lends spice to lovemaking. Don't you agree, Penelope?"

The color rose in her cheeks and she avoided meeting his eyes.

"If I agree with you you'll be suspicious of me and think I'm being amenable. If I don't agree, I won't be telling the truth," she retorted, and he began to laugh, only to stop as he remembered his cracked ribs.

"Oh, hell," he muttered. "Why did I ever go after that little devil?"

"How did you get back to Torvaig?" she asked, looking at him anxiously. This time she knew he wasn't shamming pain because it was there in his face, carving new lines down his cheeks and around his mouth.

"I discharged myself and drove here."

"Oh, Tearlach!" The name slipped out without her realizing and his eyes half opened. He smiled at this. "You might have damaged yourself permanently," she continued anxiously. "I'd better go and phone Dr. Farquhar and ask him to come and examine you."

"No, not yet. I'll be all right. Besides, there's a lot to talk about."

"But it's hurting you to talk."

"Then you talk and I'll listen, for once. Tell me about Kathleen and Ian. Mrs. Guthrie has been muttering something about them getting married and about how foolish I am to let such a lovely young woman escape."

She told him what had happened and when she had finished he gave her a shrewd probing glance.

"Are you unhappy about Ian?" he asked abruptly.

"Of course not. Kathleen was surprised when I told her that he loves her. She had always hoped he did, but when he showed no signs of telling her, it turned her off and she became desperate. That's why she fell in with her mother's plan that she should try and marry you. As Hugh put it, rather crudely, she was ripe for the picking."

"Don't I know it," he muttered. "And I didn't want to be the one to pick her. If I had it would have been all over between us within six months."

For a while there was silence in the room. Outside the wind whistled and rattled at the window. Penelope glanced at Tearlach. He seemed to be asleep, so she tried to withdraw her hand from his again. She almost had it free when his fingers curled relentlessly around hers.

"Where are you going?" he asked.

"To see if Hugh has come back."

"Do you want him to come back and stay here with you?" he asked.

"Perhaps it would be better if he did, in case you need help."

"But I thought you'd come to help me?"

"I have, but I couldn't lift you or help you to dress," she said, a little confused by the glint in his eyes.

"I can dress myself, thank you, and I'm not in such a bad way that I can't move," he replied with a touch of impatience. "I meant do you want Hugh to stay here because you like having him near you?"

"No," she answered simply.

"That's a relief. If he were here, he'd only cramp my style as he did on the yacht coming up from Mallaig," muttered Tearlach obscurely. "I can do without his youthful competition. How do you like your cottage at Achmore?"

"It's lovely."

"Would you be willing to share it?"

"It would depend on the person," she said slowly. "It's going to be my home, and although I'd be willing to take

578

in tourists during the summer, I'm not sure whether I'd want to have just anyone living with me permanently."

"I can appreciate your feelings," he said. "For many years I didn't have a home of my own, but I always wanted one. Then I learned that I'd inherited this island. I came here, saw this house and decided to make it my home. I spent a great deal of money on things to make it comfortable. I'd lived here on and off almost two years before I realized that it was no more home to me than any other place I'd lived in over the years. So I sold it."

His announcement came as a shock. For a few seconds she could only stare at him in bewilderment. Then the questions came tumbling out.

"When? Why? Who has bought it?"

"Andrew Pollock, who was one of my guests here at the end of August. He's a scion of a well-known Scottish family, which owns a brewery. He's made a career of the hotel business and has a chain of hotels, all in attractive areas of Scotland where there hasn't been adequate hotel accommodation before."

"Hugh said you'd always thought Torvaig needed a hotel," she said.

"I could have turned the house into one myself, but Andrew will make a better job of it because he knows what he's doing. Every man to his trade," he murmured.

"What is your trade?" she asked.

"Taking chances," he replied enigmatically, then seeing that she wasn't satisfied with his answer he added, "Speculating. Buying something the value of which, I think, will increase and then selling it at a profit." He paused, seeing a troubled frown on her face.

"Even your home?" she asked.

"I know you don't approve," he replied harshly, "but I am what I am and it's the only talent I have. I try to use it to the best of my ability and sometimes, I hope, to the benefit of others. A hotel on the island will benefit the tourist trade considerably."

"But where are you going to live?"

"I'm not sure. I've never been sure. That's why I had to do something about Davy and Isa. Always at the back of my mind was my knowledge of myself. I was already getting tired of Torvaig when Avis was killed. I didn't want them to become too attached to me because I knew I would have to find them a more stable home with their other relatives. Do you understand?"

"Yes, I understand now," she said quietly, thinking back to the number of times she had accused him of not loving the children. She was beginning to realize that he knew more about the meaning of the word love than she did. He dealt in realities, not romances, but that did not mean he was not motivated by love.

"Do you remember Hallowe'en?" he asked suddenly, and there was a hint of desperation in his manner now. She nodded, feeling the warmth creep into her cheeks.

"I do too," he said. "I walked into the kitchen and found you sitting there. You invited me to the dance, and suddenly that something that had always been lacking in this house, in fact in my whole life, seemed to be there."

"Oh, what was it?" she demanded, her interest caught.

"I thought, I hoped it was love. Your sort of love for me. The sort of love you give to a person no matter how old or how wealthy or how rude he is, love that doesn't care where he comes from or where he's going. On Hallowe'en it changed a cheerless dump for furniture into a home for the first time, but too late because I'd sold it."

"Oh, not too late," she assured him quickly. "Home is where the heart is. It has nothing to do with bricks and mortar. My grandmother always said that."

"And where is your heart?" He seemed to pounce on her words.

"Wherever you are, as if you didn't know," she said with a touch of asperity, which brought the teasing grin back to his face. "That is why I'm here this afternoon. But I've only just found out, so please don't rush me," she added breathlessly, as she realized how much she had committed herself.

He sank back against the pillows and breathed a deep sigh of satisfaction.

"I thought I'd never get you to admit it! Don't worry, I shan't be rushing anyone until these ribs are healed. Anyway, wooing you is something I intend to take my time over. I want to enjoy it. I've given up 'gathering rosebuds,' to quote that poem Kathleen told us about. This is forever as far as I'm concerned, but if you don't feel like that, let's call quits before we take any vows to love and to cherish."

"I'd like it to be for keeps too," she said shyly.

"That's the answer I wanted," he replied, "but don't go all amenable, will you, Penelope? I love you because you're you and you dare to twist the lion's tail. Hallowe'en was a moment of truth for me, but I couldn't be sure of you. I thought your heart was with Ian. When you returned my kisses I thought you were using me as a substitute for him. That made me angry and I was rough with you. Then you wanted Achmore—to be near him, I thought. I saw you kiss him, and in spite of what you said later, I was convinced you were in love with him. There was nothing to keep me here any longer, so I decided to go to Spain."

"You weren't coming back. You'd gone for good," she accused, remembering how clearly she had felt he would never return.

"Yes, and I might not be here if it wasn't for Davy. I suppose I ought to be grateful to the brat, just as I should be grateful to Hugh for interfering that day at Mallaig when I wanted to send you back to London. Do you realize we might never have known each other?"

"I refuse to believe that. I had to come to Torvaig. I'd have come some other way," she replied earnestly.

"We'll argue about that another time," he said with an amused glint in his eyes. "At the moment there are much more important things I want to do."

"Why did you come back?" she persisted, refusing to be put off by the altered touch of his fingers, which were not holding her hand tightly but caressing the inside of her wrist, sending queer little tingles up her arm.

"In the hospital I had time to think. I don't give up easily, but there I could see I was doing just that, giving up before I'd really tried. I'd found you, the only woman I've ever known with whom I wanted to stay, and I'd run away rather than be hurt by watching you love another man. I was giving up without a fight. I was furious with myself. I had to come back to try to win you away from Ian because I knew that if I didn't I'd be homeless for the rest of my life. My instinct to return here was right, and when I saw you walk in here this afternoon I realized I might not have to fight very hard. Penelope, do you think you could bear to share your cottage with me? After the end of November I'll have nowhere to live."

"I'm sure I can," she replied joyfully, her eyes shining with love. Then she added, in all innocence, as her practicality asserted itself, "What a good thing I've bought a double bed!"

Tearlach wanted to laugh, but he couldn't, so he groaned instead and closed his eyes. Immediately she leaned forward anxiously to push the hair back from his brow and to smooth away the line of pain. When he didn't respond she tried to withdraw, only to find that his other arm had crept around her and that she was being held down, close to him. His eyes opened and invitation gleamed in them. Desire flamed within her in answer. Giving in, she touched his mouth with her own and was lost.

This time no curious moon peered in at the window, and as the minutes lengthened, it occurred briefly to Penelope that her Viking, whom she'd long awaited, had returned to her to stay.